Wow, what a story! *I cannot believe that Schoorens wrote this book in 2021 or thereabouts, and how close it is to world events today in 2025. Secondly, I cannot believe that an American wrote this story in which Canadians ended up winning a fictional conflict with the Americans. Furthermore, being a Canadian and being familiar with Down East Washington County, Maine, and Western Charlotte County, New Brunswick, where this story is set, one can tell that the author is very familiar with the geography of the area. For these reasons, I have given the story 5 stars and would give it more if possible. Mr. Schoorens, you are one brave individual!*

–R. McGuire

ALSO BY DAVID R. SCHOORENS

Refuge: A Novel of Lost Democracy

Reviews for *Refuge: A Novel of Lost Democracy*

A powerhouse of fiction. *This book was recommended to me by a Canadian retired military officer, and the book lived up to everything he said about it - that this novel is a tour de force, a powerhouse work of fiction from a writer with a distinctive and compelling voice.*

–Max Folsom, Author

Can the world endure an autocrat in the White House? *Refuge: A Novel of Lost Democracy parallels the style of Tom Clancy's best sellers with all their precision, intensity, and scope. Like Clancy, Schoorens uses war game theory to explore the rabbit holes and dark corners into which narcissistic autocrats might drag the world.*

–Donald Mulcare, Ph.D.

A dystopian prequel not post-apocalyptic but a warning. *This amazing book is frankly terrifying in its plausibility. We can see things happening now that will lead to this. Failure to pay attention will doom us.*

–Stuart A. Halsan

A Chilling, Very Plausible Novel. A Must Read. *A very timely read, and a storyline that is chilling in its plausibility. Super first novel by an author whose work here deserves a broad audience.*

–Mark Holmes, Author

... a shocking piece of literature ... *To summarize my thoughts on the remarkable novel that is Refuge; I would say if you are a reader who is tired of reading the same old books that are lackluster and forgettable, then take a chance with this one because I promise you now that you will not be disappointed! Refuge gets five stars from me!*

–Aimee Ann, Red Headed Book Lover

Excellent and Engaging Read. *I am a Canadian living in New Brunswick. I appreciate the author's attention to detail about Canadian war history and the geography of my province. The story is fictional, but to some of us, too close to non-fiction than we would like. Americans choose their president in democratic elections. The world can only watch and wait, hoping they will select a person we can all trust. Abraham Lincoln once said something like this 'America will not fall from without, but from within.'*

–E. Ann McIntyre, Author, Canada

Engrossing and gripping novel. *An entertaining, if chilling, journey into a near future when the USA is in the grip of an authoritarian administration. Told from the standpoint of a struggle between patriotic forces determined to defend the constitution and a hardline regime prepared to go to any lengths to subjugate opposition, Refuge paints a disturbing picture of where American politics might be heading if we close our eyes to the dangers. A readable and enjoyable novel with an important message*

–Em Thompson, Author, United Kingdom

Frighteningly relevant in today's political climate. *I had the opportunity to meet David at a book signing at Root and Press in Worcester, MA. After talking with him about the book, I decided to take a chance, despite my misgivings on the subject. It was a well-written novelization of current events. It presents a plausible outcome of the poor choices we make in electing our government. I would recommend this book to anyone who likes books in the style of Tom Clancy. It's a mix of politics, military fiction, and spy craft. I think it should become required reading in today's United States. I look forward to David's next book and wish him well with his future writing!*

–C. Belcher

CAPTIVE

DAVID R. SCHOORENS

Captive

Produced and printed by Stillwater River Publications.

Visit our website at
www.StillwaterPress.com
for more information.

First Stillwater River Publications Edition.

ISBN: 978-1-968548-30-8

Library of Congress Control Number: 2026901251

1 2 3 4 5 6 7 8 9 10
Written by David R. Schoorens.
Cover design by Bob Lavoie.
Published by Stillwater River Publications,
West Warwick, RI, USA.

I am dedicating this novel to my wife, Cathy.
Without her, I would be nothing.

THE CAPTIVE

Victor Holt

Never had I known the unimaginable, visceral terror that comes from complete helplessness. That comes from knowing I was about to die.

Since that night, memory's fog obscured so many of my thoughts and actions. Yet, other things I remember with frightening clarity, such as my first thought upon regaining consciousness.

Am I alive?

Pain told me I was alive. My body felt broken. Every joint burned. My head throbbed with a monstrous, nauseating migraine. From my one functioning eye, all I saw was blackness in every direction. Questions came quickly.

Why can't I see? Why is it so dark? Blind? Eyepatch? Where's my eyepatch? I can't feel it. Was I wearing it? My glasses. I can't feel my eyeglasses. I can always feel them. Always wear them. I had them on. Where are they?

As I turned my head left and right, something scratched across my nose. The same feeling came from my balding head and ears. Some kind of fabric, stiff and heavy.

A blindfold? No. My whole head feels it. It's a bag. There's a bag over my head. It's black. That's why I can't see. Why's there a black bag over my head? Oh, fuck no!

My breathing quickened. I tried to yell, but something was in the way. Something in my mouth.

A ball? In my mouth?

Turning my head left and right, I felt a tautness across my cheeks and around to the back of my neck. It came to me that there was a gag wrapped around my head. That wasn't all. A string or a cord, wrapped around my throat, sort of like . . .

Christ! A noose around my neck? God Almighty, what the fuck is happening!

I reached for my head, but I couldn't move my arms and hands more than a fraction of an inch. I tried to launch myself up but failed. I realized the obvious.

I'm held down. Tied down. I can't move my legs. It goes across me, around my chest. I can feel it when I breathe. Rope? Strap? Tape? But what I'm on moved when I tried to get up. It must be light.

In my mind's eye came an image of me tied down to a cot, blinded by a black hood. My breathing jumped into overdrive. Sweat beaded up and ran down my face, stinging my eyes. I felt an icy knife of terror stab me in the gut. I tried to yell again, but all the gag allowed was a deep moan. I fell into panic.

I don't remember how long before what little rationality remained kicked in. From either instinct or training, a voice from inside demanded I survive.

Calm down! Breathe. Slower. Deeper. The gag's in the way. Breathe through my nose. Slower. Breathe. Yes, that's better. God, it smells bad. Rank, moldy. It's cold. Calm down. Think. Keep breathing . . . slower. Listen to my breath. Better. Okay, now, what's my condition? My status.

I began with the big question.

Am I wounded?

I mentally listed what hurt. Arms, legs. My right elbow, especially. And my nuts. Like someone kicked me there. And a headache that ranked with the worst imaginable hangover. But I hadn't been drinking that much. So, someone beat me up, but I wasn't seriously wounded. I know about being seriously wounded.

Am I dreaming?

That all this could be nothing more than a nightmare, a profoundly realistic nightmare, lent me a spark of hope.

My dreams are always in color. But everything I see is black, so . . . No. Not dreaming. The black is because of the hood. Hell, I don't even know if it's night or day!

Summing up my condition, I concluded I was alive, unless the afterlife is far different than what they claimed in Sunday School. Someone hurt me badly and left me tied up on something like a cot. Even through my clothes I felt the cot's stiff fabric. Not a hospital bed. Hospitals don't put a bag over your head.

It was quiet. No voices. No sounds. Nothing mechanical like a heating system. Nothing distant like traffic noise, birds chirping, or water running. The only sound was my own breathing. Then the quiet triggered a thought that almost sent me back into a panic.

Am I alone? Is somebody there? Stay still. Stay quiet.

A sudden thirst followed. I couldn't remember when I last had a drink. And that led to another pressing need.

I've got to piss.

Other than the last resort of letting go in my pants, there wasn't anything to do about that.

There was nothing left to do other than trying to remember what happened before all this. I'd been out for dinner. Last night, maybe. I'd gone to *Robert's* and ate at the bar like I always do when I'm alone. Can't remember what I ate or drank. Probably had my usual cocktail, a bourbon old-fashioned. Just one, I think. I hoped. So, I likely didn't get drunk.

Another customer was there. He sat at the other end of the bar. Not sure if there were other customers. Nobody sat next to me. I'm not one to sit among others anyway; there's always someone who wants to talk when I don't want to talk.

So, the place was kind of dead. Dead. Yeah, not a good word for current circumstances. Stop thinking "dead."

That guy. What did he look like? White guy. Sort of heavy set, but muscular. He ate something and watched TV. I didn't talk to him. He didn't talk to me.

Before I paid my bill, I took a leak. Then I went back to my seat, finished up my food, laid out more than enough cash, and left through the rear door to the back lot where I'd parked my truck. It was dark outside.

Walking out, I started to feel strange. Disorientated. Woozy. Not sick, not drunk, but fucking weird. I leaned up against my truck. Then . . .

Something, someone slammed me against my truck! They hit my head and pushed me down on my knees. I think I remember . . . I was in a car! Not my truck. Then everything went black.

Christ, someone took me. Kidnapped me.

Whatever self-control I had left me right then.

Am I going to die? Yes, I am.

Then came the sound of a gun.

My name is Victor Holt. Let me make a couple of things clear. That's my real name. No point in hiding that. Everyone around here knows me. They know what I wrote and what happened to me. Being kidnapped, tortured, and almost murdered will get one on the news.

Throughout this period of my life, I've tried to write down my experiences as they happened. Admittedly, my memory and interpretations are imperfect, especially the night of the kidnapping. Recollections of what happened, what I think happened, and what I want to believe happened undoubtably intermixed. Nevertheless, it's my best effort. Months of death threats that culminated in waking up on a cot with a guy holding a pistol to your head will do that to you.

I've kept parts of this story intentionally vague. Where I live, who my friends are. Road and place names, if used at all, are fictitious. Not a hint, I hope. The story's location is irrelevant in any case. What happened to me can happen to anyone, anywhere.

I've got another simple reason for being evasive. There are still people out there who want to kill me. No sense in making it easier for them.

THE CAPTOR

Jeffrey Ford

I'll be honest. Watching Holt squirm on the cot thrilled me. I held the power of life and death over another man. Nothing like it.

The kidnapping worked out according to plan. My plan. Done all on my own. Right on time, about 1 a.m., Holt started to wake up. By then, he'd been out for about four hours. He jerked around, making the cot wiggle and jump. I think he started to yell for help, but then stopped.

He'll yell soon enough, I thought.

Holt must have felt completely alone. I'll bet he had no idea I was only a few feet away. I kept silent and sat in a corner out of the light. Even with the overhead room lights on, I knew he couldn't see through that thick hood because I'd tested it.

Taking him went down easier than I imagined. Luck was with me. On his social media, he lets slip when he'd next go to *Robert's* for dinner. In the back parking lot, there was even an open spot next to his truck.

Holt sat alone at the bar. I took a stool at the other end of the bar and tried to ignore him. I know he glanced at me, but nothing hinted he somehow recognized me. Luckily, we were the only customers there.

When he went to the men's room, I got up and sat next to his stool, pretending to watch the sports channel on the television.

It only took me a second to slip the drug into his fancy cocktail. A GHB dose of exactly two grams that I'd measured on a decent kitchen balance I'd bought online. By the time Holt returned, I was back in my place. Out of the corner of my eye, I watched him drain his cocktail.

They call GHB the date rape drug. I thought about experimenting with it before taking Holt, just to see if GHB worked as advertised. Maybe not go so far as raping someone, but I decided no. I couldn't risk any complications before all this went down.

Turns out, there's no such thing as a "knock-out drug," like in the movies. Sure, there are different drugs that get someone to pass out, but they're just as likely to kill. In only a matter of minutes, GHB would seriously disorientate Holt. He might even pass out. Or die if I gave him too much. The best part about GHB, Holt won't remember much. GHB causes loss of memory.

Everything depended on timing the dose. Ideally, when he's nearly done eating. By the time he paid for his meal and walked out, the drug would hit him.

So many things could've gone wrong. And if anything did, I'd just walk away. No harm; no foul.

Nothing went wrong. Holt was a mess by the time he got to his truck. He didn't put up much of a fight. A little rough handling and he was passed out in the back of my car with the black hood over his head.

I thought, not bad for my first kidnapping. Guess I'm just good at this.

When I, that is, we, got back home, I parked inside the garage and dragged him out of the car. Hard part was getting him down to the basement. Pretty sure he got banged up being dragged down those stairs.

There's a lot of dead weight in an unconscious man about to be dead.

Holt never threw up. That sometimes happens with GHB. At

least I didn't have any puke to clean up. And it'd been a shame if he choked to death on his vomit. That's not the way I wanted him to die.

Looking at him on the cot, I kept thinking, all I need is two or three more hours, and it'll be all over.

Holt's book pissed off thousands of people. He knew that would happen. He said as much in those news interviews where he ranted about all the death threats. I didn't need to read his book to figure out he's to blame. He attacked their way of life, their place in the world. They're only defending themselves from someone who disrespects them. Holt's the threat, not them. If there's any blame, it's on Holt.

People say Holt deserves to die because he is a traitor. They like to say "executed." And like all traitors, many said Holt had to hang. As if hanging somehow legitimizes things by giving his death a sense of legal due process. They go on about hanging all the people like Holt. Make them disappear. Blow up their homes. Kill their families. Shit like that.

Screw them, I say. They're nothing more than chat room losers. Nothing but talk and no action from them. Well, I'm not just empty talk. It's fallen to me. I'm the one who'll do it. I'm the guy who'll put Holt in the ground. I will get it done. They never will.

But why me? Because I can't believe my life will amount to nothing more than being a landscaping worker or whatever comes after that. I am not ordinary. There is something larger out there for me. I don't deserve this life. I deserve more.

Holt's politics didn't matter a damn to me. I don't like people like him, but that's not the point. For me, a dead Holt is only a means to an end.

I know, just know, better things are out there for me. Someday, people will look up to the guy they discharged, turned down, and forgot. They will respect me. Fear me. Someday, I'll get what they've cheated me out of. Holt is going to get me to that day.

Honestly, before I went to *Robert's*, I'd had second thoughts about being Holt's executioner. Now with Holt laid out in front of me, it was too late for doubt. I was committed. I had no choice. One thing was for sure, it was going to be . . . messy. Stomach-turning messy.

About half an hour after he woke up, I got the show going. Act 1. Scene 1. Breaking Holt.

I moved slowly toward him. The plastic sheeting on the floor crinkled as I stepped closer. If he heard that, so much the better. As I knelt next to his head, Holt didn't move.

I took out the gun from my belt. With the muzzle pointed away, I held the revolver's hammer and cylinder less than an inch from his right ear. I brought the hammer to half-cock.

That got him! Holt knew that sound! He jerked his head and whole body.

Full cock. He heard that, too! It wasn't hard to guess what he was thinking. He was about to die, and there wasn't a damn thing he could do about it.

I turned my gun's muzzle against his temple with enough pressure so that he'd feel it even through the hood. Holt gasped and screamed as best he could through that gag.

Anticipation of death by the victim is an essential step in creating terror.

I squeezed the trigger. The hammer fell on an empty chamber. Holt convulsed. I gave it a minute to let it dawn on him that he's still alive. No doubt Holt was relieved and surprised that there was no shot.

Holt went silent. Again, I half-cocked the hammer and silently counted to five, allowing the sound of a cocking hammer to have its effect on Holt's mind. I brought it to full cock and waited again before I put the muzzle against his head again. I squeezed the trigger. Three more times I let the hammer fall on an empty chamber. I wondered if Holt was counting the trigger pulls because by the fifth time, he broke his silence. He started crying. And he'd pissed himself.

Was he thinking I'm saving a round for the last chamber?

I was. As an added flourish before the sixth round, I put my mouth next to his ear and breathed slowly and loudly. Imagine hearing heavy breathing coming out of the darkness. I thought, that'll scare the piss out of him. Well, no, that already happened.

Holt froze and stopped crying. I wasn't happy about that. I wanted him to cry. I had to know if I was getting to him! He's got to break. Beg for his life. I wanted him to surrender to me just before I put an end to him.

The opening scene was coming to an end. I stood up, took a round from my pocket, and slipped it into a chamber. Snapping the cylinder in place, I aimed at the ceiling and pulled the trigger.

Fuck! That hurt! Stupid! Forgot ear protection.

Down here, even a blank round sounds like a cannon! For a second or two, Holt must've thought I shot him. He was crying again, which is exactly what I wanted.

I sat back down and went through my mental list of tasks. Just before I kill him, I'll take off his hood. He'll see me in my mask. He'll stay strapped to the cot; no way he'll have a chance to get free. After I take out his gag, I'll tell him to read the statement I wrote, confessing all, promising him freedom if he cooperates. That done, I'll shoot him in the head. I'll get everything on video. Holt will die never seeing the face of his executioner.

After I strip his body of clothes, I'll wrap him up in the plastic sheets and then a big dark green tarp for good measure. I'll put in a couple of weights and sink him in the bay. Everything will go into the bay, one thing at a time, and in different places. The cot and any tools I've used, right down to the duct tape. Even Holt's pistol.

Of course, Holt's body will come up eventually, no matter how deep or cold the water is. As he rots, gases will build up in his body, the tarp will tear or come undone, and he'll float up. Or a fisherman will snag one surprising catch. The cops will identify him, but there's no way they'll trace it back to me. Nothing will be on the body to connect him to me.

Even the video won't connect him to me. The video background will show nothing but plastic sheets covering every inch of the basement floor, walls, and ceiling. The plastic will also catch any blood or tissue residue. I've taken every precaution. I'm very good at this.

Someday, I'll let those weaklings know who executed Holt. The video of Holt's confession, and of me ending him, will go online. Under a fake name, of course. Still details to work out after it's all done, but it'll show all those losers that someone, me, had more courage than all of them!

With my ears ringing, I went upstairs, leaving Holt to lie there in his own piss-soaked pants. He wasn't going anywhere, and I needed to prepare myself. Have a beer. Relax. Set an alarm. Watch a movie. I had one of my favorite movies ready to go. *1984*.

Come to think about it, *1984* may have set me on this course. Back in high school, junior year, I think, *1984* was part of the literature curriculum. Turns out, I really enjoyed the novel. Naturally, a book report had to be done. Me being me, getting a rise out of the teacher was more my objective than a good grade, even though I knew I could get an excellent grade if I wanted to.

I defended Big Brother's lies, violence, and the use of torture as the best ways to control the masses. I hoped my extreme, but correct views would trigger my teacher into an argument. But that didn't happen. In fact, I got a decent grade.

It being the school day's last period, the teacher had me stick around so he could explain my grade, point by point. My writing style and grammar were fine. He complemented my effort to back up my points with extra research. That wasn't the end of it, though. He called my essay not only objectionable, but disturbing.

He said something like, "especially where you say the O'Brien's torture of Winston was 'half-hearted.'" He wasn't angry; more like he didn't understand why I wrote what I did.

He should've stopped there, but he didn't. He asked me, "Are you okay? Anything troubling you? Something you want to talk about?" I told him no and to mind his own damn business. Maybe he truly wanted to help me, but I wasn't in the mood to be pitied.

Besides, I'd seen this shit before. Talk or act differently than the other kids, and the teacher thinks you're nuts. One teacher thinks that, then all of them think that. You're labelled.

Guess he pegged me as dangerous, like I was someone who'd shoot up the school. Probably it was he who called in the guidance counselors. Down in Guidance, I didn't give them an inch! I told them, yes, I thought torture was a legitimate tool of political power. Half the governments in the world agreed with me! I ended the conversation with, "It's my opinion! What are you going to do about it?"

Turns out, nothing. Not for the essay anyway. When I walked out of Guidance and told them all to "fuck off," that they could do something about. A two-day suspension.

My parents weren't happy. Upset and angry, they reached back to bring up the fights I got into in middle school. Dad asked if I was being bullied. I told him I wasn't. That wasn't entirely true. A couple of assholes had it in for me. Why I wasn't sure. Maybe because I was too much of a loner. Mom asked about drugs. I said I never did drugs. That was the truth, with a small lie hidden inside. I tried weed once and didn't like how it made me feel. Same way with booze. I don't like losing control, so even now I'm no more than a light drinker, restricting myself to an occasional beer.

When they asked how my college applications were going, I told them I wasn't going to college. That's when things got bad. I'd never seen them so angry. Screaming. Hands slapping the table. Cursing. Calling me a liar. Even tears, from Dad of all people.

I ran into my bedroom. I slammed the door shut and ignored their demands to come out. After five minutes or so, they gave up. Maybe they gave up on other things, too.

Having Mom and Dad yell at me like that, I guess I should've been pissed at them. But looking back, I don't think I was all that emotional. Sure, what they said hurt. Nobody likes being yelled at, least of all by your parents. Memories fade, but one thing stands out. It surprised me how little I cared that I hurt them.

The next morning, I played the dutiful only son and apologized. I used all the right words. We hugged each other. Even as they forgave me, I felt empty. It was just words to me. Meaningless words.

The words weren't meaningless to Mom and Dad. They weren't ready to put it all behind. The following day, they told me I'd be seeing a therapist. Dad put it this way. "Look, son, you need help. Best thing to do is get professional help." That demand rang the bell for Round Two. More screaming and swearing from me and them. The fight only stopped when me and Dad grabbed each other and started throwing punches, with Mom screeching as she tried to pull us apart.

A punch to my face reminded me that Dad did amateur boxing in his college days. He still had the skills. Sent to the floor, I surrendered and agreed to see the shrink.

The first thing I told the therapist was the same thing I told Guidance. Fuck off! Therapy didn't go on for much longer.

In the uneasy truce at home that followed, I graduated from high school and tried a semester at a local community college. I worked hard and did well by anyone's standards because I had a point to prove. I dropped out, telling my parents, "Yeah, I only did good to prove I'm no dummy." When I told them I was going to enlist in the Army, they didn't fight.

Six months after that, I was at an Army infantry boot camp.

Fort Moore, Georgia. Mom and Dad made a show of how proud they were when I graduated from basic training.

Eighteen months after that, I was out of the Army. Bastards decided I wasn't a good fit, or so they said. Administrative discharge. There I was, part of that very small fraction of Americans who enlist in the military. I had high hopes, but they kicked me out! I'll never understand why they thought I couldn't adapt to military life. That's what you get for serving your country. Their loss, as far as I was concerned.

When I got home, I started with a local landscaper while I applied to the police academy. They rejected me. My discharge status ruined my chances. I knew then I would be paying for my Army time for the rest of my life. I'd have made a great cop. They all knew I'd be great, too.

So, I had no plans except to keep working for the landscaper while living rent-free in my folks' place. They'd moved to Florida, probably to get away from me. I can't say I blame them. I've only gone down there once for a Christmas visit. I couldn't wait to head back home.

They still call every few days, asking how I am. On the phone, Mom and Dad always seem anxious. Worried. We keep things polite. We're never angry, but I don't make it easy for them. It's like we've forgotten how to talk to each other. They always end with "We love you."

Yeah, they're disappointed in me. But I think they still really love me. Do I love them? I think so, though sometimes I'm not so sure. I should love them because that is the way a son should feel about his parents, but when I say I love them, it feels reflexive. Empty. It bothers me sometimes.

Lately, I'm not even sure I need them in my life. I mean, what have they really done for me? Maybe they'd be better off without me.

None of my high school friends stayed around town. Not like I had many friends anyway. Maybe two or three people I could call friends back then. These days, they probably don't remember me.

No girlfriend either. Never seemed to get to a second date. You'd think I'd do better. I mean, I look good. I exercised regularly back then and still do. I'm fit. I'm ready.

Then there's work. Funny thing, it's the kind of job where no one sees you. You're invisible. Even when a customer thanks me, it never seems genuine. I'm just background. A shadow. They don't even look me in the eye.

Work, then home, and back to work again. That's my life. I keep my mouth shut and keep to myself. Guess I'm a loner. Whatever. Not my fault. Haven't met anyone that's worth the trouble to get to know.

One positive thing. Despite it all, I haven't gotten myself in trouble with the cops. I almost did when I started at work. One of the guys said I wasn't working quickly enough. He called me "a sorry son-of-a-bitch." I came close to beating the shit out of him right then and there, but stopped myself. I told him to go fuck himself and left it at that.

Turns out, good thing I didn't hit him. That would've brought in the police and saddled me with a record. That's another reason why the cops will never connect me to Holt. I'm not in their system.

Screw all that. I don't deserve this life. Better things are out there for me. Someday, people will look up to me, the guy they discharged, turned down, and forgot. I will get what they've cheated me out of. Holt is going to get me to that day.

Back to the movie. The newest *1984*, with Jonathan Hurt and Richard Burton. That night, I needed inspiration. If a movie can help with that, this is the one. Burton really shines in his role as O'Brien. He played it cold and understated, even during the best part when he's torturing Hurt's character, Winston. That's when we learn about their world. A world based on merciless and endless brutal power. No ideology. Only pure power. What does Burton's character say? Something about the future being a boot smashing into mankind's face. Forever.

That's how you keep power. I understand that. All those online idiots don't.

When I video Holt's confession, it'll be like what O'Brien said to Winston. He must be cured before he finally puts a bullet in his head.

My name is Jeffrey Ford. That is my real name. No point in hiding that. Everybody knows what I did. I'm the guy who put Holt on that cot.

I did my best to remember things. I wanted my story to be as accurate as possible. Funny thing, I don't know why I wrote all this down. After all, it's an after-the-fact confession. But I doubt I could get in any more trouble. I'm pretty much fucked as it is.

You know the ironic part of all this? This makes me a kind of author just like Holt.

THE COP

Harrison

Maybe I'm not like most cops. My goal in life is, or was, to live unnoticed. I'd just do my job on my way to retirement. Never dealing with a single, media-grabbing case, like a shooting or a murder, would've made me a happy man.

As it turned out, I would not be happy.

A little of my background to open the story. I live here in town. That wasn't decided on any conviction that an officer should live in the town he serves. I'd heard of a decent house in town with room enough for my wife and me, plus a couple of cookie crunchers. A fix 'er upper, but with possibilities. Long story short, we bought it, fixed it up, and live in it to this day.

Seventeen years as a cop. Eleven years as a patrol officer before promotion to Detective. All with the same police department serving a smallish suburban community by the ocean. I know my job, my town, and many of the people living here, both the good ones and not so good.

When I first met Holt, and right up until the end, I saw nothing unique in his case. That might seem strange, as hundreds of anonymous people were harassing and threatening Holt online over his work as a writer. Others demonstrated against him, doxed him, attacked his livelihood, and even attacked him a couple of times. Yet, every time I picked up his case, my training and common sense told me the threats would, in time, fade away if Holt just laid low for a while. Violence rarely results. That's particularly true in cases that don't involve the fury family members or lovers can bring. The bad guys eventually shift to a new outrage, a new target, or just get bored. Typically, only the most stupid wind up under arrest. Then again, never bet against stupidity.

Viewing Holt's case through my prism of rational, professional experience, it was the proper assessment. However, that prism also clouded my vision and blunted my imagination. I refused to entertain the possibility of what could happen. What did happen.

In the aftermath of Holt's kidnapping and attempted murder, our department, the state police, and the FBI went over every detail from my case files. In the end, their review found no error on my part. Officially, my reputation emerged intact.

Unofficially, the Chief later took me aside and said, "Detective, there's a couple of times when I think you should have, well, upped your game with Holt."

Mild criticism to be sure, said with the best of intentions, but it still hurt. I had let the Chief down. We're still on good terms with no obvious damage to our relationship, professional or personal. Still, I can't evade the fact that I misjudged Holt's case. I missed something.

My best explanation for my failure focuses on a single word. Routine.

That word describes my career in law enforcement. Traffic details, traffic accidents, DUI arrests, the odd arrest for an outstanding warrant, hundreds of details to high school games and graduations, and maybe once a month or so, a breaking and entering.

Even in a quiet town, however, a police officer sees people at their worst. The drunks, the abusers, and thieves. That decent fellow you chatted up about football yesterday turns into the guy who beats the hell out of his wife. Or his kid. Your view of humanity changes after a few domestic disturbance calls. They are the most disturbing and most dangerous of calls. When you take away the handcuffed husband or wife, and see the faces of their terrified children, your soul is scarred.

As a saving grace, the good stories far outnumber the bad. Finding a lost kid alive and unhurt or returning an elderly man with dementia who "eloped" from his caregiver. Such cases buffer me against the bad in this world. They reinforce the worthiness of what I do. For my own sake, I try to keep those cases at the front of my mind.

At times, I miss the direct contact I once had with the folks around here as a patrol officer, but being a Detective has its own rewards. The forensic work of assessing a crime scene fascinates me. Looking over a scene, identifying the evidence, and putting it all together thrills me every time. Maybe the day will come when all that bores me, and I turn into a cynical, hard-bitten cop right out of crime novels. That hasn't yet happened.

Then again, with Holt, maybe it did happen.

Routine. It's reassuring. Comforting. And if I'm honest with myself, I let routine guide my casework. Operate under the assumption that there are no original problems. Use the probabilities. Check the boxes and do not think outside of them. What's the old saying my doctor told me about medical diagnosis? When you hear hoofbeats, think of horses, not zebras. In other words, what ails the patient is most likely the most common problem, not the exotic one.

That's how I saw Holt's case. Horses. Not zebras. Just routine.

My name is Peter Harrison. That is my real name. Full title: Detective Peter Harrison. I've contributed my thoughts and experience to this story as accurately as my memory and case file notes allow. I'm no writer, and frankly, I don't know why Holt asked me to add my side of the story. At first, I refused when the request came my way. I preferred to let the official records speak for themselves. Also, I was reluctant to reveal how I personally felt about Holt. Then there was Ford. Holt's idea of including Ford's little memoir sickened me. Nevertheless, as a matter of duty, I read Ford's scribblings when I added them to the case file. Ironically, Ford's story changed my mind. Ford's words might offer an important insight into the mind of people like him. And be a message for our times.

I'll start with what I know. A man wrote a book. It pissed off people. And then things went too far.

Funny thing. I haven't read Holt's book. Maybe someday.

PART I

IN THE MONTHS BEFORE

CHAPTER ONE

REMEMBERING WHAT CAME BEFORE

Holt

Looking out from my living room at the water, for the thousandth time, I asked myself the same damn question. Victor Holt, you dumb son-of-a-bitch, why in hell did you think writing that goddamn novel was a good idea?

Maybe I should begin with why I started writing at all. Simple answer, I needed something to do. Retirement from a large defense corporation was on the horizon. Susan, my wife, would retire from the same company a couple of years later. Like typical prospective retirees, we talked about moving to a warmer place and entertaining ourselves playing golf in perpetual sunshine.

On that score, things never advanced beyond talk. Truthfully, I doubt Susan would've vetoed the idea of year-round warm beaches. And I nursed extraordinarily pleasant dreams of relaxing on sunny Floridian shores with my wife. Maybe I'm biased, but even in her early sixties, Susan was still stunning. Intensely blue eyes contrasted well with her short, now mostly grey hair. Never one to hide her age with make-up, Susan nevertheless appeared years younger than her true age.

It was me who nixed things. To me, Florida is a place to visit, not move to. And golf? Golf and fun are two things I can never put back together. After playing hundreds of rounds, I simply grew to loathe that stupid, rotten game. If given a choice between playing another round of golf or dying of a heart attack, I'd likely say, "Well, I'm excited to learn about the hereafter."

Travel became our alternative to living as a target for hurricanes. Canada, Europe, and the western United States. Maybe a truly exotic trip to Australia and New Zealand. A cruise or two every year. Throw in an extravagant Caribbean resort every couple of years. We wanted to see something of this world while we're still in very good health.

However, in between trips, I needed something else to fill my time. That's where the writing came in.

During my career, I'd often been complimented on my writing. Knowing I had the knack, the company engineers begged for my help in translating their horribly technical jargon into something understandable to lesser mortals.

The engineers knew that simplicity and clarity in messaging were increasingly critical as fewer engineers ascended to the senior executive ranks. The engineers crafted marvelous things that sailed the seas, flew across the sky, and went into space. However, they were losing status to MBA finance cyphers who saw share price and dividends as the only true marvels.

Though outside the scope of my human resources job, helping the engineers was a welcome break from mundane personnel and benefits work. Though I was a very long, long way from becoming a novelist, the seed was planted and germinated with retirement.

What to write about? My own military experience? Nothing more than a short story there, if that. Could I exploit my U.S. Army expertise to write military thrillers? That seemed promising. Yet, I didn't take that obvious track the first time out.

When inspiration, time, and opportunity did eventually come together, my first novel blended science fiction with submarines.

I begged technical help from those same prose-phobic engineers. In the process, I learned about submarine construction and operation, naval warfare, and a whole lot more about writing. Book sales didn't go much beyond the friends and family circuit, but that didn't matter. To hold in my hands my first novel was an unmatched feeling of accomplishment.

My second novel did much better. Historical fiction. *The King's Lieutenant* was inspired by Belgian King Albert I's heroic resistance against the Germans in World War I. Inspiration came from my father's family history. In 1914, Grandpa was only ten years old, living in Brussels, when Kaiser Wilhelm demanded the far weaker Belgians stand aside and allow his army to march unmolested to Paris.

Albert refused the ultimatum from his cousin, the Kaiser. The story goes that Albert said to his ministers, "Belgium is a nation, not a road." Historians may cynically dispute that account. But damn, it's hard to imagine a more eloquent and inspiring cry of resistance.

As required under the Belgian constitution, Albert took direct command of the Belgian Army. In those early days, he led his outclassed army in a magnificent fight. The Belgians disrupted the invasion timetable for the invasion of France, delaying the German advance by perhaps a week or more.

Albert never surrendered. Belgium fought on through the entire war, holding on to the *Yser Front*, a tiny sliver of unoccupied sodden land in the western extreme of Belgium, along the Franco-Belgian border. In a war cursed by criminally incompetent leaders, Albert proved to be a capable general. He was no chateau general, like those men who commanded well to the rear, safely quartered in luxurious mansions with well-supplied dining halls. Albert stayed at the front, within artillery and rifle range of the enemy. His Bavarian wife, Queen Elisabeth, served as a nurse to Belgian soldiers. Albert permitted his twelve-year-old son, Leopold, to enlist as a private.

The Rape of Belgium was no exaggeration of Allied propaganda. German officers, fearful of the Belgian partisans, *francs-tireurs*, routinely executed civilians as collective punishment. Case in point. In the first month of the war, in the old city of Dinant, panicked German reserve troops massacred 674 civilians. The Kaiser's army torched the Leuvan University library, destroying its treasures. The occupier's weapons became hunger, torture, murder, deportation, and forced labor of able-bodied Belgians. They looted Belgian industries and strategic resources.

By war's end, no one would have blamed Albert for seeking revenge upon Germany. Yet even during the war, he advocated a negotiated settlement based on a concept of "No victors. No vanquished." This is when, in my eyes at least, Albert rose to be a hero. A rare rational leader with the gift of foresight. Had the Allied powers listened to Albert, instead of humiliating Germany with crippling reparations and sanctions, and blame, perhaps a greater war would not have followed the war to end all wars.

Grandpa spent the war working as a messenger boy for the Belgian telegraph service, then run by the occupiers. The Germans paid him in bread, something far more valuable than any currency. When he talked about the war, which he rarely did, he often said, "The Germans kept me alive." Some might label Grandpa as a collaborator, but he was only a boy then. How could anyone expect him to do anything else?

For the novel, I reimagined Grandpa, Victor–I'm named for him–as a fictional character ten years older, who joined the fight as a private. Often under fire, he fights in flooded, disease-ridden trenches without relief. Belgian casualties to disease far exceeded those of the French, British, and German armies. My fictional Victor rose in rank, eventually serving as *aide de camp* to King Albert himself. Wounded twice, my character would survive the war and emigrate to the United States, marry an Irish girl, and raise two sons, only to relive the trauma of war as he saw his boys off to war against his old foe, the Germans.

A year of research went into the story, including a lengthy visit to Belgium with Susan. *The King's Lieutenant* was well received, though the sales were modest. All in all, writing *The King's Lieutenant* was wonderful fun.

Publishing both novels was not fun. I chose to self-publish. That means after writing the damned novel, the author faces the added damned expense—a couple thousand dollars—of hiring a company to print the damned thing, all the while trying to walk through a minefield of scams lurking on the web.

Then comes selling the damn thing. Only in writers' circles, a more gentile word is preferred. Promoting. If that isn't done well, you'll watch a hundred unsold copies in the basement become mold fodder.

Miracles do happen. Perhaps the book catches on with readers. It gets noticed by a great and powerful publishing house, which then descends upon the naïve author with a contract offer. That does happen. In a way, writers like me live the gambler's mantra. Almost everyone loses, but somebody's got to win.

In my case, Ed the literary agent found me. Steered by a friend toward *The King's Lieutenant,* Ed gave it a very good review and contacted me through my author website. I confess I initially disregarded his email, lumping him in with the legions of scam artists plaguing authors. Lucky for me, Ed was persistent. When we finally talked, I realized my colossal oops. Ed had a publisher in mind who'd pick up *The King's Lieutenant* and might do the same for my third novel.

Long story short, Ed saw to it that the third novel, *Democracy Lost*, was published last mid-November. A small publisher, but as it later turned out, certainly one with greater courage than the big ones.

Matching our troubled political times, *Democracy Lost* offered a plausible story of the extreme right taking power in the United States. Not through a coup. In the real world, they tried that before and came damn close to succeeding. My story imagined how the neo-fascists learned from their mistakes and took the presidency and the Congress in an election. And democracy lost.

Third time's a charm. *Democracy Lost* made good money. The publisher arranged reviews, podcasts, book signings, book expos, and interviews. It sold well, far better than I could have expected if I'd self-published. Did that result from better promotion? Yes. Partially. However, there's another reason.

My ego craved more attention. More sales. Instead of letting Ed and the publisher do their jobs, my greed set me on a dangerous path.

In a rogue promotional ploy that had its genesis more in whiskey than wisdom, I sent a copy of *Democracy Lost* to half a dozen way-out-there, far-right members of Congress, accompanied by a cheeky letter saying it was a story about patriots. Only my kind of patriots. Not theirs. The letter was, I admit, a misrepresentation. A lie. But it worked.

Last week of March, one of those Congressmen posted to his followers that *Democracy Lost* is "a must-read for anyone who loves their country." True enough, I thought, but the Congressman got the patriotic theme backwards. My readers roasted him on social media, pointing out that the book was a warning against people like him. Real patriots defend democracy. Real patriots do not advocate for dictatorship. As one reader suggested to him, "First rule of reviewing a book: read it."

Another elected right-wing firebrand defended her colleague, attacking me on social media, calling me a traitor and a rat. Stuff like that. That's when things really took off, for good and bad.

Ed and the publisher were furious at me, but their anger faded away as her call to ban *Democracy Lost* triggered an explosion in online sales.

A *New York Times* review touting my novel's value as a cautionary tale didn't hurt either. That may have got me on their bestseller list, even if only for a week. After that came national television interviews, when I made sure to sarcastically thank that particularly nasty Congresswoman. And I am very sarcastic. Sales went up again.

She fired back, gathering fellow extremists to a rally in her Congressional district. As the event's premiere attraction, they stacked up forty or so copies of *Democracy Lost*, dosed it all with lighter fluid, and struck a match. Watching the video, my first thought was, well, that helped with my next royalty check. But the smile came off my face when they burned me in effigy.

Think about it. A Congresswoman of the United States House of Representatives, sworn to "support and defend the Constitution of the United States against all enemies, foreign and domestic," burned books and then proudly posted the little fascist campfire on her official social media. The only thing missing was the brown shirt uniforms.

In her followers' eyes, I became a domestic enemy. And that's when the bad started.

Within hours of her post of the book burning rally, the social media threats started. They were brief and to the point, like threatening to cut out my heart and cut off other body parts that I'd grown rather fond of.

Threat after threat came by email through my author website. More "hope you die" social media comments hit my author social media accounts. It didn't take long for hashtags dedicated to my imminent demise to show up: #boycottholt. #holttraitor. #arrestholt. #hangholt.

If I am honest, in those first days of their hate campaign, a part of me enjoyed the negative attention. In a sense, it established me as a well-known and impactful author. And as sales spiked, it made me money.

So, I minimized the danger and ignored the threats. Writing them off as nonsense from random nutjobs, I felt certain they'd give up in a week or so. They didn't. The online trolls stayed on the attack. My initial battle plan–do not engage the enemy–didn't survive more than a week. I switched over to offensive tactics. Returning fire at the trolls with both rhetorical barrels. I thought, I'm a writer and well-educated. Use words like bullets. Hit the center mass of their egos and blast these ignorant losers down.

I learned a hard lesson. Facts, reason, and wit when battling trolls are no more effective than blanks fired in battle. Indeed, my witty responses only egged them on. The threats escalated, becoming more frequent and disturbingly more graphic. I retreated to silence, doing no more than reporting the truly nasty ones to social media platforms and blocking all I could. Perhaps sensing weakness, they continued the attack.

I was losing.

Eventually and inevitably, I asked myself, what if one of them really tried to . . . kill me? What should I do? For starters, not dying sounded like a good idea.

I did what anyone would do when facing the unknown. I searched online for what to do with a death threat. The dozen or so websites I read seemed to agree on step one: tell the cops. So, I went to the local cops with two weeks' worth of printed emails and social media screenshots.

I would learn that the police could not make the monsters go away.

CHAPTER TWO

THE COP

Holt

My association with Detective Peter Harrison began that first Monday in May. Association, not friendship. I don't think we ever became friends. That poor result is on me. Though I came to respect his dedication, from the outset I was quick to anger and often plain rude. As I saw things, I played the role of hapless victim, while I wanted Harrison to be the knight who could rescue me.

Harrison stands maybe an inch over my five-foot-ten-inch frame. With an athletic build, the only hint of his age is a smattering of randomly distributed grey in his jet-black hair. Harrison didn't need the badge and a gun to establish dominance over those he met, though they certainly helped. His handshake is enough, with a grip strong enough to send someone to the floor weeping.

Unsmiling, Harrison skipped over any niceties other than a simple introduction. All business, cold even, but courteous in a professional sort of way. Invited to take a seat at his cubicle desk, I told him my story while he patiently listened and took notes. When I showed him the printouts, I highlighted the threats that truly scared me. Without saying a word, he methodically looked over all the printouts while I sat anxiously there trying to avoid staring at him. Then came his questions.

"No one's threatened you in person, correct?"

"No. No one. Not yet anyway."

"So, all these, they were sent to you through social media or email?" I said yes.

"Nothing by regular mail?"

"No. Again, not yet."

"And you don't recognize the handle or email address of any of these people? Anything here you recognize at all? A unique phrase or expression, perhaps. Something you can connect with someone?"

"Nothing that struck me that way. So, no."

"All right. Let me ask you. Is there anyone you've argued with in the past, even over something that has nothing to do with your book? Someone with a grudge? A neighbor, perhaps."

"Nope. Not that I can remember."

Harrison laid the printouts aside. "So, Mr. Holt. Why do you think people want to hurt you?"

An obvious question for which I was unexpectedly ill-prepared. My answer was clumsy and disordered. I went from "I don't know" to "they hate my politics" until at last I recited the novel's premise. I summed things up by detailing my prank on the politicians. After I told him about the book burning, Harrison interrupted with a simple question.

"Why'd you do that?" I had no answer other than a shrug.

"So, you did it but don't know why." Harrison turned back to the printouts, shuffling them back together in a neat pile. It didn't take a rocket scientist to see he wasn't pleased with me.

Harrison acted like I imagined all detectives would. Focused. Unemotional. Not a word wasted. But I wasn't sure how to interpret his demeanor. Either he was the consummate professional, or he was supremely bored.

Apparently satisfied he had enough, Harrison offered his initial advice. "Here's what you can do now, Mr. Holt. Suspend your social media accounts." He made a strong case that the trolls were just nasty people who wouldn't act on their threats. However, what he said next was chilling.

"For now, let's assume there are multiple people threatening you. Maybe one or two aren't mentally stable. Don't respond to them. Don't engage. Don't send them over the edge."

Rather than confess that it was too late on that score, I moved on to another topic. "Detective, where does the law come down on this? I've never been through anything like this. Can you arrest someone over these?"

Harrison glanced up at the wall clock. "Understandable question. I've ten minutes until I've got to leave. It concerns another case. You got time?" I said yes.

"Just the basics for now. Let's start with insults. Most of this stuff you printed is just insults. You're a writer. Suppose someone gives your book a bad review. Calls you a hack, an amateur. Or suppose the review attacks the politics behind your book. Calling you un-American, a commie, or whatever. It's insulting, but it's their opinion. Nothing we can or should do."

"I get that. But what about threats?"

"I'm getting to that. Some seem serious. Let's start with two terms: harassment and then terroristic threats.

"Imagine a guy keeps sending you nasty, insulting messages at all hours. You never meet. He's anonymous. But you've documented every communication. You're suffering emotional distress, though none of these communications are outright threats to do you harm. We can still act. The District Attorney may decide these communications do not fall under constitutionally protected activity. Assuming we've identified the sender, the DA may charge that person with harassment, under the state's stalking law."

I interrupted Harrison. “Emotionally distressed? Goddamn right, yeah, I’m emotionally distressed.”

Nodding, Harrison said, “I can see that. Anyway, frequency is important in charging with harassment. The more frequent, the stronger the case.

“Now let’s say the guy doesn’t stop at insults. He threatens you with physical harm. Even if done one time, it ups the game. In this state, the DA could charge him with a felony. Max is five years, I believe. Another thing. With threats made over social media, there’s a new twist to the law. Cyberstalking. A misdemeanor on first conviction, but that can still put someone in prison for up to a year. With me so far?”

“Think so. Insults are insults. One insult, let it go. But a string of insults from the same person can add up to harassment. Maybe stalking. And a threat of violence, even one, could get felony charges. That correct, Detective?”

“More or less. Yes, sir.”

“Saying you’d like to see me hang, or my house burn down with me in it, those are threats. Look through that stuff I gave you. You’ll find some like that.”

“And he’s got to say *I* will hang you. I. Not something like, ‘I hope you will wind up hanged.’”

“So, the first-person personal pronoun is important, legally.”

“Ah, yeah, whatever.” I thought I detected a slight eye roll from Harrison. “Again, we don’t often identify them. ‘Course, sometimes they’re so dumb they ID themselves. Remember, we’re not talking *cum laude* types.”

I smiled at his cynical witticism. Comforting to learn my tormentors are likely not criminal masterminds, if such beings really exist. Still, dumb people will do bad things.

Harrison wrapped things up by running down a list of specific personal security measures. As he handed me his card, he said, “I’ll be briefing the Chief here and the county DA. You’ll be hearing from me soon. Call me if you have any other concerns or questions. Call me if someone threatens you. And next time, don't wait so long to tell us what's going on."

We shook hands and parted. Harrison had offered me a rational course of action. Stay calm. Don't engage. Watch my back.

That evening, I posted a social media sign-off. A "see you later if I'm still alive" message. I scrubbed my website of any mention of where I lived and redirected the email link directly to Harrison as he asked. He explained why he wanted that done.

"Monitoring your email, maybe we'll get lucky. Like they get stupid and say something that identifies their job, or location, or shit like that. My money's always on stupid."

I hated deactivating my social media. It felt shameful, cowardly, that I was surrendering part of my life to those anonymous bastards. I wanted to fight back, not lay low. I'd been trained to fight, but I retreated without offering the slightest resistance. I'd soon learn that even after going dark, the bad guys weren't done with me.

Three days after meeting Harrison and taking his cue from Congresswoman Wacko, who outed me with the book burning, a right-wing, gun-worshipping, conspiracy trafficking, radio/podcast host went on the attack against me. He wasn't a nationally known tinfoil hat type, but one right here in my home state who worked out of his basement. Hate globally, act locally.

He called himself Jack Wright and his online show *Patriot Wright*. He offered his limited following a plan of attack: protest and boycott any independent bookstore that sells my books. Unfortunately for me, he had talent at this kind of work.

That Saturday, Wright led ten or twelve angry right-wingers in a protest. He was very transparent about his plan. No need to hit every bookstore. Hit one store for a couple of hours, then move on to another before calling it quits. Just one afternoon's work. Let the news media and cell phone videos uploaded to social media spread the fear.

It worked. The stores capitulated. Within a week, all but one independent bookstore in the state dropped my books.

I don't know why, but the local news media never called me to ask my reaction.

Success attracted an ally. Another far-right personality joined Wright's campaign: a YouTube channel broadcaster named Joseph Smyth. With nearly 4,000 subscribers nationwide, he made his bread by feeding his hard-right listeners red meat messaging and deals on all sorts of prepper gear.

Soon after Wright's successful war on independent bookstores, Smyth appeared with him in a joint broadcast. Smyth urged an expanded war, arguing that their message only stays alive if the fight continues. And as in any war, they need targets.

Corporate bookstores were next. Soften them up with complaints about carrying my book. Hit them online with surges of poor ratings, which often didn't even mention my work. Then hit them with a weekend demonstration.

First up, they targeted a corporate bookstore in the state's largest city for a demonstration. Two days later, that corporation dropped my book from all their stores in the state and nationwide "for the sake of the safety of our employees and customers."

This time, the media noticed. Two local TV news stations and the city newspaper interviewed me. Did I have any response to their accusations and calls for a boycott of my books? I think my best response was this one:

"My novel defends democracy. My novel offends them. One may then suspect they're against democracy. Our democracy. The same democracy that protects their right to protest. That guarantees their right to call me unpatriotic and un-American.

"They call themselves patriots. I'd like to know if any of these, ah, gentlemen did anything for their country. Are they military veterans? Myself, I have a Purple Heart. How have they served their community? I'd like to know how they qualify themselves as patriots."

I thought I came off rather well on the TV news. Rational and reasonable, but willing to fight. Not exactly the laying low strategy Harrison recommended, but judging from the news, the public seemed to rally behind me. One independent bookstore found the courage to restore my novel to its shelves. Editorials, statements from politicians, and the like condemned Smyth and Wright.

Success is fleeting, however. My enemies, being neither rational nor reasonable, were also up for a fight. Holding the initiative, they moved on to their next target.

CHAPTER THREE

RETURN FIRE

Holt

For every action, there is an equal and opposite reaction. Though intended for objects in motion, Sir Isaac Newton's scientific law applies to human behavior as well. Rewrite it this way: For every defensive action by good people, expect bad people to hit back, but not equally. Harder. And they'll hit the most vulnerable spot first.

Here's how this law worked out for me. Authors like me customarily donate their books to public libraries. This charitable practice made target selection easy for Smyth and Wright. In calls to libraries throughout the state, they demanded my books be banned. For later celebratory broadcasts, they recorded each call. Bundling the recordings together, seasoned with profane commentary and a dash of violent rhetoric, they ran that episode in a loop. With their subscribers' emotions whipped up, Smyth and Wright issued a call to action.

"We'll show these libtard librarians what happens when they peddle the work of traitors. Today and every day this week, call your libraries. Demand to talk to the head librarian. We've listed their names and their office numbers on our website. Call them and keep calling until you get through. Don't just email them. Call them. Tell them to rip Holt's books off the shelves. And if they don't get rid of Holt's books, tell them we'll make damn sure they'll no longer be librarians.

"Then call everyone on the library's Board of Trustees. Their names and numbers are right there on the library websites. Then call your town government. Selectmen, Town Council, Mayor's office. Whatever. Call them. Keep calling, and we'll win one for true Americans.

"Remember. They're public servants. We're taxpayers and patriotic Americans. We have a right to call them. A right to petition. A right to see our tax dollars are spent the way they should be spent."

Over-the-top rhetoric, but nonetheless effective. Their followers made the calls and comment-bombed public libraries with negative online reviews. By Friday's show, Smith and Wright added direct action to their battle plan. "Tomorrow, Saturday, we'll have a live demonstration at Holt's hometown library . . ."

That morning, Carol, the town librarian, called me. I've known her since I donated my first novel. Carol defied librarian stereotypes. Outgoing, animated, and always quick with a joke, you knew when Carol was around. However, beneath that joyful personality lies a steely dedication to her profession. This would not be her first confrontation with fanatics and book banners.

"Vic, sorry to call, but those idiots who're after you. They're here, at my library. They're demonstrating. They want me to ban your books."

I was silent for a moment before using the kind of profanity one might never imagine saying in conversation with a librarian, like swearing around a nun.

"I agree wholeheartedly, Vic. Before this goes on the news, I want you to know I will never ban your books. Anyone's books, for that matter. No fucking way."

I asked how I could help. She said, "Stay home. The police are here, so not to worry." Ending the call, I tried to reassure myself that Carol would be fine.

The police are there. Carol's tough. I'll make things worse if I show up. I'll only provoke them. Do what Carol says. Stay home.

Guilt compounded by shame proved more powerful than sensible caution. I drove to the library.

The library itself could easily go unnoticed by the passerby. Just a single-story, white clapboard building hidden by a grove of trees. Only a small wooden sign by the sidewalk identifies the library. As I drove in, I saw the demonstrators waving their signs at the front door entrance. Wanting to enter as unnoticed as possible, I parked in the larger library lot on its western side. Sitting in my car, I still had a clear view of the library front.

Ten demonstrators, all with signs. *Libraries Supports Treason. Ban Holt. Holt's No Author – He's a Traitor.* They kept up a chant of "Ban Holt Now."

The TV news was dutifully covering the event. A reporter was trying to interview the demonstrators. One did oblige, but from what I could see and hear, the interview seemed to be little more than five seconds of yelling into a microphone. The others ignored the reporter, preferring to march around waving signs and keeping up their chants.

As if God were signaling His disapproval of book banning, a steady rain started.

Before getting out of my truck, I removed and pocketed my most recognizable feature. The eyepatch. It doesn't cover an empty socket or a hideous wound, but I've found it helps relieve a migraine-like pain that sometimes develops when I feel on edge. That day, Christ Almighty, I was on edge.

Walking toward the library in the rain, I realized I hadn't thought through my appearance very well. The front door was the only way in, taking me right past people who hate me. Unaware of any alternative, I kept walking until one of the cops intercepted me on the walkway. Reaching out, he turned me around, so I had my back to the protestors.

"You're Holt, aren't you?" He almost seemed to whisper.

When I nodded, he said, "Thought so. Remember seeing you with Detective Harrison." He stopped to quickly look back at the protestors, who were merrily carrying on.

"You shouldn't be here. If these . . . whatever they are, recognize you, shit, they could get ugly. Do us all a favor. Go home, Mr. Holt."

"I hear you, officer, really," I said, "but no. I can't. Carol has the guts to stand up to them. Since this thing about me, the least I can do is stand by her side."

We argued back and forth for a couple of minutes until the officer finally relented, suggesting I go in through the back door.

"Officer, look, I'm going to walk right past them and go in the front door. Don't stop me."

"Are you fuh . . . frigging crazy?" Clearly, the officer was not pleased.

"Maybe I am. But I'm going."

With that, I put my eyepatch back on, turned, and walked briskly away from him. Pissed though he was, the officer didn't stop me but followed a step behind. I walked right by the protestors, looking straight ahead, and for once, kept my mouth shut. Just as I stepped through the door, I heard one of them say, "Hey, wasn't that Holt?"

Instead of a warm greeting, Carol chewed me out. I tried to explain I was there to lend support. True to character, she wouldn't have any of it.

"Bullshit! Last goddamn thing I need is for you to show your goddamn face. I told you to stay home! You trying to pick a fight at my library? Now, what'll we do? Take a selfie with you so we can publish it on the library website?"

Carol walked away to her office. She needed a couple of minutes to calm down, time she spent throwing a book or two and swearing. Not typical librarian behavior, but Carol was the furthest thing from typical. She'd almost calmed down when the reporter and a cameraman came inside. They asked for the head librarian. One of the staff pointed toward Carol.

After the reporter's brief introduction, a still-angry Carol agreed to be interviewed. Hiding by the book stacks, I watched the reporter persuade Carol to stand by the library front desk. I listened as the reporter asked Carol for her reaction to the demonstrators. Carol gave them an off-the-cuff, perfectly eloquent repudiation of the right-wing demonstrators.

"They can protest all they want. But ban a book? Ban any books? No. Not now. Not ever. People who ban books are never the good guys."

The reporter got what he wanted and was about to leave. That is, until he saw me. He called out, "Mr. Holt? Victor Holt? You're the author they want banned, right? Could we talk to you?" I was a little surprised he recognized me. Then again, my picture was on the news, and it's in every copy of my book. Eyepatch included.

Having no place else to hide, I responded, "Yeah. I'm Victor Holt." He practically leapt toward me, not bothering to wait for me to agree to the interview. He began with the obvious question. Why was I in the library? I stumbled over an answer. "I'm, ah, here, yeah, to show support to the library and its staff and to thank them."

I should've shut up then and there, but the reporter set a sly trap for me. He asked me another inane question.

"What is your opinion of the demonstration?" That's all it took. A bait that I had to bite.

"My opinion? They've been targeting and threatening me for a while now. Online threats. Even death threats. They went after the bookstores selling my book. Now they're going after our libraries. Going after good people like Carol here.

"Let me ask you, when did we get comfortable with librarians standing in harm's way? Not just librarians. Poll workers. Scientists. Public Health professionals. Teachers. People who serve their communities and country. Now they're being targeted by ignorant fools, and we say nothing."

Shouldn't have said fools. Not smart. The news will love it, but it'll really piss off those people.

I shut up and walked away, ignoring the reporter's follow-up question as I entered Carol's office and shut the door. Carol was already there. After an awkward apology to Carol, I said it was time for me to leave. Heading back to the front door, Carol chased after me with a better idea.

"Don't be an ass, Vic." She told me to pick out a book and read it until the demonstrators left. An hour later, they did.

The libraries stood firm in the coming days. That is, almost all of them. Two libraries gave in, small ones in smaller towns nearby. For the sake of public safety, they announced the withdrawal of my books. I knew they didn't have my books. Maybe they thought they pulled a fast one over Smyth and Wright. They didn't. Smyth and Wright used them as evidence of a "massive victory."

Smyth and Wright soon shifted to a new front, targeting online retailers of my books. Within days of their latest broadcast, multiple one-star reviews of my books popped up. In a dead giveaway, these comments used the same phrases and gave little evidence they'd read the book. Though the retailer identified these faux reviews as coming from "unverified purchasers," they still counted against my ratings. That a review comes from someone who did not read it is simply galling.

Not every comment-bomb strikes the target. Retailers screen every review before it's posted. Drop an "F" bomb, and it's bounced. Violating the retailer's online community standards earns the same fate. But if an unverified purchaser keeps it clean, says not much more than the book is bad, and stays within the rules, the one-star rating stays.

Meanwhile, social media hashtags directed at me made the rounds. #boycottvicholt. #banholt. #banholtdemocracylost. #stopvholt. That's not all of them. Others infiltrated social media author groups to post insults and warnings about me.

Despite the attacks, I took solace in my continued respectable online book sales. I thought, maybe I've still got supporters out there. Or there are people buying my books for bonfires.

At home after the *Battle of the Library*, an awful realization came to me. They will not stop and will never admit defeat. All I could do, I felt then, was face whatever came next. And it did come. Smyth and Wright brought up their big guns.

Two days after the library engagement, I was enjoying a sunny morning with my morning coffee on my deck. Looking out over the water, I watched the season's first pleasure crafts sailing by. With every passing day, there'd be more boats out there sailing to nearby harbors. A brief respite from my ongoing troubles.

The doorbell's ring spoiled my peace. I went back inside and saw through the front door's glass a man standing there, holding up his identification.

CHAPTER FOUR

CRITIQUING THE AUTHOR

Harrison

It took an uncomfortably long time for Holt to open the door. When he did, I saw a wide-eyed, balding, paunchy, unshaven man with a white T-shirt, blue pajama bottoms, and ratty-looking slippers.

"Good morning, Mr. Holt. Detective Harrison. Remember me?" I held up my badge and ID just in case. Holt couldn't hide the look of surprise on his face.

"Detective, yes, I remember. Ah, yeah. Well. How are you? What's going on? How can I help you?" Holt nervously babbled on. An early morning visit by a cop does that to people. Time to assure the citizen not to worry.

"Sorry for disturbing you so early. May I come in?" Holt stopped talking, waved me in, but kept his slack-jawed, surprised expression. I decided on a little light conversation to get things going.

"Nice place you have here. Beautiful views. And I see you've taken my advice about personal security." I pointed to the drawn window shades and his truck parked facing away from the house.

"I think you can turn off the outside lights during the day." I tried to say it all with a smile.

"Ah, okay, yeah. Listen, Detective, is there something you want . . . to tell me?" Holt seemed to be struggling to recover his senses. "Is this about me going to the library? Jesus, I mean . . ."

"The library. Yeah, I know all about it from my guys and the news. Hey, is that coffee?"

"Oh, yeah. Like a cup? Let me get you a cup." That gave Holt something to do.

With a coffee in my hand, Holt led me through the house to a chair at the white deck table.

"Well, so, why are you here, Detective?"

"I'd like to talk to you about your case." Time to get down to business.

I told Holt I knew about Smyth and Wright and the protests at the bookstores. And, of course, at our town library. I rebuked him, mildly I think, for the library appearance, saying it was unnecessary exposure and could have led to confrontation. Also, I told him I'd seen his television news interview but stopped from offering an opinion. If I had, I would've said his ego did the talking, not his common sense, if he had any. At a time when he should lie low, he decided to pick a fight.

"Mr. Holt, let's start with Smyth and Wright. There's been . . ."

Holt interrupted me. "Detective, I'm no lawyer, but I guess, they, Smyth and Wright, haven't broken any laws, right? I mean, free speech."

I nodded in response and then asked Holt if he made a habit of listening to Smyth and Wright.

"No. I mean, yeah . . ." Holt rambled, saying he wanted to listen to them but decided it wouldn't do him any good. "Just makes me more, ah, anxious."

"I'm sure." To myself, I thought from what I'd seen of Holt, the word anxious described him well. Then I got back to the point of my visit. From a folder, I slipped Holt printouts from the Smyth and Wright websites. After giving him time to look them over, I gave him the bad news.

"They doxed you. Meaning they posted your home address, a picture of your home, and pictures of your truck. Registration plate and all. And they urged their followers to watch for you."

Holt did not take this well, yelling, "WHAT THE FUCK!" He yelled that again and again at an increasing volume. I let him vent before continuing. "I have more, but I'll wait for you to calm down." That took him another minute.

"You done, Mr. Holt?" He said yes, but as I recall, not in a nice way.

"Anyway, Mr. Holt. Maybe you helped dox yourself. Unintentionally, that is."

"What? You trying to blame me now?"

"No. Not at all. But your picture is in every one of your books and was all over your social media. You got yourself on the news. So, everyone knows what you look like. Plus, your books say you're from this town."

"But I never wrote or posted or said exactly where I live. How could . . ."

It was my turn to interrupt. "And I'm sure you didn't, but that may not matter. The information is out there. Let me explain." Holt stopped talking.

"You know, these days, privacy is a quaint and pretty obsolete notion. Just my opinion, but search yourself online sometimes. Your full name, birthday, marital status, voter registration, and more will come up. And your street address. It's a matter of public record. What's posted isn't always accurate, but it's a start for a determined individual. And I'm sure you've heard of Street View. Even my house is on there."

Holt seemed to settle down a little. Then I stupidly overstepped.

"Or someone just did the old-fashioned way and drove by here to take a picture." Holt did not react well to that possibility.

"What about my truck? You got any goddamn idea how they got a picture of me and my truck?"

As calmly as I could, I said, "No, but maybe you can help. Look at the background in the truck pic."

As Holt examined the picture, I told him to dismiss any thought that someone had walked or driven down and taken pictures of his truck in his driveway. "The background doesn't match your house. So, do you have any ideas?"

Still angry, Holt shoved the picture back across the deck table. "How in the fuck would I know? Jesus, I could've been anywhere."

As being nice was not working, I changed tactics to something blunter. "Holt. I'm here to fucking help you. Do you recognize where the fuck you were when this picture was taken?"

Startled, Holt responded with a muttered, weak apology.

"Okay. Let's try again. Look at the truck picture again. Any idea where you were and when?"

Refocused, Holt responded quickly. "Shit. Anyone who lives here knows that place." Holt said the pic showed him at the *Little Beach* microbrewery down the road. Their building has a distinctive, modern design. Easy to identify.

"*Little Beach*. We thought so. I go there myself. Anyway, thank you for confirming it. Now, when do you go there?"

"Okay, Detective. There's no date/time on the image. Guess they're not that dumb. Anyway, I go there a couple of times a week. Or I did before. But . . . look here. I'm wearing only a polo shirt and carrying my jacket. So, it was warm weather. That shirt. I just did the laundry this morning. Yeah, so I'm guessing it was last Sunday. That was the last time I went there. That's what I wore. I put that shirt in the laundry basket that night. It was nice that day, wasn't it? Looks like I'd just arrived. Shows me walking away from the truck. I got there at . . . just after three."

"Last Sunday, then. Three p.m." I made notes across the pic. "That could help."

Holt asked me if I thought they were waiting for me at *Little Beach,* but immediately answered his own question.

"No. That can't be. How'd they know I'd be going right then? It's not like I've got a regular habit of going for a beer on Sundays at three. I didn't tell anyone I was going. I went on impulse.

"Or they followed me there. That means they'd have to wait for me, maybe down my road someplace. No, that doesn't work either. Lot of time waiting for me on the chance I'd head out, and a good chance someone would notice them."

I complimented Holt on his analysis, agreeing it was highly unlikely someone was watching him.

"I think it's no more than a coincidence. You happened to go there when one of their fans was there. You were recognized, maybe from the news, and someone took your picture and sent it to Smyth and Wright."

Holt seemed to agree, nodding his head.

"Another thing. Their latest show got the DA's attention." I explained their broadcast included the statement, 'putting out an APB on a traitor.' The DA thinks that may meet the legal definition of a threat, and he might be able to act."

A cooperative and reasonable person would welcome this news. Not Holt.

"May? Might? Not exactly encouraging."

"Look, Holt. The DA's doing what he can. What the law allows."

It was time to wrap things up. I collected the printouts before urging Holt to be careful, watch his surroundings, and call me or 911 immediately if anything happens. I added that he should not go to *Little Beach* for a while as I handed him my card again.

Holt fell back in his chair, looked away from me, and tossed my card on a deck table before exploding. Bolting up, he kicked the chair away from the table, yelling and cursing in the extreme.

I guess he made quite a show. A neighbor came out onto her deck. Maybe embarrassed by her appearance, Holt stopped yelling. She waved, and he waved back, calling out to her, "I'm okay, Lil. Sorry. Sorry."

I stayed in my chair, trying to keep my cool. As he apologized to his neighbor, I slowly stood, spreading out my hands wide to get his attention.

"Judging from your reaction, I bet you're thinking of doing something stupid."

All he offered was a blank stare. "Stupid?"

"You're thinking of calling up Wright or Smyth. My advice: don't. I mean it. You do that, and you only confirm they got to you. That's what they want."

Holt started to object, but I cut him off. "Now it's my turn to tell you what to fucking do." Once again, I ran through the personal security measures, demanding he promise to comply.

Sufficiently cowed, Holt saw me to the front door. As we parted, I regretted being so harsh with Holt. True, he can be a jerk, but after all, his world has changed for the worse. Walking away, over my shoulder, I repeated my most important advice.

"And Vic. Don't be stupid."

CHAPTER FIVE

FIRST INTRODUCED

Ford

A long day at work usually ends with take-out for dinner, except that night when I cooked for myself, which I never enjoy. It's just more work. Especially when it's easier to pick up a grinder or heat chili or stew out of a can.

That night it was spaghetti and frozen meatballs, covered in tomato sauce from a jar. Not from scratch, like Mom used to do, but I did buy a nice Italian bread and a bagged green salad to go with it. Standing over a boiling pot of pasta, I started thinking, well, here I am, living rent-free in my parents' house after they moved permanently down to Florida. I have the whole place to myself. And I'm about to enjoy a pretty good meal. Work may be hard, but things aren't all that bad.

From in front of the stove, I could watch the news on the small counter TV attached to the underside of the cabinets. Like every other night, I ate at the kitchen breakfast bar. Then I'll flop on the couch and catch a movie. Mom and Dad are still paying for the streaming subscriptions. Maybe they forgot, but I don't think I'll remind them.

The local news was on, mostly for background noise. It's always the same old shit. A couple of shootings in the city. This or that politician with nothing important to say. The usual sports. Being a landscaper, the only part I ever paid attention to is the weather. It's nice to know if rain's coming.

As I was stirring the spaghetti sauce, a story about our town library caught my attention.

I'd never heard about Holt the writer before. The gist of the story was simple. He wrote a book that pissed off people. They protested Holt at the library. They wanted the library to ban his books, and the library said no way.

Exactly why his book got them all angry, I didn't follow, but I did catch the part when Holt talked to a reporter. Holt acted all high and mighty, going on about freedom and patriotism. About defending democracy. The news moved on to a commercial, but my thoughts lingered on the story a little longer.

Defending democracy, he says. Bullshit. He doesn't really care about democracy. He's just trying to make a buck like anyone else. He acts so superior. Just another goddamn intellectual, another elite, who thinks he's better than the rest of us. And what's with the eye-patch? He looks like a Halloween pirate. I don't care what he wrote, but I bet there's a good reason why they're pissed at him!

Democracy, my ass! What has democracy done for me?

All through dinner, I stewed about the library protest, talking out loud to myself at times. Finished with dinner, I dropped the dishes in the sink and flopped on the couch with a beer. Watch a movie and then head to bed. Big day tomorrow that'll come early.

The news said he was a local guy.

CHAPTER SIX

MESSAGE IN A BOTTLE

Holt

Sailing through my open driver's window, it smashed against my head. Shocked, blinded, I slammed on the brakes. My arms locked straight against the steering wheel. I heard tires screeching from behind. Nothing I could do but wait for the collision. And maybe die.

Seconds passed. No collision. I wasn't dead. I turned my head and looked back through a still blurry right eye. The car behind had stopped with a foot or two to spare. I felt around my head. No blood. Glasses still on. Too shaken to drive off, I shoved the truck into park.

I looked around inside my truck until I saw it. A bottle. A plastic water bottle, cap still on, full, lying at my feet. Maybe I was in a sort of shock, but I smiled, thinking it was good that it wasn't a glass bottle. In the old days, everything came in glass bottles . . .

The driver behind me roused me from my nostalgia. He drove around and up into the left lane alongside me and stopped. Looking out my still open driver's side window, I expected him to say, *Hey buddy! Are you all right? Need help?*

Nope. I got the usual road etiquette for these parts. He

screamed and swore at me. He didn't quit until another car came up behind him and blew its horn. Off he went. I sat there, in my lane, blocking, wondering what the hell had happened.

Again, I felt around my head for injuries. My head still wasn't bleeding, but I had a sore spot at the side of my left eye socket. *That'll make a nice bump.*

Another car came up from behind, blowing his horn, yelling at me as he went by. That's when I realized getting out of the way might be a good idea. I drove on and parked just off the road. I sat there, I'm not sure how long, minutes certainly, trying to clear my head and decide what to do next. Getting hit in the head while driving was new to me. Sure, I've compared middle fingers with other drivers before, but getting hit by a bottle? Why? What did I do?

My cell phone was still in its dashboard holder. I set it to record and started talking to myself.

"Was driving on the main road into town. Driver's window down. Stopped at a red light, in the right-hand lane. Light turns green, I went straight, still in the right lane.

"I saw . . . what? A white . . . pickup truck. Big one. Taller than my small pickup. Came up beside me. On my left. He didn't pass but stayed with me. That's when I got hit. Passenger in the truck must have thrown the bottle at me." I swallowed a couple of deep breaths.

"Why? Didn't cut anyone off. No. Wasn't Road rage. Something else." I stopped recording.

Maybe I shouldn't go home right now. What if they're still out there?

I headed toward the police station, deciding I'd be safer there, all the while looking for white pick-up trucks. A mile out from the station, I hit the hands-free button to call the police. I asked for Harrison.

Harrison wasn't there. I parked and walked, no, ran in and told the desk officer what happened. At least, what I could remember. He asked for another officer to take me inside. She filled out paperwork before going with me to my truck. Picking up the plastic bottle, she slipped it into an evidence envelope, said Harrison would call me, and left me out in the parking lot.

The officer's nonchalance didn't leave me with a good feeling. Like this sort of shit happens every day. She was perfunctory. A fancy word that a writer would know, meaning she did what was required and nothing more. I wanted to yell at her. *Hey, how 'bout an APB? How about trying to catch criminals? Huh? They assaulted me! You know people are after me!*

Instead, I drove home. My only consolation was that it could've been worse. It could've been a brick or a rock. Or a gun. Which was no consolation at all.

Harrison called about an hour after I got home. He promised he'd distribute a description of the white pickup, what little I provided, among local police departments and the state police. The DA was the next person he'd call. He'd send the bottle to a forensic lab for fingerprints and such. He ended the phone call with advice to be "watchful."

Watchful. Really? I unleashed against Harrison.

"Sweet Jesus Harrison! Day before yesterday, you showed me those pictures of me at *Little Beach* Brewery. Now I get whacked by a bottle. This wasn't random. I can't prove it, but I just know it. They knew who I was. They knew my truck. Wright and Smyth told all their followers to go after me. Looks like one did. They're watching me. They're after me, Harrison! What the fuck are you going to do about it?"

"My job." He hung up.

The bottle was a message. More messages will follow.

It didn't take long. The next day, in fact.

CHAPTER SEVEN

A TRIP INTO TOWN

Holt

My house sits on the seaward side of a pothole-ridden road that dead-ends at my house. Horror writers would appreciate the irony of people wanting to kill a man who lives on a dead end.

It's a two-story job with a deck facing the ocean. It's not one of those McMansion monstrosities that keep popping up around here, but a rehabbed legacy house first built at the end of the Second World War. Two small second-floor bedrooms. Two baths. No basement. There's a covered balcony off my bedroom that makes an excellent perch for viewing the waves crashing on the shore.

An old, detached one-car garage stands perpendicular to the short, paver stone driveway. Two years ago, I'd fixed the garage up rather nicely. I've never parked a car in it since. I like to say to people, my garage is the best-built storage shed around.

About one hundred feet from the seaside deck and across a slightly down-sloping lawn is a wide band of riprap rock fortifying my stretch of waterfront. Common around here, the boulders stand only two to three feet above the lawn's edge. A short span of stairs offers the easiest way over the rocks and down to the beach sand. Aged and rickety, the stairs need work. Nails tend to pop out of split, weathered wood. Its white paint now exists mostly as chips that flag in every breeze and fall one by one over the rocks. I'm certain the next big storm will take the stairs away. As badly as they need repair, I've habitually put off that project until next year and then the next.

Picky people will find the beach disappointing. Wide and sandy it is not. Strewn with rocks and seaweed, the tides push tiny seashells into ever higher and wider berms. Especially high tides submerge the entire beach, allowing waves to crash against the riprap. On the upside, the tides shoo away lingering tourists.

Scarcely past my driveway, the road's paving ends in a ragged line, petering out into a narrow plot of dirt with enough space to park four, maybe five cars. From there, a narrow foot trail winds through acres of marshy conservation land. Occasionally, people park their car in the dirt lot and set off on a little exploration through the marsh. That irritates me somewhat to see strangers parked so close to my house, but there's nothing I can do about it. It's not my land and they have legal access to the conservation land. On the plus side, I don't have to worry about someone building on that side of me.

Rather unusual for this overdeveloped coast, there are no homes on the other side of my road. A continuous, thick stand of trees entangled with bittersweet vines grants me a measure of isolation and peace. However, this won't last. All up and down the road, a developer pounded in four-foot-high wooden stakes with streaming red pennants marking which trees will live and which trees will die.

Until the builder starts work, Steve and Lillian are my only neighbors. Like me, they're year-rounders who stay on not because of a shared love of the pain winter storms bring, but for the season's solitude. For me, the peace and quiet were replaced by isolation, loneliness, and fear.

I find myself minimizing, rationalizing all that's happened.

Perhaps it's an innate self-defense mechanism, buried deep in my mind, to keep me from going crazy. From time to time, I catch myself thinking the bottle thing was a random one-off by one of those wackos who're always out there. After all, Harrison must know best. People don't act on their threats. Best to follow his advice and wait this out.

I was wrong.

At around five p.m. the day after the bottle, I did a normal thing. Needing a couple of over-the-counter meds, I drove to a pharmacy only five miles away. An ordinary, everyday errand of no consequence. It was, until I headed back home.

Only a half mile from my house, there's a T-intersection where the road into town meets my road. I slowed to the stop sign, my blinker signaling for a left turn. I saw it before I stopped.

Maybe ten feet before the stop sign, someone hammered into the ground a crude, handmade sign on two stakes. It was fairly sized, about three-by-three feet. A neon green background with big black letters. Impossible to miss. It read HOLT THE TRAITOR LIVES DOWN THERE. A thick, black arrow pointed left to where I lived. Beneath the arrow was my address.

I got out, leaving the truck running and the door open, and walked up to the sign. Dumbfounded, I stood there for I don't know how long before I called Harrison on my cell.

"Listen, Holt. Get back in your truck! Now. Police will be there in two minutes." While I waited, a few cars passed by, headed into or returning from town, paying me little attention. I tried not to look at them.

When a patrol officer arrived, his vehicle's pulsing blue lights attracted people from neighboring homes, including a guy I only knew as Doug, the homeowner across from the intersection. Another man walking his dog, a young guy, came from somewhere around the corner. I didn't know him.

As the patrol officer questioned me, Harrison and another

detective arrived. They processed the scene while the patrol officer went over to talk to Doug and the stranger with the dog. When the officer finished, Doug waved at me and went back inside his house. The stranger headed back to wherever he came from.

"They say they didn't see anything, Detective. How long the sign's been there, they couldn't say."

"Okay, fine. Go knock on the doors of the other homes in a line of sight to here. Ask them if they have a door security camera. Call me when you're done. Thanks. We got things here." The patrol officer went off to question the neighbors. Harrison asked me questions to check the facts before promising to be in touch.

"Mr. Holt, go home. Don't worry about this. Doubt more than a few people saw it." If Harrison seemed stand-offish, I had only myself to blame. Of late, I'd not been all that nice to him.

I stood out there a little while longer, staring at the cars as they crept by. Realizing how foolish I looked, I got back in my truck and drove home.

They know my truck. They know where I live. What's next?

I didn't have long to wait.

The next afternoon, Ed told me a book signing scheduled for next week had cancelled. The venue didn't want my troubling celebrity status to "attract negative attention." That was the third cancellation in the last week.

An hour after Ed, an English teacher from the local high school called. As I had done for him for the last couple of years, he'd scheduled me to speak to his senior classes about my writing experience. After forcing students to read novels written by long-dead authors, meeting a local, living author was a nice break for the kids. This time, parents complained about the possible danger I brought to their kids. Others objected to an "unpatriotic" author coming in. The school cancelled me.

Losing a book signing, that I could bear. But getting cancelled by the school, that hurt.

I'm targeted by right-wing media. They're trashing my books. They're targeting bookstores. They're attacking other people because of me. They know where I live and what truck I drive. I'm getting hateful and threatening emails all the time. Will it get worse? Yeah, of course it will.

CHAPTER EIGHT

THAT'S HIM!

Ford

Not a good end to the day, I remember thinking. I was hungry and tired and just wanted to get home. I picked up a big sausage grinder and a bag of chips for a tolerable dinner. At the intersection, only a couple of minutes from home, what I saw changed things.

Lights flashed from two cop cars stopped at the intersection. I couldn't see any accident blocking the road, but traffic stopped. Pissed, I hit the horn and yelled to the air, "Move, damn you! Move!" I hit it again. One of the cops turned to look at me and shook his head. Screw him, I said to myself. I almost flipped him off, but held back.

Standing by the cops was a man. He wore an eyepatch.

That's him! That's the fucking guy!

I couldn't believe it. Not more than ten feet away was the guy from the news; the writer guy everyone's after who wrote that book that's got them all pissed off. The guy they call a traitor. I stared at him while waiting for the traffic to move. I doubt he could see me through my tinted glass. Well, I thought, it's a small world.

What was his name? Holt, wasn't it? He lives in town. That's his truck parked on the roadside. Got his left blinker on. Nothing but maybe half a dozen homes down that way. Democracy's great defender might live down that way. Hell, he's almost a neighbor.

A cop waved at me to get going. I turned right at the stop sign, but moved slowly, trying to see what I could in the rearview mirror. After dinner, I sat myself in front of my laptop. I couldn't let go of the possibility that the man with the eyepatch lived down the road from me. A little Googling and I uncovered a couple of things.

Victor Holt does live down the end of the road. That wasn't hard to find. Two online broadcasters, Smyth and Wright, who organized the library protest, put Holt's address and a picture of his truck on their website.

Should I call those shows and tell them what I saw? No. What would that do for me? They'll thank me, pat me on the head like I was a little boy, hang up, and forget about me.

I decided to listen to their recorded shows. Find out what's going on. Besides, I was curious. And I had little else to do. Their shows bored me to tears. I'm not into politics, so I didn't give two shits about their rants on the issues of the day. The people who called into their shows didn't seem all that bright either. Then again, if I'm honest with myself, it wasn't what they said. It was how they said it. Their emotion. Their anger against all those above them. The elites, they called them. People who lord over us. They wanted to put elitists in their place. A way for real people to take their rightful place. To go up, not down anymore. I needed a way up.

CHAPTER NINE

SOCIOPATHY AND PSYCHOPATHY

Holt

The bad guys weren't done with me.

Interestingly, their approach had a certain diversity. Some haters emerged who favored an old-school, traditionalist approach. Snail mail. Detective Harrison schooled me on the telltale signs of suspicious mail. No return address. Excessive tape. Stains. Odd smell. Stuff like that. If an envelope or package looked odd, I'd send a pic to Harrison and leave the item with the post office staff, who, I hoped, would call the U.S. Postal Inspection Service. As a precaution, I secured a post office box.

As is fashionable among traditional postal terrorists, envelopes sometimes contained white powder. The first time, I idiotically opened the envelope at the post office, creating a stir for the postmaster, with police, fire, hazmat teams, and media responding. Once again, I wound up on the news. Closing the post office for a couple of days while awaiting lab tests and decontamination didn't make me any more popular around town.

Flour or baking soda weren't the only substances gifted to me. A surprising number of envelopes offered dried dog turds. At least, I hope it was from dogs.

Then there were encounters on the street. The other day, I stopped at a local drug store for a prescription refill. When I came back out, a young jerk had pinned my truck in place. Sunglasses, ballcap, sandy colored T-shirt, scraggly thin beard, and worn-out jeans.

I rapped on his passenger window. "Hey, buddy. Could you move?"

He sat there, looking straight ahead as he lit up a cigarette. I yelled some more. He ignored me. Only when I took out my phone and started taking pictures of him and his car did he move on.

Confrontations on the road are a different matter. Since Smyth and Wright unleashed their happy band, driving has become a way to meet members of the motoring public who want to hurt me. Although I've minimized driving to life's essential errands and medical appointments, I'm almost always spotted. People point at me, blow their horns, and curse me.

Rule Number One when giving the middle finger when driving: Check beforehand that the traffic pattern will allow you to depart. The obnoxious number of traffic lights on the main roads around here tends to force vehicles to travel together as a group. One moron forgot this rule. He flipped me off, but soon found himself stopped alongside me at the next red light. And then the next red light. I looked at him, smiled, waved, and took his picture. Incidents like that are almost comical.

Other road engagements were less humorous. More than a couple of times, drivers came right up behind me within a foot or two, flashing lights and blowing their horns. Nothing for me to do but keep a steady speed and hope they'd give up.

One guy didn't give up. He stayed right on my tail for at least a mile. This time, however, I acted. Turning sharply into a supermarket parking lot, he followed close behind. I hit the brakes hard. He couldn't stop in time, tapping my rear bumper, though not hard enough to crush either car or set off the airbags.

A silver subcompact. Two doors. Toyota. In-state plate. Not sure what year. The driver? Thick brown beard, about half my age, wearing a dark green T-shirt with a stylized American flag on the shoulder. Same color ball cap with sunglasses perched atop the bill.

He tried to move, but I moved faster. I stood by his door. As he tried to get out, I shoved it closed, almost catching his leg. With my phone out and camera app up, I snapped as many pics as I could of him and his car. Swearing. Oh, there was swearing. Both by me and him. Somewhere in our little conversation, I said, "I'm calling 911. Don't you fucking leave."

I guess he didn't like hearing that. He backed up onto the main road and sped away, almost causing another accident.

A cop came a minute later. I texted him the pics of the man's car and told them to contact Detective Harrison. After he talked to Harrison, the cop let me go after a very serious chewing out.

"What the hell were you thinking? An old man like you. Suppose he had a gun. We'd be here with a body bag." It went on like that for an uncomfortable stretch of time. "I'm only letting you go as a favor to Harrison."

In that moment, what the cop said didn't matter to me. I felt good. I fought back! I won! I drove away happy, my soul nourished, and my truck bearing an honorable battle scar that I will never get repaired.

Driving home, the thrill from the *Battle of the Supermarket Parking Lot* faded as the cop's reprimand replayed in my mind. While I'd won a small victory, there's no sense in drawing more fire. The officer was right. If that man had a gun, I'd be dead.

Calling that evening, Harrison went ballistic. True artistry in stringing together curses before he demanded I follow three simple rules. Number 1: Stay at home. Number 2: Do what I tell you to do. Number 3: Do not provoke. He ended with a warning. "We can't protect you if you do stupid fucking things."

My reaction, which I kept to myself, was equally simple. I do not want fear to rule my life. Yet, that's exactly what would happen.

Self-confined at home, I pulled down all the window shades and locked every window and door. Alone and disconnected in a darkened home, I didn't write. I hardly ate. Sleep did not come easily. Old movies and a bottle of premium bourbon were my only company. And the bourbon only encouraged an awful thought. There is something or someone waiting for me. What I did not know was the worst of all fears.

Isolation did not last forever. Life intercedes. On the afternoon of my third day post *Battle of the Supermarket Parking Lot*, my phone reminded me of an appointment the next morning with my therapist. Her office is twenty minutes away, near the hospital. In my mind, I conjured images of what could happen while driving. Recognition by a troll. More road rage. Violence. A house left open to vandalism.

I almost hit her office number to cancel. Too afraid to leave my house, I considered what fictitious excuse to use. Something ordinary and reasonable, which didn't make me seem crazy. I settled on the flu. I hit her number. It rang twice before I stopped the call.

"No. Not right. I need her help. Got to talk to someone." I thought, goddamn it, Harrison. Look what's happened to me by laying low. As my therapist does not have a delivery service, I planned my visit.

Harrison's security plan demands detailed planning. Check for a fully charged phone. Look through the house windows for anyone lying in wait. Check they're locked. Then plan the route. Harrison recommended I vary what roads I use to get from one place to another, but that's not always possible around here because there aren't all that many roads. So, I needed a unique road feature that would set the stalker apart from the innocent.

On GPS, double-check the route already planned to check for any traffic problems. Before opening the front door, press the key fob to remotely start the truck. Activate the house alarm. Have the house key ready in my hand and lock the door as I go out. Go straight to the truck and unlock it remotely with the same key fob. Once in the truck, lock the doors, put the key into the ignition, and start it. Hit the gas and get going immediately.

Checking my truck's undercarriage for explosive devices wasn't yet part of my security plan. But give it time. I'll get there soon.

Drive above the speed limit. Pass other vehicles whenever I can. Keep my head on a swivel, looking left and right, checking all the mirrors. Don't stop if possible. Keep moving. Arriving at the destination, park as close to the entrance as possible. Look all around before getting out. Go straight in. Task done, repeat the process in reverse, varying my route home if possible.

This time, I drove toward the business district road and took a right turn at the lights onto the main road. Down the main road, past the big shopping center, I entered that unique feature. A rotary. That's when the dark comedy started.

I circled in and went for one, then two, and then three laps without exiting. And there he was. A full-size black pickup truck, I first spotted in the town business district. He matched me lap for lap.

Fourth lap. Fifth lap. He kept with me. Once I memorized his license plate, I slowed down to a crawl. Close behind me, he did likewise. When I finally drove off the rotary, exiting toward the clinic, Black Pickup Guy continued so close I couldn't read his registration plate.

Coming up to the intersection before the clinic, I made a full stop at the green light. There was Black Pickup Guy, still behind me. I got out and took a pic of him and yelled, "The cops got your number!"

Back inside my truck, I went right. He went left.

I felt better leaving the therapist that afternoon. Talking

through my grief and fear certainly helped. But confronting that stalker had its own therapeutic value.

Sailing down my road for home, scanning for anything or anyone out of place. I parked in my driveway, locking the truck remotely as I got out. Nervous, I fumbled my house key. As I locked the door behind me, I made a mental note to get a better security system.

Self-medicating, I poured a finger of bourbon. Two sips in, I called Harrison and left a message. An anxious five minutes followed until he called back. I gave him my report of the *Battle of the Rotary*. After justifying my medical appointment, I gave him the truck's plate number and promised to text him a pic of the guy's truck. I stood in the kitchen with my phone in hand, girding myself for Harrison's wrath.

Instead, Harrison played it cool, saying he understood about the therapist appointment and promised he'd follow up on Black Pickup Guy. No yelling. No cursing.

"Vic, I get it. You need to see her. You're frustrated. You reached your limit today. Nice trick with the rotary." He even laughed a little.

"Just don't think this will discourage them. No more games. If someone is following you, drive to a police station. Or call 911. What you did could've backfired. The guy in the pickup, I'll visit him. Tonight, I think. Anyway, I've got an update for you."

Harrison gave me the latest figures on emailed threats. Over a hundred more in the last five days. He told me the police cited the guy from the supermarket parking lot.

"So, you've had your fun. Don't engage with them. Don't be stupid."

Emotionally deflated by Harrison's mild but justified reprimand, I double-checked the door and window locks and the first-floor shades drawn before going upstairs. I felt safer watching TV in my bedroom upstairs rather than the living room. My medication came along.

A little television and one, just one more bourbon, then I'll fix a half-assed canned dinner.

Watching the local news, the second one finger of bourbon became a third two-finger glass. If my therapist could see this, I knew she wouldn't like it. She'd warned me against mixing booze and antidepressants, but I wasn't in the mood to be a compliant patient. Sitting at my desk in the little alcove off the bedroom, sipping my drug of choice, I replayed the day's events.

People are threatening me. They want to kill me. They will not stop. Who are these people? What motivates someone to write a death threat?

They say liquor opens the mind to creativity, though science has yet to establish a causal relationship. However, alcohol and drug abuse correlate well with the early demise of an upsetting number of great writers and artists. I once did an online search on this topic. The first website listed fifteen writers. Another had twenty-five. The third had ninety-nine. Fitzgerald, Hemingway, and Mailer. Poe and Sinclair Lewis. Uncorking the booze may lessen inhibitions to expression and release the imagination, but eventually, alcohol sealed the coffin lid.

At least, that's my wholly unscientific view. For me, a little bourbon helped for a short time when I wrote in the evening. More than a little bourbon resulted in plain rubbish. WUI. Writing Under the Influence. So, after two pours and a third work in progress, I was well past being creative. I corked the bourbon bottle and left it on the floor, leaving the glass perched on a windowsill. I couldn't write, but I could still do research. Opening my laptop, I started with a relevant and obvious question, tapping out my thoughts as they came to me.

What kind of person writes a death threat? Most people are good.

They have a moral compass. Something in their consciousness that tells them what is wrong.

But what about people lacking any sense of right and wrong? Who are they? Unhappy. Obnoxious. Mean. Angry. Bullies. Bullied. Lonely. Close to no one. No family? Unable to control their emotions. Uneducated? Traumatized? Victimized? Crazy. Mentally ill. Sociopathic? Psychopathic? What does science say?

Sociopaths and psychopaths. Familiar terms, but few understand them beyond knowing they are bad, mean people. Among those of us with medical training limited to television crime shows, there's general agreement that a psychopath is worse than a sociopath, as in serial killer worse.

Even under the influence, you can learn something new. Turns out, sociopathy and psychopathy themselves are not accepted clinical terms. They do not appear in the *Diagnostic and Statistical Manual of Mental Disorders.* Rather, the behaviors attributed to a sociopath, or a psychopath, fall under an overall diagnosis of ASD - Antisocial Personality Disorder.

ASD's cause is unknown. Genetic? Past trauma? Perhaps both? We don't know. However, there's agreement on a long list of ASD symptoms. ASD patients tend to be angry, purposefully cruel, and impulsive. They can be manipulative, narcissistic, demonstrate little regard for danger, and not show an understanding of right from wrong. It seems logical that criminality and violence top the list. In lay terms, they are bad people.

Even though clinicians and researchers cannot agree on a precise definition of either term, there is a consensus of sorts about one factor that may distinguish a sociopath from a psychopath. Empathy.

A sociopath may still understand the difference between right and wrong, but still do wrong. In them, there is still a residue of empathy for those he or she wrongs. With a psychopath, you're out of luck. No understanding of right or wrong. No empathy. We're back to serial killers.

How prevalent is ASD? Knowing that might shed light on the odds of me running into someone with bad intentions. A simple question with no good answer. The short answer is we don't know. It doesn't help that people with ASD do not self-identify. They don't go to their primary care physician one day saying, "Hey doc. I don't know what's wrong, but I've got these feelings. I made a list of them and checked the DSM."

The first estimate I found was that 3.7% of the general population had ASD. Another estimate was a more comforting one percent. That doesn't sound so bad until you do the math. Given a population of one million, one percent is 10,000 people with ASD.

Another study suggested that of the entire ASD population, ten to twenty-five percent might be psychopaths. Splitting the difference at fifteen percent, then for every 10,000 people with ASD, roughly fifteen hundred psychopaths are lying in wait, excluding those already locked up.

Put all that on a smaller scale, perhaps one out of a hundred people you know is a sociopath or a psychopath. Not exactly a comforting thought for holiday get-togethers. I made one last note to my little essay.

Are the people who want me dead really at fault?

One day, maybe science will have enough empirical evidence to identify the causes of mental disorders like ASD. From there, effective treatments could follow. Until then, people with mental disorders, like ASD, are endemic in the population. This is an undeniable and tragic fact.

When a heinous crime is committed, the armchair psychiatrist in all of us is quick to judge the perpetrator as insane. Or we see evil at the root of the unspeakable and demand that the wicked be punished. That's the way it's always been.

Must it be that way? In those rare moments when I'm calm and rational about the people torturing me, I'm faced with a duality. Yes, I want those people punished. Harshly. How else should I feel? Who could fault me?

At the same time, I think the larger share of blame lies with the media figures and politicians who enrich their power, prestige, and wealth by propagating outrage. They know damn well what they're doing. They understand their rhetoric will inevitably trigger a few of the many. They know they're putting a match to abundant fuel. When you think about it, they are the true sociopaths who think themselves unaccountable.

In times not long ago, their message would reach thousands. With modern media, they instantly reach millions, increasing the odds that a psychopath will hear them and act.

Yes, I can blame self-serving bastards like Smyth and Wright. I can blame the book-burning Congresswoman who set this all off. I can blame them for burning down my life. In time, I could forgive those who write hate mail. But never the powerful who goaded them to action.

There's one more party to blame. Myself. Flawed, often ignorant, and stupid. I'm the one who triggered it all by sending my book to those politicians. I got from them exactly the reaction I wanted. All to sell more of my damn books.

Finished with my essay, I closed the laptop and opened the bottle. Another neat bourbon suddenly seemed appropriate.

Keep this up, and you'll wind up on that list of authors.

My deep, alcohol-induced sleep wasn't enough to prepare me for the morning.

CHAPTER TEN

SPECIAL DELIVERY

Holt

"Ed, I'm calling because I got another one."

"Another what?"

Not the thing I wanted to hear from him. "Christ, Almighty! What do you think?"

Ed didn't respond immediately. I knew he damn well knew what I meant. "Another . . . ah, death threat?"

Hungover and frustrated, I attacked. "Yeah, Ed, it's a death threat!"

"Okay. I understand. But Vic, remember what the police said. These rarely go further."

"So, when I turn up dead, maybe then you'll think at least one went, what did you say? Went further? For fuck's sake, Ed!" I kept yelling and swearing. Ed said nothing while he waited for me to exhaust myself. Staying calm in the face of emotional writers is a skill he no doubt acquired through long experience.

"Vic, okay. Help me understand." He spoke slowly and deliberately. "What is different about this one? You've never been this upset."

By going silent, I kept being a jerk. After long seconds passed without a word or a curse from me, Ed said, "Vic? You there?"

"I'm here. Listen. Yes, I've gotten hundreds of them. But this one . . . is different." I took a deep breath before saying, "Ed, sorry for my . . . whatever." My conciliatory mood didn't last for more than a couple of seconds when an image of what I found on my front step came back to mind.

"I should be used to people saying their fondest wish is for me to die. In often creative ways." Hearing no response from Ed, I further escalated an unnecessary fight.

"Listen, Ed. Don't think I'm alone in this. It's a fair bet they know you're my agent. Someday you might draw fire. But never mind, I'm sure these people won't ever threaten you. So, sorry to bother you." I held the line, half expecting Ed would hang up, but he didn't.

"Please, Vic. I want to understand. Tell me about this one . . . this death threat."

Once again, I could have acted like an adult. An adult under stress, true, but an adult. I didn't. I acted like a terrified son-of-a-bitch.

"How's it different? For starters, it's not social media, email, or a letter. It's a box. I found it this morning on my front steps. There was no box there when I went to sleep. So, someone put it there last night. Someone walked right up to my goddamn front door and put the goddamn box on my goddamn front steps! You want to know what was in the box?"

"You opened it?"

"What? Of course, I opened it! It wasn't sealed up anyway, except for Scotch tape holding the flaps shut. Like he wanted me to open it."

"Come on, Vic."

"All right, what was inside? A head. A bloody stump of a head."

"WHAT?! Did you say 'head'? What the fuck do you mean?"

Clearly, Ed finally lost his shit. Honestly, I enjoyed those few seconds before I asked myself, who is the sociopath now? Me.

"Ed, I'm sorry. I wasn't clear. You think it's a . . . human head. No, no. Not that." Again, I waited.

"Christ, what is it?"

"A fake head. A mannequin's head. With what looks like red paint applied to the neck stump. There's even an eye patch painted on it. They wrote my name across the forehead. When I first saw it, I almost shit myself."

That part is true. I first saw the box through the front door glass. Not thinking things through, I went out onto the steps in my pajamas with a full coffee cup in hand. A wise man would've left the box alone and called the police. But no, I didn't do that. Dumb ass me peeled away the tape with my free hand and looked inside.

There it was, staring straight up at me. I simultaneously jumped up and yelped like a hurt puppy. Hot coffee went all over my hand, causing a second squeal of pain, before dropping the mug and splattering coffee all over the front step, my pajamas, and the box.

"Look, Ed, sorry to come off, ah, pissed off at you. Kinda stressed these days. That's no excuse. I am sorry, Ed. But a fake head in a box isn't subtle. Someone wants to cut off my head. Didn't make for a pleasant goddamn morning."

Ed assured me he understood and asked what he could do to help. When I couldn't think of anything, he ran through the same advice he always gave me. Go to the police. Go through the personal security steps. Do what you've been told. He ended with, "And don't worry."

I hit the end call button and started pacing around my living room until I finally accepted that Ed was at least partly right. Maybe wholly right. Time to see my friend at the police station.

CHAPTER ELEVEN

MEETING WITH THE WRITER, AGAIN

Harrison

Out of the corner of my eye, I saw Holt come into the station. I was at my cubicle desk, tapping away at my computer keyboard. I didn't look up as I waved Holt toward the seat at the side of my desk.

"Morning. How's the bestselling author on this fine day in May?" I intended the sarcasm. About the weather, that is. The rain started to pour as Holt came inside the police station.

Holt didn't accept the invitation to sit down. Instead, Holt stood there and blurted out, "Great. Just great," as he dropped a large paper bag on my desk that landed with a thud.

My job requires me to know more than the basics of human emotions and behavior. But anyone could've seen something very wrong with Vic. His eyes shifted this way and that. Trembling hands. His clothes looked like he threw them on in a hurry. When Holt finally spoke, he seemed hesitant and confused.

"Look . . . Look inside, Detective. The bag. There's a, ah, box. In the bag. Someone . . . they left it. On my doorstep. I put it in the bag. This morning, they left it. The box. I found it. There's something. In the box. Open it. Look inside." Holt stopped talking, then fell into the chair. Leaning forward, his shoulders slumped, he looked away from me and at the floor. Almost whispering, he pleaded, "Go ahead, Detective. Have a look. You need to see what's in the box."

He had the look of an exhausted, defeated man. "You're not going to just tell me, are you, Vic?" He shook his head. I put on a pair of black latex gloves. Using scissors, I cut away the paper bag before getting to the box. "Okay, there's the box. Before I open it, why won't you tell me what's in the box?"

Holt wasn't talking, and there seemed to be no point in arguing. Using a pencil to hold a box flap open, I looked inside.

I admit it. What I saw startled me. Letting the box flap fall back, I looked at Holt and said, "You don't see that every day."

"No, Detective. You don't. It's fake, but it's me." Holt pointed out the drawn eyepatch and his name across the forehead. I asked about the liquid stains on the box. Holt explained about the coffee spill. "Yeah, that'd make me jump, too."

Reaching into a large desk drawer, I took out a high-end digital camera and called over to a colleague to snap pics of the box and the head from all angles with a ruler placed alongside.

Holt lingered in the chair, watching the officer work; however, we needed a more private place to talk. Tapping his arm, I led Holt to the conference room and closed the door.

"Vic, Officer Grimes will process the head. Meanwhile, I've got questions for you. You okay with that?"

Holt went through all that happened, from the discovery of the box to spilling the coffee, how and where he touched it, to putting it in the bag and driving to the station. I took notes and asked Holt to read them to make sure we didn't miss anything.

I ended with, "You didn't see anyone put the box on your steps. And coming here, you didn't see anyone around your house. You didn't see anyone following you here."

"Ah, no, I don't think so."

"Okay. I think I've got a good picture of things." I closed my notebook and leaned back in the chair.

Holt looked a little surprised at that and said, "Well, that's all you're going to do? What's . . ." I preempted him.

"This is the part where I assure you the box and its contents will undergo a forensic examination for fingerprints, DNA, and other things in the hope of identifying who put it all together." I was about to continue with my summation when Holt stood up and interrupted me. Rudely.

"Jesus, Detective, do you not understand? They dropped it at my front door. The front door of my house! They walked right up to my door last night! For fuck's sake, they . . ." He must have gotten a little loud. I saw a couple of faces turning my way from outside the conference room.

I put up my hands and said in a calmer tone than his, "For fuck's sake, I do get that, Vic. Now, are you going to help me do my job?" Holt was pissed. Maybe I'd have felt the same way. Holt nodded.

First off, I thanked Holt for safeguarding the box by putting it in a paper bag and not taking the dummy head out of the box. "Okay. Let me give you my initial observations. Let's begin with the obvious. They didn't mail it or have it shipped. Guess whoever sent it isn't that stupid. Did you notice the logo on the box?" Holt said no.

"Looks like they, ah, repurposed an old box from an online store," I told him. I saw part of a shipping label and bar code still on the box. "Odds are against it, but that partial label might help us trace the box back to its original user." Holt seemed calmer. Encouraged, I continued.

I explained we might be able to pick up something from the head, such as a manufacturer name, maybe a lot number, and of course, fingerprints. To lighten the mood, I deadpanned, "Course, I'm not an expert on mannequins."

Not appreciating humor at a time like this, Holt got out of the chair and started to walk away. Before he finished his second step toward the door, I got his attention back.

"Stick around. We're not done." I didn't yell. Just a firm tone, what they called from my early patrol officer days, a "command voice." Holt sat back down. I locked my eyes on his eye.

"Look, Vic, let's talk about your case, starting with how many threats you have received." I gave him the figures he already knew. "Since April 21, the first death threat, one hundred thirty-three threatening emails have been sent to your author website. Twenty-nine are unambiguous death threats. Now what have we done with them?"

A quick update, I thought, might improve the demeanor of this nervous citizen. Starting with all the dumb threats, the ones who used unencrypted Gmail or Yahoo accounts, I assured Holt that we identified twenty-two individuals.

"So that's the dummies. They got angry and acted out. Our county DA has the identity of those in his jurisdiction. The same goes for the DA's offices outside our county. Doubt you need to worry about them. Police contacted every single one. Like this local one. Old guy. He 'bout shit his pants when we knocked on the door. I'll bet he thought of himself as a law-abiding citizen. He was until then. His case is before the DA."

Next up were the smarter ones. "As I told you before, we're not sure how many fit into the category of skilled, ah, threateners."

Skilled meant they had a fair understanding of the technology they used. It's possible to send anonymous, near-untraceable email using one of half a dozen or so providers that mask the IP address that is normally tagged to every email. Nothing illegal about that. They help clients establish VPNs—Virtual Private Networks—that are essential to organizations wishing to protect their trade secrets and such. Anyone can get VPNs. But like anything made for a good purpose, it can be used for bad.

Holt said something cynical, to which I fired back. "By the way, your publisher got two hundred eleven threatening emails. The worst of those, thirty-three to date, threatened violence toward the publisher's building and employees. Since your publisher is in another jurisdiction, the police there are taking care of it. Tell me, have you given any thought as to their situation, Mr. Holt?"

Holt didn't respond other than casting his eyes down. I took it as a "no." Holt came back to the death threats against him from persons unknown. "Can't we do anything about the encrypted ones?"

Even with encryption, I explained, there are options. A single anonymous threat likely won't match a single person, but with a statistically significant number of threats with matching grammatical patterns, misspellings, repetitions, or unique phrases, it might point us to a single, yet unidentified, author.

"That puts us a big step closer to identification. And again, they make mistakes. Maybe they say something that betrays their identity. Work, town name, veteran status, and so on."

"Like you said, Detective. You're betting on stupid."

"That I am." I shifted the conversation to another aspect of the insults. Something I found amusing.

"There are, let's say, certain commonalities to insults. Especially those with, ah, an anatomical theme. Asshole, Goddamn asshole. Fucking asshole. Goddamn fucking asshole. You know, we did a statistical analysis of each of them."

"You're kidding. You counted how many times someone called me an asshole?"

"Seriously, we did. Determine the frequency of specific, perhaps unique words or phrases, use them as a kind of marker, and we might identify patterns. Patterns might indicate a single person. And frequent insults from the same person could lead to cyberstalking charges."

"You're not going to tell me how many times?"

"I'd rather not. I don't think it'd do you any good. Anyway, all this sound about right?"

He mumbled, "I guess so." Holt sounded like an eye-rolling teenager who couldn't care less about what I told him. It was time to snap back at him.

"You know, we put a lot of work into this." What I held back from saying was he's pissing off the very people who can best help him. Disgusted with Holt, I excused myself, telling him to stay in my seat while I went to take a leak.

When I came back to the conference room, I showed Holt a piece of paper inside a plastic evidence bag. "Officer Grimes found this. A letter under the dummy head. Guess you didn't see it before."

"No, I didn't. What does it say?"

"Nothing good. It says, 'You will die on a chopping block like all traitors.' He misspelled 'chopping.' Used only one 'p.' All caps. Typewritten. Old school. Anyway, this is good. More evidence.

"Look, as I see it, someone who types out a death threat, on a typewriter, spent more time thinking about it than someone spends on a social media post or an email. Put the paper in, set up the typewriter, hit the keys and put it in an envelope with a stamp and go to a mailbox. That takes time. Time for them to, well, reconsider things.

"Emailing or posting accommodates impulsive acts. Just hit the send button. So, I'll take a mailed old-school threat more seriously."

Apparently not in a mood to accept any good news, Holt shot back that the police couldn't possibly know of all the threats that might be on Telegram or 4chan or any of those other extremist-serving websites.

"You're right. Do you want me to say only stuff that makes you feel good, or do you prefer honest answers?"

Holt didn't answer but glanced away.

"I'll take that as you want honest. All right. Law enforcement in general has limited resources for monitoring the web, and again, you're not the highest priority. When we've got politicians and judges and outspoken celebrities being threatened all the time and, well, you're not at the top of the pile."

Holt didn't say a word but stared at the wall, avoiding eye contact. I wasn't done with Holt yet. "Now, do you remember what I told you about how the law views threats?"

Still fixed on the wall, Holt said, "Yeah, I do. Real threats can be prosecuted. Insults, no."

I wrapped up things by talking about the gift left on Holt's doorstep. "The box, the head, and the typed letter goes to the state forensics lab today. They'll examine the letter for typographic evidence, like imperfections in the key strikes that could link it to a specific typewriter. Like in emails, they'll also look for writing patterns. Characteristic punctuation and grammatical mistakes. Hell, whoever wrote this might be threatening other people. A serial threatener. Is that a word, my writer friend?"

Still distracted, Holt said, "It is now."

"They'll try to get fingerprints and DNA off the paper letter and the box. Match that against their database. 'Course, only people who'd been arrested before will be in the database. Always a chance, though."

I asked Holt if he had time for another question. "Aside from this box with the head, anything else, anything unusual around your house?"

"No, nothing really."

"Nothing . . . really? Well, Vic, if you remember that there is something else, and you want to talk more, give me a call."

Holt wasn't done. He asked about guns.

CHAPTER TWELVE

PERSONAL FIREPOWER

Holt

I hadn't added to my arsenal of one weapon, the same one I bought years ago. A simple over and under 12 gauge for trap shooting. With the 00 buckshot shells I'd since bought, it would be especially lethal. However, I wanted other options.

Three weeks ago, I'd taken the Department of Public Safety handgun certificate test. I passed, and two days ago, the handgun certificate arrived in the mail. Commonly known as the DPS Card, I could now go to any gun shop in the state and legally buy a handgun and ammunition.

Purportedly, the DPS Card test ensures prospective handgun owners understand the safe operation of their new weapon. Not exactly a challenging test, in my opinion. Fifty multiple-choice questions, requiring a score of eighty to pass. The questions offer choices A through C with not terribly imaginative distractors. Get ten wrong, and you still pass. There are TV game shows that require greater intellectual acumen.

I took the test at a nearby gun store. Ten minutes and I was done. The employee behind the counter said he'd send it on to the state for scoring. He asked how I did.

"I'm sure I passed. Pretty easy. Too easy if you ask me."

"Well, it's not meant to be hard. We've got guns to sell. I mean, you want a gun, right?"

At least he was honest. Thanks to Army training, I'm sure I could still break down and reassemble a weapon. Of course, one can't expect the same standards for the civilian world, though to me, the paper test only screens out people who'd have trouble identifying which end the bullets come out.

Passing a paper test is a low bar for ownership of a deadly weapon. No pistol range time under instruction is required. To get a driver's license, there's a written exam plus an eye exam, proof of auto insurance, and a real-live driving test in an actual car. But to buy a handgun, no practical test is required.

The only other hoop to jump through before buying a handgun is the background check form and a seven-day waiting period.

When I told Harrison I had the DPS Card, he didn't seem all that pleased. "Well, Vic, if you do, ah, you've never owned one before, right?"

"No, never have. Fired handguns before." I started reviewing my experience, but Harrison cut me off.

"In your experience, though, you've never used a gun in a confrontation with another human being. Even during military service."

"Yes, that's true. No. Not with a handgun. Never."

Harrison leaned back in the chair, as if he needed a moment to assess things. "Okay, Vic, if you buy one, please promise me you'll enroll in a shooting course." I started to object, saying I had extensive time on Army ranges with the sidearm of those days, the tried and true .45 caliber Model 1911.

Harrison stopped me. "I know, and that's fine. But it's been how many years? About forty? Wouldn't want you to buy one and only then figure out you're no good. Let's face it, you're four decades older and down one eye."

I said, "Okay, I see your point. I'll take a course. Any recommendation on what kind of gun?"

"You thinking of carrying one around for self-protection? Getting a concealed carry permit? With all that's happening?"

"Might make sense," I said it almost apologetically.

"Then let's talk about that, Vic." He paused for a second, shaking his head. "You'll get the permit, given your situation. But it's not like I look forward to another nervous citizen going around everywhere with a gun.

"Let me tell you, when I retire, I'm going to enjoy not carrying a gun. Pain in the ass. Aside from my service weapon, I don't keep a gun at home. I don't like them. They make more problems than anything else."

I didn't say anything, but I remember thinking that was an odd thing for a cop to say. Then again, I don't know but one cop - Harrison. My expression must've betrayed my thoughts.

"Didn't expect to hear that from a police officer, did you, Vic? Let me tell you, I'm not the only cop who feels this way."

Harrison waved his hand toward his colleagues in the main room. "We've all made traffic stops or gone on domestic disturbance calls. Especially those. Most dangerous thing we do. Highly emotional situation. Too many times, there's a gun in a drawer somewhere.

"I know, I know, you hear all sorts of stories about people using a gun to successfully defend themselves. Well, those are stories. Anecdotes. Nothing more. The data tells the story about people who screwed up with a gun. Or used it to kill themselves.

"Real evidence, statistics, show a handgun in the home endangers the owner and his family more than anyone else. The gun becomes the go-to thing to settle any dispute. It correlates with higher rates of suicide. You're a writer. You know how to do research."

Harrison indulged in his own past.

"I've unholstered my weapon only twice. My patrol officer days. Had it out, ready to shoot, and would've done it. Training kicks in. Believe me, though, when I tell you, I'm thankful I didn't shoot. If I can make it to retirement without . . . yeah . . ."

Leaning toward me, Harrison restored himself to the matter at hand.

"You asked about the type of gun. Try out different kinds at a gun store with an indoor range. Me? I'd stick to a revolver. Simple. Never jams. Easy maintenance. Get a small frame one. Better for concealed carry. Anyway, if you can't defend yourself with five or six rounds, shit, you'll be dead anyway." He said that last part with a bit of a smile. Maybe he was trying to lighten the moment, but I didn't catch on.

"And don't get one of those stupid magnum revolvers, like in the old *Dirty Harry* movies." I promised I wouldn't. Harrison replied, "Good, because they're pretty much useless. They're really for guys who want a bigger dick."

I got that joke.

"The permit to carry concealed. Hang on a second."

Harrison left for a moment before returning with pamphlets on the state gun laws. Purchasing regulations. The use of firearms in self-defense. And an application for a concealed carry permit.

"Vic, read these, and I mean read them carefully. Especially the part about defending yourself. Most people get it wrong. Let's start with defending yourself in your home. Ever hear about the *Castle Doctrine?*" I said I hadn't.

"I'll keep it simple. People say a man's home is his castle. They say you should be able to defend your home. Simple idea, right?" I nodded.

"Well, we've got our own version of *The Castle Doctrine*. Damn poor title if you ask me. Confuses people. Anyway, sure, you can use a gun to defend yourself and your family against an intruder. But you can't shoot someone on your front lawn. Bad guy outside, you stay inside. Basically, both you and the intruder must be inside, and you have no avenue of escape, and you are in imminent threat of life and limb. Understand?"

"Seems pretty clear."

"Really, you think it's clear. My best advice. If you shoot someone inside your home, be prepared to explain to a guy like me your every step.

"Now, there's another law that applies to concealed carry. Our take on the *Stand Your Ground* law. Another stupid name. Frankly, I hear about too many people who buy a gun, get the concealed carry permit, then go around town thinking they can shoot anyone who threatens them at any time. And believe me, they do. Always claim self-defense. It comes as a real shock to them when they're charged with a crime."

"Not sure I follow."

"Fair enough. Let's try again. The law imposes a duty upon someone carrying a gun, even with a permit. It's called a duty to retreat. If there is a way for the gun owner to retreat, escape danger, he must do that before using deadly force. You understand?"

"I think so."

"You think so. Christ, come on, Vic. You already have people threatening your life. I want to know if you understand. Try again."

Rightly rebuked, I corrected myself. "Duty to retreat. Yes, I understand that. If I can run away, I run away. If I'm about to die, then I can shoot."

"That's better. Remember, under state law, the last option is lethal force." Or as Harrison put it, "You've got to be on the verge of meeting Saint Peter."

I promised to give the pamphlets a thorough reading.

"Please, Vic. Jesus, the people I see. For them, the gun becomes their hammer, and every problem becomes a nail."

"Another thing, Vic. Once again, your address is easy to find. Town property tax rolls, voter registration . . . all open sources.

'Course, there's probably more people named 'Holt,' but, hell, your books let everyone know you live in this town. And it's a small town. So, one minute online and anyone can find you."

"That supposed to make me feel better, Detective?" I tried to say that in a funny way, but it was Harrison's turn not to catch the humor.

"Vic, do your best to remain calm. I know that's not easy, but try. Remember, it's extremely rare that a death threat is acted upon. They've still committed a serious crime, and if we catch them, they'll be prosecuted. They may only want to scare you. Don't let them."

"Christ, too late. Mission accomplished."

"Meaning you are scared. Look, I'll send a police car by your place a few times over the coming days and nights. But that's about all I can do. Unless we catch a break from the forensic tests."

I stood up, stopped for a moment, nodded thanks, shook his hand, and left.

Harrison had one last thing to say as I turned for the door. "Hey, Vic, save us all this trouble. Next book, write a kids' book."

I had to smile at that one.

He's right; I've got to calm down. Shouldn't piss off Harrison. He may be my only friend in all this.

Driving back home, I was alone with my thoughts, trying to figure out my next step. That is, until my fuel gauge warning dinged.

After I filled up, I pulled out of the convenience market onto the road home. A deep blue family van was coming on, maybe faster than I thought. Anxious about getting home, I pulled out ahead of him, turning left toward the traffic light by the store. The light turned red. The van stopped very close behind me.

From behind me, I heard yelling and cursing. In the rear-view mirror, I could see the van driver giving me the finger. That wasn't unusual, especially these days. I let it go. The light turned green.

He stayed right on my tail up to the next red light. And the one after that. As we approached the next intersection, I had enough of him. I went right toward a shoreline road. He followed. I went left at the next intersection, then left again toward the main road. He followed. Stopping at the light, he was still right behind me, almost kissing bumper to bumper.

I went right on the red and then took an immediate left. Two more lefts brought me, us, right back to the main road. There he was, right behind me. At the stop, I turned right as fast as I dared. So did he.

After a few hundred yards, I pulled a sudden U-turn. I headed for the police station, only a mile or so away. He followed. Hoping I wouldn't be seen by the cops who'd just seen me, I pulled into the police station parking lot. Blue Van Guy just kept going down the road. I guess he didn't want a confrontation in front of the cops. Neither did I.

It took a while for my hands to stop shaking before I headed for home. Meanwhile, I had time to think about what happened. Was it another Smyth and Wright guy threatening me, or was it nothing more than road rage, if a tad over-the-top? I couldn't be certain of anything other than I'd be safer at home.

One good thing did come from Blue Van Guy. He got me off my ass to call my home alarm company for an upgrade. The platinum plan level of security for the especially fearful. Remote door locks, alarms everywhere, plus security cameras with motion sensors. If I had done that earlier, we would've caught the guy with the fake head on video.

There was another thought Blue Van Guy suggested. *If I had a gun, would I have . . .*

CHAPTER THIRTEEN

PARANOIA RISING

Holt

The first post-fake-head morning, I awoke determined to brush things off and get back to work. Rather than imagining the gruesome ways people wanted to kill me, writing would force me to concentrate on how to kill off my fictional characters.

By midday, after hours sitting at my desk, zero progress had been made. My mind wasn't in the game. I easily distracted myself with irrelevant research or funny animal videos. Or worse, the news. What I did manage to tap out was pure rubbish, even by first draft standards. Getting up from my desk chair and walking randomly about, I wondered aloud to myself. "Guess you've got a nice case of writer's block."

No, it's not writer's block. Not of the typical kind.

It was fear. A primal fear straight out of the primitive brain. Fear of being hurt. Fear of being murdered. At the same time, another part of my brain held a residue of a paratrooper, reminding me I'd felt fear before. To be precise, my only brush with combat forty years ago.

I got through it back then; I can get through it now. Focus. What am I afraid of?

Doodling stray thoughts across a pad, my self-analysis realized fair results. Harm to myself headed the list, but coming in a close second was something more subtle, yet more terrifying. The idea that my life is no longer my own. I have lost control of my fate to people who will not stop.

Contemplating my doom wasn't all that fun, so I set the day on a different course: learning something about the science behind my fears.

Here's what I found from the *National Library of Medicine*: neuroscience identifies fear as an acute stress factor. In response, the brain's amygdala circuits become highly active, which in turn interferes with the functioning of the brain's prefrontal cortex, the center of cognition.

Compounding the situation, the prefrontal cortex is especially sensitive to acute stress. In other words, a little fear goes a long way toward messing up higher-level functioning, making it difficult to plan or reason. Or be creative, as in writing. Fear, therefore, can contribute to writer's block. If I get a handle on the fear somehow, maybe the writing unblocks.

To tone down the fear, I went back to Harrison's advice. The vast majority of threats are not acted upon. Criminal masterminds only exist in superhero comics. Criminals are not Mensa candidates. They are often just plain stupid and compensate with cruelty.

Another thing about the criminal mind, Harrison passed to me. The typical criminal's egotistical compulsion to brag frequently trips them up. Showing off with social media video posts got more than one January 6 rioter identified and convicted. Logically, the Bottle or Fake Head Guys might follow precedent. So, I searched all over social media. Alas, no joy. All I did was elevate my paranoia. Then again, as the old saying goes, just because you're paranoid doesn't mean someone isn't after you.

My second post-head day went much the same. No research.

No writing. No nothing. By the third morning, as a concession to physical safety and security, I exiled myself to the second floor, making only brief forays downstairs to the kitchen. I kept around my desk, mostly surfing the web for whatever came to mind, which again was mostly cute puppy videos.

That afternoon, however, there was a literal ray of sunshine. The weather turned beautiful. I thought fresh air might cure what ails me. With my laptop ready, I relaxed on the lounge chair of the master bedroom balcony. It was comfortably warm with a steady, light breeze. A wonderful view of the sea and of Montrose Island. Placed by nature almost one thousand yards offshore, the island is a tiny scrape of rock. At high tide, only an acre at most stays above the sea. On that small spot of land is a small sparkplug-looking lighthouse.

The beach is no more than a hundred feet in front of my house. In times before, Susan and I watched from the deck and the balcony the occasional couple strolling innocently along the beach, often with a dog playing with the seashells or a piece of driftwood. A couple of times a week every summer, men and boys waded into the water to harvest the conch shellfish from the near-shore bottom. If the wind was right, we heard them talking, often in Spanish or Portuguese. Day and night, other fishermen took station on the beach, casting away.

Idyllic is a good word to describe where I live. I've said to friends that if heaven exists, when I die, I won't notice. I'll just be here.

My earthly heaven is gone. Now I conjure danger from those same beachgoers and fishermen. Whole families, with their kids, suddenly turn on me with guns drawn. The pet dogs become attack dogs with a taste for my throat. The anglers become assassins, pulling pistols from their tackle boxes.

That afternoon, stunning views and fresh air didn't rid me of fears or change my reality. Lying on the lounge chair that afternoon, unable to write, I finally asked myself the obvious question: If I stopped writing, wouldn't my troubles all go away?

Until then, I hadn't seriously considered that logical option. Is it worth my life to keep at something that is more a hobby than a career? Financially, writing isn't critical. I'm well off. There's no mortgage. No car payments. I've got investments. My social security. Three years ago, I retired with a very nice 401(k). Plus, Susan's considerable retirement assets remain untouched. All I need to do is send out a press release announcing the end of my writing career and stop sales of that troublesome book.

Fleeing my home was another option. Sell everything and find a nice little place far away. Move to the Maritimes. New Brunswick, Prince Edward Island, and Nova Scotia are beautiful places. Then again, it gets cold there on a regular basis.

How about a place that's always warm? The Antilles, perhaps. I heard Bonaire is nice. Grenada? Wouldn't that be ironic? Exactly where isn't important, as long as it's tropical with fantastic white sand beaches. And restaurants with bars. Live an excellent life with my head still attached to my shoulders. No worries. No troubles. No threats.

No purpose.

Writing is the best gig I've ever had. I'm my own boss. I set my own hours. No commuting. I get to be a Creative. An Artist. I birth stories out of pure thought. What could be better? I like writing. It's what I do now. I don't want to stop. Writing is what I do for no other reason than I need something to do. Most importantly, my writing career is just starting to take off. That's the upside.

The downside? These days, writing carries with it the possibility of my bloody murder. And if I withdrew from that life, would the danger end? The question answered itself. No, these people will not stop.

Stay on the course, continue to write, and stay where I am. The best outcome, perhaps the only one, is to outlast them. And not get killed in the meantime.

Once again, that night's sleep did not come easily. Even with the house alarm and lights on outside and inside, every little noise set me on edge. A wind-blown screen tapping against a window became someone trying to break in. A creak of wood became a murderer coming up the stairs. With every sound, a sudden stab of terror ran through my gut, turning this old man in his sixties back into a six-year-old running for Mom and Dad, pleading for them to chase the monsters away.

In my world, however, monsters are real. They're not vampires or demons. Nor vengeful angels. Rather, they are the guy driving the pick-up truck behind me. The restaurant patron drinking coffee, looking at me from the next table, or the lady on the gym treadmill right behind me. My monsters are everyday people who, under different circumstances, might have become my friends. My monsters are here, they're real, yet possess the most perfect camouflage. They are ordinary.

In this fitful night, my monsters came.

CHAPTER FOURTEEN

MY END

Holt

Almost to the minute, I restlessly shifted position from one side to the other side and then onto my back. Unable to calm my mind, I was about to admit defeat and find a book to read in hopes of dozing off. My bladder had another idea. As I finished my business, I saw headlight beams coming down the road toward my house. Keeping the bathroom light off, I watched out the window as the car stopped near the road's end, half on pavement and half on dirt, headlights on and engine running. The seconds ticked by. The car didn't move.

Since I last saw Harrison, I'd brought my 12 gauge up to my bedroom, leaning it up in the corner by the nightstand. On the same nightstand, I left open a small box of classic but effective 00 buckshot shotgun shells. I kept the shotgun unloaded. To this nervous old man, leaving it loaded only invited an accident. Next to the shells, I kept my eyeglasses, a flashlight with fresh batteries, and my cell phone, charging continuously.

I went back into the bedroom for my shotgun and a handful of shells, slipping them into my robe's pocket. Checking the scene from the bathroom window once more, I saw the car still hadn't moved. As scared as I was, I halted at the top of the stairs, took a couple of deep breaths, and slowly headed down the stairs, one step at a time, tightly grasping the handrail in one hand and the shotgun in the other. Finally, standing in the foyer, I loaded both barrels and snapped the breech closed.

With a lethal weapon in hand, I flipped the outdoor lights off and then on. The car didn't drive away. I flashed the lights again. Still, the car didn't go away.

Opening the front door, I presented myself on the steps. An old man in an open bathrobe and worn-out slippers, tattered pajama bottoms, holding a shotgun. An old man who'd forgotten his eyeglasses. No doubt a terrifying sight to any trespasser.

Seconds later, the car backed up into my driveway. Raising the shotgun to my shoulder, I leveled it at the car's rear window. Resetting my stance to counter the recoil, my finger moved inside the trigger guard to lightly touch the trigger. If their door opens . . . another second . . .

The car went forward and turned left without incident or urgency. I'll never know if the driver skedaddled because he saw a man with a gun. Or he was a poor lost soul who never saw me at all and was only trying to turn around.

Standing outside on the steps, I lowered the 12 gauge and watched the car drive out of sight. Relief washed over me. At least tonight, I thought, I wouldn't shoot anyone.

Back inside, I locked the door and went a couple of steps into the foyer before breaking the shotgun breech. But I couldn't unload the shells. My hands trembled so. No little tremor, but a full-on spasm. I let the shells slide back in the barrels. Standing there in the dark, I took a deep breath or two before trying again. This time, I successfully unloaded it and dropped the shells in my robe pocket, hearing them clink against the spare shells. I walked back upstairs, one careful step after another.

Closing the breech, I stood up the shotgun in the bedroom

corner. The shells from my robe pocket went one by one back in the paper box before I sat down on the bed. Then the shakes started again, this time in a whole-body convulsion. It passed within seconds, and I fell back across the bed.

What the fuck just happened? What the fuck was I going to do?

I knew the obvious answer. Yes, I was about to kill someone. I chose confrontation when I could have stayed safely inside. Even with my unimproved home security system, one button would have alerted the police. But I was stupid. Irrational. Terrified by trivial events, like a car turning around. That's the fiction writer's curse. You have one hell of an imagination, especially for bad things.

By then, sleeping was out of the question. I sat up in bed, a bed I hadn't made in two weeks, stuffed a couple of extra pillows behind my back, and grabbed the remote from the nightstand for a late-night distraction.

I found an old movie. An awful romance story between . . . I don't remember. You'd think an utterly forgettable movie featuring long-deceased actors would've eased me off to sleep. Not at all. Not for a moment did drowsiness come.

After wasting another hour of my life surfing the cable channels, I mulled over the possibility of taking a shower, something I hadn't done in the last three or four days. Then a memory of the classic movie *Psycho* came to mind. *So, no shower.*

I shut off the TV, got out of bed, and sat in the bedroom chair near the window. Sitting there alone in the dark, I felt every one of my years. Never mind the thinning and gray hair, or the soft middle that overflowed my belt line too much. Nor the noticeable drooping of tissue from my triceps, hints of sagging chins, and the beginnings of a wrinkled neck. The generalized aches and pains. The sensitivity to cold and sudden urges to nap.

How I acted made me old. Slow to sit down; even slower to get up. Always anticipating random spasms of pain with every movement. Knees that sometimes rebelled at going downstairs. And going upstairs. And someday soon, falling on the stairs.

When I was young, I stayed in good shape. Even after leaving the service, I kept up Army PT exercises for about ten years. Mostly running, rounded out by quick rounds of weightlifting at a nearby gym. Then I just stopped. I don't know why. Maybe I got bored with the gym's hamster wheel-like routine. Or maybe I found donuts to be a greater attraction.

When I hit sixty, the cusp of old age, I ditched the donuts and went back to the gym three or four times a week. The result: my weight dropped back to around 190 pounds. BP leveled off at a pretty good 122/80. I felt firmer, more toned. And the gym helped offset a once-a-week visit to a microbrewery down the road. My medical history didn't hurt either. No history of heart disease or cancer. I never smoked. No chronic conditions, aside from manageable gastric reflux.

"If you're not getting older, you're dead." That's the timeless wisdom of Tom Petty. A couple of years ago, I thumbtacked a meme of that quote on the wall by my desk. Being a writer, I suppose I should've found a more worldly thinker to quote, but Petty's seven simple words serve well enough. There's no escaping the indignities that come with getting old. And I appreciated the irony in Mr. Petty's words. Not a well man in his last years, he died four days shy of his 67th birthday. A great talent lost. And here I am, not far from that milestone.

Sitting in the bedroom chair and obsessing about my age did me no good, so I shifted focus to the shoreline, deciding I'd find peace by watching a new day come over the sea. Cliché though it is, I'd always felt the dawn coming up over the water was like watching a whole world reborn, bringing new possibilities.

Not this dawn, however. My scrambled mind couldn't let go of the threats. Smyth and Wright. The library. The bottle. The lawn sign calling me a traitor. The guy driving that blue van. The parking lot. The bloody fake head.

What kind of sick bastard made that bloody head? He's still out there somewhere. He came right up to my door. What if he breaks in next time? Then what? Is he out there, right now?

Do what Harrison said. Any trouble, call the cops. Stay inside. Don't go out. Don't go shopping. Lock the doors. Don't keep to any regular habits. Don't go online. Don't look for the people who want to hurt me. Kill me.

How in the world will this old man, all alone, deal with what might happen?

I looked away from the water at the device in the bedroom corner. And the shells. The shotgun would stay there until I moved it. Or used it.

Without deliberate thought, I stood up from the chair and went to the nightstand. My right hand picked up a shell and took it back to my chair.

I held the shell close to my face, admiring the simplicity of its design and the precision of its manufacture. Caressing the smooth, shiny brass base that reached almost a third of its length, I ran my finger across the bottom, sensing the circular valley in the brass that surrounded the primer. I gently squeezed the fluted red plastic hull. Shaking the shell, I heard the rattle of the lead shot inside. The heavy lead balls would easily escape the shell's crimped end. Closing my palm around the shell, I buried the shell from my sight.

This could be my end. My way out. How very easy. One shell. Open the shotgun's breech with my right thumb. Load the shell into the lower barrel. Snap the breech closed. Turn the weapon around. Safety off. Lay my fingertip on the trigger. Say goodbye. That's all it would take.

I picked up the shotgun, loaded the shell, and sat on the bed, facing the seaside window.

Funny how the mind works. Only moments away from sending a lead shot through my brain, I became oddly logical, thinking through the consequences in a detached sort of way.

I can't let someone find me in this rotten old robe in a dirty house. What about the mess I'd make? Someone must clean that up. Clean me off the walls and windows. I really shouldn't put someone through that.

Then, what about the house? Who gets it after me? I should get my attorney to update my will before I do this. I don't want anyone to think I left behind a legal mess as well. My affairs need to be tidied up and orderly before I . . . before I what?

The dawn came while I sat there, holding the end of me in my hands. I looked out at the water, maybe thinking this would be my one last look.

That morning, nature provided a rare treat. The sunlight's first minutes left a dim, pinkish glow across the eastern sky that attenuated as it reached across the sky to the west. The water was as flat calm as I'd ever seen it. Hardly any clouds. No boats underway. A last glimpse of a world at peace.

Something moved me. Someone spoke to me. I put the shotgun down across the bed. I think it was Susan.

CHAPTER FIFTEEN

SUSAN

Holt

I'm angry at you, Susan.

Susan died a year ago last March. I don't understand why I can be angry with my dead wife. Sure, I'm angry at the guy who killed her. I'm angry at God all the time. But Susan?

A month after she died, I coincidentally had an annual physical with my primary care doctor at the Veterans Administration clinic. I could've rescheduled it, but I didn't, perhaps because I unconsciously knew I needed to talk to someone. That fifteen-minute appointment turned into something like an hour.

Telling the doctor about Susan's death, I started off in an almost matter-of-fact manner. After her condolences, she gently took hold of my hand, asking all the questions this doctor-patient situation required, but I could see in her eyes . . . something. Hurt, genuine sadness, and empathy.

I acted like a tough old soldier, claiming I was fine. Until my facade fell all at once. My words fumbled and stopped. Anguish swept over me, suddenly and without reserve. I collapsed, crying like I'd never cried before, nearly slipping from the exam table onto the floor.

My doctor patiently waited for me to recover, handing me a small box of tissues to wipe away my tears before wiping away her own. Once I settled down, she began counseling me on how to deal with my troubles.

"It's called situational depression. It's a normal reaction to the loss of a loved one. It takes time to deal with grief. Vic, above all else, I want you to know that you're not alone." That's when she referred me to my therapist.

"I've worked with her before. Clinical psychologist. She's very good. Please follow up with her. She can help you." I agreed.

"It helps to talk to someone you don't know. Say things you need to say without being judged. That's something that family or friends, even with the best intentions, often can't do. You understand?"

"Yeah, I think so."

"Good. Before you see her, let's talk about things you can start doing right away. Things that don't require medication. I'll get to that option in a minute.

"Regular exercise can help with depression." I said I had been a regular at the gym before Susan died, "I haven't gone, well, since then." I stopped to check if I was still in control of my emotions before continuing. "But I'll start again. I promise."

"Good. It's important to stay active. Promise me you'll write up a plan for each day. Workout routines, writing, walking outside, fixing things. Whatever you can do to stay active. And talk to your friends. Meet them for lunch or dinner. Social interaction is important. You don't have to talk to them about Susan. Just talk to them. And put in that plan time to be alone. To think, meditate, and read. Or cry."

"Cry? Guess I'm pretty good at that." That got a chuckle out of her.

"The good, I mean only good news out of all this, is that most people come out of their grief. I'm not trying to minimize things. It'll never completely go away, of course."

She handed me the business card for the therapist. "Call her."

A prescription for an antidepressant came next. "*Lexapro*. I'll call this into a pharmacy before you leave. Get it today. Start taking the prescribed dose today. Start at ten milligrams per day: same time every day. See how that goes. We can increase the dosage if need be. Understand?"

"Yes. Seems simple enough."

"*Lexapro* needs about four weeks to have clinical effects. Don't stop taking it unless I tell you to stop, even if you feel better. Call us immediately if your mood takes a turn for the worse. And you're going to see me again in two weeks, okay? Just to check in."

I had a feeling she was saving the best for last.

"One more thing. No alcohol. I mean none. Alcohol works against the *Lexapro*." The reaction on my face didn't make her happy. I went along with her demand, if only half-heartedly.

The therapist first saw me for an hour a week later. The first couple of months, I saw her once a week, then twice a month, until it became once a month.

Whether it was the antidepressant regimen, the therapy, or both together, really didn't matter to me. All I know is I was better able to cope. I don't remember all that the therapist said, especially in the first few sessions. But I did latch onto the stages of grief concept.

Shock and denial of the death come first, but not immediately. Grief's time clock differs from one person to the next. For me, the shock of it all first came a week after the funeral. I was trying to do laundry. I'd gathered everything up, put the clothes in, and turned on the washing machine. It all started just fine. An everyday task.

I collapsed on the floor, sobbing. Susan always did the laundry. That was her thing. She was gone. Forever. I would never see her again. Susan was dead.

It took me ten minutes to get up off the floor. I said aloud, "Someday that'll make a funny story." Though there were other episodes like that, over time their frequency lessened. Small tasks and the most fleeting of memories still set my grief in motion.

A gap persisted between intellectually understanding that my wife died and emotionally accepting it. Numb to the loss, as experts may call it, is a common aspect of denial. In my case, denial started to fade when I discovered I wasn't reaching across the bed for her.

So far as I know, I pretty much skipped through the second stage of bargaining. There wasn't anything I could've done to save her. Human error and the unforgivable mathematics of force equals mass times acceleration.

It was a Friday. February 4th. 1:35 p.m. On the main road through the town business district, a driver crossed from his lane into hers. A head-on collision. His heavy-duty pickup had more than three times the mass of her compact car. The cops figured he was just over the speed limit at fifty. Susan was driving, maybe forty-five. Combined collision speed of ninety-five.

That man survived the crash with a couple of broken ribs and a smashed wrist. He left Susan so badly mutilated that I had no choice but a closed-casket wake.

He admitted to the cops that he was checking his phone when he collided with Susan. They cited him, of course, but the DA decided against any criminal charges, such as vehicular manslaughter. His clean record was a mitigating factor, according to the DA. And maybe, an unsaid degree of there by the grace of God go I. We've all done something like the driver did with his phone.

Although friends and strangers criticized the DA's decision, I kept silent. But beneath that mask, I seethed. And my anger almost cost me my soul.

For weeks afterward, I obsessed with the idea of dispensing my own justice: killing the man who killed my wife of twenty-six years. I wanted him dead. I needed him dead. Stone cold fucking dead. Surely a vengeful husband had the right.

Refining every step, I meticulously played out his murder in my mind. I knew where he lived. I'd chosen where I'd corner him. How I'd kill him. How quickly I'd kill him. Then my wife's killer almost beat me to it.

Grace, who worked at the front desk of my dentist's office, happened to live across the street from him. I think three months after Susan died, I ran into Grace at a convenience store in town. With all good intentions, Grace asked how I was. I offered her a curt "Fine; I gotta go." Though I did my best to signal I wanted the conversation to stop, Grace had another idea. She took hold of my arm. Fixed in place, I stood there silently, holding a jug of milk, as she said there was something I might want to know.

"Vic, you know, ah, that guy who . . . well, anyway, something happened to him last week." I didn't respond. I stood there staring at her, thinking, does she have any idea I do not want to talk about the man who killed my wife? Who I want to kill?

"He attempted suicide. Took a bottle of drugs. Over-the-counter stuff. I don't know exactly what. Anyway, the thing is, his wife found him; called 911. He didn't die, but could die anyway. It really messed up his liver. He might need a transplant. I just thought you should know."

So, you waited until a random meeting at a store to tell me this? Why? Do you think this . . . helps?

Not saying a word, I turned away from her, paid for the milk, and walked out. Turns out, Grace was only half right. Word gets around in a small town. His liver wasn't destroyed. Damaged, but still functional. He would live.

Should I have taken his attempted suicide as an admission of guilt? A plea for forgiveness? That he attempted suicide even after knowing there would be no charges, did that show his despair and torment? Is it a reason to forgive him? They say forgiveness is the surest path to saving oneself. And if I did, would that bring me peace?

I'm not sure when my murderous fantasy left me. It wasn't a conscious decision. Nor did I sense one of God's angels touching my shoulder, giving me the grace to let it go. I don't believe in God anyway. Maybe I had a less spiritual reason. Perhaps I just grew tired of planning the man's murder. Perhaps I began to scare myself. The man who killed Susan will never know how close he came to a bullet.

In the weeks following her cremation and funeral, I kept myself at home, fearing chance meetings with more acquaintances and friends. I didn't want to deal with anyone else saying how sorry they were about Susan.

They meant well. As anyone would, they struggled for the right words. I'd thank them and say the words a widower is expected to say. There were times, however, I wanted to say something closer to the mark when they asked how I was doing.

How am I doing? How would you be doing? Or something like, *Oh, I'm fine. You know, Susan being dead isn't as bad as I thought it would be.* Or simply, *leave me the fuck alone!*

That last wish came true. There was no one left to talk to. My friends were mostly her friends. Though they called me often in those early days, that soon tapered off. Can't say I blamed them. I'm sure they thought it was best to leave me to myself for a while. Anyway, they've got their own lives. Truth be told, I didn't often try to reach out to them. I could have, but I didn't. Because I was stupid or scared. Or both.

I had no family to turn to. My folks passed away years ago. Dad had a heart attack. Mom passed in her sleep. I still have my younger brother Henry up near Bangor, Maine. He is married with two children, Steven and LeAnne. A good man, I love him, but when Susan died, he'd already been well into an early onset of dementia. His wife, Amelia, was Henry's full-time caregiver.

Though Amelia didn't mention it, I knew the awful burden a long trip for the funeral would put on her, let alone the long car trip back. Even a routine day caring for Henry was staggering labor. As close as Henry had been to Susan, we agreed it would be best for Henry to forgo the funeral. I told Amelia that Susan would understand. I cried as I hung up, as I realized that by any measure, Henry had already departed this Earth. I needed to see Henry. The old Henry.

There were happier times.

I was only a year or so into what looked like a promising career with Electric Boat, the submarine builder in Groton, Connecticut. I'd taken my Boston University M.B.A. and experience with the telecom industry in a new direction, which offered stability, something rare in the telecom industry.

EB would be building Navy submarines for decades to come. Dynamic and sexy EB is not, but I'd had enough chaos with telecom, when I'd often worry if my company would be alive the next day. Settling down into a career with a sense of permanence didn't preclude ambition. I still coveted a senior executive position with all its rewards.

Imagine my surprise at a meeting at the EB shipyard when I saw Susan's familiar face across the table. I'd last seen her almost ten years before. Startled, I asked her name twice. There she was, my old friend from the University of Massachusetts Dartmouth days, back when they called it Southeastern Massachusetts University.

We were just friends then, but good friends. After the Army, I used my VA benefits to pursue a B.S. in economics. Susan majored in mechanical engineering. I first met Susan in a general education course. English Literature, I think it was. Then she appeared in my calculus classes. We'd see each other in the *Rathskeller* for beers or at off-campus parties, always with other people. Neither of us thought to take things beyond that. Maybe that's why we were always at ease with each other. We could, and did, talk about anything.

Susan was a year behind me. After graduation, I went into telecom. A year later, in 1989, she wrote to tell me she was heading for Officer Candidate School in the Navy. I wrote back to tell her how proud I was of her. As the Navy OCS was at a nearby naval base, I even attended her graduation and commissioning ceremony.

Her next stop was as an Engineering Officer aboard the *USS Missouri*, BB-63. She wrote again—people wrote actual letters in those days—to catch me up on things. She wrote about the challenges of her job aboard the historic battleship. "One day, you're working on the latest hi-tech missile and sensor systems. Next day, you're dealing with a propulsion system from the 1940s." She loved the job.

Then came *Desert Storm*. In the first hour of the campaign, Susan watched *Missouri's* cruise missiles fly from their armored deck launch tubes. Even while buried deep in the engineering spaces, she felt down to her bones the shattering tremor from the 16-inch guns as they fired at Iraqi targets in the desert.

I closely followed the war's progress on CNN and whatever other sources I could find. I wrote to Susan four or five times, never confessing my worry about her. Though there was no safer place to be than aboard an Iowa-class battleship, accidents happen. And in combat, sometimes even a weak enemy can land a lucky punch.

At the war's end, I was relieved to hear from her. All was well, and she was headed home. That was the last time I heard from Susan for years.

It was only when we met again at EB that I found out what happened to her. After the war, the *Missouri* sailed home to be decommissioned. Susan got a new engineering assignment ashore at the naval base in Hampton Roads. As life tends to play out, she met a fellow naval officer, they married, and had a beautiful daughter.

A heart condition took their child and their marriage. Near the end of her military obligation, by then, Susan chose a new path. The design division of Electric Boat. The work was interesting at times, but there was much wasted time in the back-and-forth correspondence between her division and the Navy. Still, that didn't bother her. Like me, she was looking for a quieter life.

Reconnected, things moved quickly. Get-togethers became dates, leading to an accepted proposal of marriage. Susan had one codicil. "You should know. I'm not sure I can . . . cope . . . with having another child. Just too much."

We never had children. No, this was not an empathetic sacrifice in recognition of Susan's loss. Honestly, I was indifferent to kids. I selfishly thought children might be a distraction to my career ambitions.

These days, I'm of a different mind. Not having kids is my only regret from my time with her. I could have used a son or a daughter to hold me up, to help me, to lean on. To know that fragments of Susan survived.

Acceptance is the final stage of grief, the experts say. All I know is I'm not there yet.

Yes, Susan, I am still angry at you for dying, but that will fade. I love you. I could use your help. Especially now.

CHAPTER SIXTEEN

LEAVING MY HOUSE

Holt

I had an appointment with my therapist. My first post-shotgun suicide appointment.

After carrying out my personal security plan, I headed out. The trip took half an hour. No incidents. No one followed me. I did manage a small psychological success before heading out. I showered. The *Psycho* maniac, stabbing me while I shampooed what little hair I had, didn't materialize.

No surprise, but that therapy session went longer than previous ones. I'd lost significant ground, but we stopped a complete fall. Surprisingly controlled and unemotional, I gave my therapist the whole story. Every detail, every thought that came into my head as I came close to using the shotgun against my own head.

"Vic, can you tell me why you did not do it?"

I told her Susan stopped me. "I know that sounds bizarre, but Christ." She said she believed me. Then came a question I should've anticipated. As she handed me a box of tissues, she asked, "Vic, you are taking your antidepressants, right?"

Honesty comes easily after you've confessed to almost turning a gun on yourself. "Ah, no. I stopped."

"Really. For how long?"

"About a week. I was, before the fake head, feeling better so, I, ah . . ."

One expects sympathy and understanding from mental health care professionals, especially their own. However, she did not respond with a compassionate correction. Instead, I got a chewing out that rivaled anything I'd suffered back in Army basic training.

"As a clinician, let me frame my response in a way someone like you will understand." I raised my head to look her in the eye. "Dumb fucking idea! You were told not to do that! Absolutely fucking dumb idea!" I had no idea she could yell like that.

"The meds work. They're why you were feeling good. Jesus, did you not stop and think that being off your meds, combined with that head in a box, the car showing up at night, maybe had something to do with why you almost killed yourself?"

I had no answer.

"Get back on them. Today. And don't even think of stopping again until I fucking tell you to. You got that?"

My therapist took no shit from anyone yet knew exactly when to hold your hand or wipe away a tear. I liked her immensely. When I got back home, I practically ran for the bathroom medicine case, and washed down a full dose of antidepressants.

I needed that kick in the ass. She was right. Things needed to be set right. And looking around my home, one thing needed to be set right immediately. It was a shithole. Changing into gym clothes, I maniacally cleaned the house. Dusted and vacuumed. Cleaned bathrooms. Cleaned dishes. Changed bed sheets. Ran the laundry. Everything short of polishing the silver.

Cleaning the refrigerator revealed a more serious problem. It was empty, save for random condiments. No eggs, no milk, no fresh or frozen or even leftover meat. Same story in the cupboards. No bread. Not even canned vegetables or stews. No pasta and no sauce. No nothing.

There are two options. Starve or go out.

While starving would help shed those unwanted pounds, I'm more in favor of eating. To eat, I needed to buy food. That meant a trip to the supermarket. An errand with all its risks. Deciding to wait until tomorrow morning, I ordered pizza online. Stay inside tonight. As a sign of how far I'd fallen, when the delivery guy showed up, I wondered if he was really an assassin.

Another restless night of little sleep followed. In the morning, I stared once again into the refrigerator, thinking that a man with any foresight would've signed up for a food delivery service.

Screw it. Got no choice. Go to the supermarket.

Ten minutes away is the town's independent supermarket. My first impulse was to make it a quick trip. Dash inside and pick up only the absolute essentials. My second and better thought was, well, that's dumb. Get everything imaginable; otherwise, I'll have to go out again. And again.

Thank God I've got plenty of wine, beer, and bourbon. No need for a second stop at the liquor store. Shit, no. I can't drink alcohol. The antidepressants. So much for that happy thought.

In a concession to security or paranoia, I put on sunglasses and a ball cap before heading to the market. The eyepatch would stay at home. My diminished hygiene had one beneficial byproduct. A fair amount of beard growth helped obscure my identity. Then again, even after nearly a week, the beard didn't come out well. Grey and a bit patchy. God, I thought, I look like such an old man.

Walking into the market, fear competed with the silliness I felt with the amateur hour disguise. Up and down the aisles I went, stuffing my cart with every conceivable staple and luxury, when of all people, I ran into Harrison. He must have sensed my surprise. Of course, when I asked him what the hell he was doing here, that likely tipped him off.

"Same as you. Shopping. What else would I be doing here?"

After explaining he was on a "honey do" errand, he led me and my overfilled shopping cart to a quiet spot by the market florist shop.

"So, how are you doing, Vic? For real. No bullshit."

Suppressing a smartass answer, I lied. "Fine. Better, I think. Just needed a few things." I think I even managed to fake a smile.

"A few things? What, for the Apocalypse?" Harrison laughed, pointing to my shopping cart overflowing with milk, eggs, bread, meats, sausages, fresh vegetables, canned food of every variety, pasta sauce, spaghetti, vanilla ice cream, and all sorts of other comforting goodies.

"Anyway, so any unusual deliveries or mail? Everything OK around your place?"

You mean like when I came within a hair of killing myself?

"No, I mean yeah, Detective. Pretty quiet."

After an awkward couple of seconds staring at each other, I stammered out that I'd better get going before the ice cream melts and said goodbye. As I headed to the one open checkout aisle, Harrison let me go with a reminder that he'd be in touch.

With a month of groceries in my truck, I headed back, fast. Down my road in a cloud of dust. A quick wave to Lillian, standing on her front porch. In earlier times, I would have chatted with her. However, my security plan demanded a measure of rudeness.

Frantically unloading the truck, I somehow managed not to drop any grocery bags. After piling all of them on the front steps, I locked the truck and unlocked the front door. Into the foyer went the bags, sometimes not so gently. All the while, I had this feeling Lil was watching me.

Christ, what she must think of me these days.

I sat down at the kitchen table to catch my breath and sanity. I didn't know why, but seeing Harrison seemed to set something off. Embarrassment?

Feeling safe inside, I moved with deliberate slowness in putting away the groceries, leaving the ice cream at even greater mortal risk. Finally done, I convinced myself of the critical need for my personal and time-honored medication. The over-the-counter pharmaceutical is derived from grain, corn, and the biological process of anaerobic fermentation of complex sugars. I poured two fingers of bourbon over ice, leaving the bottle out and uncapped, in case I dispensed an insufficient dosage.

At the first sip, I inconveniently remembered the warnings from my VA doc and therapist. Alcohol by itself may lead to impaired judgment. Mixing alcohol with antidepressants may worsen feelings of depression and anxiety since the alcohol may counteract the drugs.

The doctor, the therapist, and the prescription label used the word "may."

On the second sip, I dwelled on the meaning of "may." May is not certain. As a verb, it can mean possibility. In pharmacology, it could mean not everyone. May might not mean me. May might mean bourbon will help lighten the mood with nothing more than its usual effects. May might . . .

As I put the glass in the kitchen sink and gently tipped it over, I mourned the passage down the drain of a chilled full measure of my painfully expensive favorite bourbon. Capped, I put the bottle back in the liquor cabinet.

A pity. One of the top ten bourbons.

CHAPTER SEVENTEEN

UNWELCOME VISITORS

Holt

I can't explain why I slept better that night. Certainly, the antidepressants hadn't had enough time to kick back in. All I know is I did sleep well. Somewhat refreshed in body and mind, I cooked myself a decent breakfast of corned beef hash and fried eggs. With a second cup of coffee in hand, I took a stab at writing. I surprised myself with eight good pages in under two hours. Then again, as Hemingway supposedly said, the first draft of anything is shit. Nevertheless, any shit's better than no shit at all.

Those pages put me roughly halfway through my latest novel. Working title of *Surfmen*. A historical fiction about the United States Lifesaving Service, circa 1900. The USLSS had an extensive presence then along the Atlantic and Pacific coasts, as well as the Great Lakes. I saw it as a potentially great adventure story about the men who crewed those open surfboats, rowing them out into freezing heavy surf and seas to rescue sailors off grounded and sinking ships. Wooden boats and iron men.

To celebrate my progress on that breezy, sunny Saturday, I decided to grill up a nice lunch. A burger and a brat on the deck grill, accompanied by a sizeable bag of chips. I'd enjoy lunch up on the balcony. Shielded on both sides, I felt safer up there. Plus, I can still watch over the beach and the bay.

I'd just flipped a burger and turned a brat when I heard cars coming down the road. Before my troubles, I wouldn't have given that a second thought. But these days . . . *I need to see who's here.*

Something told me I shouldn't show myself. I went down the deck stairs and kept close to the house wall, walking through grass that I'd long neglected to mow. Peeking from around the house corner, I could see the cars. Two sedans and a quad cab pickup truck. They'd parked in a line abreast on the dirt end of my road.

A dozen people came out of the vehicles. All men, it seemed. Young men. Twenties, thirties, maybe two or three in their forties. Oddly, they all dressed the same, like they were in a sort of half-assed uniform. Black hoodie and khaki cargo pants. Military-style boots. Khaki ballcaps. Dark sunglasses. Each one had a white cloth, a gaiter, pulled up over their mouths and noses. Over white skin.

Every black hoodie had the same logo splashed across the entire chest. Two concentric circles of red and blue around a white background. Above the logo were words in white which I couldn't make out. Beneath the outer circles was an American flag. Cutting through the white center of the logo were two black lines running closely parallel to each other. They looked like lightning bolts.

I muttered, "Oh, fuck" as realization struck. The lightning bolts are right from the SS. Schutzstaffel. The Nazi SS. Nazi symbols above an American flag.

The gang assembled on the road at the head of my driveway. One of them took the lead, telling the others to wait there. He walked down the driveway to my front door. On the steps, he rang the doorbell repeatedly and knocked loudly on the door.

"Mr. Holt! Mr. Holt! Please come out. We want to talk to you. Mr. Holt! We know you're here. Your truck's here. We're not going to hurt you! Holt!" So focused was he on my front door, he hadn't seen me around the corner. Nor had the others. Yet.

In hindsight, a rational person would've taken the safe way out. Slink back to the deck, go inside, and call the cops. However, my rationality was in short supply. Instead, absolute, irrational fury welled up inside me.

What's this fucking guy doing? Who're these fuckin' people? On my land. My house. Broad daylight. I've had enough!

"Hey! You! Who the hell are you? What the fuck do you want?" I came out from behind the corner. Screaming at him, I went up the three steps of my stoop to face him. I got nose to nose, eye to eye. Not exactly civilized on my part, but it fit the moment.

Startled, the stranger jerked his head away from me. "You Holt?"

I kept screaming. "What's your name? I don't fucking know you! You're on my property! What the fuck do you want?"

He didn't answer other than to say in a tone calmer than mine, "You'll see."

Retreating to his followers about thirty feet away, he lined them up at the end of my driveway. One had a big, green canvas bag hanging off his shoulder that looked like an old Army duffel bag. He dumped the bag's contents over my lawn at the road's edge.

My book! That's my book!

Duffel Bag Guy then knelt and neatly stacked them into a pyramid. I left my front door and walked about halfway to them. Again, not a smart thing to do. I was alone, in only a T-shirt, sweatpants, and sandals. Facing me were twelve menacingly dressed men. But I was reacting, not thinking. Instinct? Reflex? No, anger. Real, honest-to-God, I-want-to-hurt-somebody-really-fucking-bad rage.

The group's leader walked back to stand in front of me, face to face. He put his right arm straight out, showing the palm of his hand, only inches from my chest. "Hold it right there, Holt."

"FUCK YOU!" You'd think a bestselling author would show greater wit. In lieu of words, I replied in a different way that had its own eloquence.

I backed up half a step. With my left hand, I grabbed his outstretched wrist, twisted his arm before pulling him forward a little, getting him off balance, helped by the driveway's slight upward incline. Then I stepped forward, taking back that half step while sending the heel of my right palm into his sternum. I let go of his right wrist. He stumbled backwards a couple of feet but did not fall. The whole maneuver took hardly two seconds.

I readied to parry his response with my right knee smashing into his balls and follow that with my fist to his throat. I may be an old man, but Army training lasts a lifetime. Rule number one: do not fight fair.

As their leader steadied himself, two others stepped forward to flank him. Someone yelled, "Holt. Stop! Stop, or we'll fuck you up!" Surprisingly, the leader held up a hand to keep them in place. He stood there with his arms at his side.

Stalemate. Me against three, with reserves. Not the time to see an ICU from the patient's point of view. Or the inside of a coffin. Time for a different approach.

I could've retreated inside my house, locked the door, and called the cops. I could have gotten my shotgun. Instead, I walked back toward my house and sat down on my stoop, facing them as they stood at the end of my driveway near the pile of my books.

Out of my pocket came a weapon potentially more powerful than a shotgun—my cell phone. I turned on the camera/video app and videoed the entire bunch from the steps. I demanded they identify themselves and explain what they were doing. I threw in a promise they'd be on the television news with a healthy dose of insults and sarcasm. I called them cowards, morons, maggots, idiots, and those were the clean insults. Sufficiently provoked, I hoped they'd reveal their faces from behind the gaiters. Looking back, I'm surprised they didn't beat me to death then and there.

They didn't react. I'll give them this. They were disciplined. Aside from curses, they stayed in formation. After a minute, their leader got the ball rolling. Pointing to Duffel Bag Guy, he said, "Okay, do it."

Duffel Bag Guy squirted a can of lighter fluid all over the books. Another man approached with a long-necked butane lighter. Woosh! Even on my stoop, I felt the flash of heat. The flames built quickly from the bottom to the top.

For the next act in their fascist play, they lined up in a single file, facing the fire, shoulder to shoulder with their right arms in a raised stiff-arm salute. Chants of "Sieg Heil" alternated with "White Power!"

There was no need for me to add further commentary to the video. They're burning a pile of books. My book. A book burning right in front of me. In front of my house. A book burning by Neo-Fucking-Nazis. American-Fucking-Nazis. Goddamn white supremacists burning books in the United States of America. Inspired by that goddamn Congresswoman, no doubt.

It was time to do something. I got up and walked halfway toward them. With as big a smile as I could manage, I panned the phone around, yelling, "Well, boys, thanks for buying my book. Thank you! I'll be looking forward to my next royalty check."

Their leader, no, their Little Führer was a better label, turned to me and said, "Please allow me, Holt." He calmly made a sweeping motion toward his followers as he quoted from *Henry V*. "We few. We happy few. We band of brothers. For he today that sheds his blood with me, shall be my brother; be he ne'er so vile . . .

"I could go on, Holt. I'm sure you recognize it." I did. Shakespeare. *Henry V. Act IV*. The Saint Crispin's Day Speech. Not an ordinary Neo-Nazi. A literate Neo-Nazi.

Little Führer then transitioned from Shakespeare to something more like Goebbels. Speaking across his file of men, he said, "Holt, your book insults patriotic Americans everywhere. It's un-American! It applauds treason. It betrays your own disloyalty and treason. We're here to demand—DEMAND—you stop writing filthy lies. Stop selling your book! If you don't stop, we'll be back!"

He then almost whispered a warning to me. "We've made our point. Do what we say, and nothing will happen."

I couldn't let all that go without a smartass reply. "I'm un-American? That coming from what, a Nazi?" I took a couple of steps toward Little Führer, keeping the phone pointed in his direction.

"What you're doing, burning books, a 19th-century German Jewish poet, Heinrich Heine, said something about this. 'Where they burn books, they will also, in the end, burn human beings.'

"You worship people who did exactly that. They burned books. Then they burned people. Millions of people." I repeated the quote twice more, but to no effect. I should've realized that empathy and reflection are not inherent qualities of Nazis.

I shifted back to Little Führer. "And that Band of Brothers bullshit. Let me tell you, I served in a real Band of Brothers. Look at the plate on my truck. Purple Heart. 82nd Airborne. There's a bronze star that goes with it."

I wasn't done with the rest. "And you all, I'll bet none of you ever served. Closest you came was to play army when you were little boys."

That struck a nerve with Little Führer. "Fuck you! I served in the Army. I was decorated . . ."

Before he could finish, I snapped, "Decorated with what? An Iron Cross?" If Little Führer answered, I didn't hear him. I sat back down on my stoop and said in a quieter voice, "Knock this shit off. Go away, you goddamn cowards."

Not done, the Nazis began chanting, "FUCK YOU HOLT!" Finally seeing the futility of arguing with them, I let them play out their little demonstration, figuring their voices would eventually die out along with the bonfire.

I was again videoing the Nazis and the burning books when someone tugged at my arm. Startled, I hadn't seen Lillian walk up to me.

"Vic, sorry, listen, I called 911. Police are on the way. You, okay? Need any help?"

"No. Thanks, Lil. You should go back home. I'll be all right."

"Not just yet, Vic." I watched my seventy-year-old neighbor take a wide path over to the Nazis' cars, taking pics of their registration tags with her phone. All the while, I could hear her husband Steve yelling at her from their porch. "Lillian! Get back here, goddammit!" Still in a Bledsoe boot from a fall off a ladder two weeks ago, Steve couldn't walk over and drag his wife out of harm's way. As if she'd let him.

Her task done, Lil turned back for her house, but not before giving the finger to the Nazis.

Well done, Lil. You're one brave lady.

The police arrived as Lil stepped onto her porch. Two patrol vehicles with lights going full tilt stopped about fifty or so feet away, blocking the road. I waved at the two cops walking toward us.

At that point, the Nazis probably realized their tactical error. Having deployed themselves near the end of a narrow, dead-end road, they had no escape route by vehicle. Unless they tried to run away through the woods or down the beach, the Nazis were trapped.

Two more cop cars arrived. After ordering me to go inside, the cops went to work. They took the Nazis' IDs and searched them and their cars for weapons and whatever else might be of interest. The cops took folding knives from almost all of them. I knew the knives weren't necessarily illegal. When the cops took a pistol from one of the Nazis, I thought, now that's got to be illegal. I so wanted to see the cops drag at least one Nazi off in cuffs.

As the questioning of my visitors continued, one cop came to my door. After I let her in, she asked if I was okay, if the Nazis assaulted me, if they threatened me, or if they damaged my property.

I shook my head. "No, officer, they didn't assault me. Other than burning a patch of grass, nothing was damaged. Did they threaten me? Yes, they did. They said if I didn't stop writing, they'd be back. Seems like a threat to me."

She asked, "Did the one with the gun use it in any way to threaten you? Did he take it out? Did he lift his sweatshirt to make sure you saw it? Did any of them point a knife in your direction?"

How I wish I could've said YES! HE DID! "No, he didn't. None of them showed a weapon to me."

She made a final note before giving me the disappointing news. Other than citing them for trespassing and disorderly conduct, there wasn't much else they could do. I asked her about the Nazi with the gun.

"Yeah, we're taking all the knives and the gun with us to the station. The guy with the gun showed us a permit to carry concealed. We'll confirm the permit is authentic. If it is, we'll have to return the weapon to him."

The officer interrupted me when I started telling her about the other death threats I've had. "Yeah, I know all about that. Look, Detective Harrison is on his way here. He should get here in a minute. You can tell him what happened. We're going to detain these . . . people . . . right here so Harrison can question them. Now, stay inside your house. When we're all done here, I'm sure Harrison will talk to you. Okay, Mr. Holt?" I agreed.

Oh, shit! The grill!

The burger and the brat were far gone. As in carbonized. Leaving my ruined lunch on the grill, I went back inside. From an upstairs window, I watched as Harrison interrogated each Nazi in turn. As the cops escorted the Nazis away, Harrison knocked on my door.

CHAPTER EIGHTEEN

DEBRIEFING THE VICTIM

Harrison

Holt didn't look all that well when he opened the door.

"Hi, Vic. You, ah, okay?" Holt invited me in, and we sat down at his dining room table. I pointed at the bourbon and ice he'd poured himself. "A tad early in the day for that, don't you think?"

Holt turned away from me, defiantly taking a sip of his whiskey before asking, "Well, Detective. Not so sure about that. As they say, it's five o'clock somewhere. Would you like one?"

"What do you say, Vic, we put that aside until I'm finished."

"Gee, Detective. A cocktail seems appropriate when celebrating the arrest of Nazis. But if you insist." Holt put his glass in the sink before coming back to the table.

Ignoring Holt's flippant response, I had him go through every step he took during the confrontation, from first seeing them, to the confrontation on his front steps, to hitting the head Nazi, the book burning, and up to when the first cops arrived. Holt ended by sending me his video of the Nazis from his phone.

Holt's manner then changed. He became reserved, even meek. I felt sorry for him, thinking he's scared and maybe finally realizes his vulnerability. Bad men came to his house today and made it clear they'd be back.

Looking away from me, Holt asked, "Do I need to worry, Detective? I mean, legally? Like, did I do anything wrong?"

"Vic, you're worried about when you pushed that guy back?" Holt whispered, "Yeah."

"Well, don't. They trespassed onto your property. When you shoved him, you were pretty much restrained. He made no mention of it anyway. As I see it, self-defense. No, Vic. I'm not going to arrest you." Holt nodded his head and exhaled long and loudly, no doubt relieved.

"Anyway, Vic, let me tell you what I found out." Laughing a little, I said, "First time for me, interrogating Nazis." Before I debriefed Holt, I promised that an officer would be stationed at the top of the road for at least the next twenty-four hours, starting now.

"I'm sure the DA will be interested. Not every day he gets to investigate Nazis. We know their names and where they live. I'll call the police in their towns. I doubt they'll come back."

"Detective, do you think they're connected to the threats? I mean, it seems like a possibility."

Agreeing, I told Holt I'd be checking them for criminal records, especially any that had a history of making threats, as well as looking through social media for any mention of this demonstration. "Guys like that like to brag."

"They from around here? Can you tell me that?"

"None from here in town. Except for five, no six, all are from in-state. That's all I can say now."

"Their gang. What's their name?"

"They said they belong to . . ." I looked down through my notes, saying, "Want to get this right. Yeah, the National Socialist Action Group."

Holt smiled before saying, "National Socialist Action Group.

NSAG. Catchy name." Holt took out his smartphone, saying, "Let's see what the internet has to say about them."

Holding up my hand to cut him off, I told Holt I'd already done a quick search on my own phone. "The Southern Poverty Law Center lists them as a hate group. They got chapters in each of the Northeastern states. Kind of a new group. I need to research them more."

Vic asked for the leader's name before mentioning that he claimed to be an Army veteran who might be familiar with Shakespeare.

"An Army veteran. I didn't know that. It'll be interesting to find out about his service record. Thanks, Vic. But no, I won't tell you his name. Won't do you any good. That's interesting about Shakespeare, but it seems a little trivial. Anything else you overheard that might be useful?" When Vic said he couldn't think of anything else, I left him with a warning.

"Look, Vic. Leave the research to us. I promise I'll get all I can on NSAG. Anything significant, I'll let you know. Meantime, you trying to do my job will not help . . . your frame of mind. Understand?"

I closed my notepad. The real message I had for Mr. Victor Holt came next. "Next time, if this does happen again, stay inside and call us. Not a smart move going out there, Vic."

When he started to object, I let him have it. "Jesus H. Christ! Listen to me! If they come again, stay inside your house and call 911." Vic stared at me in silence. I needed to say more.

"Think, Vic. What if you went after that guy with a gun? He might have put you in a body bag." I looked down at his hands. "Look at you. Your hands are shaking." He was sweating too. Perhaps against better judgment, I went to the sink and brought back his glass of bourbon. Holt held it in both hands. As he sipped, I continued.

"It's called a flight or fight response. Adrenaline is running around in you right now. I've seen this before. Bet you have too. But an old guy like you, probably been a while since you'd been in a fight. So, sit down. Take deep breaths. Watch TV. And next time, do the flight, not the fight."

Maybe that little witticism of mine did the trick. Vic promised no repeat performance. Before I left, I suggested he get away for a while, like a week on Cape Cod or go up to Vermont.

Holt didn't take to my suggestion, saying it was high vacation season, and the traffic would be a pain in the ass. And finding a decent hotel wouldn't be easy. Absolutely true, but it was a dodge on his part. He was scared to stay in his house. And just as scared to go away.

At least he said something nice to me as I left. "Thanks for your concern, Detective. Your help. Means a lot."

CHAPTER NINETEEN

URGENT FURY

Holt

I wasn't entirely truthful with the NSAG Nazis, though I'm not sure lying to their kind is a sin. I think Jesus would understand.

After Harrison's casual mention of my combat experience, and after my dust-up with NSAG, memories of Army days came to the fore. Add to that Little Führer's incomparable obscenity of calling his rotten gang a Band of Brothers.

Dr. Stephen Ambrose's history of Easy Company of the 101st Airborne popularized the real Band of Brothers. In a chaotic jump, those men parachuted into Normandy and nonetheless achieved their objectives. They continued to fight the Nazis from D-Day on through Operation Market Garden, the Battle of the Bulge, and the final battles inside Germany itself, all the way to Hitler's Eagle's Nest. In every imaginable sense, they were heroes. Especially the ones buried over there.

My being a paratrooper is true. I was 82nd Airborne. My combat experience, however brief, came during *Operation Urgent Fury*, the 1983 invasion of the Caribbean Island of Grenada. Unlike Easy Company, I didn't parachute under fire. Landing at already secured Point Salines Airport at the island's southernmost point, we walked down the transport aircraft ramp onto the tarmac.

As it would turn out, my entire combat experience lasted only seconds. I didn't lead my squad into action nor fire a shot in anger. The wound I suffered went deeper than a maimed eye. A profound feeling of frustration, of failure, which troubles me to this day.

My enlistment in the Army did not please my parents. Graduating salutatorian from high school in '78, I brushed aside letters of acceptance to three universities and generous scholarships to boot. My decision wasn't easy for my parents to accept.

Dad tried to understand. In 1952, he'd seen combat as a M26 Pershing tank gunner in Korea. I wrongly expected he'd be sympathetic to my decision. I can still see him sitting in his living room chair as he tried to talk me out of enlisting. Dad didn't get angry—he rarely did. He clearly and methodically stated his case that I was making a mistake.

"Victor, I'm trying to understand, but you have to help me." Dad reminded me I'd lose the scholarships. He talked about how hard Army life could be in ways I couldn't possibly imagine, especially for an infantryman. And war was always a possibility. Seeking compromise, he asked me to think about college and a Reserve Officers' Training Corps program. Or Officer Candidate School after college.

I countered, unfairly, I think, with his own Army stories. "Dad, your Army days, you always talked about how . . . tight . . . everyone was with each other. How you felt like being part of something larger than yourself. You always say enlisted guys get the job done. Maybe I'm naive, but I don't want to miss that."

"Yes, I said those things. Maybe I should've had more foresight." Dad chuckled and put down his cigarette in the ashtray. "But know this. I skipped over the bad parts. A lot of bad happened in Korea."

Even then, he didn't counter with stories of buddies lost in Korea. For reasons I didn't understand then, it was a line he wouldn't cross.

We talked about my enlisting a couple more times over the following days, but in the end, he relented. "Well, son. All right. If that's what you want." He stood, and we shook hands. "Now, go convince your mother."

I took a go-slow approach with Mom, leaving hints until she finally sat me down to ask a direct question. "Are you sure the Army is right for you?"

I assured her I'd asked myself the same question repeatedly. Nervously, I launched into my well-rehearsed pitch of how the Army will help me grow. I had it all planned out, point by point. She stopped me almost as soon as I started.

"Victor, I've heard all this from Dad already. He accepts it. I won't stand in your way either. But I can't let this go by without saying how . . . disappointed I am. How, you know, this scares me. You know why, I think."

I did. Mom's older brother, Michael, the uncle I only knew from old pictures, was killed in action in November of 1944. On the wall by our fireplace hung a somewhat faded framed photo of him in uniform, taken before he shipped off to the European Theatre. He stood close to his father and mother, my grandparents, and his sister. My preteen Mom stood with her arm around Grandma. It was the last photo taken of him.

Next to the photo was a framed Purple Heart medal.

I didn't fully realize it then, but my decision hurt Mom terribly. She had lost her brother to war, and there I was, asking her to take on the same terrible burden borne by her parents. Mom must have pictured in her mind another posthumous Purple Heart, hung carefully on the wall, side by side with her brother's.

How many times throughout history have sons and daughters

put their mothers and fathers through such emotions? Pride conflicted with the fear of what may come.

After boot camp came advanced infantry training, often led by old hands who fought in Vietnam. I absorbed all I could, steadily advanced, and in my third active-duty year was selected for Airborne School. I earned my Parachutist Badge and went on to the 82nd Airborne Division. The Screaming Eagles.

Whenever I could, I enrolled in on-base college classes, setting my sights on an associate degree. Working around deployments and training to keep up with classes wasn't easy. Nevertheless, dreams of Officer Candidate School were not far from my mind. By my fifth year, I made it to staff sergeant and was assigned as a squad leader.

Then came *Operation Urgent Fury*. October 1983.

On the 19th, the division was alerted. Down at my level, they first described the alert as another division readiness exercise. Things changed just before midnight on October 24. Not a drill. Real-world combat. An opposed rescue operation of American medical students on the island of Grenada, a place that maybe none of us had ever heard of. A rescue operation, not a full-on invasion, but with an emphasis on the word opposed.

After years of training, for the first time, I would lead men into battle. My squad. Nine men and me. The exhilaration I felt was matched only by the fear that I would not do my job well.

When we got to Pope Air Force Base, all geared up, the operation's scope expanded. Assembled at a place known as the "Green Ramp," we got our official orders. Invade Grenada. Eliminate the communist resistance. Restore order. Rescue the American medical students on the island. Restore a Western Allied government and liberate the people from Cuban and communist oppression. Seemed clear to me, though I'd never heard of Grenada before.

In the years following the invasion, harsh things have been said about *Urgent Fury's* hurried and sometimes flawed execution. To be fair, the *Urgent Fury* planners had no contingency plans whatsoever for invading Grenada. In fact, operational planning started from scratch on October 21, with D-Day scheduled for four days later. There were bound to be problems.

From my narrow perspective as a lowly squad leader, all I saw were gaps in intel and planning, which led to indecision. Frustrated, I vented a couple of times to a more senior NCO. He finally had enough and set me straight.

"Holt, shut up. Keep your concerns to yourself. Doubt will not help your men. Show them confidence."

He was right. It was poor behavior on my part. Accepting confusion is a part of war, especially for paratroopers. Unexpected things happen. Things will go wrong. Our Company Commander, a captain named Winoski, spoke to us before we went aboard the transport aircraft. He was clear on that point, saying, "Flexibility, gentlemen. We'll adapt to whatever the situation demands." As troubling as the lack of intel was, I respected his directness and honesty.

Case in point. We had zero military maps of Grenada. In fact, we had no maps of any kind. The story goes that an officer went into Fayetteville and bought a tourist map. He put a grid system over it and made copies. We only got these ersatz tourist/tactical maps as we boarded the aircraft taking us to war.

There were other embarrassing equipment, training, and communication failures. Mistakes were made at all levels. Let's include my own.

Marching with my company through the somewhat chaotic assembly area at Pope, we already had a standard ammo outfit and all the other kit required by the book: Six 30-round magazines in two pouches with a seventh in the M16, for a total of 210 rounds. Grenades stayed in storage crates until we landed. But by then, I allowed my doubts about higher-level planning to cloud my judgement. The result was a classic tactical error arising from combat inexperience.

With fifteen or twenty minutes left before boarding, I saw tables stocked with ammunition of all kinds, ours for the taking. I persuaded my lieutenant that "it'd be a good idea, sir, for the men to grab extra M16 ammo, so we've got enough for three days, like they said. You've seen how things are. No guarantee of resupply anytime soon." He agreed, but it was a foolish suggestion. Our men greedily grabbed more M16 ammo, extra 60 mm mortar rounds, and belts of ammo for the M60 machine guns, plus almost everyone grabbed a M72 light antitank rocket launcher. And of course, more rations.

Well supplied but now overburdened, my men looked more like pack animals than soldiers; a couple staggered under the weight of their equipment as they boarded the aircraft. I had discarded the wisdom of the old hands who trained me. More is not always better, meaning more weight to hump through the tropical countryside. And to top it all off, we'd find our battledress uniforms sucked in a tropical climate. Tropical weight uniforms were nowhere to be found.

The first C-141 transport aircraft arrived at Pope at 0400. At 1000, we were in the air. Even then, it hadn't been decided if we'd parachute in or land and then disembark, which is called an air-landing assault. The Brigade Commander wanted preparations made for both contingencies and ordered the aircraft be rigged for parachute assault enroute. That didn't prove to be practical. In any event, it didn't matter, thank God, because we didn't need to jump.

That 25th of October at roughly 1400, we landed at Point Salines airport and taxied to a stop alongside other C-141s and C-130s. We hoisted our gear and walked down the aircraft's rear ramp onto the tarmac. A rather anticlimactic entry into war. No parachute jumps into history. There was a good reason for that.

The 1st and 2nd battalions of the 75th Ranger Regiment had parachuted in well before us to secure Point Salines airport. The Ranger assault was timed to be simultaneous with a helicopter-borne Marine Corps seizure of the Pearls airport on the northeastern coast, a somewhat primitive airfield consisting of a cinderblock terminal and a fuel facility.

Standing there on the tarmac in the disagreeable heat, I said to the lieutenant commanding my platoon, "Well, Rangers did their job." He agreed, perhaps as relieved as I at not being shot down. While getting ourselves sorted out, Captain Winoski called everyone together.

"Here's the latest. We'll get our orders soon. Until then, check your gear and hang tight. For now, look around." He waved a pointed finger to the edge of the airfield behind us.

"Over there, that's a ZU-23 anti-aircraft gun. There are two or three more around. If you keep looking, you'll see piles of steel beams and junked cars. The enemy put them across the airstrip as obstacles against landing aircraft. It almost worked.

"As the Rangers were flying in, they spotted the obstacles. They couldn't land like we did, like the plan called for. They had to circle around and replan their assault. About forty to forty-five minutes later, the Rangers did a low-level parachute assault. From five hundred feet. Lowest since World War II. The sun was up. No tactical surprise. You all know what that means. They caught all sorts of fire from the Cubans.

"That did not stop the Rangers! Under sniper fire, they hotwired a bulldozer to push the obstacles clear. They secured the high ground around the airport. They fought back a Cuban counterattack backed up by Soviet built BTR-60 armored personnel carriers.

"Why am I telling you this? First, when you see a Ranger, thank him. He's already saved your life. Second, take a lesson from the Rangers. They did not stop. They adapted. They improvised.

They accomplished their mission. The Rangers led the way! Let's do the same."

We needed to hear that, especially at my squad level view of war. The captain's one-minute speech made up for some of my doubts. For the rest of the day, we checked and rechecked our gear, rested, and watched more of our Brigade arrive that evening and through the night.

On the morning of the 26th, we advanced. Battalion ordered our company to proceed northward from the airport toward the village of Grand Anse, about three kilometers northeast of the airport. Our lieutenant briefed my platoon's NCOs on our line of advance.

"We take point. Hump it over to the airport perimeter to pick up a dead-end road, here." He pointed to a faint line on a tourist map. "We move east along the airstrip, then head north through some scrub to meet this road that goes through the village of Calliste." He traced the road with his finger. "No, I don't have the name of the road, but it leads directly to a T-intersection less than 300 meters further. We clear the buildings on either side. Secure the intersection and another one about thirty meters to the west. Charlie Company will pass through us to Calliste village.

"Intel indicates Cuban soldiers of unknown strength and disposition are in Calliste. Be advised, there are hundreds of civilians in the area."

The lieutenant must've sensed our collective unease with the lack of hard intel. "Look, I'd like better intel too. So, all I can say is, you see an enemy, engage them. Get prisoners when possible. We need intel from them. And watch out for the civilians."

Another sergeant asked the lieutenant, "Sir, the civilians we'll pass by. Can we ask them about the Cubans?"

"Sure. Go ahead. But I've got no word about their, ah, sympathies."

My squad moved on the right flank of our platoon's advance.

After marching through the low brush around the airport perimeter, we reached the dead-end road. Another 250 or so meters in a direct line ahead was the intersection. I led my squad as we advanced, pausing only to clear a couple of buildings along the way.

No Cubans. No Grenadian soldiers. Just scared civilians.

The lieutenant ordered my squad to take a defensive position along a thick tree line at the southeast corner of the intersection. After ordering my troopers to take their positions, I waved my alpha fire team leaders over to me.

Maybe my arm motions tipped off a communist soldier that I was a leader and therefore a primary target. I'll never know. Whoever he was, he threw a grenade in my direction. It fell short, thirty feet away. I'm not even sure I heard it go off. Grenade fragments hit me and only me. No fragment was serious except one. A half-centimeter-sized piece of steel skirted my nose and entered the inside corner of my left eye, about where the tear duct is. At that angle, it went in behind the eyeball.

I dropped instantly, pressing my left hand over my eye. What happened next was then and still is foggy. I don't think I screamed or anything like that. I felt burning, but not pain. That came later. I do remember swearing loudly and someone yelling, "Medic! Medic! Holt is hit!"

My troopers returned fire. Everybody must've emptied a mag into the trees and bushes. I thought, oh well, we've got extra ammo. Then I heard, "CEASE FIRE! CEASE FIRE!"

My team leader held up my head while applying a wound dressing from my kit over my eye. "Sergeant Holt. Medic's here. Hang tight." He kept talking as our medic put a new dressing over my eye and shot me with a dose of morphine.

What words were spoken, I remember only in bits and pieces. It went something like, "Mike, your squad now. Status? Any other wounded?"

"No, Sergeant. No other casualties. We heard screaming from inside the trees. Two enemy KIA. Men are out looking for more. We saw movement. Maybe retreating Cubans. I don't know. I got this, Sergeant."

Sometime during my evacuation from the battlefield, the pain finally overcame the shock and the morphine. Now that I'm a writer, I should have a unique and elegant way of describing pain to a reader. I could write 'searing pain.' That's accurate because it felt like someone put a red-hot piece of metal inside my head—that's what a grenade fragment is—but it's also a cliché. I could say, imagine the pain of hitting your thumb with a ballpeen hammer. Then imagine the hammer hitting your eye. Now multiply the pain by ten, and you're in the ballpark.

Let's just say it hurt worse than any fucking thing I'd felt before or since and leave it at that. Within the hour, I was under surgical care at the 44th Medical Brigade's field hospital. By that evening, stabilized, heavily sedated, I was MEDEVAC'd from Point Salines to a stateside hospital ophthalmic surgery unit.

Think for a second about what it would feel like for surgical instruments to go in behind your eyeball. Now imagine moving your eyeball out of its socket and laying it down across your cheek. No surprise to me that I spent a good deal of time in the hospital under a heavy dose of painkillers. A huge surgical patch covered the eye, reinforced in place by gauze bindings around my head. A special strap device kept my head in place. When I finally came around, I got the word from the surgeon.

"Sergeant, we removed the fragment. We saved your left eyeball. There's still enough blood flow to keep it viable. No prosthetic eye is necessary at this time. But I'm afraid there's no chance you will regain sight in your left eye. The grenade fragment destroyed the optic nerve. I am sorry."

He gave me a moment to let that sink in, then continued, saying the frag hit the optic nerve precisely at the point where the superior and inferior rectus muscles controlling movement come together. So, in addition to the loss of sight, voluntary movement of the eye wasn't possible.

"We stabilized the eyeball in one position, facing straight ahead. As I said, the eyeball itself wasn't seriously damaged, except for partial detachment of the retina. It may surprise you to know the eyeball will still see things, even if poorly; it just won't be able to send visual signals to the brain." He wrapped up with a talk on the postoperative care of the wound and therapy I'd receive. There wasn't much for me to say other than to thank him.

It is odd to think my eye still works fairly well at focusing images on the retina, but can't send a nerve impulse to my brain. And it can't move. Rather disconcerting to people when they see my working right eye move normally, while the other one stares straight ahead.

It could have been worse.

Had I kneeled on the ground five centimeters to my right, the fragment would've missed me. Two centimeters to my left, the fragment cuts through my sinus cavities and likely on to the frontal lobe of my brain, damaging the brain matter that holds my personality. Or kills me outright. No more than a slight tilt or turn of my head, or a tiny change in angle or elevation between the enemy and me, an entirely different future. Or no future at all.

Sheer chance often determines the fate of soldiers. During recovery, I devoured story after story of highly trained men wounded or killed because of a step to the left or to the right. Their fate was determined not by their martial skills, but by the most insignificant of decisions or movements. By random probabilities, as in my case, of the dispersal of steel shards. Given all I learned, my only conclusion was that it's best not to think about such things.

Losing eyesight meant the loss of something else. My Army career. Military medical separation from duty. Staying in the service was impossible. With all due respect to the pirates of old, half blind men do not make good soldiers, no matter how fierce one looks with an eyepatch.

Eventually, the Medical Evaluation Board settled on permanent medical retirement. Loss of an eye put me above the thirty percent disability threshold. Being a service-connected injury—no shit, combat—I was awarded a lifelong DOD/Veterans Administration monthly disability benefit, with an added combat-related disability benefit. Not a great dollar amount, but it helped. And I get free VA medical care forever.

Within two months, I was awarded a Purple Heart. Everyone wounded in combat gets one. Without doubt, a high honor. The Army also sent me a Bronze Star. Again, a high honor. I appreciated the recognition, but the Bronze Star left me embarrassed. There was nothing valorous in what I did. I never personally engaged the enemy in battle, nor did I lead my men into a fight, but nonetheless, I got a Bronze Star, something I've always felt was undeserved.

Nineteen soldiers and sailors lost their lives in *Urgent Fury*. On the few occasions people asked to see my medal, I remind them of the nineteen as a way of explaining why I keep it buried in a drawer somewhere.

Since Grenada, I've heard all the stories of how *Operation Urgent Fury* was, in the words of a former Air Force Combat Controller I once knew who was there, an "absolute and complete fucking goat-rope." I decided long ago it was best to leave all the second-guessing and punditry to the big-picture historians and analysts.

I was just a staff sergeant. My big picture went only as far as I could see, hear, and smell. I saw *Urgent Fury* from the ground up, not as others did from their elevated and faraway desks. Leaving aside how it all turned out for me, I'm proud to have been a part of *Urgent Fury*. With only four days to plan a major operation, the American military nonetheless prevailed.

We engaged the enemy in a fierce battle and won. We got the American civilians out. Our forces adapted and successfully liberated the people from communism and restored order. Even forty years later, grateful Grenadians remember we helped them put in place a democracy that continues to this day.

My war was over. I suppose I should be happy that I entered combat, however briefly, and came out alive. Yet, my ego feels a wound unacknowledged by the Purple Heart. Denied the chance to prove myself as a soldier in combat, I've carried a kind of guilt or shame that comes with not discovering if I would have measured up. That I let my troopers down. To be sure, it's an irrational response to a situation entirely outside of my control, but it never leaves me.

On the lighter side, I gained a new kind of sinus duct, allowing me to amuse friends by holding my nose to blow a gust of air and tiny drops of snot out of a unique orifice.

CHAPTER TWENTY

THAT'S WHAT NEIGHBORS ARE FOR

Holt

Harrison was barely in his car when Lillian came knocking at my door. With a wide smile on her face, Lil said, "Hi, Vic. Interesting day, wasn't it?" I stood there at the open door, staring, not saying a word.

"Vic? You okay?" Her touch on my arm brought me back to this world.

"Ah, yeah. Sorry. Jesus, Lil. I'm sorry. I'm okay. Ah, yeah, interesting day." My attempt at laughing it off fell flat.

She shook her head. "Interesting? I meant that sarcastically. And no, you're not okay."

Head down, nodding, I said, "Well, Lil, I, ah . . . Not every day Nazis burn books in your front yard."

Suddenly remembering what Lil did during the Nazi demonstration, I said as I held out my hand, "Lillian, thanks for checking on me during all . . . that. Thanks for calling the cops."

"Quite all right, Vic. Someone had to show some common sense." As she took my hand in both her hands, it occurred to me that Lil and Steve were involved in all this shit now. And it was my fault.

"Hey, Steve and I want you to come over to dinner tonight. Pork shoulder, veggies, and potato salad. You like that, right? We've got more than we can eat. Looks like you could stand some company, too."

I tried to demur, but Lil insisted. "Oh, Vic. Don't be such a shit. You're coming over." Then Steve chimed in, yelling from their porch. "Vic, be here at five. I'll have an old-fashioned ready for you!"

I yelled back, "Right, Steve, if it's no trouble."

"Trouble? Look!" He pointed down to his foot. "Goddamn boot comes off tomorrow. And because of it, I haven't been able to go anywhere or see anybody. Except for Lil. And I need a goddamn break from her." I couldn't help but smile.

Lil cocked her head to me, smiled, and said, "See what I put up with. Be there at five."

Still numb from the day's events, I headed for the couch, hoping to clear my mind. I never made it because a glance at the wall clock told me I had to get cleaned up, find something remotely decent to wear, and grab a bottle of wine. Perfectly routine tasks, but on a less-than-routine day.

I hadn't made a social visit to their house since Susan died. It took an attack by the Nazis to prompt this occasion. More importantly for this visit, I needed to plan for what I'd say to Lil and Steve. NSAG's visit was sure to come up in conversation.

Nice people, Lil and Steve. And great neighbors. Something more than being polite and respectful of property boundaries. If you need help, they're there for you. But their most important quality is the ability to mind their own business. Now they won't be able to do that. In this fight, they're potentially collateral damage. I thought, I can't let them become combatants.

Precisely at five, I was at their door, showered and shaved, dressed in grey slacks, loafers, a blue short-sleeved Oxford shirt, and a matching and totally unnecessary navy-blue blazer. Fitting their casual lifestyle, Lil and Steve stayed in their T-shirts and shorts, their sandals kicked aside, save for Steve's very large gray boot. Lil was quick to say I didn't have to get all dressed up, as she stripped me of my blazer.

Steve greeted me with a handshake known for a grip bordering on crushing. A strong, fit man even into his mid-seventies, I'd often wonder how a man seven years older than me still had a flat stomach and a near full head of hair, grey though it may be. Lil matched Steve in age, yet there was one word that couldn't be applied to Steve but matched Lil. Elegant.

Five minutes after I arrived, Steve handed me a perfectly mixed old-fashioned. Two shots of a smooth locally distilled bourbon, half a shot of water, a dab of simple syrup, a teaspoon of orange bitters, and a garnish of blood orange, run once along the highball glass rim before being plopped in. Plus, a gourmet cherry. Heaven. I thought, antidepressants be damned.

Lil and Steve had their traditional vodka martinis. Iced down in a shaker, three olives and the slightest spray of dry vermouth. Long ago, Steve corrected me when I said the vermouth seemed superfluous. "Young man, if we fail to add a second liquor, then it is not a cocktail. It doesn't matter that you need a gas chromatograph to find molecules characteristic of vermouth in this solution. That little spray makes it a cocktail. There are rules, you know."

Steve had a graduate degree in organic chemistry. He'd retired after forty years teaching chemistry at the town high school. Add to that a dozen or so years as an adjunct at a nearby community college. He first met Lillian when they worked at the same high school. Back then, she worked as a guidance counselor before moving on to administration, eventually serving as the principal of a middle school. Lil retired two academic years ago. I remember how Lil explained her retirement to Susan, and it reflected the times.

"I've had enough. Maybe I could've gone on for two or three more years, but these last two years . . . Life's too short to put up with all the bullshit. They made us heroes when COVID started. Then they made us villains. All over . . . politics. There're some people in town I'll never forgive. So, I've decided, I'm done."

Before tonight's dinner started, the small talk continued, absent any mention of the book burning. I was helping them with the final place settings when a gunshot went off.

My arms jerked, knocking a wine glass off the table. It shattered on the tile floor, scattering shards of glass. I screamed, "FUCK! GET DOWN!"

Two terrified faces stared at me as I crouched on the floor.

"Christ, I'm sorry, Vic. I, ah, that pot. I'm sorry. You okay?" I looked behind me. A heavy black cooking pot was on the floor, tipped over, and corn scattered everywhere. I realized that's what I heard. Not gunfire.

We all stood frozen in place. Mortified, I apologized. "Lil, no, it's my fault. I thought it was. . . sorry. Damn, I'm so sorry."

"You thought what, Vic?"

"It's fine, guys. Just, ah, the noise, well, startled me. That's all. Let me help clean things up."

Lil took a couple of steps toward me from the kitchen island. "No, you sit down at the table. Me and Steve will clean it up. Don't worry. Go on now, sit down, Vic. Please."

I had no words. Embarrassed, I sat down at my place at the table, ignoring my cocktail. Within a minute, Steve had cleaned up the glass shards. Lil had scooped off the floor what would've been a delicious side of her specially seasoned corn. Done, Lil took her seat. She put her hand on mine and leaned forward to look me in the eye.

"Well, Vic, I told you. You're not okay." Squeezing and then patting my hand, she continued. "It's all right. Later, after dinner, we can talk, if you like. No worries. So, let's get going with dinner. Don't forget your cocktail there."

The pork shoulder was as I expected. Wonderful. First boiled. Then baked, coated in mustard and brown sugar. In my humble opinion, beef is overrated. Pork is a tastier and far more interesting staple of life. And the sides? Garlic mashed potatoes, baked carrots with onions, and peas cooked up as a quick replacement for the seasoned corn.

Dinner conversation started off rather less seasoned than the dinner, with bland and cautious talk about the weather, our hopes for the summer, and Steve and Lil's travel plans. We avoided the awkwardness of my evident problems, though I knew Lil and Steve wanted to talk to me about the book burning. They had a stake in things, too, but I wanted to wait until after dinner.

After I helped Lil clear the table, Steve filled our wine glasses with a nice, sharp sparkling rosé. I really wanted a second old-fashioned. Or maybe a couple shots of straight bourbon, neat, but wine was the more rational choice.

"Guys. Let's have the wine on the porch, if it's not too much trouble. I want to fill you in on what's been going on."

I told them everything. The letters, emails, and social media posts. Smyth and Wright. The lawn sign. The bottle that was thrown at me. My escapade at the rotary. I wrapped things up with the mannequin head and a summation of the investigation to date. They sat there as silent as stones, ignoring their wine.

"Lil. Before I forget, again, thank you for helping today. You're a brave woman. Calling the police. Checking on me while the Nazis were still here. But please, don't do that again."

"Don't do what?"

"I mean, don't get involved. The last thing I want is for either of you to get hurt because of my troubles."

Leave it to Lil to break the tension. Laughing, she countered,

"Come on, Vic. I didn't do anything. I wasn't being 'brave.' Hell, I've faced more dangerous middle schoolers than those cretins."

Both Steve and I smiled at that crack. Lil wasn't done. "I don't suppose the police told you who they were. Maybe I know them from school days. Now that'd be funny, wouldn't it, Vic? You know what teachers say. Every felon in a prison cell was once in a classroom."

Steve shook his head at that, pretending to be irritated with his wife. Glancing my way, he said, "Can't tell her anything. You want some more wine there?"

"I'm not driving. Yes, please." After he gave me a more than healthy pour, Steve asked, "So what do you know about those Neo-Nazis?" I told them what little Harrison told me about NSAG. Lil summed things up by cursing NSAG. Steve did the same and then asked the big question.

"So, what'll you do now?"

"What'll I do?" I stopped to take a sip, no gulp, of wine. "I'm going to keep writing. Keep selling the book they hate. Write new ones. I'm not moving either. Sorry, but I guess you'll have a bothersome neighbor for a while. I intend to fight back."

Worried that I did nothing more than unnerve them, I shut up. They don't need troubles next door, especially at their age. Then Lil did something unexpected. Lil cheered.

"Fight? Excellent! I was afraid you . . . okay, wait, you'd better define what you mean by 'fight.' And I want to know how we can help."

"We, my dear?" I wasn't sure if Lil's lust for combat had left Steve shaken, or if he was just trying to be funny.

Lil wouldn't listen to my plea that they stay out of it. We went round and round on that score for a while until I finally accepted that I had to give Lil a position on this battlefield. As in the rear with the gear.

"Seems word got out. Big news that the Nazis invaded our

town. *The Herald Journal*, a couple of other local papers, and a TV reporter called me before I came over for dinner. Not sure how they got my number. Maybe from earlier interviews. Anyway, I told them I needed time to get my head straight. I'll follow up with them tomorrow."

"Bringing in the news. That could provoke, you know, the Nazis. And those nuts on the radio."

"You're right, Steve. It's a risk, but I doubt I could keep the media away anyway. I expect they'd come right to my house whether I want them to or not. A risk, but maybe favorable publicity will help.

"For Smyth and Wright and NSAG, I've got an idea. Lawyers. I'll be calling Anthony, my attorney, tomorrow morning to talk about a civil lawsuit against Smyth and Wright for harassment. And this NSAG bunch. Get a restraining order or whatever they do."

We sat quietly until I said, "Sorry to be such a buzzkill."

"No, no, all that sounds good. But is that all? Is there anything else?"

"What do you mean, Lil?"

"As I see it, lawsuits take time. And you have no idea if these . . . terrorists . . . that's what they are, terrorists, who burned your book will face any criminal charges. Even if they're charged, that'll also take time."

"Lil, honey, there's nothing Vic can do about all that."

Lil snapped back to Steve, "I know that! It's just that, maybe there's something we should do in the meantime."

"Again, Lil. We?"

"Yes, Steve. We."

Over the next hour and another bottle of wine, I steered them through all the conceivable options, from full combat to bunkering in, all while trying to gently persuade them to stay out of the way. Making joint defense plans while drunk is not a good idea. Until, however, a simple but powerful argument came to mind.

"Look, guys, if you get too involved, you'll ruin my one great advantage."

"Advantage? What the hell do you mean by that? We can defend ourselves, and we're willing to help defend you!"

"Lil, I love and respect you guys, but don't let the wine do the talking." I don't think she liked hearing that. On the other hand, Steve chuckled.

"My advantage? Being alone is my advantage. With Susan gone, I've got no family. No kids. So, it's just me. Think about it, what makes someone vulnerable to death threats?"

Steve answered. "When someone they love could get hurt."

"Exactly!"

"Then your plan is to fight this out all alone. Vic, that just doesn't sound very smart. You are going to need help, no matter . . ."

I cut Lil off. "Not entirely alone. Don't forget the police."

Lil almost seemed angry at me, as if I were denying her the pleasure of striking back at the kind of people who drove her from a job she loved.

Before Lil could continue her objections, I laid out the essentials of an expanded media campaign. "First thing, I'll get my agent onboard. Send out press releases about the book burning. Get me on news shows, podcasts, author talks, book signings, and book fairs as he can, anywhere in New England."

"Won't they go after your agent, too?" Lil seemed doubtful of my on-the-fly plan.

"Might. They've already threatened my publisher. Look. If Ed, he's my agent, wants to separate from me, I won't stop him. I'll just do all those things on my own."

"So, Vic, the core of your plan is what? Attack with legal action and use a media campaign to build public sympathy."

"Yeah, Steve. In a nutshell. And become as visible as possible. Get out there. Be seen. Show them their harassment isn't working. Live my life."

Lil sat turned away from me, her arms crossed. Steve seemed to be in a better mood. He took the bottle of wine in his hand and added another dose to all our glasses. Smiling, he said, "You know, they say if a wine glass is not empty before you fill it again, it only counts as one glass."

"Then, Steve, it's not the glasses, but the bottles we need to count." I pointed to the two empty bottles of expensive rosé wine. It was time for me to bring this discussion to a close before the wine did.

"I do need you to keep a watchful eye. Watch your house. Watch my house. Keep your home alarm on. See anything unusual, call the cops. If something happens like what happened today, don't come out. Call the cops, but don't come out."

Lil was not happy. "But can't we do anything for you? Come on, there must be something. Like run errands for you so you're not as . . . exposed."

"Thank you, Lil. That's nice to offer. Maybe I'll need that. But getting out there, running errands, that's part of the plan. I'm done being shut up inside. If I need milk, I'll get my own milk. That's the point. I want to get out there and be seen. Right now, I think it's important I show them they can't make me a prisoner in my own house."

We drained our glasses in silence. I made my goodbyes and walked back to my house, swerving only once or twice.

There are all sorts of movies out there where bad guys do something over-the-top bad to the main character. Murder his family or some other atrocity. Then it turns out the main character is a legendary retired Special Forces or CIA super-agent with expertise in killing people in both straightforward and imaginative ways. Naturally, he takes revenge, killing all the bad guys along with a dozen more accomplices for good measure. The lead villain is always the last to die, usually right after the main character reveals himself with a pithy catchphrase. Different titles. Different actors. Same movie.

That night, I started to watch one of those films, but I couldn't get to the end. All it did was remind me of my own precarious situation and that I lack that special, lethal skill set.

I am not that kind of man. I'm a scared, ordinary man. Sure, I was a soldier. I learned then how to control my fears, like when jumping out of a perfectly good airplane. But that was forty years ago. That I might die while going to get milk, that's another kind of dread.

Falling into bed, I remember thinking, no matter what my fears, my fight begins tomorrow.

CHAPTER TWENTY-ONE

PREPARING THE BATTLEFIELD

Holt

"Vic, you know it's Sunday. Pretty damn early for Sunday."

"Yes, Ed. Sorry. But something's happened."

Without giving Ed a chance to say another word, I launched into the book burning and sent him the video I took of NSAG.

"Ed, I need your help. I'm gonna fight this."

"My help? Shouldn't this be something for the police?" Ed sounded less than enthusiastic.

"Like I just told you, the police have already been here. There's only so much they can do. But I want to use this get more publicity, so . . ." Ed interrupted me.

"Why in hell do you want publicity? Christ almighty, Vic. The cops told you to lay low."

I let the moment hang in silence before I spoke. "Look, Ed. I did stay out of sight, and look what happened. Anyway, like it or not, this morning the local TV media are on their way here. I'm not going to stop them. But we can use this book burning to get people on my side. I need public support."

"Support for what?"

"To fight back. Look, I'm not going to hide inside. I'm going to live my life. So, here's what you can do. I've sent you videos I took of the book burning. Use my videos with a press release to all the newspapers in New England. And the big papers out of Washington, New York, and Chicago. Then ABC, CBS, NBC, MSNBC, CNN. And FOX. Get me interviews. It's what agents do, right, Ed?"

"I mean, you sure that's a good idea, Vic?" I replied with confidence, I hope. "Yes, quite sure."

"Okay, let me get this straight." I could hear the irritation in Ed's voice. "The cops told you stay out of sight. Instead, you want to go after these guys, head on. In the open. You want to make yourself a target."

"Yes, that sums it up nicely."

"You're going to get yourself in trouble."

"I'm already in trouble. Oh, and send that release to our entire Congressional delegation, the Governor, my state legislators, the AG, and my town police."

Ed turned me down. In response, I gave him an ultimatum. "Ed, you've got a decision to make. You can help me. Or you can end our relationship. I'll be the first to say there is risk to you. Personal risk. But first, let me appeal to your business sense.

"Public support could lead to increased sales. Think of sales as a metric for measuring victory. I was a best-selling author. New York Times bestseller. I had a pretty good social media following. So, I'm a decent enough revenue stream for you and the publisher. Remember how sales jumped after that wacko Congresswoman burned my book? The same thing's going to happen. More book sales. Even these days, Nazis aren't all that popular. As long as I don't go too far, like suggesting people gun down a couple of Nazis. Then again, shooting Nazis is always popular."

Ed didn't appreciate the humor. I let him yell it out for a minute, then offered my terms. "It's a simple binary decision. Help me, or resign as my agent. The choice is yours. What's your pleasure?"

"I'll call you back."

"Good. I need your decision this morning. Bye."

Next, I called Anthony, my lawyer. It took me a good five minutes to brief him on the harassment, the Nazis, and Smyth and Wright.

"Anthony, I'm done hiding away. I want to take legal action against them. Smyth and Wright. And NSAG. Hell, I want to sue that fucking Congresswoman! Can't we begin with, what do you call it, a cease-and-desist letter? Get them to stop talking about me?"

"Well, it's complicated," Anthony asked me to come to his office and more thoroughly explain all that's happened. "I'll tell you right off, Vic, if I'm not the kind of lawyer for this, I'll refer you to someone else. Fair enough?"

We made an appointment for the afternoon.

After I hung up with Anthony, I crossed the social media Rubicon. I reactivated all my social media accounts. With minor variations, the opening salvo post went like this:

Victor Holt here. Author of Democracy Lost.

I'm Back. Sorry for being away, but I've been harassed and threatened with death by extremist trolls. I tried ignoring them, but that didn't work. They kept at it. Now, Nazis are after me. Honest to God, American-born Nazis! The National Socialist Action Group. NSAG. They burned a pile of my book Democracy Lost right in my front yard!

I'm done being quiet. I'm done hiding.

Have a look at the video I took of their fascist book burning. Do you know any of these terrorists? If you recognize any of them, call your local police.

Spread the word! Share this post!

Thank you to all my supporters and readers!

As an added visual, I paired still pictures of the National Socialist Action Group book burning with a historical image of the real

Nazis burning books back in the 30s. Each time I clicked on *Post*, I felt like I'd slapped another Nazi across the face. Of course, it's easy to be brave from an online sanctuary.

I knew my posts represented a risk/reward calculation. I risked enraging someone out there who would do me harm. With luck, the reward might be public exposure of a Nazi, which might cost him friends, family, and perhaps employment. For the moment, though, the exhilaration I felt at striking back more than exceeded my fears.

My posts and calls finished; I waited for the local television news to show up. It wasn't a long wait. A quick sit-down interview in the house, followed by a showing of the book burn pile, which was then dampened by a light rain. Lastly, I made sure they had my video of the Nazis. All done in twenty-five minutes. It was pretty much "repeat as necessary" as the other reporters showed up.

When my latest step into local media was done, I headed for the gym. *I won't fight this fight from inside my house. The fight begins with being seen.*

On the way to the gym, I remembered the prayer of soldiers and astronauts.

God, I hope I didn't fuck up.

CHAPTER TWENTY-TWO

A WAY UP

Ford

My crew had just gotten back from a job site when the boss said, "Hey, Jeff. Would you come into my office for a sec?" I got a cold chill in my gut; a stab in my stomach of I don't know what. I went into her office thinking something bad was going to happen.

Beth Johansen. She owns this landscaping company. We hardscape patios, build outdoor kitchens and firepits, and plant every kind of shrub or flower bed imaginable. This time of year, we worked straight out.

If you ask me, Beth is a great boss. Always quick to compliment. Keeps her temper in front of others. If you screwed up, she'd take you to someplace private, explain things, and demand it not happen again. I went through that once. The right amount of stone didn't get on a truck for a patio job. Four pallets were needed, but only three got on the truck. We lost time and money when one of the crew took the truck back to get the missing pallet. Beth didn't like that.

Other bosses would've yelled, swore, and insulted me. Even fired me. Not Beth. She went over the added costs to her company, the missed deadline for the client, and the time it could cost other projects downstream. She stayed calm and kept to the facts.

"All right, Jeff. Well, let's just call this a mistake and move on from here." That was it. No yelling. She even shook my hand. Maybe because I liked her, I offered no excuses, admitting I screwed up and promised it wouldn't happen again. In the back of my mind, I thought, well, that's a first for you, Jeff; you took responsibility. Since then, every day I went to work, I made damn sure there'd be no more mistakes.

What I said to her back then wasn't entirely true. The pallet thing wasn't my fault. The job supervisor, Glenn, told me to put three pallets on the truck. Three. Not four. I know he did. When Beth confronted him, Glenn lied and pinned the blame on me. I know he lied. I promised myself I'd get back at him, someday, somehow.

"Shut the door, please, Jeff, and have a seat. Need some coffee?" The boss wanting the door closed was another bad sign.

"No, Ma'am. I'm all set with coffee." I sat down in the chair in front of her desk. She poured herself a cup, laughed a little, and said, "Still with the Ma'am stuff? You make me feel old!"

"Sorry, Ma'am. Ah, yeah. Mrs. Johansen. Boss. Yeah, so you want to talk to me?"

Beth turned away from the coffee pot, almost spilling the cup all over herself. She looked embarrassed.

"Oh, shit, I'm sorry. No, no, you're not in trouble. I'm sorry if I gave you that impression. I've got something for you." With a big smile, Beth sat down, reached into her desk drawer, and handed me a small manila envelope. "Go on. Open it."

I pulled three new one-hundred-dollar bills halfway out. "What the fuck?" I meant to say that to myself, but it slipped out.

Laughing, Beth said, "Jeff, that's yours. A little, off-the-books bonus. You've been working hard, very hard, for us. Always on time. Never seen you slack off. Always getting the others to keep up the pace. Taking all that overtime without question. You've never given me any hint of drug use or alcohol. Nothing like that. Wish I could say that about everyone." During my time here, Beth fired three or four guys for drugs.

"I thought you deserved a reward. Anyway, keep this between us. Don't tell the other guys. Liable to cause, ah, trouble." I agreed, though I wasn't sure I understood why I couldn't tell the others.

"Now let's discuss your future."

Beth told me that next week there'd be an opening for a supervisor, and she wanted me to fill that slot. More responsibility, but more money. And it'd be year-round work. During the winter, supervisors work in the office and store. So, even more money.

"This is how it'll work. I'll set you up on the schedule for a couple of jobs coming up. I'll pick the crew. I want to see how you do. It's kind of a probationary period, but your increased pay starts right then. You'll learn that things can change with your coworkers when you're the boss. I want to be sure you're comfortable in this new situation. You follow?"

I heard her words, but I wasn't sure I believed this was happening. She was offering me a promotion. I didn't know what to say.

"Ah, hello? Jeff?"

Guess she said that a couple of times before I said anything. "Yeah, sorry. Wow. Ah, thank you."

"Does that mean you're accepting the supervisor job?"

I smiled, something I don't do that often. "Yes, I am. I do. I mean, I'm accepting this job."

"Excellent!" She held out her hand, and we shook on it.

Leaving her office, it occurred to me this promotion might be the start of something. If I do well as a job site supervisor, then maybe I will become a manager. There's good money and a future for me here.

My first thought was to call my folks. Then just as quickly, I decided not to, thinking I should wait to see how things turned out. Besides, I suspected, I'm not sure they'd care.

On the way home, deciding to celebrate, I splurged some of my extra money on take-out chicken parmesan from a pizza place downtown. And a nice beer from the microbrewery down the road. At home, with the chicken parm and beer on the coffee table, I clicked on the local news.

Hoisting the beer, I toasted Mom and Dad. “Thanks for leaving the big LED television here while you escaped to Florida. Least you could do.”

I was in time for the weather report. The weather forecast is important to landscapers. Rain makes for a difficult day. Fortunately, good weather for tomorrow and the rest of the work week. Then something more interesting followed the weather news.

It’s always surprising when a news story happens right around the corner. Let alone one about a bunch of Nazis who came near here and burned a pile of books. The news played Holt’s video of the Nazis, and I replayed it more than twice. The books burned, and the Nazi’s gave their stiff-arm salutes. Naturally, they interviewed Holt. The same guy from earlier news stories. The same guy I saw standing on the side of the road. I started yelling.

“So, Nazis came after you! Too fucking bad! You wrote that book! Your own fucking fault! What an idiot. What’d you think’s gonna happen, you stupid motherfucker!” Then I switched targets.

“Look at those dumb bastards. Playing all big and tough. Burning books. What’s that supposed to do? The real Nazis, they did things. They knew what to do, and they did it. Not these guys. Holt won’t stop. He’ll keep doing what he’s doing. Nothing changes! Nothing fucking changes!”

I finally shut up and went back to my dinner, angry that the news spoiled my celebration. Over the last of my chicken parmesan, I muttered to myself, “Nothing changes. They didn’t scare him. They can’t stop him.

“I could.”

CHAPTER TWENTY-THREE

THIS WILL NOT HELP

Harrison

The Monday morning after the Nazis came to town, I found myself headed to my cubicle at the station. Before I'd reached my desk, the Chief intercepted me. After having seen the news reports of the neo-Nazi book burning, the Chief told me to make that case my top priority. He said he'd already gotten "calls from town council members. They're upset, so get on it, Pete."

Naturally, I promised to do just that. But first things first. The weekend left me with police reports documenting three less exotic incidents. I attacked them first. I wanted my desk cleared of routine issues and distractions before I focused on Holt vs. the Nazis.

When reviewing police reports, I am the second set of more experienced eyes on the paperwork and the responding officers' investigative and arrest procedure. My job was to identify any inconsistencies in the reports before they were passed on to the Chief.

A few of my colleagues were habitually cursory in this shared responsibility. I doubted they read more than the first ten words before signing off. I try to carefully check every entry and word written by the officer, spelling included. That irritated my fellow detectives on occasion. As one said to me, "Pete, you're wasting your time. There's no need to be so damn . . . meticulous." I didn't listen to him. Someday, my "meticulous" nature might save me, and this department, from unnecessary grief.

Fortunately, lawbreakers had a slow weekend. I had only three patrol officer reports to look over. A DUI here, a domestic assault arrest there, and a traffic stop that uncovered a guy wanted on a bench warrant. With those reports done, I started on Holt's case.

Detaining NSAG created a stack of paperwork, which, of course, I double-checked for accuracy and completeness. Checking their criminal records yielded a surprise. No ex-cons turned up. Aside from low-level misdemeanors, none had a previous felony conviction. You'd think a member of a Nazi organization would've had at least one serious brush with the law. Then again, this was unfamiliar investigative territory for me.

That finding alone troubled me. Until they appeared at Holt's place, these NSAGs were pretty much law-abiding citizens. Any one of us might know them as a fellow parishioner, a coworker, or a friendly guy at the neighborhood bar, completely unaware they'd found common cause with history's worst monsters. We want them to look like monsters, not like ordinary folk. Not like us.

Why or how these people turned into hateful scum, I didn't have the training, experience, or time to understand. I investigate and arrest, if warranted. I act after the fact of a crime, not before. My job is not to understand the genesis of their radicalization, but to deal with the consequences.

There are those who do try to understand them. For decades, the FBI investigated domestic extremists, from the KKK and Weatherman Underground of the sixties to the Patriot Front and Proud Boys of today. I had zero knowledge of the FBI's activities in this field, though I recalled attending a regional law enforcement conference a couple of years ago. The Deputy Commander of the FBI's Hostage Rescue Team briefed us on HRT's recruitment, training, capabilities, and activities. During the Q&A that followed, he offhandedly said that the lion's share of HRT's activities dealt with far-right domestic extremists. Militia groups and the like. The FBI seemed like the logical next call.

My call to the local FBI office was brief and disappointing. When I pimped the agent for what they knew on NSAG, he only said it was a new group, and the FBI didn't have much. He did gush over my having identified NSAG members, including at least one leader. It seemed I already knew more about NSAG than the FBI. In fairness, NSAG hadn't done anything bad enough to attract serious federal attention. I sent them a copy of my file.

Next was a series of calls to other jurisdictions to make sure they have got the word on their residents who live a second life as a Nazi. Responses varied. For a couple of those police departments, I imagined their NSAG notes going no further than into a file that wouldn't see the light of day.

After lunch, I briefed the DA, hoping he'd get so pissed off that actual Nazis came to his jurisdiction, he might order me to arrest the whole bunch. Of course, that didn't happen. Instead, I was told to keep the DA office informed and investigate further. His lukewarm reaction left me with the feeling that all this work would amount to nothing.

Hanging up with the DA, frustrated, I caught myself saying a little too loudly, "All this over a fucking book!" Heads in the station turned my way. It was time to check up on Holt. But first, more coffee and a little reflection.

My detective side understands Holt is the victim of a series of crimes. I am to gather evidence of each offense and dispassionately analyze the facts. Eventually, it may be possible to identify and arrest the perpetrators of the threats.

Holt has not broken the law. He's a scared old man, so I

shouldn't expect everything he says or does to be rational or nice. My job does not require that I like the victim. Holt makes that easy when he doesn't follow my advice.

A case in point. This morning, I found out Holt reactivated his social media after the book burning. That blindsided me and went against my advice to stay out of sight. Fortunately, his posts announcing his return weren't the ravings of a madman. He soberly posted the details of the book burning before flatly stating his intention to fight back. No surprise, his return prompted return fire from people, not his fans. There was a pleasing number of supportive comments, but those seemed to tail off as others attacked them. Five or six of the hateful comments qualified as threats, but I was relieved Holt didn't match stupid comments with more stupidity.

When I reached him, Holt said he was busy and to call him back in an hour.

"Busy? Really? Too busy to hear what I'm doing about NSAG?"

Holt said he had "one last new interview" to do and then he'd be free, "like I said, in an hour or so. So, if you don't mind." I clicked off the call without saying a word.

Yeah, he can be an asshole.

CHAPTER TWENTY-FOUR

I FIGHT. WE FIGHT

Holt

No one killed me at the gym on Monday afternoon. Not being murdered is a good way to wind down the day.

Ed didn't resign. Another good thing. We've had our disagreements, but when something needs to be done, Ed gets it done. Late Sunday night, Ed called to bring me up to speed on the media campaign. Videoconference interviews with the national television networks will start on Tuesday. CNN at 8 a.m., followed by MSNBC and ABC every half hour. Ed told me they already had my book-burning video.

He'd also emailed the video to half a dozen podcasters I'd worked with before. "Nothing back from them yet. But don't get your hopes up. They may not want to do this. Makes them a target, and just about all of them are one-person shops. I've got other ideas for podcasts. Just give me time." I was pleased Ed joined the fight with such vigor.

"Look, Vic. In the interviews, just be yourself. No, something better than your usual self. Be matter of fact. Don't get pissed off. Smile a lot. Understand?"

After I got off the phone with Ed, I wrote up a simple prepared statement for the network interviews.

To those who continue to threaten and harass me, to the neo-Nazis who burned my books at my front door, I will not stop writing. I will not withdraw the novel that triggered you. Not from any store or event. In fact, I will work harder at promoting it. You tried to terrorize me. You have failed. You have already lost.

Brief, firm, and without sarcasm. It made my intentions clear, though it risked antagonizing my enemies even more. Then again, anything I say or do will piss them off. I practiced saying the statement in front of a full-length mirror. Though I felt a little silly, my presentation had to be good if I was to get the attention I wanted from friends and supporters. And enemies.

After the last Tuesday interview, I called Anthony. He wanted a breakfast meeting for eight o'clock tomorrow. "There's someone you should meet. An attorney who has relevant legal expertise."

Wednesday morning, I dressed as formally as I did these days, meaning casual but clean. Polo shirt with khaki slacks and loafers. With a worn manila folder in hand, I set out for the meeting place, the *Sunrise Café* in town. An appropriate choice, as I borrowed the name for a setting in the novel NSAG torched. A somewhat upscale breakfast nook, it is always busy and always good. Best of all, the background noise stayed within a reasonable decibel range.

Anthony was already in the café when I came through the door. Seated with him was the attorney he wanted me to meet.

Greetings and introductions were made, seats taken, and the coffee poured. All the while, I prayed my recently acquired but ever-present anxiety about public spaces did not show. Hard to let go of the thought of enemies all around, waiting for their chance. A crazy notion, but not all that crazy considering my world didn't make a damn bit of sense right now.

"Ms. Llewelyn, call me Vic. May I call you by your first name? Do you prefer, Bron or Bronny?"

"Bron. I prefer Bron. Bronny is something my family calls me."

Anthony got things going. "Vic, I'll let Bron explain her role. As I told you, she has legal experience that might fit your case."

Bron was about to speak when the waiter came over to collect orders. Bron went first, ordering Eggs Benedict with ham on a sliced Portuguese bolo bread. While she ordered, I took further stock of her. Almost my height. Wiry, but not exactly skinny. Her attire struck me as fitting for an attorney. Silver wire frame glasses. A darkish grey business suit with a white blouse and barely noticeable gold earrings. Hair trimmed short. Judging from her shock of grey hair, she looked to be in her fifties. No smiles from her yet.

Anthony ordered a ham and cheese omelet. I went for something more grandiose. "The corned beef hash, homemade, with three fried eggs, over medium, grilled English muffin, and a side order of bacon with a large orange juice."

"Well, Vic, I'm glad to see fighting Nazis hasn't diminished your appetite."

"Yeah, yeah. Cut me some slack, Tony. Haven't exactly been out and about lately. You know, with people wanting me dead, this could be my last meal." I said the last part with a wide smile. Anthony snickered a little. Bron, on the other hand, kept a stone face.

Anthony nodded toward Bron. "Mr. Holt, while we're waiting for the food, let me explain why I am suited to this case." She didn't wait for me to respond.

"Fifteen years with a district attorney's office in a county outside Philadelphia. A prosecutor. Well over a hundred of my cases involved charges of harassment and threats, in one form or another, often accompanied by other charges. Mind you, these were criminal proceedings. Ninety percent of the defendants pleaded out. The ten percent that went to trial, I won. Penalties ran the spectrum, from restraining orders, fines, restitution, and incarceration. Now, how this . . ."

I interrupted. "Okay. For fifteen years. How long ago was that?"

At least outwardly, Bron forgave me for my rudeness. "If you're wondering if I am still current, put your mind at ease. The law on harassment hasn't changed much, save for new laws pertaining to cyber harassment and bullying."

"You'd know better than me. Sorry for the interruption. Please continue."

"Thank you. After the DA work, I did six years as a defense attorney. That exposed me to a wide variety of cases, but it included clients facing harassment charges. Particularly, harassment and threats made over the internet. So, I come with the perspective of both sides.

"These past years, I'm a junior partner with the legal firm Howard, Leslie, and Jacobson."

I couldn't stop myself from thinking, at least she didn't say Dewey, Cheatum, and Howe. God rest *The Three Stooges*.

She continued, unaware of my mental lapse into classic slapstick comedy. "Now, at some point, the DA may criminally charge anyone who threatened you with violations of the state's harassment and terrorist threat law. Anthony told me Detective Peter Harrison is handling your case."

"How much do you guys know about all the threats I've gotten?"

Anthony answered. "Detective Harrison gave me a quick rundown on the online threats, quoting, let's say, the more colorful ones. And he told me about the mannequin head and the Nazis showing up at your house. I passed all I learned on to Bron."

Not skipping a beat, Bron said, "So, criminal violations, like death threats, go to the police and the DA. I'm here to look at civil action. Our firm does civil matters exclusively. It's obviously too early to recommend a well-defined plan. But I can offer a general framework. Subject to change, of course. May I?"

I glanced at Anthony, who shifted his attention to his coffee, before I looked back at Bron. "Sure. Go ahead."

Bron explained the first step would be cease-and-desist letters, better known in legal circles as a stop harassment letter. The purpose is to put the offenders on notice that they're violating the law. It makes it difficult for them to squirm out of responsibility by later claiming they didn't know or understand that what they were doing was illegal.

"We can do this quickly, especially since the harassment you're facing involves inciting threats to property and life. We're on solid legal ground."

"You mean, Bron, hit Smyth and Wright with this letter?" I didn't let her answer before starting a small rant. "Because, Jesus, I hope you do. I downloaded their latest broadcasts. They cheered for the Nazis! Egged on their listeners to follow NSAG's example . . ."

Bron held up her hand to get me to stop. "You know, Victor . . ."

"It's Vic."

"Very well. Vic. Maybe it'd be a good idea to lay off listening to them." Her rebuke shut me up. She continued, explaining that the better approach with Smyth and Wright is to petition a judge to issue a cease-and-desist order.

"Quick explanation. A letter is just a letter. It can't compel someone to change their behavior. An order from a court, well, that can compel. Ignore a court order, and the judge can issue a bench warrant for arrest. Cease and desist court orders are well-suited to cases like yours. Ones that may involve libel or defamation or perhaps character assassination. Because the harassment is ongoing, I'm confident we can get an order.

"It'll go like this. We petition a judge, get the court order, plus a restraining order to keep them away from you. I don't think it'll take long."

"But, Bron, what if they don't cease or desist. Or, I mean, what if Smyth and Wright, and the people who listen to them, keep coming after me?"

Then she brought out the big guns. "While a judge mulls over issuing a bench warrant, we hit them with a civil suit seeking damages. Not just Smyth and Wright. We could file against anyone threatening you, but that might not always be, ah, practical or appropriate."

On that point, I sensed a shift in her tone. Bron may have been about to explain before I cut her off.

"Not practical. Bron, I think I know why. I don't think any of these people have much money, Smyth and Wright included. No offense, but I think you're saying it wouldn't be worth it. Financially, I mean. For me. And for you."

Bron didn't bat an eye at my suggestion that money is the deciding factor. "Well, Vic, now that you've brought it up. Let's talk about money."

As if on cue, breakfast arrived at the table, momentarily sparing us from a delicate discussion, if only for a minute. Between bites of Eggs Benedict, Bron went at it again.

"Let's start with legal fees. Sometimes my firm operates on a contingency fee basis. You've heard those injury attorney commercials. 'You don't pay unless we win!' Sometimes we do that, but that's almost always when the defendant has deep pockets. Insurance companies and such. With Smyth and Wright, no deep pockets.

"My firm would demand I charge you our usual rates. The kind of rates we charge our wealthy clients. Corporate types. We're very good at what we do and deserve to be compensated accordingly."

She took another bite. I didn't lift my fork for fear of choking on the hash, anticipating what all this might cost me. Or that this legal fight would end right here and now.

Pointing her fork at the Eggs Benedict while chewing, Bron said, "Mmm. Wow. This is really good. Eggs done perfectly." She put her fork down and got back to business.

"Anyway, I have an idea. Care to hear it, Vic?" Bron's suddenly smiling face hinted that a joke was about to be played on me. Judging from Anthony's smiling face, he was her co-conspirator. They had a surprise headed my way. I nodded to Bron.

"Good. Here's the plan. I take your case, but work on my own time, not the firm's time. I'll help you go after those bastards. The harassers, the Nazis. The lot. I'll get court orders. Restraining orders. Civil suits. No matter what assets they have or don't have. I'll join your fight."

Then I knew I liked her, but just to test her a little, I asked, "Define 'win' please."

"Winning means the justice system, civil and criminal, puts enough of these guys in financial ruin or in jail, or both. Their example should deter others of their kind."

Encouraged, I took a healthy bite of hash and eggs. I swallowed my food before I asked the big question. "What will you charge?"

"Nothing. *Pro bono*."

I stammered out my words with specks of breakfast, "What? Did you say p*ro bono*?" It took me a moment to grasp what she said before I asked, "How can . . . why would you do that?"

"Oh, it wouldn't be just me. I've got a dozen eager law students I could recruit. You see, I teach a law class. I haven't talked to them yet, but I can't imagine they'd turn down the chance to go after this NSAG. And Smyth and Wright. A real-world case right in their backyard. A case that fits our political times."

She's a steely-eyed killer. Good. That's what I need.

"One last point, Vic. Though I'll stick to civil proceedings, should I uncover anything that could lead to criminal charges, I won't hesitate to clue in Harrison."

I looked at Anthony with a face that must have said, please help me decide! He smiled back, nodding in the affirmative before he said, "Vic, if you want to fight back, that is, fight back in court, this is the deal you want. I'll be a part of it too. Don't worry about my fee."

"I, ah, I'm a bit overwhelmed by all this." As I kept at my hash, eggs, and bacon, the most important question finally dawned on me.

"You've said how it could be done. But you've not said why."

Bron pushed aside her plate and straightened up in her chair. She repeated my question, speaking each word with a deliberate slowness. "Why do I want to do this?"

"Things in this country are . . . not well. No, that's not right. Dangerous is a better word. Things are dangerous. Look at what's happened to you. You write a work of fiction, and before long, Nazis, American-born Nazis, are burning books in your front yard. Nazis who took their cue from a duly elected member of the Congress of the United States.

"Nazis. It infuriates me to my core. You see, my grandfather fought real Nazis. German Nazis. He died fighting them in Holland and these fu . . . Sorry, I don't mean to swear; it's unprofessional, but . . ."

"Don't worry about that, Bron. You can say fuckers if you like. I use it all the time."

Bron's professional demeanor broke into a chuckle. "Well, okay. Anyway, I can't stand by and watch these, ah, fuckers, thank you, desecrate the service and sacrifice of my granddad and all his fellow soldiers. I will not let that happen. Does that make sense, Vic?"

"Yes, it does. Well said, Bron." A feeling, lately unfamiliar, returned to me. Connection to another human being. Someone who could lift me up. Something I hadn't felt since I lost Susan. For a fleeting moment, I felt at peace.

The three of us refocused on breakfast. I asked the waiter to bring me more coffee and the bill. "I got this, guys. Least I can do."

After I paid the bill, we lingered over the coffee, chatting about the things people usually talk about over breakfast. Sports, the weather. Stuff like that. I, maybe we, needed a break from the legal tension. And part of me didn't want to spoil it all by bringing up another issue.

"Anthony, Bron, I agree to the plan. I want you to help me." I took a healthy sip of the now lukewarm coffee before I continued. "There's something you should understand."

"Which is?" asked Bron.

"When all this started, I shut down all my social media. Harrison said to. I kept a low profile. Well, not always. There're other incidents that I'll tell you about later that the police already know about.

"Right after the book burning, I restarted my social media accounts. Here's a copy of what I posted yesterday." I reached into my folder and gave Bron a copy of my post. She read it over, nodded slightly, and handed it to Anthony.

"And yeah, the post includes still images and video of the Nazis." After a last sip of my coffee, I continued. "Tony, this is where you say that's a risky move. Then I say, yes, it adds to the risk, but I think it's a risk worth taking."

Bron surprised me. "Vic, I already saw the post. As your attorney, I strongly advise against doing that in the future without allowing me to review any posts beforehand. I want your word on that."

"Okay, I promise. But I got to say, it felt good to post that."

"I'm sure it did." Bron stopped to sip her coffee.

I felt compelled to explain my reasoning behind my reemergence into life. "Staying quiet didn't help me. They doxed anyway.

The online threats continued. They went after the bookstores. And the town library. I got hit with a bottle while driving. The fake head at my front door. NSAG came to my house. This staying out of sight isn't working. They're not done with me.

"So, I'm changing strategy. It means getting media attention. I've done interviews at my place about NSAG. Local news and then national news interviews . . ." Anthony cut me off.

"Yeah, Vic. We've seen them." Anthony didn't continue after that, which unnerved me. I asked, "Well, what did you think?"

"Actually, I thought they went well. You didn't yell or swear. You kept to the facts. You even seemed gracious to the reporters. That must've been an effort for you. I mean, being gracious." Anthony wasn't pleased.

"It was, Tony. Now, is my media activity going to change your mind about representing me?"

After a very long and painful pause, Bron said, "No, it doesn't change my mind. Getting public support is important, and to get that, you need media coverage."

Anthony chimed in, unmasking his irritation with me. "Next time, clear it with us first. Christ almighty, Vic. This puts an even bigger target on your back. Sure, you'll get public support and sympathy, but do you remember the old joke about where you find sympathy in the dictionary?"

I did. Between shit and syphilis.

"Don't count on support being deep and long-lasting. At best, it'll be shallow and brief. People quickly forget things. And it could backfire. No, not could. Will. Send these radicals over the edge. They'll try to hit back. But you know that, don't you?" Anthony pushed away his empty breakfast plate and laid down the law.

"Look, Vic. Going forward, let's try to work together, as a team, on a media plan."

There was still one fragment of hash browns on my plate.

Picking it up, I chewed on it slowly, creating a silence I needed to diminish the tension created by Tony's criticism.

"Agreed, Tony. I promise. Another thing. I'm done being held up in my house. I'm going to live my life. I will be seen. And yes, I know that's risky." They nodded their acquiescence to their new client's wishes to live a life worth living.

"Now, Anthony, Bron, what's the next step?"

Bron spoke. "When I leave here, I'll go meet with Detective Harrison. I'll look over all the evidence he has. That is, anything he can let me see, and anything you've given him. You don't need to come with me."

"I thought you'd only be doing this on your off time."

"I am. I took the day off. Next is NSAG's scene of the crime. After I'm done with the detective, I'll come to your place. I want to see where they burned your books."

Bron spoke about how she'd integrate her students into the case, such as having them write the cease-and-desist letter to Smyth and Wright while she lines up a judge to issue an order.

"And same for NSAG once we know more about them. I'll keep you informed."

"Okay, sounds great. Thanks, guys. I feel much better."

Bron and I shared cell numbers before saying goodbye. As I turned away, I remembered something Bron had said about her grandfather.

"Bron, when you come by my house, set aside a little time. If you don't mind, I'd like to hear more about your grandfather."

CHAPTER TWENTY-FIVE

THE STEELY EYED KILLER

Holt

After breakfast with Anthony and Bron, I wanted a quiet, relaxing day at home with nothing to do but wait for Bron to drop by. Instead, I did something dumb. I checked my reactivated social media accounts.

Though I'd posted it only a couple of days before, I was itching to see the reaction to my NSAG campfire post. As always, I left my page open to public comments. Though I expected lots of insulting comments, it shocked me how many there are in "lots."

Interpreting the comment "Likes" emojis proved confusing. A "Like" seemed straightforward, as did the "Cares" and "Sad." Of the sixteen hundred in total and climbing, roughly half were those first three. I counted them as supportive. Not so much the other half. "Angry" or "Haha" emojis were likely not fans of my work. They likely supported the Nazi side.

The comments interested me more. These numbered two hundred eighty-three and kept climbing as I read them. With that volume, all I could do was glance through them and occasionally type out a quick thanks to supporters. I did not thank those who wished me a quick trip to hell. Then there were the outright threats.

Since my first book, I've promoted my work using social media. To this day, I still don't have a clue how it works. I know every commenter leaves behind their "handle" or online account name. That in turn requires an email address. Somewhere along the way, their actual name could be uncovered. Maybe.

It's always an option to report threatening comments to the social media platform. If the platform found the comment violated their community standards policy, it could be taken down, and the commenter could be suspended from posting. Sometimes they enforce their rules. Sometimes they don't. That day, I didn't report anyone, thinking it better to leave them up and let their vile words betray their own despicable nature. Who knows? Maybe my supporters will do the job for me.

Of course, shaming someone who has no shame is a poor tactic. When I had more time, I'd take screenshots for Bron and Detective Harrison.

They call these people trolls. According to Norse mythology, the trolls of old lived in the dark of mountain caves. They dined on hapless humans and unlucky goats that wandered by. Today's online trolls are equally hideous, though their tastes have evolved from human flesh to human emotion. Trolls feast on politics, lies, racism, outrage, and hatred. My post was as tasty to them as a herd of goats. Like the mythical ones, today's trolls are insatiable.

So, you're back for more abuse. We'll oblige. Traitor! That was the nicest one. Was it a threat of physical abuse, or merely name-calling?

Got rope from the hardware store. Looking for a tree. Either this guy is threatening to hang me, or he's putting up a backyard swing for his kids.

Slow learner. You know what will happen. This one is ambiguous enough to stay just within the legal lines.

Watch your back. Edging closer to a more definitive threat. Or is it just advice to be careful?

*We've had enough out of you, f****** ass****. We'll ruin you!* Best case, it's a vulgar threat to my business and not to me as a person. Profanity in comments is not allowed by most platforms. On others, it's part of the experience.

Stop writing now! You'll never sell another book! Everyone is a critic.

You're way to liberal! Whoever wrote this comment impeached himself in two ways: grammatically and ideologically. First, it's "too," not "to." Second, when did defending democracy become a liberal thing instead of an American thing?

Calling me a cockroach, a rat, or vermin was a popular expression, often linked to the verb exterminate. It's an old trick. Like the Nazis of old, classifying me in their followers' minds as less than human eases the transition to violence. A bug or a rat is easier to kill. In the jargon of Army days, they were preparing the battlefield.

Most comments went on like that. None crossed the legal line by saying *I am going to kill you.* Personal pronouns are important here; they grant a prosecutor the specificity needed in court. Given enough time, I knew one or two would eventually oblige by saying "I." Amazing how much I've learned about the law in the last few months.

Then one appeared that stopped me cold.

Glad your bitch wife got killed. You can join her soon.

From my heart to my stomach, a cold, raw feeling ran through me, followed by a reflexive stab of fear, like the flash of terror I felt moments after being wounded.

Frozen at my desk, my mind a blank, I couldn't form a coherent thought. As if nothing else existed, my world shrank to those eleven words. I read it again, slowly, disbelieving what I saw, unable to comprehend how a human being could write something so despicable. So inhuman.

Slamming my fist against the desk, I screamed, "You fucker! You goddamn motherfucker! You piece of shit—who are you?" His handle was *stonepatriot4394*.

I clicked the reply to icon and typed out my own threat. A clear and unambiguous death threat.

You cruel, sadistic animal. Fuck you! I'll find out who you are. I will kill...

I stopped. No, that isn't true. I did not stop myself. Susan stopped me. Not literally. I didn't hear her voice or an angelic choir telling me to stop. I don't understand how, but she spoke to me again, through the grief that is always with me and the pain reignited by that troll. And during that contest for dominance between rage and rationality, somewhere in my brain, crucial nerve cells carried her message. Susan was still at work, nudging my consciousness toward another approach.

I walked away from the desk and headed downstairs. Standing before the doors to the deck, I stared at a peaceful view I'd taken thousands of times before. Calmer, I went back upstairs to backspace away my incomplete post. In its place, I entered a more measured thought.

By attacking my deceased wife, you've lost. You have shown the world how troubled you are, so I need not say more.

Though it violated my policy of not engaging, in this case, my response seemed fitting. I made a print screen image for Bron and Harrison. I'd wait until Bron had seen *stonepatriot4394* before reporting him.

I shut down my laptop, needing time to calm down before Bron arrived. That proved problematic as I paced from the front door to the deck doors and back again. Grief and anger battled it out before I somehow managed to quiet myself enough, so I seemed normal... and not a murderous psychotic.

Self-medication seemed appropriate. Meaning day drinking against doctor's orders. With a gin and tonic prescription in hand, at around three o'clock, I wandered out on the deck, staying under the awning as a light rain returned. As the calming effect of the rain's rhythm and the gin began to take effect, Bron called.

"I'm still in town. I'd like to come over to your house and brief you on my meeting with Harrison. Have a look at the scene. Be there in five minutes, okay?" Of course, I said. I needed company more than I needed a second G&T. Just in case, though, I left the cocktail fixings on the kitchen counter.

When she arrived, we did the obligatory pleasantries, including offers of coffee and a tour of the house. "Not now. Thanks. Maybe later. We've got some ground to cover."

"Okay, Bron, but before we do that, we should look over the burn site before the rain washes it away." Standing by the now damp ashes of my novel, she took pics while updating me on the book burners.

"Haven't forgotten about NSAG. Harrison said they're a new group, according to the FBI. They shared what information he had. Not much though." Bron turned to me and said, "A couple of my students agreed to research them. They might be able to outdo the FBI."

That task done, we went back inside and set up at the dining room table. A large folder from her briefcase dropped on the table. Bron pointed to the folder, saying Harrison provided her with copies of all the printouts of the threats I gave him, plus police reports, and copies of the photos of the mannequin head.

"I'm up to speed with Harrison. Very cooperative. Though frankly, Vic, I got the feeling he doesn't like dealing with you. You got any idea why?"

"Really. Nope. Not a clue. Did he say something about me?" Bron seemed less than amused by my sarcasm.

"Don't bullshit me. Harrison thinks you're stubborn.

Uncooperative. Well, I can write that off to your state of mind. But the man cares about you. Really. So, for your own sake, be nice to Harrison. Anyway, that brings up how you'll deal with me."

I had the feeling a hammer was about to fall. "In any matter, small or large, you will give me the facts undiluted. You understand?" Bron didn't wait for me to answer.

"Two more things. First, I know your agent is working on more media interviews. You will check with me on every media interaction before committing. TV, radio, podcasts, newspapers, book signings, author talks. Whatever. Second, if you call the police about anything, your next call is to me. Clear?" This time, I responded in the affirmative.

"It'll take me a couple of days to examine what Harrison gave me. Here's what I'm looking for. Was there an increase in harassment and threats following the Smyth and Wright broadcasts? Do the threats share the same words and phrases used by Smyth and Wright? If I can establish such a relationship, that leads to the big next step."

"Lawsuit?"

"Yes. Smyth and Wright go first. NSAG will come later. We'll need time, not much, I think, to research them. Their membership, structure, funding. Likely, it'll be a bigger case. Also, I want to find out the DA's intentions regarding NSAG. For now, it's Smyth and Wright. Who knows? We might uncover a connection between Smyth and Wright with NSAG. Agreed?"

I nodded my ascent, admiring her focus and determination. A picture came to mind of her leading a cavalry charge, her saber drawn, as yet unbloodied.

"Now about the cease-and-desist court order against Smyth and Wright." Bron already called the court to request a hearing. She guessed the hearing would take place within days.

I had to say something dumb, as if I hadn't been listening to her. “Okay, sounds good, but what legal grounds do we have for a judge to issue an order?”

With a hint of exasperation in her voice, Brain said, “Grounds? Vic, these guys are threatening your livelihood. And inciting others to threaten your life. So, yeah, we have grounds for an order. You know, by the time we’re finished, you’ll learn about the law. Maybe then you could consider a safer job, like a paralegal, instead of being a writer.”

“Yeah, Harrison dropped the same hint. I’ll take that under advisement.”

Bron talked about the discovery process in civil cases, keeping it simple for my untrained mind. Bottom line: the defendants must come clean with any case-related communication or documents.

When I asked how long a civil suit could take, Bron shrugged her shoulders, saying, “Difficult to say. Maybe a couple of years. Many variables. They could appeal the order, for example. I’m sure their lawyers will advise them to shut up about you, which is exactly what we want them to do, but we keep the pressure on. They may even settle out of court. Getting to court may not matter anyway.”

“Not matter? What does that mean?”

“A lawsuit is the biggest gun we have against Smyth and Wright, or any other harassers. A suit forces them to hire lawyers. Lawyers are expensive. If they refuse to settle, if they want this to drag on to a court date, then on to appeals, well, it’s going to cost them. Strikes me these aren’t guys who have money lying around.

There was something unsettling to me about her plan. Maybe Bron sensed this in me. She slowed things down. “You know, Vic. Maybe coffee would be a good idea, if you don’t mind.”

As I was putting the coffee machine to work, I asked Bron, “What you said, that’s a harsh indictment of our legal system. I mean, people always talk about having their day in court. Rings hollow, really. Only certain people get that. Rich people who can afford lawyers."

"And you're just becoming aware of that truth, Vic?"

I returned to the table with two coffee mugs. Seated, I said, "So, our plan is to impoverish them?" After stirring sugar and cream, I continued. "Maybe I'm naïve, but it doesn't take a legal scholar to know the rich have an advantage in, well, everything. But that's not what I'm trying to say."

"Okay, Vic, spill it. What do you want to say? What is it you want the legal system to do for you?"

I shocked myself at how quickly I answered. "I want them, the Nazis and Smyth and Wright and all the goddamn people threatening me . . . and all the people who cheer them on, the guy who attacked Susan, I want them . . ." I stopped talking, too frightened to say what I wanted to say.

"You want them, what?"

In a low voice, calmly but firmly, I replied, "Dead. I want them dead."

I remember looking straight at Bron when I said that, looking for her reaction. Only she didn't react. Bron was about to say something when I clumsily walked back my murderous fantasy.

"I'm sorry, Bron. Stupid thing to say. Doesn't help us. Okay, that's how I feel, but that, well, no. What I want and what can be done are two different things. I'll settle for justice. I don't care if we take them for every cent, or the DA arrests them, I want them brought to account so everyone knows how awful they are."

I expected a scolding, but she did the unexpected. "No need to apologize. You're not the first client to wish death upon the person causing them pain. This is where I say to a distraught client, yes, I understand. You're emotional, and you've got reason to be so, but it's important, publicly and in court, and online, and with the media, that you do not express those desires ever again. Not even privately."

Bron diverted to another line of questioning. "You said something about . . . Susan."

I told Bron all about Susan. Everything, from our life together and how her life ended. That must have lasted a good five minutes. Bron could have prodded me to get to the point, but she waited patiently while I worked out my emotions.

"Here, I'm sorry. Let me show you what I mean." I showed her the comment from *stonepatriot4394*. I told her how close I was to replying with my own threat, but somehow Susan stopped me. I told her about the shotgun and Susan. Expecting Bron to think I was crazy for believing my dead wife somehow communicated with me, Bron's response surprised me.

"I'd feel the same way, Vic. I'm glad Susan was there for you." She turned back toward the screen and said, "We'll get that fucker."

CHAPTER TWENTY-SIX

CARING FOR ANOTHER ONCE AGAIN

Holt

After we finished with all things legal, Bron hung around. It didn't seem strange to me. Perhaps it was a little surprising that we easily transitioned from legal plans to trading opinions about the best restaurants in the area, sights to see, and places we'd seen in the world. Here I was, with my new lawyer, and I was speaking to her as if she were an old friend.

Personal things came up, such as our family histories, beginning with Bron's. In the mid-1870s, her people emigrated from Wales to America. Like so many of the Welsh, they worked in the mines of Northeastern Pennsylvania, including her great-grandfather, Ivor. Bron told me of his legend.

"Ivor was active in union organizing. Even met the legendary John L. Lewis once. Anyway, Ivor died in a mining accident. They say mine executives arranged for the accident. Probably no truth to that, but it makes for a colorful family story." He was only thirty-six when he died in 1933, during the Great Depression.

Ivor left behind a wife and two children, a girl and a boy, ages fourteen and sixteen. In 1944, that boy, David Ivor Llewelyn, Bron's grandfather, was killed in action in the European Theater.

He had a young wife and a boy. David's son would become Bron's father. "No siblings. Mom died ten years ago. Dad died at forty-nine years old. It seems in my family, the men die young."

"My family's been spared that," I told Bron of how my grandfather Victor found himself under German occupation during World War I. Victor was only a boy then, but enough of his story survived that it inspired *The King's Lieutenant*. After the war, Victor came to America and married an Irish girl. Two girls and one boy. My dad.

When I got to my own story, I began with my Army days, a short story that ended with Grenada. Susan was a much longer story. It didn't seem at all odd to talk to Bron about her.

As the conversation lagged, I suggested she couldn't leave without going down to the beach and taking in the ocean view. She agreed, pushing aside my warning that the wet grass would leave her with sodden shoes. "I need the air anyway. Might wake me up a little."

From the garage, I got her a pair of slip-on rubber boots, the pair Susan used. "No sense in ruining your shoes. Try these. See if they fit." Though a tad too big, Bron didn't mind. I gave her a light jacket in case the rain popped up again.

Standing on the beach, I gave her the one-minute geography lecture I always give guests. I began with the most prominent offshore feature of my little place of heaven, Montrose Island Light. "There's talk of fixing it up. Rebuild the old lightkeeper's house and make it open to guests. Use the proceeds to keep it in shape. Well, just talk now, but it'd be nice. Anyway, you should see it at night. Pretty powerful light."

Bron hardly said a word as we awkwardly walked south along the beach, avoiding the berms of seashells and seaweed. Pointing across the water, I launched into an off-the-cuff history lesson.

"Over there, on the point where there's a bunch of those mansions." I directed Bron toward an elevated point about a mile away.

"That's where, before white people got here, Native Americans, they had a village there. For centuries, they held annual gatherings there with other tribes. They'd trade and feast. Do what any person would do. That changed in 1675. A war started. You can guess how it ended."

Once on the history lecture circuit, it's hard for me to stop. Bron got a one-minute summation of the King Philip's War before I realized I was talking too much. "Christ, I'm sorry. I'm talking too much, and you've got things to do. But one more thing. If you could see beyond that point, there's a channel leading to a picturesque village harbor. Try imagining this. Up until 1820, slave ships passed right by here and into that harbor. The slave traders there made a fortune in West African slaves."

"You're kidding. Slaves? Here? In this state?"

"Yup. In my mind's eye, I can almost see those ships sailing right by here." I stopped, shaking my head. "All that. . . all that misery. Went right by here. Anyway, Bron. Maybe there's a book in all that. Fiction. Or non-fiction. What do you think?"

She smiled back at me. "Sounds like you're already thinking about it."

We timed our return to the house well, as the rain started again. Back inside, I saw it was five thirty. I asked her about dinner, offering to cook something or order out, but she demurred, saying she'd pick up something on the way home. A short plea from me for takeout delivered here met with surprisingly little resistance.

Taking a menu out of a kitchen drawer, I recommended a pizza place in town that delivered. We settled on a pepperoni and Italian sausage, which she insisted on paying for. Waiting for the pizza, we picked up our conversation, though this time Bron did the talking.

"Maybe you should know something about me. After all I know about you now." Without a word, Bron went to the fridge, took out a corked bottle of Chardonnay, and by trial and error found two wine glasses in the kitchen cupboards. With both of us supplied with two generous pours, she began.

Bron was married to another attorney in a district attorney's office back in Pennsylvania. A demanding job that entirely consumed them both. "Maybe other couples can deal with it, but we couldn't. We drifted away from each other."

Eventually, reluctantly, they reached the same regrettable conclusion that neither wanted. Their careers made for an unworkable life together. The first suggestion of divorce came from Bron. She was also the one to resign from the DA's office.

"I just couldn't ask him to give up what he was so damn good at. Besides, I knew I could easily sign up with another firm. Which turned out to be the case." Then Bron said something I can't forget.

"So, we dissolved our life together over our work. Stupid of us, really. Rather not make that mistake again." Bron took a sip of wine before continuing. "One saving grace, for us at least, we spared ourselves the, ah, complication of children." I almost asked her why no children, but wisely stopped myself, knowing from personal experience I hadn't the right to ask.

Bron declined my offer of another glass of wine or a coffee. "No thanks. Time for me to go."

I held her back for another minute with a question. "Bron, I'd like your, ah, opinion about something. It's not a legal or a personal question. It's something that's been bothering me."

"Okay, Vic. Go ahead."

"Here we are in the 21st century. You'd think, by now, we'd be more, well, enlightened. Yet Nazis came to my door. Worse, American-born Nazis! Your grandfather and millions of other men defeated the Nazis. So many lost their lives. But Nazis are back. How can that be?"

Bron sat back, took a moment, and said, "Don't have an answer for that one. Not my field. Yeah, I guess, while we defeated the Nazis themselves, we did not defeat the, ah, hatred, the evil, which created them. The hate has always been here. Always will be here. Mix hatred and ignorance together, and this is the result. I know that's simplistic. Maybe your question is better suited for a philosopher, a priest, or a rabbi. I'm just a lawyer. What I do know is it's our fight now."

One thought was left unsaid. As a generation that fought dies out, the human condition ensures all their sacrifice and loss will be forgotten, and the same atrocities and tragedies will play out once more.

Escorting her to the door, she said, "Don't concern yourself with how you looked on TV. Remember, these are only our opening shots."

"They're going to come after me, aren't they? The Nazis and all those others, I mean."

"Yes, Vic. They will."

I shook her hand goodbye. She looked at me and smiled. I stood by the door until she drove away. Legal issues were not on my mind.

CHAPTER TWENTY-SEVEN

MISFIRE

Holt

Four days after Bron and I stood together on the beach, the court issued cease-and-desist orders against Smyth and Wright. Bron called with the news, the first good news I'd gotten in I didn't know how long.

Over the following week, like a child eagerly counting the days till Christmas and the greatest gifts ever, I listened to the Smyth and Wright broadcasts. Sooner or later, I imagined, they'd perform an on-air *mea culpa*. An admission of fault. A plea for forgiveness and a groveling retreat. They'd beg their followers to back off. If they couldn't find the love of Jesus in their hearts, I'd settle for the fear of me. And Bron, my steely-eyed killer.

On the first broadcast after the cease-and-desist order, Wright and Smyth kept to the usual drivel, without saying anything about me. Same on the second and third broadcasts. By the fourth, it seemed my dream of their on-air unconditional surrender would forever remain a fantasy; a wish that would never happen.

Steeled against further disappointment with a freshly mixed

bourbon old-fashioned, I watched their show on my laptop for a fifth time. It went something like this.

"Fellow patriots, I'm here today with my, ah, friend, Jack Wright. We want to . . . to talk to you about something. Ah, something serious that came to our, both our, attention about, what, I guess five or six days ago. A week, let's say."

It was unusual that he stumbled on the opening line. He seemed subdued. Halting. Not his usual smooth self. Then Smyth went quiet for two or three seconds. Dead broadcast air always seems longer than it is.

"Listen, we've both been served a court order. An official court order to cease and desist." As Smyth paused, I felt both relief and worry.

"The court says we've got to stop talking about that local writer and his book. You know the guy I'm talking about. I can't say his name, but you know what we've said. You joined us in protests. You saw that . . . man, all over the news. Local and even national. Like CNN. You know, the Communist News Network." A nervous joke that perhaps they needed more than their audience.

"Here's the thing. If we violate that order, well, you can guess what'll happen. So, that's why we haven't talked about that guy. We needed time to, yeah, how shall I put this, evaluate our position. We talked to our lawyer. He told us what our options are."

Sensing victory, I slapped my hand down on the desk and whooped so loudly you'd have thought Tom Brady was back with the Pats and they'd won their seventh Super Bowl with a touchdown in the last seconds.

Smyth's course then took an unexpected tack. "We've got a plan. A plan to fight back against Mr. Victor Holt and his lefty lawyers."

As he said that, I was taking a celebratory sip—no, swig is more accurate—of my cocktail. I almost spat it all out. Fate's referees called for a penalty on Tom. No touchdown. With Wright repeatedly chiming in with a "yup" or a "that's right," Smyth announced they would not obey the court order.

"What's the worst that can happen to us? Maybe the judge locks us up for a week. Maybe Holt will sue us. That doesn't matter. It'll take, what, years before it ever gets to court? We don't have much for him to get anyway. Hell, we aren't getting rich off this show, let me tell you." They both shared a laugh.

"And you know what? WE WILL WIN! How do I know that? Because we are righteous. Yes, my friends, righteous. We've said it before. We do what is right for the country. We do battle with those who would betray us all. We will . . ."

He went on with his crap for a full minute more. I didn't catch every word, nor did I want to. Bottom line: Against complaints of defamation and libel in civil court, they will claim status as journalists and argue for protection under the First Amendment. Bron had already briefed me on this possibility of a free speech defense. "They could even win, but here's how we counter them."

She explained that if we connect specifics of their on-air speech to specific threats and incidents of harassment, and we could show they knew of that connection but persisted, that gives us our best chance for a win in civil court. As she said, "Journalists do not engage in threats."

As I drained my old-fashioned, Smyth made his final pitch to his fans.

"My friends and patriots don't stop what you're doing. Continue the fight for our freedoms. Continue the fight against the radical lunatic communists around here. Continue the fight of real Americans! Don't give them an inch! Don't give that guy Holt a moment's rest. Stay peaceful. Don't hurt him, but keep up the fight. As for us, Jack and I will take what comes. This fight is just too damn important. So, until next time, God bless you, and the United States of America, and God damn the liberals and communists."

That ended the show. Having recorded it, I wanted to listen to it once more before calling Bron. Instead, I opted for another cocktail. After the second old-fashioned and an old movie, I fell asleep on the couch. Calling Bron would have to wait until tomorrow.

CHAPTER TWENTY-EIGHT

IT GOT WORSE

Holt

When I finally reached Bron, sometime around eleven, she was deep in other matters and couldn't talk long. We quickly agreed to meet after she got out of work.

"How about we meet at that microbrewery near you at six. Make that six thirty."

"You mean *Little Beach*? That'd be fine. You know where it is?"

"Vaguely. But GPS knows. Six thirty. Bye."

My anxiety-driven mind consumed me for the rest of the day. I worried I said something wrong, and she was upset with me. I kept that up until I reminded myself that Bron has a real job. Rebuking myself, I thought, you're acting like you just got a noncommittal answer from a girl you asked out to the prom!

There I was at the brewery, early at quarter past six. Showered and shaved, dressed in the best casual clothes I had, eyepatch included. Sitting at a high-top table in their indoor greenhouse garden, I felt terribly nervous, and not because I was out in public. As my attorney, Bron's legal acumen should have been my greatest concern. It wasn't. To be honest, what mattered most to me then was what she thought of me.

I checked my watch for the God knows fifth or sixth time. By 6:40, I was nearly convinced that Bron stood me up.

Of course, right then, Bron walked into the greenhouse. Relieved, I waved and called out to her with a happy, "Hi, Bron. Just a little rain, eh?"

Only minutes before, the rain came on with an Old Testament ferocity. She shook her head and did her best to wipe the rain from her suit coat, cursing herself for not having an umbrella or a raincoat. We shook hands like two professionals, a greeting that left me emotionally disappointed. Seated, her dignity restored, she asked, "Wow. Nice place. What was it before? A garden store?"

"Close. A nursery. Plants and shrubs and gardening stuff."

In as suave and gallant a manner as my awkward nature allowed, I asked if we should order a drink. Waving one hand toward the bar in the next room, I offered my other hand to help her from the chair and escorted her to the counter. As we stood in line, I gave her the rundown of the place.

"They bought this building and all the land from the old nursery that used to be here. Plus, the property's other two buildings. One in back, they turned into the actual brewery. In the fields, they'll be growing brewing ingredients. Hops, fruit, stuff like that. This is the old garden store. We're in the greenhouse. They turned it into a quiet little room off the main beer hall. There're great views off the two decks, when it isn't raining, plus a wide-open patch of ground below with Adirondacks and tables. Food trucks. Live entertainment. Families come here all the time."

Bron got to the point. "And the beer?" I asked for her preferences and offered my recommendations. A Belgian-style lager for me and a double IPA for her. Back at our spot in the former greenhouse and after the first sip, Bron skipped any further pleasantries and got right to business. Or tried to before I interrupted her.

"Wait. Something I want to ask. When I called earlier, you said you were seeing the judge today, during working hours. I thought you'd be managing my case on your own time. I don't want to get you in trouble with . . . "

Brons' turn to interrupt. "An hour here and there. Use my PTO. You know, Pretend Time Off. Don't worry. My concern. Now, can I continue?" I sensed a flash of irritation from her.

Bron began with the disappointing news. Since we're suing Smyth and Wright, the judge saw no reason arrest them on a bench warrant for violating the court order. He did take a middle ground, fining them a thousand dollars each.

"I argued otherwise, but the judge believes civil action by us will be enough."

"What about NSAG?"

"That requires more research. Maybe a week to ten days. I need to know more about how . . ."

A woman came up behind me. Probably middle-aged, dressed in tight old jeans, a white baseball cap over a chaotic mass of shoulder-length brown hair, and a red T-shirt with a meme printed across it that I didn't catch. I had no idea who she was.

She slid over to my right and stood only inches from me, holding in one hand a half-empty glass of beer. Her other hand grasped our table as she swayed side to side and fore to aft. *She's plowed.*

"Hey, I seen you. You're that, ah, guy on TV! One-eyed guy. Yeah."

I do not like dealing with drunks. "I beg your pardon."

"Yeah, you're that guy the Nas . . . Natzees is after. I saw it. One-eyed guy. On the news. Well, let me tell ya . . ."

Oh, please. I wish you wouldn't.

I turned my good eye away and tried to ignore her, preferring to look at Bron, who wasn't hiding her disgust in the slightest. I hadn't faced a drunk in a long time, let alone an unidentified female drunk. I was lost for words. Drunks, however, are never lost for words.

"Listen, far as I'm fuckin' concerned, you got what you fuckin' deserved!" More swaying. More slurring. She jerked her beer hand toward me, sloshing beer over the table. "Ya know what, they shoulda burned your fuckin' house. Burned it right fuckin' down. With you in it, far as I'm concerned. You . . . unpatriotic, fuckin' traitor!"

With all the self-control I could muster, I stood up and faced her. We almost collided. She was slightly shorter than me. Thinking I'd established dominance in both stature and sobriety, I locked eyes with her and said, "Ma'am, please go back to your seat. We don't want trouble."

Wrong words, if there are ever any right words for drunks. "Trouble? You want fuckin' trouble, old man?" Drunk Lady poked my shoulder with her free hand.

Bron had enough. She warned Drunk Lady to sit back down, or she'd be in legal trouble. Bron was about to say something else, but Drunk Lady didn't let Bron finish.

"Woah. Calm down, lady. I'm jus' talkin' here!" She switched back to me. "You got this . . . bitch here to stand up for you? What a man!" She turned to face Bron again.

"Yeah, you heard me, bitch! This guy here, I bet you're fuckin' him. Yeah, ya won't be fuckin' him much more. We're gonna take care of him. Fuck you!"

Drunk Lady pitched the last of her beer across Bron's face. I shoved Drunk Lady away with my arm, hard, and stood between her and Bron. Her glass fell to the stone floor and shattered. I was more than a little surprised she stayed on her feet.

By then, we had the undivided attention of everyone in the brewery. I screamed at Drunk Lady, "Shut the hell up! Go away. Now!"

Drunk Lady staggered back, but against all odds, and alcohol, remained standing. She didn't go away. She turned and grabbed another customer's empty pint glass off a table and hurled it at

Bron. The glass hit Bron in her face, across her right cheek. Bron fell off her high-top chair onto the stone floor.

Kneeling by Bron, I lifted her head in my hand. There was blood, but she was still conscious. I yelled at someone to call the police and an ambulance. Almost everyone, however, sat frozen in the chairs. A few skedaddled. Others did what people do these days. They took out their cell phones. We'd later see their videos on social media.

Bron waved me off, saying, "Okay, I'm okay. Barely hit me." But it didn't barely hit her, judging from the mark on her face. The glass hit Bron squarely on her right cheek, an inch or so below her eye. As I helped Bron sit up on the floor, another woman knelt to help steady Bron. I didn't need to see the drops of blood on Bron's face to know the next thing I was going to do.

Other than wobbling, Drunk Lady hadn't moved. I went toward her, intent on beating the shit out of her. Good fortune intervened to save me from myself.

Someone, I think an employee, grabbed Drunk Lady from behind, wrenching her arms behind her back. Kicking her legs out from underneath, he pinned Drunk Lady to the stone floor. At that same moment, a big, bearded man got between me and the person I wanted to send to an ICU. Or a morgue.

"Vic! Don't! We got this." It was Nate, the owner of *Little Beach*. He knew me from a book signing I'd held at his establishment. Nate put both his beefy hands on my chest, nudging me back a step or two.

Nate is built like a linebacker. Me charging through him to get to that woman was not going to happen. I put my arms down, signaling to Nate my newfound nonviolent intentions. Drunk Lady had shut up, still held down on the floor. Looking around, only three or four unmoving and silent customers remained in the greenhouse. I think I mumbled an apology to Nate and all present. All this was a new experience for me. My first bar fight. I didn't know what to do next.

Until I did. With Nate carefully watching me, I squatted down by Drunk Lady's ear and whispered, "Ma'am, you've got no idea how bad things will get for you."

Drunk Lady had poked the bear, that bear being Bron.

I went back to Bron, thankful to see the stranger still attending to her. Bron wanted to get back up on her chair, but I told her to stay on the floor until the ambulance arrived. She complied, but not without protest. Nate came over with a first aid kit and held an ice pack to Bron's face.

Three police cruisers arrived with an ambulance a minute behind them. I watched as two cops handcuffed Drunk Lady and escorted her to the back seat of a cruiser. Belligerent, she cursed the cops while kicking at anything within reach. While one cop stayed with Drunk Lady, the other two got statements from me, Nate, his employees, and witnesses who bothered to stick around.

Meanwhile, the EMTs checked out Bron, giving her another chemical cold pack to hold against her swelling face while taking her vital signs. Checking for any other head wounds, they asked if she had lost consciousness. Bron said no. Before they could place her on a gurney, Bron demanded the police take a statement from her. First thing, she identified herself as my attorney before detailing the assault, moment by moment. Meanwhile, the police collected the weaponized pint glass and took pics of Bron's facial injury.

"Okay, Counselor, I think we got a pretty good picture of what happened. I imagine you know the drill. Now, please cooperate with the EMTs here. They're taking you to the ER."

"I'm fine. I don't need to go to any ER!" The EMTs weren't listening. They strapped her in the gurney and rolled her out. I threw in my two cents. "Bullshit, Bron. You have a head injury. You need to be checked out. Cooperate. I'll follow you to the ER."

Bron surrendered. As they wheeled her out, I heard Nate tell his patrons to clear the way and "put those goddamn phones away." I made a mental note to thank Nate later.

Before he got back in his vehicle, an officer turned to me. "I remember you, Mr. Holt. From the station and that thing with burning books. I'll give a full report of all this to Detective Harrison. She came after you because of your book, right?" I said yes.

The cop had the final words. "Unprovoked assault. On an attorney no less. I wouldn't give that drunk a snowball's chance."

Later, I sat in the hospital waiting room alone with my thoughts. *My book. My troubles. My plan to fight. My fault Bron is hurt.*

Finally released with a cold pack and a pain meds prescription, she headed straight for the ER exit doors, offering only curt responses to my questions. Once in my truck, she told me to drive her back to the brewery so she could get her car and drive home. That was not going to happen.

"Drive yourself home? No, Bron. No way. You had a head injury. You had a shock. No way, no fucking way, am I going to let you drive yourself home. You'll be a danger to yourself and any other poor bastard on the road. I'm driving you home now. Tomorrow, first thing, I'll get your car and drive it to your place. I'll take an Uber home from there."

We argued back and forth until she finally handed me her keys. We exited the parking lot, heading north. In the silence that followed, I reflected on what I learned from this bar fight. If arguing with a drunk is futile, arguing with a lawyer—someone professionally trained in argument—represents a new level of challenge. My momentary pride in besting a lawyer faded quickly.

"Bron. This is my fault. I should've met you at my house. I thought a public place would be safe. I'm sorry." Bron didn't cut me any slack.

"Oh, for fuck's sake, Vic. Stop that! You didn't do anything wrong. Not your fault. That drunk is at fault. And she'll pay for it." Her harsh tone silenced me. I had no idea what to say. Then came her summation.

"Let's be clear about all this. In case you're wondering, I'm still your lawyer, and I'm still in this fight." All I could think was, I'm liking her even more.

"Hey, Vic. Do you know where you're going?"

"Oh, yeah. Bron, where do you live?"

Maybe it was the way I said it, but Bron started to laugh. "And I'm the one with the head injury. Head for Old Town Wharf."

"You were going to let me keep driving, weren't you?" We both started laughing to the point of watery eyes.

As I turned around, Bron had something else to say. "Listen, I want to thank you for, well, holding off that goddamn woman." When I protested that I really didn't do anything, that anyone else would've done the same, that the brewery staff held Drunk Lady until the cops got there, Bron wouldn't hear of it.

"No, you're wrong. Not everyone would've. I mean it. Thank you."

"Well, okay. Next time, I'll let you beat the shit out of the drunk."

Reaching Old Town Wharf, I parked in her condo lot. Escorting her to the complex's door and elevator, I politely demanded that I hold her arm to keep her steady, repeatedly asking if she was all right. An awkward moment ensued as we stood face to face in the lobby. Bron thanked me once more. Then she did something unexpected but welcome. As we said goodnight, she kissed me on the cheek.

After retrieving Bron's car in the morning, I'd have another errand to run.

CHAPTER TWENTY-NINE

OUT AND ABOUT

Holt

Through a drizzly and overcast morning, I drove the two miles to *Little Beach*. Out of my truck and into her car, I started out for her condo. I felt safer in her car. Little chance someone would recognize me. Just to be sure, the eyepatch came off.

Halfway there, my cell rang. *Bron!* I kept driving while I took her call. Firing questions at a machine gun rate of fire, and at almost the same deafening volume. I must have sounded like a madman, asking about how she felt, whether she was in pain, her injury, if she was going to her office, and that she should stay home and rest.

Bron didn't respond right away. "Ah, can you hear me, Bron? Bron?"

Bron spoke slowly. "Yes, Vic. Yes, I can hear you. Jesus. Slow down, cowboy. Good thing I've got pain meds here because you're about to give me a migraine."

I did as commanded. Bron assured me she was fine. Not to worry. No serious pain. She was home, taking the day off, having called in sick for the first time. All I said was, "Thank Christ. I was very worried."

"Really? Well, I'm fine. And thanks for getting my car." She switched topics. "When you get to my place, call me. I'll buzz you in. Come up, and we'll talk more then." Bron hung up.

Once in her condo, Bron offered me a coffee in exchange for her car keys. While it was brewing, she gave me the nickel tour, pointing out the two bedrooms and the two baths before leading me out to the balcony. A beautiful harbor view even in light rain and fog. I kept glancing at her injured face, trying not to look obvious. Still a fair bruise, but the swelling was almost gone. It was good to see her up and about.

Being the respectful guest, I complimented her décor and the artwork on her walls. In truth, the furniture struck me as rather ordinary, and the artwork was what one expected for any seaside home. Framed prints of sailboats and lighthouses. That is, until she showed off the work of a local artist. Two small original oils that captured local eating establishments. More specifically, the neon signs of well-known breakfast and lunch diners.

"These are nice. I love diners, but that one's gone."

"Yeah, I know. Cardinal Street Diner. Too bad. I ate there myself. On my way to being a regular. Something about food in a real diner. Glad someone preserved a part of it as a painting. Got it from an art club in town."

We had our coffee at the kitchen breakfast bar. "So, let the lawyer in me pick up from when I was . . . interrupted."

For the eventual lawsuit against NSAG, she and her team of law students needed at least another week to research NSAG's basic structure and leadership. In ten days, a draft motion for a court order cease and desist could be done. She'll also ask the court for a restraining order targeting not only the NSAG members who came on my property, but anyone associated with NSAG. She then talked in general terms about the planned lawsuit.

"We'll seek damages and punitive penalties. Doubt they have secret Cayman Island bank accounts, but anything they have is fair game. The chance of a big judgment, plus the legal bills, might cause them to fold their tent. That is, until they crawl out from under another rock."

Smyth and Wright weren't forgotten. Though disappointed the judge didn't issue a bench warrant for their arrest, Bron planned to increase the damages sought by the lawsuit, plus argue for far greater penalties for ignoring, even flaunting, the court order. Summing up, she added a cautionary note. "This'll still be a rough road. Remember, this will take a long time."

After saying I understood, I steered the remainder of our conversation toward irrelevant topics, but inevitably, it came to the brewery fight. I asked what her intentions were vis-à-vis Drunk Lady.

"Charges are filed. Felony charge of assault. She spent last night locked up. This afternoon, I think she'll face a magistrate. After she enters a plea, bail will be set. Or she'll be denied bail. I've set in motion a restraining order against her coming near you and me. Either way, her legal predicament is best described, translated into Latin, as "*Ea fucked*."

I stared back at her, dumbfounded. "Huh? No, can't be. You mean all my life I've been swearing in Latin without knowing it?"

"Appears to be the case." After a second or two, she dropped her stone-faced expression as her composure broke into laughter. "Got ya!"

I shook my head in a gesture of faux disappointment and said, "All right, all right, is there a proper legal term or what?"

"Oh, yes. *Ea eruditionis habes*. That's the correct translation of 'she is fucked.' Well, it's not exactly proper legalese. Or proper Latin. The proper legal terms I can apply to her are charged and soon-to-be convicted felon."

"Well, you learn something every day."

"I guess you do. *Ea eruditionis habes*. Old law school joke. At least at my law school."

Then Bron got serious. "Vic, about yesterday. I want you to understand something. When I say 'thank you' for what you did, I mean it. Really. Almost all the people there turned away, but you didn't. You confronted her. But then you held back. Furious as you were, you didn't let yourself, how shall I say this, go too far."

While I politely waved away her words, I instinctively knew my next words might determine the course of our relationship. Even this quickly, there was a feeling emerging; I wanted, or needed, something more than being another client to Bron. Was it a genuine attraction? Or a desperate need to be part of someone else's life, to fill the void left by Susan?

I looked away toward the balcony view, sipping my coffee to give myself time to think. "I don't know about that, Bron. Nate, the owner, had something to do with holding me back. Literally. Anyway, if you're suggesting I deliberately made, I guess, a moral or rational decision not to escalate, you're wrong. That lady was a threat. She attacked someone I know. Attacked you. So, I reacted. That's it."

"Tell me, Vic. Were you going to hurt her?"

"If Nate, the owner, hadn't gotten between me and her, well, and I'm glad he did because . . . because I'd have beaten her to a bloody fucking pulp. That's what I wanted to do. Then I'd be the one who's *Ea erudite . . . whatever.*"

She countered. "Maybe even without Nate, you wouldn't have. Something we can't ever know. By the way, the masculine pronoun would be *Ipse*, as in *Ipse eruditionis habes*."

"Smart ass."

Staying silent for a moment, I looked down at the counter and away from Bron. I said, "Yes, I wanted to hurt her. And hurt her badly. And Bron, I don't know how far I would've gone."

"Sounds like there's something more you want to say, Vic."

I nodded and unemotionally said, "There is. I could've killed her. Why? Partly because of all the shit I've been through. Take it all out on her. But mostly," I halted. "Because she hurt, ah, you."

I got up from the stool, fearing I'd gone too far. "Maybe I should go."

"No, no. Please, sit back down." I hesitated but did so.

"Vic, I think I heard you're seeing a therapist. That right?" I said I'm still seeing her.

"Good." Bron put her hand over mine and held it tight. I sat there, surprised. And pleased. "See her as soon as possible to talk over what happened. What you told me. I'm not saying this as your attorney, but as a friend."

I promised I would.

"I'm well enough to drive. Oh, yeah, your truck. Let's go pick it up."

Twenty-five minutes later, standing together by my truck, I expected that I'd thank her for the lift and say, "See you later." That and a platonic handshake were as far as my social contingency planning took me. Bron scrapped those plans.

And thank God she did. She firmly held my hand, at first with one hand and then the other, before once more kissing me on the cheek. The kiss seemed more than a friendly peck on the cheek, or so I imagined it. But then Bron followed with a full-on embrace. Not knowing what to do, I hugged her back. She released me far sooner than I wanted.

"Vic, again, thanks so much."

Terrified, I went to my go-to in dangerous social situations. Make a joke about it. "I look at it this way. I saved you from doing the same to her."

Bron smiled, nodded, and I continued. "You don't need anyone to leap to your rescue. I know that about you. The circumstances required me to do something. That's all."

Should I invite her to spend time here? For maybe two seconds, the thought lingered. It was the best two seconds I'd had in a very long time. Bron, however, had another idea.

"Okay, well, I've got to get back home. Call you later."

As she started toward her car, she said, "You're going to call your therapist, right?"

"You bet." I waved goodbye.

I'm violating my own rule. Fighting back requires that I cannot be in fear of harm coming to someone close. And I have that second errand.

CHAPTER THIRTY

THE PURCHASE

Ford

Do I need a gun?

That question troubled me. There are other ways to get the job done. Yet, when push comes to shove, nothing speaks louder than a gun. Besides, I felt safer having one. Sort of like having an insurance policy against the unexpected.

How do I get a gun?

The answer came down to whether I get one illegally or legally. I had no clue how to get a gun illegally. I didn't know any criminals at all, let alone any who sold guns. I could've tried stealing one myself, but where? A gun store? Someone's house? That seemed stupid to commit a crime to get ready for another crime. True, buying a gun legally leaves a paperwork trail behind, but I can explain that away.

I went to a gun store and took the state-required paper test on handgun safety. A couple of weeks later, the results came in—I passed—and my Department of Public Safety Firearm Card arrived in the mail. I needed that card to buy a handgun. Do the paperwork, pay for it, and once the waiting period is over, go back and pick it up. All legal and proper.

What kind of handgun?

My first time on the Army base range, I earned the pistol marksmanship ribbon. The Army's pistol was a semi-automatic, but I wanted something simpler with fewer moving parts that didn't need any more maintenance than regular cleaning. Anyway, chances are I'd only use it once. To me, a revolver fits the bill. Easy to shoot and clean. They never fail.

At the library, I found a reference book on firearms. In less than an hour, I had the general specs on a suitable gun. Revolver, short barrel, preferably a .38, maybe a .357. The next step was to select a gun store. Online, I found one that had a suitable revolver in stock and an indoor pistol range. I wanted a "one-stop shopping" experience, where I could buy the pistol and practice with it, while involving as few people as possible.

I went to the store with a range one day after work. In the display case was a Smith & Wesson .38 Special, small frame, two-inch barrel, black finish, five rounds, and rubber grip. Just like what the police detectives on the old cop shows carried.

The perfect choice, until I saw it cost nearly $600. Silly of me, but I didn't want to spend that kind of money on something I may only use once. I looked around for a cheaper alternative, and it was a good thing I did. In the store's case of used guns, I saw a used .38 Special at around half the price. All I wanted was something that worked. Though dinged up here and there, and a four-inch barrel instead of a two-inch, it would do the job.

Things went quickly. I showed the guy behind the counter my driver's license and DPS Card. He brought out the gun, checked its operation, and handed it to me. It felt comfortable. I think he wanted to ask me more questions, probably to see if he could upsell me on a more expensive model, but I cut it short. Handing back the revolver, I took four one-hundred-dollar bills out of my wallet and laid them on the counter.

"I know there's paperwork to fill out, and there's a background check. How long will it take before I can pick it up?" He said there's a mandated seven-day waiting period. After that, give them a call to pick it up.

"Any chance of getting some range time with it right now?"

That didn't prove to be a problem. He gave me another form to fill out and directed me to a cubicle to watch a range safety video. After setting me up in a range lane, the guy called me on the intercom to pick up the gun and a box of twenty rounds from what reminded me of a drive-up bank teller's steel drawer.

Twenty rounds went down range, twenty-five feet to the target's five concentric rings. None went outside any of the circles. Thirteen rounds hit within the center two rings. The rest went either below or up and to the right. I thought, at least my time in the Army was good for something.

The clerk congratulated me on the good shooting and started to lecture me on the groupings above and below. I didn't pay attention. My marksmanship was good enough for what I wanted to do. My target would be much closer than twenty-five feet.

The last thing he said was, "I'll make sure the weapon is clean when you pick it up. It'll come with a carry case. Included in the price. You might want to consider buying a lock for the box. And trigger lock too. Anyway, here're your receipts and copies of the background check forms. See you in about a week, Mr. Ford."

Another step closer.

CHAPTER THIRTY-ONE

THE HAMMER

Holt

Confused. That word understates my fragile emotions. A sense of danger with brief feelings of elation offered by Bron. The way she held my hands. The way she kissed me once more. How she held me close.

Wandering around the house after seeing off Bron, I tried to make sense of the opposing notions running through my mind. The devil's side reminded me that Bron was my attorney and protector. My building romantic feelings for her were childish and stemmed from loneliness. The angel of my better nature refused to discard a beautiful possibility that Bron had feelings for me. Back and forth they battled until my angel delivered the *coup de grace* to my devil. An old man needs joy in his life, if only because he has less time.

I felt good. Good despite the brewery fight. Good despite, well, everything. Best of all, it wasn't only because of the antidepressants. It was because of Bron. And that thought reminded me of Bron's demand that I call my therapist. That call did not go well.

My therapist offered to see me right away after I pleaded a

crisis. Then I stupidly declined, saying I was too busy today and asked for a time the next day. She did not like that.

"Really? You say you're in crisis, but in the same breath, you say you're too busy today. That, Vic, doesn't sound like a crisis."

She had me there. My "crisis" had more to do with assuring Bron I was okay. My admission that I shouldn't have used the word "crisis" did not go over well either.

"What word should you have used?" I countered with "important." Her silence told me my new word choice didn't impress her either.

"Very well. Important. While the term crisis warrants immediate attention, important means we can wait until the next open appointment. I think I learned that in grad school. But you're in luck. Someone cancelled. I'll see you tomorrow at 5 p.m."

Sarcasm sent and received. I started to thank her when she interrupted. "Look, Vic. This only works if you are honest with me. So, first question. Are you back on the antidepressants?" I said yes. That was an honest answer.

"Second question. Since our last session, has something happened where you considered harming yourself or others?"

I said no. That was half honest. Or half lie. No, I hadn't thought of suicide since that morning when I held that shotgun shell in my hand. But harming others? I'd come within a single step of beating the shit out of Drunk Lady. She'd need to know about my flirtation with manslaughter.

Hanging up, a nagging security question came to mind. Should I get rid of my shotgun? I could take it to a local gun store and sell it on consignment. Or I could give it to Steve and Lil for safekeeping. But they would ask why. And if I told them the truth, I'd scare the crap out of them. Pouring myself another cup of coffee, I went upstairs to my desk to write a quick analysis of the shotgun question.

Fact: My life has been threatened. There'll be more threats. They've come to my door—the fake head and the Little Führer.

Conclusion: Should someone break in, I'm within my rights to use deadly force to defend myself if there is an imminent threat and I have no other option. Therefore, I need the shotgun.

Fact: You considered suicide using the shotgun.

Conclusion: The shotgun is possibly more of a threat to me than anyone else.

Well, I got myself there.

As I drank the last of my coffee, I decided the shotgun would stay. There's an old saying. Better to have it and not need it than to need it and not have it. Whatever the "it" happens to be. A raincoat, extra food in the pantry, or a lethal weapon. Besides, I'm in therapy and on antidepressants, so maybe turning the weapon on myself was not a significant possibility.

In any case, I wanted a more flexible arsenal. My application for a concealed carry permit was ready to go to the Office of the Attorney General. I'd affirmatively checked the box, "Has the applicant demonstrated a specific articulable risk to life, limb, or property? If so, has the applicant demonstrated how a pistol permit will decrease the risk?" People keep threatening to kill me in all sorts of ways. So, yes, there's a specific articulable risk to life, limb, or property.

I'd checked every other box save one. The Certification of Qualification. That requires a legally qualified range officer to certify that I met the minimum qualification score. One might think that shouldn't be a problem. I'd scored as an expert in the Army. Of course, that was before I lost use of an eye in Grenada. I hadn't fired a handgun in the four decades since. A little practice seemed to be in order.

Buying a handgun for self-protection was that afternoon's errand and one I did not take lightly. Given my recent notoriety, gun stores were possibly hostile territory. I had to assume people there might not be fans of my work. Hell, if having a beer at a brewery triggered a fight, at a gun store . . .

I face different possibilities. Perhaps no one will notice me. I'd go in and out unrecognized with a minimum of fuss. However, it was possible, even probable, that someone would recognize and approach me. Should that happen, I could leave immediately. Or try a bolder, confrontational response.

I went with bold. Go in, eyepatch and all. I wouldn't shy away from anyone who spotted me. If my new approach was to be seen, what better place than a gun store? My driver's license and DPS Card identified me anyway.

Looking around the counter with the twenty-something sales guy, I found the weapon I wanted. A small frame, .38 caliber, five-round double-action revolver, black finish with a 2-inch barrel. Barely weighed a pound. No hammer to snag on a holster when drawing it out. As an added feature, it already had a laser on the rubber grip to aid in targeting. As the literature said, it was designed for concealed carry. Plus, this pistol was exactly what Detective Harrison suggested. Then again, his best advice was not to buy a gun at all.

"I'll take it." A possible fate determined by three words. The gun could save my life at the cost of taking another's. Or end my life in a confrontation. Or by my own hand.

While filling out the paperwork, I noticed something familiar in the glass cabinet. A Model 1911A1 .45 caliber pistol, not at all different from the one I carried into that forest's edge in Grenada. Breaking my own rule of getting in and out quickly, I asked the clerk to let me have a look at the 1911.

"It's previously owned, but in excellent shape. A couple of scratches, but otherwise the finish is in excellent shape. Almost like it's right out of the factory." As he handed me the weapon, he asked, "Are you familiar with this weapon?"

While manipulating the pistol's slide a couple of times—*smooth, just the right tension*–I answered reflexively, without thinking, "Yes. Army."

The clerk didn't respond. He looked straight at me, cocked his head, and glanced down again at the form. He said, "Oh. You're that guy. I heard of you."

Too preoccupied with the nostalgic feeling of holding something so familiar, I didn't bother confirming his suspicions. Or even look at him. After slipping an empty magazine in and out of the pistol a couple of times, I finally looked up at him and said, "You've heard of me?"

I handed back the 1911. "Well, son, what've you heard?"

There was firmness in my voice. Even anger. Controlled anger, but I felt it was there. Leaning slightly over the counter, with my hands spread apart on the countertop, I stared at him before I opened with a change in tactics.

"Come now. I won't take offense." I said it with a hint of a grin. Maybe facing a one-eyed, self-professed veteran with possible anger issues flustered the clerk. Stumbling for a direct answer, he gave up and launched into a pro and con review of the two weapons. I waited until he was done, ignoring all that he said before.

"Son, I understand what you're saying. I really do. Thank you. But I'm quite familiar with a 1911. I want it instead of the revolver."

"Okay, sir, but if you're looking for a concealed carry, well, the .38 is far better, like I was just . . ."

"I know. Like you just said. And I appreciate the advice. But it's my call. When I pick the 1911 up, I'll need another magazine. No, two extra magazines. And ammunition. Plus, a shoulder holster set up and a decent waist holster." I handed over my credit card.

"Oh, when I pick it up, do you have an NRA instructor here? I'd like to shoot for qualification. For my concealed carry permit, you understand."

"Yes, sir. I can set you up in his appointment book." We settled on two days later at eleven.

"Excellent. Now, could I get in some practice right now?"

"Sure. Only one other customer on the range."

I hadn't fired a handgun, or even picked one up, since my military discharge, but as I stood in my lane box with the pistol and one hundred rounds of ammo, the memories came back. The faint smell of gun oil. The near-perfect fit in my hand. The steel's coolness and the rough texture of the pistol grip in my right palm. The weapon's nicked, parkerized flat green, grey finish. A comfortable, familiar feeling grew within me.

I slipped a magazine with seven rounds into the pistol. Holding the weapon in my right hand and keeping it low and pointed down range, I drew back on the slide with my left hand to put a round in the chamber. I could almost hear my old Army range instructor, as if he were standing beside me.

Right hand on the grip with index finger outside the trigger guard, thumb up. All four fingers of the left hand covering the right hand's three fingers, with the left thumb going forward parallel to the frame. Hold the grip firmly. Lock wrists. Bend your elbows slightly. With your right thumb, push down and release the safety. Raise the weapon and get a sight picture. Don't anticipate the shot. Don't make a "now" shot.

I fired. Nervous, excited, I lowered the weapon and breathed slowly before setting a steady pace. One shot roughly every three seconds. With the seventh round, the slide locked to the rear, rendering the weapon safe. Tilting the weapon slightly to the right, I thumbed the magazine release button and caught the magazine in my cupped left hand.

Forty years had evaporated. I said out loud to myself, "Like riding a bike."

Not quite, though. Though my hands became those of my youth, my one functional eye remained in the here and now. Sighting with my aged right eye, and through prescription eyeglasses, the sight picture was blurry. The target score confirmed my diminished skill. Only four hits in the 5X center mass area, which outlined where the heart would be. Mixed results for the other three shots. One would've clipped the target's ribs. One went south of the 5X and into the belly. And the last one went to parts unknown.

Rather embarrassing for a crack shot soldier. Still, not bad. If it ever came to a fight, my best hope might be that the noise would scare them off.

On the upside, aiming the pistol, wearing my black eyepatch, I looked pretty badass.

Over the next hour, I fired at a slower pace. My accuracy improved with better groupings. But I knew that in a real fight, I wouldn't have time to take careful aim. Point and shoot and blast out a whole magazine.

A story from my father came to mind. He'd served alongside an old sergeant major who'd picked up an interesting shooting trick in his time. Dad's unit had rotated off the line in Korea. At a hastily constructed range, Dad watched the sergeant major fire his sidearm with a machine gun rate of fire. Bullseye seven times. The old hand did it again with the same results.

When Dad asked how he learned how to do that, the sergeant said, "Kid, I was in Burma in the last one. Not much going on, and we were godawful bored. Yeah, boredom is mostly what I remember from Burma. We needed something to do, so me and a couple of guys would load up a jeep with ammo and shoot shit and shoot fast. We got pretty good."

With enough ammo left for two full magazines, I experimented with fast firing. Pausing after the first round, I shot the remaining six at a pace of one shot per second. I tried to shoot even faster with the last magazine, which earned me a rebuke over the range PA system.

The data did not support the hypothesis that fast shooting leads to greater accuracy. I policed my space and returned the weapon to the clerk. I should've thanked the clerk and left the gun store. But I had to be a jerk. "Now, son, you owe me an answer. What've heard about me?"

"Sir, I, ah, don't, I mean, didn't mean anything by what I said, sir. Just that I saw you on the news. And, well . . . people are after you. Maybe that's why you want . . ."

I interrupted. "Want a gun? You know, you seem like a decent enough guy. And you're, how shall I put this? Curious? Concerned? Why is this old man buying a gun? An old man who is facing death threats. Who had Nazis come to his door."

Judging by the clerk's expression, I wasn't entirely calm. He couldn't look at me. His distress must've been noticed by a colleague who walked over and asked if there was anything he could do.

"Yes, sir. There is. Here's how you can help me." I raised my voice to something more than an indoor voice.

"Tell people I was here. Victor Holt. The writer guy who had Nazis come to his house and burn a pile of his books. The guy on the news with all these death threats. Tell everyone I bought a firearm. A big, powerful firearm."

Pausing to look around at the other customers, I continued. "This seems like a popular place. So, please. Tell everyone. I was here. Tell them what I bought. Get the word out. It'd be a big help to me. You understand?"

Neither of the clerks said a word. Guess customers don't often act this way. With as expressionless a face as I could hold together, I said to them, "Hell, boys. Get out your phones and take a pic of me! A selfie with me. Put it on your website for all I care!"

Wouldn't you know, the kid did just that. I faked a smile for the camera. As a final gesture, I tossed a couple of my author business cards on the counter.

"Remember, my friends, let everybody know. Holt was here!" I wished them a good day and walked out.

On the drive back home, I pumped my fist into the air a couple of times and let out a whoop. I felt good, like I won an engagement. However, by the time I got back home, as the surge of adrenaline and endorphins faded away, doubt and remorse reemerged.

The kid in the store; did he do anything wrong? No. Just doing his job. He said he recognized me from the news. That's all. He didn't judge me. He didn't challenge or insult me. All he did was try to help me buy what I wanted, and I turned into an asshole.

Because he worked in a gun store, without evidence or cause, I assumed that he and everyone there were enemies. My smug self-satisfaction faded away entirely by the time I finished a hastily prepared cocktail of ginger ale and bourbon.

That poor kid. He didn't deserve to catch shit from me. I was wrong.

The empty highball glass dropped into the sink, surprising me that it didn't shatter. Being in no mood to make a proper dinner, I settled for a couple of boiled hot dogs and baked beans. Fifteen minutes later, I was making my second highball. To help process my thoughts, or so I lied to myself.

Publicly showing myself says I am not afraid, and the death threats are not working. Prodding the gun store clerks to tell all their friends, real or online, that I was there adds to my visibility. Eventually, the Nazis and whoever put that dummy head on my steps will hear of it. With luck, before anyone comes up to my door in the dead of night, they'll be deterred by an image in their mind of a .45 caliber pistol aimed at their face.

The second highball reinforced that instinct. That is, until it came to me, the downside of my little show might trigger.

I cannot face my enemies alone. I need allies. True, the police can protect me, and Bron would advocate for me. And Steve and Lil, I suppose, could watch my back. The news interviews Ed arranged generated awareness and sympathy. There were favorable statements by public officials. A handful of supportive letters to the editor in the local paper, as well as well-meaning comments on social media. But such expressions are fleeting. The story moves on by the next day, or hour, or minute. It's human nature to forget. It was fanciful at best to think that strangers would defend the barricades for me.

What I did in the gun store won't bring me allies. Nobody likes a jerk. I was blowing it.

CHAPTER THIRTY-TWO

A PIECE OF THE PUZZLE

Ford

"What's this, Cory?"

Standing in the dirt less than a foot away from him, I held up a tiny zip-lock bag to his face. Inside the bag was a white powder. Wide-eyed, Cory looked down and patted all his pockets. Then I knew it was his. Grabbing Cory by the arm before he could say anything, I hauled him to the other side of the truck, out of sight from everyone else.

Whispering, I said to Cory, "Found this on the ground right by you. Wasn't there before. It's yours, isn't it?" Cory didn't answer. He kept looking anywhere but at me.

When he didn't answer, I pinned him against the truck, putting my forearm across his throat, maybe too much because he struggled to breathe. With his eyes bulging out, Cory tried to bat my arm away but couldn't. I didn't care.

No longer whispering, I said, "You going to answer me?" I think he got a "yes" out. I let my arm fall from his throat, but kept him up against the truck.

"Jeff. Please. Wait." Coughing, Cory got out, "Not what you think."

"White powder in a plastic bag. You think I'm fuckin' stupid? It's cocaine." I shoved him harder back against the truck.

"You brought drugs to a job. Goddamn it. I'm calling the boss. She hates drugs. You know that! She's fired druggies before. She'll fire you, too. Then she'll call the cops." I slammed him one more time before stepping away to call the boss.

Cory started crying. I heard him say, "It's . . . it's . . . not cocaine."

I held up the baggie, pretending to look it over carefully. "Not cocaine? Really? I've never seen cocaine for real, but this sure looks like it." That was true. My television is the closest I'd ever come to cocaine.

"Tell me what it is!" It took him a couple of tries, but he blurted out, "GHB."

"GBH? What's that?" Cory corrected me. "No, no. It's G . . . H . . . B. Date rape drug."

Once Cory started talking, he couldn't shut up. He told me what it's used for, excusing his crime by claiming he is so awkward with girls that GHB was the only way he'd ever get laid. Put the right dose in the girl's drink, he explained, "She'll get drowsy. Might even pass out. Next morning, she won't remember anything. Amnesia. At least that's what I've heard."

"You sick shit." I slapped him across the face. Cory fell to the ground, putting up his hands as a shield against another hit. I got down on my knees and grabbed his collar. "You're a real piece of shit. You'd drug a girl and then rape her? What the fuck is wrong with you?"

I'm not the most balanced individual. I'm aware of that. My sense of right and wrong is, how shall I put it? Challenged. Yet there I was, angry and disgusted with Cory. I took out my cell phone. One call and he's fired. But I didn't do what I should have done. Another possibility came to mind. I stood up and put my phone back in its belt holder.

Cory said the GHB made them drowsy. Maybe knock someone

out. Amnesia. They won't know what happened when they woke up. Could use this . . .

Glancing left and right, I saw no one was around. I pulled Cory up on his feet. I asked, this time in a softer voice, "Where'd you get it?" Eager to keep out of trouble, Cory claimed he knew a dealer but couldn't say more because the guy would come after him.

"How much is in the bag? Dose-wise, I mean."

"There's eight grams in there. One, maybe two grams a dose. More than four grams could kill somebody. Guess about four doses. For ordinary-sized people."

"How long does it last?" Cory said one to four hours, depending on the individual and the dose.

"Listen, Jeff. Can you pretend this didn't happen? Look, if you want money, I can get you some. This goes to the cops; they'll kick me out of college. Shit, I haven't even used it yet. Not once." Cory was still so scared that he was shaking.

I knew I had him. "Here's the deal, Cory." His eyes filled with tears, Cory nodded.

"I'll get rid of this stuff. I won't tell the boss, but you'll work harder than you ever have. Don't say a word about this. To anyone. At the end of this season, you leave for college and never come back. If I hear about someone getting date raped, well, I'll find a way of getting your name to the cops. Clear?"

"Yeah. I, ah, I understand." He straightened up. Like the weak boy he was, he held out his hand like he wanted to thank me. I didn't shake his hand. I said, "Get back to work. Remember what I said."

Cory ran away from me, grabbing a shovel to join the other two workers. I stood there watching him as he furiously attacked the pile of mulch. I slipped the little plastic Ziplock into my front pocket and patted it, wondering if a big piece of the puzzle was solved.

CHAPTER THIRTY-THREE

THE SLOG

Holt

Before going to bed that night, I made two wise decisions. First, I didn't make a third highball. Second, I didn't check my social media. I needed more sleep and less outrage.

In the morning, with a large cup of dangerously hot coffee in hand, suited up in workout clothes for a trip to the gym, I began the day with a routine task. Online, I checked my bank accounts and other investment accounts. Before long, however, my wisdom evaporated as the mouse cursor hovered over links to my social media. I hadn't looked at my page since the *Battle of the Little Beach Brewery*. Rationalizing a poor decision with a need to answer a specific question, I clicked on the icon.

Comments blazed with red-hot hate. They called me a traitor, a commie, or both at the same time. Frequent calls for my arrest and execution; hanging being the preferred method. Pervert frequently showed up, though the connection between my work and the accusation was lost on me. Zoological analogies abounded. I am a rat, a bug in need of squashing, a snake, a worm, a parasite, or any one of the slimy, slithering creatures on this Earth. And, of course, time-honored, straightforward profanity. Breezing through the comments without responding, I paused only to take screenshots of those that crossed the line to threats.

I had a well-defined target in mind. I kept scrolling, looking for . . . *I found it!* A comment that appeared only in the last few minutes.

Heard about you giving shit to my friends at the gun store. Can't wait to see you hang!

Within half an hour, a dozen or more comments about the gun store popped up. I sat back, considering the inference I could draw. Likely, the gun store staff did as I hoped. They told someone who likely told someone else, who told someone else . . . and around it went.

Whether publicity about my new pistol would achieve the deterrence I wanted, I had no way of knowing. Unless I got shot. Then I'd know deterrence failed.

An hour at my laptop was long enough. I turned it off and headed out for the gym. After my usual household security routine, I got in my truck. A couple of miles away from the gym, my phone went off. It was Bron.

Before I could say good morning, Bron cut me off. "Hello, Vic? Can you hear me? Yes? Okay. Listen, I'm out in the street. We evacuated my office building. Someone called in a bomb threat."

Oh, shit. I pulled over into a funeral home's parking lot that happened to be along my route. Bron continued talking, assuring me she was all right, the police and fire department were on scene, and the whole thing was certainly a hoax. Then she said the bomb threat was connected to me.

"Are you okay?" I was loud. Surprises bring that out in me. Bron again said she was fine.

"Thank Christ. Hey, what do you mean, I'm connected to the call?"

"Oh, yeah. He knew my firm represents you. Hang on a second,

Vic." I heard someone talking to Bron, though I couldn't make out the words over the traffic noise.

"Ah, looks like we can go back in. Anyway, how're you?"

"I'm, well, fine, I guess. Pretty boring day. That is, until you called. Going to the gym. Jesus, Bron, I don't know what to say. You're sure you're all right?"

"Again, I'm fine. Look, things like this, sometimes they're the cost of doing business. It's happened before. Pretty rare, but it does happen. Always some pissed-off crank out there."

Bron continued with a string of platitudes. Don't worry. I'm fine. No need for me to do anything. "Go to the gym; watch your surroundings. But this is the fight we're in. I'll call you tonight after work. Bye."

Flummoxed by the morning's events, I sat there in the parking lot wondering if there was a certain irony about being parked at a funeral home. With nothing else to do, I drove on to the gym.

Turned out my worry of being recognized and confronted at the gym was groundless. More troubling was the temptation I faced every time I left the gym. The best donuts in the whole damn world are only a quarter of a mile away from the gym. Turn left, I go home. Turn right, I get two enormous honey-dipped donuts that are to die for.

I turned right.

Half an hour later, I'd turned onto my road, anticipating a minor gastronomic wonder of two enormous gourmet donuts paired with a cup of delicious black tea. If Michelin gave stars to donut shops, that place would be a one-star. Maybe two.

On the final approach to my home, my hopes for a peaceful breakfast were dashed. A small group of casually dressed strangers stood waiting for me at the head of my driveway. I stopped before my driveway, angling the truck to the right so I could speak directly to them through an open window, but far enough away that . . . *that what?*

Not NSAG. No black hoodies. But . . . damn them! I don't need visitors.

I yelled, "Who the hell are you?" Not very nice, I'll admit. A "Can I help you?" would've been more polite, but there are times when impoliteness is a more effective approach. Like when there's a group of unknown people at your home.

A woman, dressed in grey slacks and a pink polo shirt, held up her hand and started to close the gap between herself and my truck.

"Look, you can stop right there! Who are you and why are you here?" Pink Polo Lady kept coming.

"Hello. You must be Mr. Holt. We just want to talk to you. We have something . . ."

"I said, stop right there! So, stop . . . the fuck . . . right there!" Officially angry by this point, I shifted the truck into reverse, holding it in place with the brake, ready to retreat. I checked that my cell phone had the camera app up. I wished I had that pistol before remembering pistols are hammers, and then every problem becomes a nail.

"Mr. Holt. There's no need for that kind of language." By then, she was only ten feet away, while the other five had moved only a few feet closer.

"You don't like my language?" A rant followed, questioning why they were here. Oh, yeah, I said fuck a lot.

Holding up her hands spread wide, she stopped walking but kept talking. "Mr. Holt, please, we just want to talk."

I let loose another barrage of F-bombs. This time, with greater effect. She and her little band retreated to where they started. Seeing that she finally got the message, I considered my situation: I'm unarmed and outnumbered, though they don't look dangerous. Best to keep them away.

"You want to talk? Let me tell you how that's going to happen."

I pointed to a big Suburban parked on the other side of the

road. "That your car? All of you! Walk back to it and stand in front of it. Do not go inside the vehicle or behind it. Stay where I can see you and stay there until I tell you to move. When you do that, I'll park my truck in my driveway."

They bickered among themselves. I couldn't hear them, but it seemed Pink Polo Lady took the lead and persuaded them to do as I ordered. I parked in the driveway, opened the truck door, and left it open as I got out.

"You! In the pink shirt! You want to talk to me? Walk across the road. Just you! I'll tell you when to stop!" I had to give her credit. Even in the face of a madman, she didn't hesitate. While two of Pink Polo Lady's companions started videoing the scene, I did likewise. When I got them all on video, I tossed my phone onto the driver's seat.

When she got to about six feet from me, in a more moderate tone, I said, "Okay, that's close enough."

Though I didn't catch her name, Pink Polo Lady then identified herself as the president of the Town Council. Three of her companions were also on the Council. The remaining two represented both the organized political parties in town. Perhaps as a politician's habit, she emphasized the bipartisanship of her group. After apologizing for showing up unannounced, she claimed multiple attempts to call me didn't get through.

That was likely true. Except for people I know, I ignored or blocked calls from anyone unfamiliar.

"Look, I'm not answering calls or emails from people I don't know. You can guess why. I mean, a bunch of Nazis burned my book in my yard. You know all that, but you show up, no warning. So, what in holy hell did you expect me to think?"

"Please, Mr. Holt. This isn't easy. Let me explain. We're here out of concern for our town and its citizens."

"Really? Am I one of those citizens you're concerned about?"

Apparently not. While she claimed they were sympathetic to

my situation and found the Nazi demonstration "abhorrent," the Town Council unanimously believed the resulting media coverage damaged the town's image and frightened the town residents.

"Frankly, Mr. Holt, people are worried that, ah, you've become, well, a magnet for trouble. First, the library, and then what happened here. We hate that, but people are scared. There's been enough of that kind of violence going on in the country. We see it almost every night on the news. We don't want the violence to come here. We're afraid innocent people will get hurt."

I stood there dumbfounded, asking myself if she really said that it's my fault. Angry, I said, "Innocent people? You mean me? Cause I'm the only innocent one around here who's gotten hurt!"

"That's why we're here, Mr. Holt. We don't want anyone to get hurt. Including you."

"Then what will the Town Council do about those Nazis?"

"That's the police's job. What will the Council do? We've come here to ask you to do something." She paused, as if waiting for me to say . . . anything. My silence seemed to unnerve her.

"Mr. Holt, it's not easy to ask this. But it's in the town's best interest. To keep the peace, you understand. I, I mean we, hope you'll help us. Help the people, that is." My rolling eyes must've betrayed what I was thinking. *Get on with it! Say it!*

"We'd like you to withdraw your book from the library, and stop selling it, at least for a while, until things calm down. And sign a press release to that effect." She motioned to one of the others to bring the press release copy to her. "We hope that this . . . concession will stop all this. Do you understand, Mr. Holt?"

I could have countered that I'm the innocent party. That they're asking me to suspend my livelihood. They're asking me to surrender to extremists, all for the sake of peace. Their peace. The same plea was made by appeasers across history. I could have fired back with all that and more. Instead, I chose a better response.

"No."

In life, I've found that a one-word negative response leaves the recipient with little room to maneuver. All she could do was parrot my response.

"No?"

"No." I shut and locked my truck door, walked to my house, and went inside. Looking back through the door glass, I saw her still standing in my driveway, press release in hand, with no idea what to do next, except leave.

A minute later, they all left. I said to myself, "Looks like I won't be finding any allies in town government."

After a cup of black tea and the donuts, I went upstairs for a shower, hoping that would also calm me down. Before I had a chance to turn on the shower, a knock at my door made me jump. I pulled up my sweatpants, put back on my rank sweatshirt, and went downstairs. When I looked through the front door glass from the stairs, I saw Steve.

"Well, hi neighbor! How are you?"

"Fine, Steve. Fine. I see the boot is off. Want to come in?

"Thanks, but I can't. And don't bullshit me. I watched the whole thing with you and our illustrious town leaders, but we can talk about all that over dinner and cocktails. Tonight, at five. That is, if you don't have anything else on your busy social calendar."

After a moment of confusion, I said, "Dinner? Again? You guys don't have to. Really, I'm fine."

"Chuck roast. Fall off the bone chuck roast, drowning in onions and gravy, with mashed potatoes and baked carrots with more onions. Simple, but delicious. I'll have the cocktails ready. Come on, my friend, don't think about it. Just say yes." I said yes.

I hadn't had a chuck roast in years. It was as promised; well beyond delicious. After the plates were cleared, this time without me dropping glasses to the floor, we adjourned to their three-season room for another round of cocktails. Lil got to the heart of the matter.

"I hear you met our old friend Marie today. Marie Ballenger. Our Town Council president."

"You guys know her?"

"I guess you could say that, but my dear wife is being sarcastic. Marie isn't a friend."

"Sounds like there's a story you guys want to tell me."

Steve nodded and put down his drink on the small table next to his chair. He turned to Lil and asked her, "Shall I start, or you?"

Not being reticent about such things, Lil started. "We've known her for a long time. Three decades thereabouts. Didn't take all those years to learn it's best to avoid her."

I asked why. Like opening the cork on a shaken bottle of champagne too quickly, Lil's disgust with Marie gushed out.

"Runs a hardware store in town. Does very well, I have to say. But she's a real goddamn busybody. Polite and everything. To your face, that is. Likes to flaunt her connections and who she knows. Too slick by half. You know what she is? She's a change jinglier, as my uncle used to say."

When I confessed I didn't understand the expression, Lil clarified. "Change jinglier. An old saying that I think goes back to the Great Depression days. It's what my uncle called self-important people. They'd talk to you with one hand in their pocket, jingling silver dollars, making sure you knew they had money. That they're better than you."

By then, Steve seemed agitated. "Lil, the point, please."

"Vic, first let me say, you telling Marie to fuck off, all I can say is, kudos to you. She needs to be told that. But I didn't ask you over here just to say that. I want to warn you about her."

"Christ Almighty, Lil. We talked about this. Get on with it."

Lil turned on him. "I will! Vic doesn't know that Marie, for all her charm, can be one vengeful goddamn bitch."

"Bitch, my dear?"

"Yes, Steve, a bitch she is, but I can say that, not you." Though

I thought Lil was trying to lighten the mood, her pejorative for Marie ignited a side debate between the two, while I sat there unsure of how to take all this in. I decided to intervene.

"Okay, you two. Let's get back on track. Lil, what do you want to tell me about Marie?"

"Yes, sorry. Marie." Lil collected her thoughts, aided by another sip of her cocktail.

"Most people say she's a charming person. They'd be right. She's an expert at reading a room. People come away feeling she listened to them. But her real talent is telling people exactly what they want to hear."

Lil was on a roll. "That's made her popular around town. Probably why she's been such a successful local politician. She's not dishonest, but not exactly honest either. You follow me?"

"Maybe. Maybe not. Keep going."

"I know that sounds like a typical politician. I'll grant you that. But there's another side to her."

Steve interjected, "This is why you've got to be careful around her, Vic."

Lil stared straight ahead and said, "You going to let me finish? I planned this as a monologue. You'll get your chance."

"Damn right I will." Steve sat back, waiting for his moment.

"So, Vic. Anyway, there're stories about her. How she's used her friends in town government to go after people on the QT. Say you need the building inspector to look at something, but you're on her shit list, well . . ."

Lil paused to lift her arms in mock exasperation as she said, "Could be a long time before the building inspector comes by. Same goes for business licenses. Permits. Zoning decisions. Stuff like that. The more those stories go around, the more people want to stay on her good side."

"As of today, I don't think I'm on her good side." Laughing, Steve confirmed my suspicion. "No, my friend. Definitely not!"

"So, what should I do? Any recommendations? Aside from, of course, not asking for a business license or a building permit."

It was Steve's turn. He told me a slim majority on the Town Council wanted to pass a resolution condemning the group that demonstrated at the library and reaffirming a commitment to protect books, not ban them. Marie stopped it.

"She argued a resolution would just get things more heated and maybe make the Town Council a target. All it would do is scare people. Stuff like that. Same argument about the book burning. Marie squashed a resolution against the Nazis. Imagine that. Afraid to officially say Nazis are . . . bad." Steve shook his head in disgust.

All this was new to me. "Wait, Steve, how do you know this? I don't doubt your word, but . . ."

"Clearly, my friend, you don't go to Town Council meetings. Or read through the meeting transcripts they post online. Of course, it helps I've got a couple friends on the inside." I suffered Steve's mild rebuke of my lack of civic responsibility without comment while he continued. "And I know how Marie works. She'll keep hammering on you until she gets her way."

Steve shifted his focus to our shared view of the shoreline. Sipping my cocktail, I needed time to take all this in before I came up with *the* question.

"Okay. So, you're telling me the Town Council, mostly Marie that is, decided not to officially condemn Nazis. And if I don't do as she asked, withdraw my book, she'll come after me. I got that right?" Steve nodded.

"Don't suppose you know why?"

Steve shook his head before looking back at me and saying, "I don't know. The thing you have got to understand about her is that Marie acts in Marie's best interests, while claiming she's acting in the town's best interests. It's always about her. I say that from long association with her."

Steve got up from his chair and paced, leaving the cocktail on the small table. To me, Steve seemed to struggle with his thoughts, as if he were trying to sort out two conflicting notions. He eventually said, "Maybe I'm being unfair. One thing I'm sure of is, she's not in sympathy with Nazis."

As Steve sat back down, Lil summed things up. "Marie is just plain scared of them. Look what they've done to you. If the Council condemned them, they might come after her because she is president of the Council."

Steve added a different topic. "Perhaps. Then again, Vic, maybe Marie is being honest when she says people in town are scared. Let me ask you. You ever hear of an online group from around town called *Coastal Neighbors*?" I said no.

"Since the library thing, even more so since the Nazis, a lot of people around here want you to shut up about your book."

Without thinking, I said, "That include you two?"

Lil reacted angrily. "No! No effing way! Jesus, Vic."

"Easy, my dear. Vic didn't mean anything by that. Let's cut him some slack."

Realizing my error, I apologized and asked about what people were saying online. While not mentioning anything specific or naming names, Steve gave me the gist of it.

"Comments. Hardly a scientifically sound data collection methodology. It doesn't help that people will say almost anything online if they're anonymous. That said, by my quick count, roughly six or seven out of ten commenters want you to give in. And of those, maybe a third want you out of town."

"Well, I'm not moving. If people around here don't like me, I can live with that. Lil. Steve. Look, first, thanks for all you've already done. But I don't want you guys to get involved. Not directly. It's my fight after all. I can't . . ."

Lil didn't let me finish. "Like hell you can't! No way. There's got to be things we can do to help!"

A mental image came to my mind of Lil and Steve manning the trenches against an invading horde of Neo-Nazis, rifles blazing. I drained off my cocktail to give me time to think.

When Lil had her Irish up like this, I learned it was best to smile and not say a word. Fortunately, Steve was well-experienced in this situation. He shifted focus back to the online group.

"Vic, there's something else. And it's harsh, but it's more a measure of the people who wrote the comments than you. Human nature, I suppose. People put their heads down. Appease the bully. Wish it away."

"Christ Almighty, Steve. Get to the point!" Lil was never lost for words.

"Are they threatening me? Cause if they are, I'm sort of used to that by now."

Steve shook his head as he said, "No. None are threatening you. That said, the common thread is that most of them, not all, think you brought this on yourself. That you're the cause of your trouble."

Rarely in my life has the word "astonished" seemed appropriate. This was one.

"Me? I'm the cause? Are they saying that? Jesus. Nazis came to my fucking house. I didn't invite them! And they blame me?" I might've said even more colorful things. Either out of wisdom or a touch of fear, Steve and Lil let me vent before speaking again.

"Like another drink there, Vic?" Steve barely got that question out before I stumbled over my response. "Yeah. Ah, no. A third cocktail won't help. Thanks, but no thanks."

"Good, because I wasn't really offering one anyway. Last thing you need." I set my empty cocktail glass on the table by my chair.

"What I need, Steve, Lil, is advice. What do I do now, I mean, with people in the town blaming me? Wanting me gone. Got any ideas?"

Lil spoke first. "As a matter of fact, we do."

In a kind of tag team relay, Steve and Lil outlined their

proposed counteroffensive. They'd write a letter to the editor of the local weekly paper defending me. Their message would be posted on *Coastal Neighbors*. Other letters to the Town Council members demanding adoption of a resolution against NSAG and the extremist protestors at the library. Simply put, Steve and Lil wanted to turn local public opinion in my favor.

Lil had a special plan for Marie. "You let us deal with her. Like we said, we've known her for a long time. Matter of fact, we know all the Council members. They'll hear from us, face to face."

Steve reminded Lil of her big gun. "Oh, yes. We have a Town Council election coming up. Vic, you are the first voter in town to hear that I will be running for Council. And by God, this old woman will win. How's that sound?"

I didn't know what to say. I should have told them not to put themselves in the line of fire. Instead, I asked the obvious question. "Lil, you think you can win?"

"I will win. Don't fuckin' doubt that." Lil got a laugh when I suggested that it be her campaign slogan.

Steve had the evening's last word when he walked with me back to my house.

"Don't be too harsh with people in town, Vic. See things from their point of view. They're scared and legitimately so. It doesn't make them bad people. Just makes them typical people."

"I hear you, Steve."

"Do you?" Steve surprised me with that challenge. It must have shown on my face.

"Look. We'll help defend you, but there's something you, and us, must keep in mind. About our future."

We stopped halfway. "Okay, Steve. You've got something to say."

"That I do." Steve stood facing me, quietly allowing a long few seconds to pass before speaking.

"Someday, you'll be at the supermarket in town, and you'll see coming down the aisle a guy with whom you had words over this book of yours. You'll recognize each other. What then? Do you act decently to him? Or pick up the fight where you left off? Even if you win in court, even if the police arrest the people attacking you, that will not be the end of it. Those people will still be here.

"You know as well as anyone, things are not well in this country. Look at the news." Steve turned away to stare at the seashore. I'd never seen him like this. I knew for certain it wasn't the cocktails talking. He wasn't angry; more pained than anything.

His voice quivered as he continued. "All the political violence. We may not be in a civil war. Technically at least, but sometimes it seems more like The Troubles in Northern Ireland back when. Yes, they're scared. You're scared. I'm scared."

Still facing the water, Steve put his hand on my shoulder in a fatherly sort of way.

"We must find a way to reconcile. Truth and Reconciliation. Isn't that what the South Africans did after apartheid? We must learn again how to live with each other. So, here's how I see it. Victory in this fight of yours is not the destruction of your enemies. Victory, as I see it, is reconciliation with your enemies. I mean, your hero from that book of yours, who was it? The one about World War I? The King."

"*The King's Lieutenant?* You mean King Albert?"

"Yes. King Albert. What did Albert say at the war's end? 'No victors. No vanquished.' Somehow, that's where we need to land if we're ever to put things back together.

"Anyway, Vic. I don't know if I've made a damn bit of sense. But try to understand. Try to find a way. Try to reconcile. Otherwise, we win the war but lose the peace."

Steve tapped me on the shoulder; we shook hands and parted. I watched Steve all the way to make sure he made it back home before I headed for my door. As he reached the stairs to his door, I yelled out after him.

"Hey, Steve. Any idea how we do this reconciliation?"

"Nope. Not a goddamn clue."

CHAPTER THIRTY-FOUR

PERCHANCE TO DREAM

Ford

The young man knelt on the wet ground. In the near freezing cold, he had no coat or hat. All he had was a tattered and torn black woolen shirt and filthy grey pants. His pitiful shoes were worn down to almost paper-thin soles. Standing behind him, only an arm's length away from him, I stared at the back of his head.

At the edge of a deep pit in the sandy soil, the man waited to join the fifty or more crumpled, warped, bloody bodies, spattered with blood, gore, dirt, and mud. He heard moaning and crying from the few still alive. Children, women, and men. Somehow, I knew he saw his family among the murdered.

I am also a young man, but I wear a grey, blood-stained tunic and trousers, with mud-smeared black leather boots which reached to below my knees. On the right arm cuff is a black band, embroidered with silver gothic lettering. I am *Schutzstaffel.* The SS. The executioner.

Though resigned to his death, the man turned his head to face me. I saw his exhausted, sad eyes. He turned away from me to face the pit again. With my right hand, I pressed my small black pistol against the back of the kneeling man's neck.

Someone standing at my side says, "Go on, my friend. This must be done. It's our job. This is for the good."

Without looking at my comrade, I smiled, nodded my agreement, and pulled the trigger. My hand recoiled slightly. As the man fell into the pit, my uniform caught droplets of blood.

That the dead man was alive again, kneeling at the pit as before, somehow did not surprise me. I held a pistol to his neck, but a different kind of pistol. My uniform had changed. A tan blouse, adorned with a brown leather belt across my chest. A red star stitched below the sleeve cuff. Like before, blood spattered on my uniform. I am the executioner again.

I hear another voice at my side saying, "Go on, my friend. This must be done. It's our job. This is for the good."

I smiled and fired. The kneeling man crumpled into the pit. He lay facing me. I saw that a bloody exit wound had ripped away his cheekbone and half his upper jaw.

This time, the dead man spoke. "You killed me. You killed my wife and son. They told you murder is your patriotic duty. To save your people, you must kill my people. They said God was with you. They said . . . "

As the dead man's voice faded, I stood at the pit's edge alongside my other selves, as SS executioner and as Soviet sergeant. Together, we laughed at the dead man's words. Now I knelt at the pit's edge. I felt the cold metal of a pistol muzzle on my neck.

Astonished, I screamed, bolting upright in my bed, gasping, clutching the sweat-soaked bed sheet, the room's horizon swaying. In that first second of consciousness, I had no idea where I was, even who I was.

A dream. A nightmare. The most vivid nightmare I'd ever had. I sat up on the side of the bed, letting the bed sheet fall away. A minute, maybe more, passed before I moved again to grab my robe off the footboard and stand up.

"Jesus, what happened?"

Walking into the kitchen, the wall clock said it was three in the morning. Opening my dad's liquor cabinet, I grabbed a bottle of whiskey he'd left behind, thinking, Christ, I need something. I reached for a glass from the cabinet shelf. And then I stopped. I put the glass back down, shaking my head. I said to the room, "No. That won't help." *But what do I do now?*

I didn't understand exactly why, but I knew I had to find the man I "killed." I knew his face. I knew it from a picture. An old photograph from the Holocaust. The Nazi death squads on the Russian front. Using my laptop, I raced through online images. Within a minute, I found it.

A grainy black and white photo I'd seen before. A man, probably middle-aged, on his knees at the edge of a pit. On the dirt spoil of a mass grave, a yard or so behind the man, stood a bespectacled Nazi. Dressed in an ordinary uniform save for the riding boots and crop pants, the Nazi is aiming a pistol at his next victim. Behind the uniformed man is a ragged line of nine or ten comrades who seem bored by the whole exercise. Convinced of the properness of their executions, the Nazis routinely photographed themselves as they murdered the innocents.

The photo caught the kneeling man just as he looked upward and to his left. Across his gaunt face, his expression is calm, seemingly detached from his fate. The photo captured his haunting stare a second before he died. Was he looking for loved ones? Or was he looking at his murderers, using his eyes as his last weapon, to burn inside them a lasting and final accusation.

Is that what Holt will do? Will he look me in the eye as he dies?

I shut my laptop. My hands were shaking.

Why dream about this? Why this image? Why this nightmare? What does it mean? Why am I an SS Sergeant, and then a Sergeant of Stalin's secret police?

The morning hours went by, and I settled down. With the dawn, it became clearer why my SS doppelganger murdered that man. In my dream, I felt certain of the correctness, the legality, and the morality of this murder. It was justifiable. It was a step toward a worthy goal that must be attained by any means.

Long ago, I'd read somewhere that the purpose of dreams is not well understood. Ordinary dreams may be nothing more than a rehash of the day's events as they are processed into memory. They're not messages from Angels. Or Demons. They cannot foretell the future any more than a deck of tarot cards.

This was a nightmare, not an ordinary dream. Nightmares stemming from past trauma can be triggered by stress and anxiety. At least, that is what a quick online search claimed. Okay, I thought, planning the kidnapping and murder–no, execution–of Holt is causing me stress.

I dreamed of playing the executioner's role. And I dreamed I was successful. That seemed logical to me, if dreams can be logical. I am the killer, and Holt is the man falling dead into the pit.

Shouldn't I listen to the dream?

CHAPTER THIRTY-FIVE

BRON

Holt

No victors. No vanquished. At war's end, it was King Albert's plea to the Allies. An appeal from the leader of a nation that had suffered grievously from the Germans. Perhaps he feared Allied vengeance upon a defeated Germany would only fuel the German people with a fire for revenge. He was right. Belgium would burn once more. On May 10, 1940, Nazi Germany invaded Belgium.

Steve asked me to heed the wisdom of Albert. Win my war but do not lose the peace. Fight off those threatening me, but find a path toward reconciliation. No matter how successful I am, they will still be here. And I must still live among them.

However, before there can be reconciliation, the war must be won.

Bron updated me regularly on the latest legal news, even when there was no news. Though well-intentioned, this routine only reinforced my opinion of our legal system: only lawyers understand it. Common sense and the law seem barely acquainted and are often not on speaking terms. Above all else, the law moves slowly.

"Courts are busy, Vic. It's like draining an Olympic swimming pool with a garden hose. It'll get done, but it takes time."

Bron and I cheered the legal news regarding Drunk Lady from *Little Beach.* She pled guilty. I did not cheer when Bron told me Drunk Lady was released pending sentencing. It was more like a WTF moment. Halfway through a rant over why a violent offender gets to go home for a couple of months, Bron set me straight.

"Real-world law is not TV law. There's rightly a high bar to keep someone in custody. She has no prior offenses, posted bond, and will wear an ankle bracelet until her court date."

"What if she comes after you? Or me? What's to stop her?"

"A restraining order. No contact with me or you. None. There's nothing unusual in this outcome."

Without thinking, I said something risky. I told Bron about the 1911 pistol I bought for protection and the expected concealed carry permit.

"You have the pistol now?" When I told her I'd pick it up tomorrow, a sharp, tense feeling came to my stomach. I feared this was a mistake; that she'd be pissed. Instead, she was nonchalant about the gun.

"Okay, I don't blame you. Really. Just for my sake, and yours, make sure you understand the law. Where and when you can use a weapon to defend yourself." After assuring her I'd already studied the law carefully and had a long talk with Detective Harrison, I shifted topics to something more routine.

"Bron, I do appreciate these calls to keep me up to speed. They help. Anyway, I think we should, ah, meet, well, face to face someplace. Once a week, if we can. Might make for easier communication." I shrank inside. Even back in high school, I'd never been smooth when asking a girl out.

"Face to face? You mean like a dinner meeting?"

"Yeah, I mean, it'd be in keeping with my plan to be seen out and about. I know a couple of nice places close by. Besides, tomorrow's Friday. Might as well enjoy things."

"And I won't get beat up again, like last time?" The way she deadpanned the question, I sensed a refusal was certain.

"No, I promise you." A response bordering on flippant. Yeah, I thought, this is going nowhere.

"So, Vic, let me make sure I understand what you're asking. You are my client. I am your attorney. Dinners between attorney and client aren't unusual. No ethical issues. We'll have to talk about business. Just so you understand."

Dinner conversation turned out to be five minutes of business followed by two hours of what two people talk about on an evening out. Frivolous remarks about the restaurant décor, favorite movies, and music. Vodka martinis started the evening, followed by an appetizer of baked stuffed quahogs, entrees of baked tautog and steak *Del Monico*, capped off with liqueurs and beignets with a small scoop of vanilla ice cream.

All done and dishes taken away, the two of us nursing the aperitifs, Bron leaned forward and said, "Vic, I have to say, this was excellent. There can't be many places this good around here."

"Actually, there are. Highest per capita distribution of fine dining establishments of any state. New York included. And even if that statistic is faulty, that's what I believe, and I'm sticking to it."

Bron giggled and looked out into the night at the small marina by the restaurant. There was a peaceful look about her, framed by what I saw as a smile of satisfaction.

"You know, Vic. I'm glad we didn't talk much about business. Frankly, I needed a night out. A normal night out. No law. No court issues. Thank you. I hope you don't mind my saying that. It's been a while."

"Not at all, Bron. I certainly don't mind. Same here. Yeah. It's been . . . a while."

"A while?" She said those two words slowly. Straight faced, emotion wiped away.

"Oh, ah, nothing. Jesus, nothing, Bron. It's just that, well, I haven't been out to dinner in a long time. That's all I meant."

With a teasing smile, Bron said, "Well, Vic, what do you think I meant?"

For a fleeting moment, I felt accused. In my mind's eye, I saw myself in the courtroom dock. And there was Bron, in a black barrister's gown and dull white wig, intent on a ruthless cross-examination. Why my mind transported me to an English court of law, I hadn't the foggiest. Lost, I had no idea what to say. After an uncomfortable pause, I let my guard down.

"Bron, please, I'm trying to say something. It's this. I'm happy to be out having dinner. That's for obvious reasons. It's, ah, been a while, as I've said, that I've been out at all. So, I'm just happy to be out . . . not alone and out with someone else."

Bron laughed as she shook her head. "Don't worry. Just kidding with you. I understand. It's been difficult for you. So much has happened." I think she wanted to say something else, but I interrupted her.

"Out with you. Out at dinner with you, Bron."

I expected a rebuke that I'd violated the compact between attorney and client. Whatever hopes I had would be smashed.

She didn't tear my dream apart. Maybe she somehow sensed my feelings, my worry. Bron looked at me, straight in the face, grinning, and reached out to hold my hand in a way it hadn't been held in ages. Not since I lost Susan.

CHAPTER THIRTY-SIX

A NEW LIFE

Holt

"Morning, Bron. Coffee's ready. There's cream and milk. Bacon's about done. Hope you like your eggs scrambled." Dressed in a robe, Susan's robe, Bron leaned against me, softly laying her head on my shoulder.

"Scrambled is fine. Nothing like waking up to the aroma of coffee and bacon."

"You're right. Nothing like it." Especially this breakfast, I thought.

Last night I started a new life. I wanted it to happen. I needed it to happen. Yet I began the evening certain it would not happen, so beyond any rational possibility it bordered on the infinitesimal. I figured she'd eat breakfast, get cleaned up and dressed, then leave for her harborside condo. Last night would prove to be an illusion which would fade as quickly as it appeared.

Bron surprised me. She set a pace for a slow, leisurely morning. We ate, then we enjoyed a second cup of coffee out on the deck. She stayed in Susan's robe, while I joined her in my pajamas and slippers. It was a beautiful Saturday morning, warm and clear. We sat in the Adirondack chairs, with a small table between us, enjoying the peace of the flat calm waters.

To fill the time, and to selfishly delay her departure, I brought out the binoculars and pointed out a distant flagpole on the shore south of us.

"Look down the beach that way. That big place with a huge deck. It juts out from the beach. There's a flagpole by the rocks. You'll see a flag flying. Got it?" A breeze obliged, fluffing the flag out almost in full.

"Yeah, I see it! What's that? A black, what, an animal? A lion? You know it, Vic?"

"Yeah. Every summer day at dawn, that guy puts out a different flag. That one's the Flag of Flanders. Belgium."

Bron smiled and said something like, "Wow, cool. How, ah, appropriate. Think he knows your family came from Belgium?" I said I doubted that.

Minutes passed as Bron sat silently. Naturally, I took this as a bad sign. That she was thinking about things, about us, trying to figure out a good time to say goodbye and head for home. I couldn't have been more wrong.

"Vic, I want to, talk. About us. Is that okay?" I nodded, anxiously anticipating a brutal end to this new life.

"I'm sixty. Healthy, but sixty. So, I don't have time to waste. There's no point in waiting. No point in letting something good go by. And Vic, what I have here, what we have, is good. I found out last night. I've known it for a while now.

"So, let me ask you . . . we haven't known each other for very long. But long enough as far as I'm concerned. I care for you, Victor Holt." She let that hang in the air for a while before asking me the big question. "Do you care about me? Enough that we could make something here?"

That was a moment I wanted to hold on to and never let it go.

"Bron, yes. I care about you. More than that."

A suave, debonaire man would've kissed her then and there. I tried. I got up from my rocking chair to close the space between us with a kiss. As I leaned toward her, I bumped into the little table between the rockers, jostling a mug and spilling coffee onto the deck. Red-faced, I repositioned the table to clear the way for a more successful attempt. The trouble was, she was too busy laughing to make this anything like a romantic moment. Fortunately, she threw me a lifeline.

"Well, Vic. That's good. I feel the same way. I don't know why, but I do."

Bron stood from her chair. I rose to meet her, and we embraced. With her head resting on my shoulder, she asked a question I'd been dreading.

"Vic, what about Susan? You think . . ."

I answered immediately. "Think that she'd mind? No, I'm sure she wouldn't." I asked Born to sit down. Looking into her eyes, I said, "I loved Susan. Still do. Before that, we were friends. We lived a long life together. We wanted to go all the way to the end. That was our plan. I never thought . . . never crossed my mind that . . . she'd die. So, yes, I'll always love her. I want you to know, I love you."

"I just don't want you to think that I want to . . . could replace her."

"Christ, no. Look, it's like you said. We're closer to the end than the beginning. And you know, I don't think Susan would object to us living what's left the best way we can."

"Thank you, Victor. I was, ah, well, worried about that."

"Don't be." I held her face in my hands, this time without jostling the table, and kissed her once again before asking, "Another coffee?" Such a romantic.

I returned to the deck with two cups of fresh coffee with cream and sugar, along with a wet dishrag to clean up the earlier spill.

Both of us stood leaning against the deck rail, sipping our coffee, when I saw something odd on the grass below.

By the corner of my house closest to the conservation land was a wooden pole about three feet long, driven into the ground. Something hung from the pole. Without a word to Bron, I stepped across the deck and down onto the lawn to inspect whatever it was.

It was a brown burlap bag, sewn up and stuffed with what seemed like dead grass in its lower half. The upper half was twisted into a ball about the size of a fist. Twine ran down from a nail at the top of the pole and then wound around the base of the ball. A crude, thin line of white paint illustrated an unsmiling mouth. Two white X's marked the doll's eyes. Sloppily painted across its chest was my name: Holt. The doll was my effigy hanging by the neck.

Looking back at Bron, I started to blurt out something, but stopped, thinking I must keep calm. Stay in control. I took a deep breath before telling her to please get inside the house. Naturally, she came toward me. I went back on the deck, grasped her arm, and led her inside, locking the deck doors and drawing down the shades.

Bron isn't the kind of person to stand idly by. She demanded to know what I saw. After fumbling through a description of the doll, she told me to call the police. I did so as we went upstairs to get dressed. While on the phone with the police dispatcher, I looked through the windows on all sides of the house. For all I knew, someone could still be out there.

When the police arrived, they searched the area, photographed the scene, and removed the effigy as evidence. After routine questions, they left.

Aside from identifying herself to the police, Bron didn't say anything until the cops were gone.

"This is like the mannequin head, isn't it, Vic?"

"Yeah, pretty much. You okay?"

"Think so. Unnerved somewhat. I mean, someone came here last night, while we were both here, upstairs, in the bedroom, and stuck that thing in the ground."

That's when my steely-eyed killer found her footing once more. "Anything else? Like something tagged or broken?"

"The cops didn't say, but then I didn't ask," Bron suggested we both walk around the house, the garage, and my truck. Nothing seemed out of order. When I said I should take her home, she refused, saying, "I'm staying. Besides, I, that is, we need to let this settle down."

I apologized for what happened. Bron would have none of that. "They did this. Not you. Nothing to apologize for."

When I asked for her thoughts on possible suspects, she said, "Well, yeah, the usual suspects. NSAG for one. Or any of the fans of Smyth and Wright. And whoever left the mannequin's head. They're the logical suspects. Until the police come up with forensic evidence from the doll, best not to speculate."

"Listen, as long as we're talking about threats, how about you? Your firm had a bomb threat. Was that threat directed at you personally?"

"Oh, yes. The partners had me listen to the threat on voicemail. Guess that unnerved them. Bastards didn't say a word about my safety. Now, enough of all that."

After sitting in silence for a while, the conversation shifted to lighter fare, as if we were back to being two ordinary people enjoying a beautiful weekend. That led me to suggest we go to a nearby seaside village for a walk and lunch. Considering the effigy, I recommended we spend the night at her condo. Bron agreed that it might be wise.

Lying next to her that night while she slept, the reality of my endangered life came back to mind. I'd told Steve and Lil about why I could fight back against these extremists. Why wasn't I as vulnerable as one might think? Being alone was my shield. I risked only my life and no one else's.

That's all changed. My shield was gone.

I love Bron. She loves me. I had a decision to make. Do I dare put her at risk? They've already threatened and assaulted her. They came to my house while she was here.

What right do I have to put her in danger?

CHAPTER THIRTY-SEVEN

THE BEACH PARTY

Holt

A good week followed the *Day of the Effigy*.

Only days after that scare, Bron suggested she move in with me. Just part-time for now. She started shuttling between her law office, condo, and my home. As Bron said when she dropped off a sizeable overnight bag, "No point in wasting time." I certainly didn't stand in her way.

On another front, Steve and Lil's letter to the editor was published online in each of the weekly newspapers for our and the surrounding towns. One letter even made its way to the state's largest, and only, newspaper. Lil posted the same letter on *Coastal Neighbors*.

As I feared, Steve and Lil caught more than a little online hell from their fellow townies. Outwardly, it mattered little to Steve and Lil. As Steve put it, "To hell with them. Got too many friends to keep track of anyway. Need to delete a few."

Steve and Lil also used their personal connections with the Town Council members to wrangle an unscheduled Thursday evening Council meeting. I went along. Honestly, I'm not sure if my pitch had any impact. I spoke like a high-brow academic, lecturing them on the U.S. Constitution and the historical lessons of appeasement.

Being more in tune with the town, Steve and Lil spoke to them as friends, reminding them of their shared pasts. A more emotional, but more effective plea. In a minor victory, a majority agreed to reintroduce the resolution condemning the Nazi book burning at the next regularly scheduled Council meeting.

Then there was Marie. She spoke not a word more than required by the Council rules of conduct. I asked Lil if Marie's muted behavior might bode well, but she shot that notion down. "I don't think so. When she's quiet, she's thinking how to get back at you."

I put that dark thought aside once the last words were said. We went home together and celebrated with a Chinese takeout dinner. That night, I went to sleep feeling more secure than I had in a long while.

I woke up at six a.m. to a beautiful sunny Friday morning. A clear sky and little wind. My weather app forecasted a scorcher, hitting close to ninety, but with a fair breeze developing later in the day. A good omen.

Plan of the day: shower and shave, breakfast of over-medium fried eggs and corned beef hash, followed by writing and then light, escapist reading. Bron was working and wouldn't get here until later that night.

Ed's latest email about surprisingly good book sales continued my lucky streak. Perhaps the publicity we'd arranged sparked sympathy or solidarity. Or the paperbacks were needed as fuel for more fires.

Good sales news put me in a writing frame of mind. A couple of hours racing through a list of research topics. Then an hour and a half tapping away on my laptop, resulting in another two thousand first draft words to *Surfmen*. A plot twist. A little more richness to one character. A couple of witty lines. Not bad at all, even in normal times.

The writing isn't the best part of historical fiction. For me, it's what I learn through research. For this one, the historical setting is locally focused. I'd been gathering every word I could find on the United States Lifesaving Service from the late 1800s to the early 1900s. The story weaves characters together as they face a climactic shipwreck. Fascinating stuff to a history buff like me.

As in most historical fiction, some of my characters are inspired by actual people. Others are created entirely out of my imagination. This morning, I decided on the fate of one of the imagined characters. Nothing is more fulfilling than to build every detail of a character's life and then kill them.

Reading over the draft, I corrected the obvious typos, redundancies, and grammatical issues. After saving and backing up the file, I did an important thing. I gave it a rest. I've found it helped to walk away from the story for a while. Plot holes and other inconsistencies will still be there waiting for me when editing starts for real. I took a seat on the balcony.

Yes, I thought, someone might try to kill me later, so why not enjoy life now? Sitting on the beach in the sun with a good read was what the doctor and antidepressants ordered.

In my experience, trips to the beach often make the logistics of the Normandy Invasion seem only slightly more daunting. From the bedroom, I got a ball cap, a rash guard shirt, and swim trunks. From the upstairs bath, I picked up a bottle of sunblock, a chapstick, and a pill bottle with ibuprofen and acetaminophen. Down to the basement to get a beach towel and a collapsible cooler, plus ice, three beers, and a couple of sodas from the basement fridge. Then off to the garage, where I kept the beach gear. Sand shoes, collapsible chair, and sunshade with poles and stakes. Last stop was the living room for the binoculars, a post-apocalyptic paperback novel, and my always fully charged cell phone. I loaded the gear into a wheeled pull cart for this expedition's sortie to the beach.

And one more thing. An acknowledgement of my new reality. A .45 caliber Model 1911A1 pistol, packed in a small black nylon range bag, with one magazine in the weapon. I tossed the pistol bag into the hand cart, along with my wallet. In it was my brand-new concealed carry permit.

Miracle of miracles, having passed my qualification shoot with a barely satisfactory score, I handed the concealed carry permit application to Detective Harrison. Somehow, Detective Harrison fast-tracked my permit. I picked it up yesterday. Harrison's only words to me were, "Remember, Vic. A gun is a hammer, and every problem becomes a nail."

On the beach, I set up the sunshade on a sandy spot in front of my house. I planted myself in the chair, a cool, not cold beer resting in the chair's arm sleeve, and the paperback in my hand. The binoculars hung off the left side of my chair. By my right side, over the chair's back, hung the pistol bag.

One thing was missing. Bron. I called her from the beach, but she couldn't skip work. That turned out to be fortunate.

Around eleven, after an hour of lazily reading about the fictional end of civilization, I saw the not-so-fictional apocalypse walking toward me. At first, all I could make out was maybe a couple of dozen people, men and women, dispersed in groups of three or four. No kids.

Glassing them with binoculars, still a hundred yards north of me, they seemed no different than the typical beach goers around here. Just more of them. They came with all the usual equipment, except for larger-than-usual coolers. A big, wheeled wagon carried more beach stuff, which they pulled with increasing frustration over the rocks and shells. As they got within thirty or so yards, I used the binoculars again. They were wearing the same white T-shirts.

Fuck me! It's NSAG! I had only seconds to decide what to do.

No time to pack up everything. They won't just walk by. They'll recognize me. Stay here, and something bad will happen. Move. Now.

Leaving the sunshade, chair and all the other beach gear behind, I pocketed my wallet and phone before grabbing the pistol bag. I decided against taking out the pistol.

As I started up the stairs over the rocks, I heard him. "Holt! Surprised to see us?" It was Little Führer, jogging up to me. He stopped only feet away, at the bottom of the stairs. He grinned, leaned up toward me, and held out his hand.

"No hard feelings there, Holt. Are we good?"

"No." Keeping my eyes on him, I walked over the stairs onto my lawn. Little Führer kept his place, still grinning. As he followed me up the rickety wooden stairs, he called after me.

"Hey buddy, no need to go. We're gonna have a little party here. Stick around! Have some fun! We still want to talk to you."

I yelled back over my shoulder, "No!" I kept walking. Little Führer turned to his crew. "Hey, guys! I don't think Holt wants us here. He must think he owns the whole fucking beach!" Laughter and curses came from the NSAG crew.

Three or four men joined Little Führer. They moved as a group, keeping pace with me across the lawn, yelling after me. I couldn't clearly hear what they said, but I'd heard enough. They wanted a fight.

Halfway to the house, sweating heavily now, I picked up the pace. NSAG was only about ten feet behind me, and I had a long way to go. I wouldn't make it to the house before they caught up with me.

Still walking with my back to them, I unzipped the pistol bag with my shaking hands. I took out the pistol and dropped the bag. Walking slower, I pulled back the slide to chamber a round and turned around.

There's something about that metal-on-metal sound of

readying a pistol that drowns out all other sounds. They stopped immediately.

Holding the pistol flat across my chest, I said, "Back up. Get off my land."

Little Führer held his arms out front with open hands. His widening eyes told me he didn't expect to be facing death this day. They all stopped.

"Hey, Holt! What the fuck! No need for that!" Squatting down, I picked up the range bag and, without looking, tossed it up onto the deck. Backing up one foot at a time, I kept the pistol close to my chest. My hands still trembled. I was well and truly scared.

Reaching the deck stairs, I turned to walk up one slow step at a time. As I got to the top of the stairs, one NSAG fool broke ranks and rushed the steps.

A nail. I've got a hammer.

In an unthinking move, I raised the gun in a two-handed grip, its hammer already cocked back, patiently awaiting word from the trigger. Aiming down the stairs at a stupid man's chest—center mass—my finger moved to the trigger. Two pounds of pressure, and he dies.

"Back . . . the . . . fuck . . . up!" He stopped.

"Mike! Get off those stairs, Mike. Now!" It was Little Führer. "I said now!" Mike delayed only a second or two before obeying orders. Turning around, he flipped the bird all the way down.

Even in retreat, Little Führer had to have the final say. "Holt. We're gonna have our party now. If we're too loud, too fucking bad." They all started back to the beach. I lowered the pistol to my side.

I had to sit down. Panting, sweating, I planted myself on the deck table bench. Just as I laid the pistol down on the table, vomit filled my mouth. Leaping for the deck railing, I let it all go onto the grass. Most of it anyway.

The reality of almost killing that man had hit me. One trigger squeeze, and he would have died, and my own life changed for the worse. And for all I know, I might've panicked and shot the rest of them. Two pounds of pressure away from charges of manslaughter or murder in the second degree. Decades to build a life; an instant to destroy one.

As I wiped my mouth with my hand and took a deep breath, I realized I'd stupidly left a cocked and loaded weapon on the table. Before picking up the pistol, I carefully thought through all the steps of rendering the weapon safe and kept doing that until I calmed down. That took a while.

With my right hand, I thumbed the magazine release, finger held outside the trigger guard. I pulled the slide back with my left hand until it found its notch, locking it safely and ejecting the round in the chamber. Ignoring the round as it fell off the table and onto the deck, I looked inside the chamber to confirm the obvious. Now with an empty chamber, I pushed the slide stop down to let it spring forward. Putting my left thumb between the hammer and the firing plate, I eased the hammer down with my right thumb. Before putting the now safe and unloaded pistol back in the range bag, I picked up the ejected round and loaded it back into the magazine. Pleased I hadn't shot myself accidentally, I put the pistol back in the range bag, leaving it on the deck table.

By then, NSAG had set up umbrellas and chairs, appropriating my chair, sunshade and towels. Beers cracked open, accompanied by heavy metal music, loud enough that everyone up and down the shore must've heard it.

The flag of the United States went up, alongside their very own NSAG flag, which looked like a large mock-up of their hoodie logo. That's when they all turned toward me and chanted "FUCK YOU HOLT!" Again, and again. Then NSAG brought out something I thought I'd never see in my lifetime.

NSAG unfurled a huge Nazi swastika flag.

The shock and disbelief of witnessing this obscenity to human civilization lasted only a moment before being swept away by red-hot anger. Without thinking, I reached for the range bag.

They are nails; I have a hammer.

Whether my impulse was serious or merely a murderous fantasy, I can't be sure. The moment passed. I did not go down to the beach. I sat back down and called the police. Until they arrived, I recorded NSAG on my phone. In ten or twelve minutes, the cops were talking to me on my deck.

I pointed to the range bag. "You should know my pistol is right there, officer. It's unloaded. Didn't fire it. But I brought it with me, just in case."

After examining my pistol to confirm it was safe, one cop asked me how I used the weapon. I told him everything. Almost. I didn't tell him I'd leveled the weapon at that man, Mike's chest. I lied. I don't know why I lied. A lie of omission, perhaps excusable under the circumstances, but a lie which nonetheless was a crime.

"Officer, you must know these people were here before. They're violating a restraining order by coming . . ." He interrupted me. "Yeah. We know all about that. The book burning."

When asked if NSAG complied with my demand to leave my property, I said yes, but only after I displayed the pistol.

"So, you were sitting down on the beach. You saw them coming. You had your pistol with you, but you left the beach. Four of them followed you to your house. They trespassed, but they didn't assault you. But when they saw your pistol, they went back to the beach."

"Yes, but they came on my property. And there's the restraining order. Can't you do something about them now?"

"Mr. Holt, we'll go down and talk to them. Make a report. Someone else will sort out the restraining order." He motioned to his partner and said, "Come on. Let's get this done."

While the first cop seemed blasé about NSAG, the other cop lingered long enough to say, "Like anyone else, they have a right to the beach. If it's any comfort, they can't camp out overnight. Town ordinance against that."

"I understand about the beach access. Moot point about them overnighting, officer." I added, "Tide will come in around seven tonight. It'll be a real high one. King tide. That'll drown any campsite."

"Good. Wish we had an ordinance against that goddamn Nazi flag. Free speech, I guess. Above my pay grade. Anyway, we'll tell them to keep the music down and stay off your property. After we leave, if anything happens, call us."

Thanking him, I watched him as he caught up with his partner. From what I could see, NSAG seemed cooperative. NSAG turned down the music. After only ten minutes or so, the cops headed back to me.

Before the cops left, they asked me if there was anything else I wanted to add to my statement. I said, "No, officer. Nothing." I lied again. The officers departed. As they left, I called Bron. She arrived an hour after I called her. No niceties, she acted more as my prospective criminal defense attorney. In the living room, I went through every step of the incident, including the full story of Mike and the pistol. All the while, NSAG partied hard down on the beach.

I said to Bron, "I might've shot him if he hadn't stopped. Christ, if their leader hadn't told him to stop." Even without that part of the story, Bron thought the police response was rather cursory. "Not that it's, in this circumstance, a bad thing. Don't understand why they didn't arrest the ones who trespassed."

"Okay, suppose it goes to court. How's that gonna turn out?" As tired and scared as I was, I'm not sure I understood or even heard all Bron said. But I got enough.

But if it did go to court, NSAG's Little Führer could claim he held out his hand in friendship; an attempt to make amends. I was hostile and showed a weapon. His friends then moved to protect him.

Her defense argument would rest upon my very reasonable fear of harm from NSAG. These same men threatened me during the book burning. They were known to carry knives, and one of them had a concealed carry permit. Four of them trespassed even after I warned them. I did not display my weapon until I'd reached my house. She'd argue self-defense. Mike had charged up the stairs, but I did not shoot. NSAG trespassed in violation of a restraining order and were confronted by the outnumbered property owner and licensed gun owner.

"Besides, Vic. Damn few potential jurors like Nazis, or so we could hope."

"At the same time, Vic, the court may find you threatened unarmed men with a firearm when they had not overtly threatened you. And you didn't include that in your statement to the police. Though I would argue you were defending your home, you were not in your home. You had an avenue of escape. You could have gone inside and locked the doors. Or simply run away."

My dismal expression must have tipped her off. "After the cops talked to NSAG, it's strange the cops didn't ask you about pointing the pistol at that guy Mike. You'd think NSAG would've told the police about that. I guess they didn't. So, Vic, maybe there's little reason to worry about all this."

Her legal tasks done, Bron said she had news. "Looks like I'll have more time to work on your case."

"Huh? What do you mean?"

"The firm partners had a late-night meeting yesterday. After I'd gone home. They demanded I drop your case." That same cold stab of fear went through my stomach.

"I resigned," Bron said that offhandedly, as if she'd said nothing more serious than it would be raining today. On the other hand, I was not calm. "What?"

"Relax, Vic. Not as bad as it sounds."

"Not as bad . . . Bron. What the fuck!"

"Vic, don't worry. I'm still going to represent you. Like I said, I've even more time available."

"Bron, come on. How can you not be upset? I'm not worried about me. You, I'm worried about."

"Don't. I'm fine. Here's how it all happened."

Bron gave the whole truth and nothing but the truth. The bomb threat, accompanied by threatening phone calls and emails, spooked the partners. For the safety of their staff, they told Bron that she must end my case. When Bron refused, they gave her two options. Resign or be fired.

"Well, I'm no fool. If I decide to look for another job, a resignation doesn't look as bad." Bron ended the news by mentioning she'd given them two weeks' notice and accepted a decent severance package. "No doubt to persuade me not to sue them."

When I asked what she'd do now, she had the barebones of a plan. "Oh, not much for now." Finish up loose ends at the firm, maybe pick up legal work with Anthony, and continue with the law school gig. "I'm not worried. You shouldn't be worried . . ."

"Well, I am. Jesus, I feel like I'm . . ."

"Somehow responsible? We've had this talk before. My decision. If cowards run that firm, well, to hell with them." Bron leaned across the table and said, "Besides, I'll need more time off anyway if I'm ever to move in with you." She leaned forward and kissed me.

"Well, honey, got to go. My soon-to-be former office expects me for a meeting." She laughed that off, kissed me one more time, and went out the door.

I stayed sitting on an Adirondack rocker, keeping watch on NSAG until they left. NSAG did their best to be irritating. They'd see me and give me the finger. No surprise the music got louder after the cops left. I let that go. They'd make a show of darting up to the lawn, then quickly back away. It became a popular sport to piss on my beach roses. The number of beer cans thrown onto my lawn grew by the hour.

For my sanity's sake, I decided on a simple rule. Call the cops only if they did something serious, like trying to rush up and kill me. Until that happens, let them enjoy the beach.

As I predicted, the band of happy, drunken Nazis kept the party going until high tide came in at about 7 p.m. NSAG packed things up, including my sunshade, chair, and cart. They left behind every form of garbage imaginable before starting their drunken trek back to their cars. As one last gesture of defiance, half of them formed a line on my lawn and renewed the chorus of "FUCK HOLT!" But in the end, they left.

Throughout the night, the hammer stayed on my nightstand, waiting for a nail to appear.

PART II

THE LONG NIGHT

CHAPTER THIRTY-EIGHT

WHY AND HOW

Ford

It'd been a shitty day. A hardscaping project I was supervising went south. We used a small front-end loader tractor to even out the ground for the customer's new patio. The idiot operating the tractor didn't see the boulder buried under a berm of dirt we had to move. The result: the boulder didn't move, and the scoop snapped. Expensive to fix.

The tractor operator caught hell from me. Maybe I shouldn't have screamed at him, but I wasn't about to let all this fall back on me. He didn't like it when I showed him how the boulder was peeking out from the dirt on the reverse side and asked why he didn't check first. He got so pissed at me that he walked off the job. The broken tractor scoop was bad enough, but losing a worker when we're already short-handed was worse.

When I called the boss about the broken scoop. I told her the tractor operator screwed up and walked off the job. She cut me off, yelling, "Listen, Jeff. You should've checked that berm, too! That's what a supervisor does!" She told me to have the guys come in tomorrow morning, Saturday, to get the job back on track. They didn't like that. To hell with them, I thought. It wasn't my fault.

My short time as a supervisor hadn't been easy. Some things went well. Some things did not. This broken scoop job was way into the category of not well. The equipment will get fixed. The rest of the crew is dependable, but I'll have to watch them like hawks.

When the day finally ended, I got home pissed, frustrated, and exhausted. I tried to move on. Flop down on the couch with a takeout sandwich, chips, and a beer. Watch TV and try to forget about the day. But I couldn't shake an uneasy feeling about my future.

As much as I tried to dismiss my doubts, I couldn't get rid of the feeling that maybe she's already washed me out as a supervisor. The boss was angry. She'd never yelled at me like that before. The possibility that she'd fire me over something that wasn't my fault only made me angrier. And if I get fired—I won't accept being demoted—then what comes next? What jobs are out there for me? Jobs worthy of me.

I didn't know. I had no idea what to do.

That realization became a kind of parasite infecting my thoughts, untreatable, leaving me damaged and certain my future was dying. That night, my bed partner was a building despair that I faced a life alone working a meaningless job. Unwanted and wholly dependent on my parents for a place to live. And what if that ended? What if they flat-out abandoned me and kicked me out of this house? Do they really care about their disappointment of a son? Will I wind up on the street?

A break needed to come my way. Something had to happen to get me what I knew I was due. But that break wouldn't fall from the sky. I had to make that break myself.

Unable to sleep, I got up and found myself wandering from room to room, desperately trying to calm my mind. I needed that perfect opportunity that couldn't come to me by chance. I had to make that opportunity happen. Then I remembered a question that had been rattling around in my head for weeks.

Was Holt my opportunity? Perhaps, but I was still uncertain. I'll confess that until that night, I saw taking out Holt as more of a fantasy than a reality. But there I was. Facing a dead end in my job and maybe my whole life. It seemed as good a time as any to try and find the answer.

I grabbed a legal sheet and a pen from my dad's desk, reminding myself to burn any notes or doodling in the fireplace. I wrote the word WHY in caps and circled it. My thinking was that a good explanation of Why might help answer the question of How. I wrote my thoughts out like I was writing an essay for school. It went something like this.

> *Why kill Holt? Simple. I can't waste my life in a boring job. There's something greater for me. My life will count for something. The Army didn't give me a fair chance. I don't want college. I must make my own chances. That starts with showing people what I can do. That I'm better than they are. That I can do what they can't. Or won't. Killing Holt shows up all those do-nothing cowards. Killing Holt will bring meaning to my life.*
>
> *No one else can be involved. All credit must go to me. Besides, involving anyone else only increases the chances of being caught. I'm not on a suicide mission. I gain nothing if I'm caught or killed.*
>
> *Holt must die in a way that has maximum effect. That means terror. People must see the terror on Holt's face as he dies badly. People will then fear me.*

All that led to How. I started jotting things down on how I imagined the killing playing out.

Drive-by shooting won't do. Too quick. Too many things I couldn't control.

When I take Holt, I'll use the GHB to get him under control. Take him to a controlled space, like my basement. Heavy plastic sheets along the floor, walls, and ceiling, all stapled in place. Tie him up on the cot. Scare him. I've got a gun. Force him to read a statement confessing his crimes. Make sure the video records his face. Then shoot him.

Question: Is a gunshot to the head really a good idea?

Dramatic, yes. But messy. Lots to clean up. Use a big knife and cut his head off? How do you cut off someone's head? Maybe just cut his throat and keep cutting. Even more blood to clean up.

But if I don't shoot or knife him, how do I kill him? Poison? I could give him the rest of the GHB and hope he stops breathing. That won't work. The problem with a quick death is that it is quick. I want people to see him struggling. Victor Holt must die violently.

Hanging? Fighting to breathe would make a good video. But I'd have to get him off the cot. That might give him a chance to get free. A garotte? Maybe. But how do you use a garotte?

Then it hit me.

Suffocate Holt. Put a plastic bag tightly over his head. A clear plastic bag so everyone can see his face. Use duct tape to seal it tight around his neck. He'll scream until he can't scream anymore. The best part: it's clean. Suffocation leaves no mess. No matter how much I clean up in the basement, with blood, there will always be some left.

How do I get rid of his body?

I'll strip his body of clothing and anything that might identify him. Then roll him from the cot onto the plastic sheets that cover the basement floor. Roll him up again in extra plastic sheets. Seal the sheets with more duct tape. Wrap him again in a dark green tarp using heavy tie down straps. To get the body upstairs, I'll use the straps to haul it up the basement stairs, carefully, one step at a time. Drag him to the garage. Put him in my SUV. It means heavy lifting, but I'm in good shape.

Bury him or throw him in the water? If I bury him, that means he's always there, waiting to be found. So, burying him in the dirt doesn't work. If I dump him in the ocean, weighed down with rocks, he'll go to the bottom. Maybe the currents take him out to sea. Maybe the fish eat him. Anyway, he'll rot. It could be days before he floats up. Someone might report him missing by then, but that won't matter.

Everything in the basement gets thrown out. I'll burn his clothes. I'll throw into the ocean the camera, tripod, and cot, and anything else Holt or I touched. Except my gun. I'll keep that. Never know when I might need it.

But where do I sink him? I can't just roll him off the beach. I can't be seen, so I need a secluded spot. The water must be deep.

I had to think about that for a while. I didn't have so much as a rowboat. Renting a boat leaves behind a paper trail. Plus I know nothing about boats. Dropping him off one of the bridges around here was a possibility, but I decided against it. Someone's sure to drive by and see me. I also remembered reading somewhere that they have closed-circuit cameras up on all the bridges.

So, boats, bridges, and beaches are out. I needed a place where I could manhandle his body out of the car and drop him directly into deep water without being seen. A place close by. Not a good idea to drive around very long late at night with a body in my car.

Turns out, there was a place like that. A place where I used to jump off into the water when I was a kid. The old ferry landing!

Long ago, before they built Collin Bridge, a ferry operated from the same landing. They made it out of huge granite blocks. Concrete walls right by very deep water. The tides are strong. Though there's a small park there now, there are no lights and only one way in and out. Only two homes around there. It's hardly a two-minute drive from my place. If I can, I'll dump him at night just as the tide starts to go out.

Dropping the pen, I said aloud to myself, "Okay, genius, but how do you grab him?"

Can't do a straight-forward home invasion. If it's me against him, I'd lose. It'd be noisy breaking down his front door or crashing through a window. Does he have a home alarm? I have a gun, but what if Holt does? I don't want a fair fight. Kidnapping Holt away from his home is the only option.

Get him as he leaves home? No. He doesn't work and doesn't have a routine like a commuter. I'd have to

> *secretly watch his house from a hideaway somewhere in sight of his place. Maybe the beach. Or the woods across the road from his house. Squatting in the woods would get me nothing more than a bad tick infection. Where'd I park? How'd I get to my car once I saw him leave? When can I do this? I got to work. Then I'd have to follow him to a place that I knew nothing about.*

Nothing made any sense. No matter how many times I ran through all the possible ways I could kidnap him, it came down to this: I had no way of knowing where he'd be and when he'd be there. Time and place. Unless I had that information, my plan was useless.

Little sleep came to me that night as I fixated on a simple question.

How do I kidnap him?

CHAPTER THIRTY-NINE

THE LAST LINK

Holt

Bron's move into my home was taking longer than I wanted. I called her to see how she was coming along.

"Everything's going well. Almost done handing over my cases. I should be done by the end of this week. Oh, you'll like this. Tomorrow we're filing a suit against NSAG. When I say we, I mean me, assisted by a couple of my law students. One told me he wanted a neo-Nazi hunting trophy for his wall."

Bron went on to update me on NSAG's violation of the restraining order, saying she called the judge who issued the order. "I expect he won't be pleased."

"Sounds great, Bron. But, you know, you could work from here. I've got space. You can use my desk . . ."

"Yeah, nice of you to offer, but I still need my office at the firm. And I've got a workstation set up in my condo. And anyway, I'm way behind in packing up my stuff from the condo. And if I moved in before I got all this done, well, I'm afraid you'd be too much of a, ah, distraction. Understand?"

It was a shame she couldn't see how I smiled.

"So, Vic, this weekend, I'll finish packing up. Movers are

coming on Saturday to pick up the heavy stuff for storage. Time for me to get back to work. Love you. Bye."

Thoughts of Saturday night to come left me on a positive note. Meanwhile, I continued my campaign to resume a normal life.

Tuesday started with a little writing and more research. Breakfast and lunch were hasty, light, and tasteless affairs, followed by a late afternoon of unwisely scrolling through online hate. By the time I scrolled over the twentieth accusation of treason, it struck me that staying inside all day was hardly in keeping with an aggressive resumption of normalcy.

Screw it! I want a cocktail. I'm going out for dinner!

I picked one of my former usual places. *Robert's.* Nothing fancy. A comfortable tavern on the main drag in the Harbor Park part of town. Within sight of the water, it's a legacy establishment from another era. It had a worn feeling, inside and out, that took a customer back decades. Décor defined by a random collection of old beer and liquor logos, long since abandoned by their sponsors, was displayed behind the long, wood-grained bar. The bar chairs cracked green leather upholstery had long ago exceeded their life span. Here and there, rust-colored water stains marked several of the overhead ceiling tiles. By the front door, the nearly paper-thin floor tiles are worn clean of color.

Most interesting was a wall-mounted collection of old photographs. Harbor Park in the old days, before the hurricane ninety years ago wiped away the amusement park, roller-skating arena, and almost all the homes. And nearly a hundred lives.

I loved the place.

Decent cocktails. Burgers, sandwiches, and a selection of tasty entrées. Fish and chips or steak and fries. Sometimes a special of ribs. Good, solid comfort food. And inexpensive.

At this time of year, the clientele is a mix of townie regulars, summer residents, and stray tourists. Fridays and weekends are usually the busiest nights. It being Tuesday, I anticipated, correctly, not many patrons would be there. There was a party of two at the first high-top table. At the far end of the bar sat three other guys, side by side. I took a bar stool at the other end.

God, it felt good to get out! More than good. Liberated! Freed from my self-imposed imprisonment. Eating a bacon cheeseburger—it'd been so long since I had one—a side of fries and a cold mug of a local brew, I watched a game on the television. Third inning, Red Sox versus Baltimore at Camden Yards. Scored tied, 1 to 1. The Baltimore hitter sent one into the right field stands, and all I could do was smile and laugh. Not that I'm a Sox or Orioles fan. Those days ended long ago. The game's just too damn slow for my taste. That night, however, I'd felt as happy watching a cricket match in Scotland.

Shifting on my stool, a reminder of what I carried under my jacket bumped into the bar edge. A shoulder holster with my pistol. At least the light rain allowed me the pretense of wearing a light jacket to cover the weapon. This was my first time carrying concealed in public. Though perfectly legal, it unnerved me. On one hand, I had to be able to defend myself, and my hidden cannon could do that very well. On the other hand, it scared the shit out of me. Theoretically, being armed should lessen my anxiety. However, that theory wasn't supported by my feelings. I'd reach inside the jacket and anxiously tap the pistol with my fingers to make sure everything was okay.

After dinner was done and cleared away, I ordered a coffee and a dessert. Cheesecake with a scoop of vanilla ice cream. My favorite. Time taken for dessert meant more exposure, but I was determined to linger in my rediscovered happiness, believing if I am to die soon, I might as well die sated.

A crashing noise startled me and quickly left me with a wide smile. Bursting through the kitchen entry doors came a big man dressed in a white work shirt and black pants. It was Hank, the chef and owner. Years ago, when he took over the restaurant,

Hank kept the old name out of respect for the former owner. Hank was a well-known character around town, a local version of Shakespeare's Falstaff. Boisterous, beefy, and the nicest guy you'd ever meet. He slapped me on the back as he slid onto the barstool next to me.

"Jesus! Vic! Great to see you! Been a while, hasn't it?"

We spent the next few minutes catching up on things. Susan and I had been regulars, showing up twice, sometimes three times a month. Along the way, we got to know Hank and his perpetual girlfriend, Janice. When I asked him once when they'd finally get married, Hank gave me the same answer he always did. "Someday. Not today. Someday."

The conversation paused as Hank got serious. He grabbed hold of my hand as it rested on the bar and asked, "How are things, Vic? I mean, with what's been going on with you." He wasn't going to let go until I answered.

When most people ask questions like that, they typically want to get the subject out of the way, to check a box for their sense of morality, and then move on to something lighter and more comfortable. With Hank, on this night, he looked genuinely worried about me.

"I'm, ah, okay. Thanks for asking. Yeah, really." Hank didn't release his grip.

"You seem, well, a little less than okay, Vic. If you don't mind me saying." It was time for honesty on my part.

"Shows that much, huh? Well, I guess you'd be right. Not been easy, since Susan, ah, and all this shit . . ." I stopped to check my self-control and carefully select my words. Hank filled the void.

"Yeah. A fine lady. I'm so sorry, Vic."

Hank didn't have to say anything. Few had offered me the gift of committed friendship as did this good soul. When Susan was killed, like many others, Hank came to the wake and the funeral. Unlike all the others, Hank took that extra step. Every day for a couple of weeks afterward, he dropped off a prepared meal at my house. Sometimes I'd greet him at the door. Or I'd find a casserole dish on the front step with a note that said, "Thinking of you. Hank." Later, I'd return the cleaned dishes to his restaurant, always making a point of thanking him in person and offering to pay. He shrugged off every offer, saying that "this is just what people do."

"Yeah, guess I'm, ah, still trying to deal with Susan. I'm told it's normal. Been seeing a therapist. But, yeah, I'm okay. Well, better. Then there's what's been happening lately. The book, I mean. I'm sure you heard."

Sitting on the barstool, Hank stayed quiet and patiently waited for me to answer. I wanted to be honest but lie enough to spare him the worst details.

"Oh yeah. I heard." Hank didn't look away. "Saw the news about the book burning. Listen, I talked to a couple of cops in town, including Harrison. He comes here. You know him, right? Anyway, I've got at least an idea of what's going on with you. Sorry, man. Look, anything I can do?"

"Thanks, Hank. Really. No, really, I don't think so."

I sipped my coffee before continuing. "Matter of fact, I've got a good lawyer who hates the bastards more than me. And there's Detective Harrison. He's got my back. So, I think, with their help, and time, this will eventually, ah, wind down."

Hank said, "Good. Glad to hear it. Hey, this is a bar. Guys get to talking. If I ever hear anything, I'll let Harrison know."

I thanked him again. Then Hank's smile disappeared. "Jesus, Vic, maybe I should have come over. See how you're doing. I'm sorry."

I gently brushed his guilt aside. "No, no, please don't think that. What's to be sorry about? Goes the other way too, you know. Really, Hank, coming out to see me right now, to talk to me, it means, yeah, it helps. A whole lot."

Hank modestly dismissed my sentiment as well and said, "I've got to get back to work." We shook hands, and Hank clasped my shoulder. He had something else to say.

"I want you to understand something, Vic. There're people around here, more than maybe you think, who support you. I've heard it. Just wanted you to know that. I'll see you again, here, right?"

"Yes. I'll be back." I held out my hand for one more handshake. Grasping his hand with both of mine, in a trembling voice, I said, "And thanks, Hank. See you later." With that, Hank disappeared into the kitchen. It was time for me to leave. When I put my card on the table, the barkeep gave it back to me. "Hank said it's on the house."

Tearing up, I told the barkeep, "Hank's already done so much for me. I really, I just can't let him do that. Here." I took out three twenties and laid them on the bar. "That should be enough. Thank you. You keep the change." Walking out into the twilight, I felt less alone.

As was my habit, my cynicism dragged me down from that emotional high. If there are people in town who support me, where have they been? The question answered itself. They've stayed hidden and silent. Silence. Silence in the face of . . . evil? As I pulled into my driveway, a quote struggled to be remembered. Fragments from Dr. King. Something about the silence of good people. All evil needs is the silence of good people.

Good people see evil but often fear openly condemning evil. A head in the sand is safer. It's simply human nature. Most turn away and try to get on with their lives while hoping someone else makes the monsters go away.

Doffing my street clothes for pajamas, I sat myself in front of my laptop. On my reactivated Social media accounts, I posted a long note of thanks to Hank and *Robert's*, saying I'd be back on Thursday night.

CHAPTER FORTY

FINDING THE KEY

Ford

The boss didn't fire me, but she made it clear my permanent promotion to supervisor was in serious doubt. Saying I treated the tractor operator poorly and made her staffing problem worse. Shorthanded and with big money jobs on the line, maybe she couldn't afford to immediately fire me.

Once this job ended, I felt certain the boss would let me go.

Slamming down a breakfast of a bagel and coffee, I checked Holt's social media on my phone. He'd restarted his media a few days ago, and I was simply curious if he had anything to say. He did. He gave me the answer. Holt posted that tomorrow night, Thursday, he'd have dinner at a local restaurant, *Robert's*. Like a gift from heaven, I had both time and place for Holt.

The irony, I thought. The answer to when and where to take Holt did not come to me in my dreams. The answer came from Holt himself.

I'd never eaten at *Robert's*, but I knew it wasn't a fancy place. At any of those higher-end places in town, I would've been out of place; stuck out like a sore thumb. Also, Holt's post didn't say anything about going with someone else. Another plus, because my plan required Holt to be alone.

Was I really going to do this? I don't recall thinking through any kind of answer then, but I do remember jumping up from the table to puke in the kitchen sink. When the last spasm ended, with vomited fragments of bagel mixed with coffee in the sink, I wiped my mouth with a paper towel. Nausea triggered by reality. Staring over the sink through the window, I realized this was no longer a game. Things had to happen quickly, if they were to happen at all.

Straightening myself, I took a deep breath, hoping to settle my mind and stomach. The wall clock told me I was going to be late for work if I didn't leave immediately.

On the drive to work, I decided to recon *Robert's* after work. Pick a spot to park. Check the neighborhood. Look for security cameras. Go inside and have dinner. Buy a beer and nurse it slowly. Watch the staff. Look over the customers. Are there high-tops? A bar? Table or booth seats? I wanted to find out as much as I could.

Then came my pep talk. If it turns out *Robert's* won't work, I'll lose nothing by waiting for another place and time. If Holt doesn't show tomorrow, no harm, no foul. If he did show and I couldn't take him, then I can still go back to the drawing board. I'm the one in charge. I will always have the initiative. I'm the one with all the time in the world.

If I do abort, I'll carry on with my normal life. A normal life that had started to fall apart.

CHAPTER FORTY-ONE

DRESS REHEARSAL

Ford

At seven that night, after sunset, I took a seat at the far end of the bar, next to the wall. From there, I silently assessed the entire joint while sipping a beer, waiting for my order of a burger and fries.

In the back was a gravel parking lot, though with only limited spaces. On two sides, solid plank fencing obscured the view of the lot from surrounding homes. The lot entrance had no gate. The one weak spotlight left much of the lot in the dark. A streetlight by the lot entrance didn't add much light either. No security camera that I saw, anywhere around the building. No camera visible from the single-story office building across the street. Customers could enter the restaurant from the lot through a back door, as well as the front door on the street.

Inside, the place was a typical neighborhood bar. Half a dozen tables in a one-step lower dining area as you came in. A bar that went three-quarters the length of the upper room. High-tops and small tables in the bar area by the windows on the street side. Behind the bar, booze bottles against the wall. A couple of TVs.

Restrooms off an aisle that led past the bar and kitchen. The back entrance was at the end of that same aisle.

Based on this investigation, I came up with two critical conditions. First, the back lot is the best place to take him. It's shielded and dark. Therefore, Holt must park in the back lot, and I must be certain he does. I'll arrive at the restaurant ahead of him. When I see him come in, I'll slip outside to check where he parked. Everyone knows what his truck looks like. If possible, I'll move my car next to his truck. If he parks in the street, it's game over. No point in kidnapping him right in front of all the neighbors.

Second, it must be a slow night. The fewer people around, the better.

I'd already considered an alternative, an easy way out. As he leaves the restaurant, follow him out and shoot him. Then where he parked wouldn't matter. Then again, Holt might have a gun. He could shoot me first and that is definitely not the outcome I want.

Ambushing him wasn't what I wanted. He needs to die in the right way. He needs to suffer. I want him to confess. And record it all.

Munching on the last of my fries, I thought about how I'd dose him with the GHB. Things could go sideways when dosing Holt. To state the obvious, somehow I had to slip the dose into his drink and do so completely unnoticed by Holt or anyone else. So, I set two more important conditions.

First, he must come alone and eat alone, away from any others. Buddying up to him at the bar and then dosing him when he's distracted would be a monumentally bad idea. Someone might see us together and later tell the cops I was the last person to have seen him. I must be as invisible as possible and still get to his drink.

Second, the dose must be timed to within five to ten minutes before he leaves. Five would be best. Yet I had zero control over that. The best I could hope for is he'd do something like walk away from his seat for a minute or two. If that happens, and after I dose him, I'd leave ahead of him and wait outside in my car. If I'm lucky,

Holt gets very groggy as he reaches his car. I take him then, stuff him into my car, and get the hell out of there.

Though being a novice to major crimes like kidnapping, I appreciated not everything can be precisely planned out or anticipated. I could always abort, even after he gets the GHB.

His truck was one detail I couldn't do anything about. Going back afterwards with Holt's keys and driving the truck away was an unnecessary risk and just plain stupid. Why let someone see me with his keys and his truck? The day after he disappears, I'm sure someone will notice Holt's truck in the parking lot. By then it won't matter. Holt will be dead.

After paying for my dinner in cash, I left *Robert's. This will work; time to get the GHB doses ready.*

CHAPTER FORTY-TWO

EXECUTION

Ford

My plan fell apart.

Grabbing Holt went well. Holt happened to park his truck right next to my SUV. He came alone. It was a slow night. Holt went to the john just before he finished and paid. I walked by his bar stool and slipped the GHB into his unfinished drink, a move I'd practiced at home with a little envelope of folded paper and sugar as a stand-in for GHB.

I waited for him in the parking lot. Holt was staggering by the time he came outside. A couple of smacks and a shove, and I had him passed out in the back with a black hood over his head and covered by a dark green tarp. All in all, this part of the plan worked out better than I could've hoped.

The only surprise was that Holt had worn his gun. That was the first thing I took from him. A nice piece, I thought, but it had to go into the bay with everything else.

Getting him downstairs from the garage wasn't easy, but it was only a matter of lifting a heavy weight. Or a soon to be dead weight. He collected scrapes and bruises on the way down. Not that he'd ever notice.

For the first couple of hours, I had him strapped to the cot, laying him on his side. I saw no point in him choking to death on his own vomit. True, dead is still dead, but I wanted the show.

By eleven, he was still out cold. Figuring by then there was little chance that he'd throw up, I rolled up the hood just enough so I could put the gag on. My best guess was around midnight, an hour later, he'd wake up, and then I could get to work breaking him.

Holt woke up right on time. Judging from his crying and moaning, and urine-soaked pants, my midnight mind games with the pistol worked. After checking he was still secured to the cot, I went upstairs for my little movie break while the darkness and his fears broke him even more.

When I later went back down into the basement, with my mask back on, I saw Holt wasn't moving. For a second, I thought he'd already died, a horrible disappointment, until I saw his head jerk.

Honestly, I couldn't help but smile.

Just before I gave him his orders, and the false promise of freedom if he complied, it came to me that I'd fucked up.

Flat on his back and all tied up, Holt wouldn't be able to read the confession. Those were my words, and just as important as his death. Without my script, the world wouldn't know Holt's crimes. They wouldn't understand why he needed to die. No one would see the good in his execution. But lying flat on his back and his arms duct taped to his sides, Holt couldn't hold the paper up to see and read it. Lying flat, if I freed his arms so he could hold the paper and read it, the paper would get in the way of a clear recording of Holt's face. People wouldn't see the terror in his eyes.

I changed my plan on-the-fly. I'd get Holt off the cot so he could sit up with his arms freed enough to hold the script lower than his face, as if he were reading a morning paper resting on his lap. Lucky for me, there were metal folding chairs in the corner that my parents had left behind. I simply re-taped him to the chair.

Still wacked-out from the drug, Holt hardly resisted when I

cut his chest, arms and legs free of the cot. I kept his legs bound together at his ankles. The tricky part was retaping his arms. It was too dangerous to leave his entire arms unbound. I taped his wrists together before I wrapped duct tape around the chair back and his upper arms. That still left his forearms free at the elbow so he could hold the paper in his bound hands.

Aside from this repositioning, the plan remained the same. After he finished reading, I'd slip that plastic bag over his head and tape it tight around his neck. The world will see him suffocate to death.

It was time. I readied the camera before I took off his hood. The gag stayed in. His eyes went wide, looking every which way. He was breathing fast, as if he'd fallen into ice-cold water. I slapped him gently across the face to get his attention. When his eyes focused on me, I gave him his orders. That turned out to be harder for me than I expected. Excited, nervous, I stumbled over my first words. After I cleared my throat and took a deep breath, I started over.

"Holt, I know this is hard, but you need to do what I tell you, and then everything will be fine." I did my best to speak clearly and slowly, even friendly like. Kindness. Empathy.

Holt stayed fixed on what little he could see of my face—my eyes. I couldn't help but imagine what Holt saw. Here he is, bound up, hungover, looking up at a man in a black sweatshirt, black gloves, and a turtleneck, his face hidden by a black balaclava. Except his eyes.

"That's it, my friend. Slower, yeah. Breathe slower. That's it. Don't worry. Good. Good." I kept that up for a minute or two, talking to him like he was a frightened, helpless child. Which, in a way, he was.

"That's better. Good. Okay, please listen to me. I'm going to hand you a sheet of paper. Please hold it in both your hands. Then I'll remove the gag. Do not yell or say anything, or the gag goes back in. When I tell you, read what is on the paper. Word for word.

Do not say anything that is not in the script. Please, read it clearly and loudly. I will record everything. That's all I want. When you're done, I'll cut enough tape so you can go up the stairs. I'll blindfold and gag you again, sorry, but I will let you go. I'll help you leave. This all ends. No worries." I let that sink in.

"But, if you try anything, you know I have a gun. I will shoot you if you try anything. I don't want to, but I will if you force me to. Now, nod yes if you understand." Holt nodded.

After setting the camera on the tripod, I handed him the script and removed the gag, dropping it on the floor. I got behind the camera.

"Okay, Holt. Start. Ah, please."

CHAPTER FORTY-THREE

ABOUT TO DIE

Holt

I don't clearly remember everything about that night. How could I? The drug and a concussion left gaps. Add to that, surviving memories mixed with my nightmares, making it hard to know anything for certain. That said, I've done what I can to put things back together.

The hood coming off shocked me. If I could lobotomize the memory of that first blurry sight of him, I'd do it myself with a rusty icepick. A man close to my face, wearing a black mask. A man I did not know, who tortured me.

He spoke to me, but I struggled to hear, let alone understand. Something was wrong with my right ear. My thoughts were a dribble of nonsensical words. Though barely conscious, I sensed being taken off the cot and then tied up on a chair.

Whatever he did to me was wearing off. As the minutes passed, I began to understand his words. He kept telling me to calm down, stay quiet and not yell. I did as he said. I had no choice. As confused as I was, one thing was clear to me. If I didn't do something, anything, he would kill me.

He pushed a sheet of paper into my hands. When the gag came

out, I reflexively went into a coughing fit. When that subsided, I looked down at the paper as he kept talking. I'm sure he said he'd let me go if I read the words on the paper out loud. And just as sure he'd kill me as soon as I finished.

Buy time. Read the paper.

I acted confused, which wasn't hard to do. I mumbled, stumbled over and repeated words. I'd bring the paper close to my face, almost touching my nose, then hold it as far away as I could, leaving everything out of focus. That part was no act. My glasses were gone. I was buying time. And discovering things.

My hands. They're free. My arms. I can move my elbows. What else?

Fidgeting this way and that, I noticed my feet were flat on the floor, but I couldn't spread them apart. They were tied together at my ankles, but I could move my feet forward and back. The backside of my thighs felt an edge. I tried to lean forward from my hips, but I couldn't. My back was stuck to whatever I was sitting on. I swayed left and right a little. It seemed to move a little with me, up off the floor.

A chair. A light metal chair.

I stalled. I asked for water. He refused. When I asked for my glasses, I think he said, "Look, do the best you fucking can!"

I tried to sum up my situation. I'm tied to a flimsy metal chair. Maybe a folding chair. My upper arms are tied down at my sides. Forearms and hands are free but tied together at the wrists. My lower legs can bend at the knee. Feet tied at the ankles, but both feet were flat on the floor, and I could move them. In front of me, there's a tiny camera mounted on a stand. He's kneeling close behind the camera, maybe three feet or so away. Right behind him was a concrete wall.

Desperation gave me an idea.

I needed him to come closer. Come out from behind the camera. How? Piss him off. I stopped reading. He swore and yelled,

"Read it. Louder!" I delayed, then spoke in a whisper. He yelled again. I coughed, whispered, demanded my glasses again, anything to anger him.

While he focused on my lack of focus, I inched my feet backwards under the chair as far as I could. Heels up and on the balls of my feet. He came out from behind the camera and got only inches away from my face.

Now!

It's taken me a while to reconstruct, but my attack went something like this.

From my feet, I pushed up and threw my forearms up and out. I grabbed what must have been his shirt and pulled it down. I held on as he tried to back away, his arms wrapping around me. His move must have brought my head straight into his chin. He fell backward. Knocking aside the camera, we crashed together, chair and all, hitting the concrete wall. The back of his head hit the basement wall. Hard. My head and face must have slid right over his and into the wall, with a nasty abrasion above my forehead resulting.

On top of him, I furiously attacked his face with my hands. I clawed until my fingers found his eyes. Though I still suffering from an addled mind, there was no mistaking the feeling of my bare thumb going in and behind an eyeball. When he screamed, a scream like I'd never heard before, he used his hands not to hit back at me but to cover his face. I know from experience there is no wound so debilitating as one to the eye.

Grabbing his mask, I rocked his head back and forth, slamming it against the wall and then the floor as we slid down. I kept at it, smashing his head I don't know how many times. Through the mask's fabric, my hands felt something warm and sticky. Head wounds are like that. Blood vessels there do not constrict around a wound. The mask was soaked in blood.

His screams muted into moans until he went silent. His arms

fell limp to his sides. Passed out or dead, I didn't care which. It was time to go.

Letting his head drop, with my teeth I tried to tear at the tape around my wrists, but I could barely reach it. My ankles were also out of reach. Panicking that he'd wake up with me still taped to the chair, I maniacally twisted in the chair. I tried to smash the chair against the wall and the floor. All that did was to cause me more pain.

I don't know how, but the tape from across my chest and the chair finally ripped. The chair fell away. Curling up into a ball, I tore at the ankle tape. My arms and my legs were freed. Only my wrists were still bound.

I stood up but immediately collapsed on top of my still unconscious torturer, my legs exhausted and numb. Lying at his side, I felt dizzy, near fainting. An ugly, shattering scream came from me.

Don't faint! Get out!

I'm hazy about how I did this, but I must've crawled to and then up the stairs all the way to the top. When I looked back down, a blood trail mixing mine and his marked my path on the stairs, the wall and the railing.

The basement door stood between me and escape. On my knees at the top step, I reached up, turned the knob and fell forward through the opened door. Hauling my lower half over the threshold, I stood up but fell against the hallway wall and slid to the floor. Turning my head to look across the hallway, I saw the kitchen. I thought, or must have thought, kitchen . . . knives. Get a knife.

Crawling over to the kitchen, I used the entryway frame to pull myself up, inches at a time until I stood, woozy, leaning on the frame. I remember standing there for probably no more than a minute, before I started easing myself past the refrigerator and along the counter.

Frantically yanking open the drawers, I searched for a knife. A couple of drawers came completely out and crashed on the floor. Then there it was all along. A big, wooden knife block. I drew out the biggest knife I could find.

And that was stupid. When I tried to flip that goddamn saber of a knife around in my hands to cut away the tape around my wrists, I clumsily dropped it on the floor. After a whispered curse, I drew out a paring knife from the block. That proved easier to maneuver. I cut about an inch through the tape, enough so I used my teeth to tear away the rest.

Armed with the paring knife, I went back into the hallway and found the way to salvation. The front door, to my left, was only steps away. I moved toward the door, but it wouldn't open. Locked somehow. Stupidly, I kept turning and pulling on the doorknob until I saw the deadbolt.

Outside! I'm outside! Run! Run!

I had no idea where I was. I was in a neighborhood. One house after another on both sides of the street. New houses.

Go! He's coming! He's got to be coming!

The streetlights were on. Porch lights too. I dropped onto the pavement, tripped up by my own feet. The knife went somewhere. I got up on all fours, deciding on flight rather than finding the knife and fight.

Over the trees, in the distance, I saw a string of white lights in the sky.

Lights? I know those! The bridge! I'm near the fucking Collin Bridge! I'm near home!

Struggling back onto my feet, terror's knife went through my gut as I saw I hadn't gone far. I was in the street, but in front of the still open door of his house. Stumbling and swaying, I decided to make noise.

Yelling for help as loud as I could, I went toward a house across the street, smashing my whole body into its front door. I kept yelling as my fists struck the door. No response, I wobbled over to the next door, falling twice on the way. Again, not a sound. A third house. Again, nothing. I fell again in the driveway of a fourth house.

Flat on my belly, I couldn't move. My vision seemed to be collapsing. No, don't! He'll catch me! He'll kill me! I don't know if I yelled those words or just thought them. I was all alone and about to pass out.

A hand, maybe two, grabbed me, turned me over, and pinned me to the ground. I'm done. It's him.

Lights. I remember lots of lights. White lights. Blue and red lights. Then, sirens and people yelling. On my belly again, someone grabbed my arms and pulled them behind my back. Something around my hands . . . my wrists. Something metal. I looked around. People were all around me.

A flashlight blinded me. "Who are you? What's your name?" *My name? I know that.*

"Ah, Holt. Victor, ah, Holt."

That broke the mental logjam. They were police. Maybe all of them. Rapidly and likely incoherently, I told them all I could.

Standing before me was one cop I recognized. Harrison, dressed in sweatpants and a T-shirt, with a badge hanging from a lanyard around his neck. I remember thinking something silly, that this is just like on TV.

"Oh, hi, Detective Harrison. Someone tried to kill me. In their basement. Hey, what time is it? Someone must've caught you at home."

"Almost two a.m. Mr. Holt, Vic, which house? Which house where you held in?"

"That one, I think." I pointed to a house a couple of doors down the road on the other side of the street. A darkened house with its front door wide open.

CHAPTER FORTY-FOUR

END OF LIFE PLANS

Ford

When I came to, I couldn't remember. I felt detached from myself. I have no idea how I climbed the stairs. Strangely, I don't remember any pain. Maybe I was in shock, whatever that is. I do remember standing at the top of the basement stairs staring at the blood pooling at my feet. Drop by drop, the pool expanded until it covered about half a floor tile. My first clear thought was I'd better clean up the mess. My parents won't like blood over their nice tile floor.

Seeing the front door open brought me back to reality. I flung the door shut and went back to the kitchen without thinking about what the open door meant.

All the house lights were off, but enough light came in from the streetlights, so it wasn't completely dark inside. It then struck me that I literally wasn't seeing things clearly. Unfocused and off-center. My eye. Something was very wrong with my eye.

That realization surged the pain all at once. My neck. My head. My eye. God, my right eye felt on fire. I yanked off the balaclava in one motion and threw it to the floor, sending blood spatter across the wall and floor. Had my eye been completely out of its socket, I might've sent it against the wall.

With my right hand covering my eye, I felt all over my head and face with my left hand. When I brought my left hand down, it was coated in blood. Completely covered. That sight will never leave me.

The noise from outside, yelling and police sirens, triggered me to remember what happened.

Holt! Holt got away! He beat the shit out of me and got away!

Through the fancy white window curtains that mom was so proud of, I saw silhouettes moving to the front door and around back. Even with one eye and suffering from what I learned later was a concussion and skull fracture, I knew who they were. Cops. Their guns were out. One had a rifle.

With my bloody left hand, I took the pistol from the small of my back. That wasn't easy. I'm right-handed. Why Holt hadn't grabbed my gun, I never found out. I stood there, looking at the blood-smeared pistol in my hand, afraid to take my hand away from my eye, when the cops banged on the front door.

"POLICE! OPEN THE DOOR!"

Even in the hallway's dim light, I had a clear view of the front door. It shook every time they pounded their fists on it. I knew that in seconds they'd come crashing through a door that wasn't even locked.

It's over. I failed. Blood and DNA all over the place. The video. And Holt himself. They'll come in and arrest me. No defense. Kidnapping and attempted murder. Life in prison. What will that be like? No, that's not what I want.

In those few seconds, I chose my end.

A lecture from high school chemistry class flashed from memory. My teacher was talking about the chemistry of combustion. To get a combustion reaction going, fuel and oxygen had to be in the right ratio. An ignition source would supply enough energy–activation energy–to set off the reaction. For half a second, I felt good, recalling that I got an A in that class when most kids did poorly.

I needed time. I had only one means to delay the police. Leaning against the wall with no thought of cover, I aimed at the door. I fired two shots. The cops yelled and then went silent. Shooting bought me time, even if only a minute. When they did come in, they'd be shooting. That's what I wanted.

I backed up into the kitchen until I stood in front of the gas stove. I turned all the burners on and went back into the hallway. Natural gas was the fuel. The pistol would be my ignition device. But I needed more fuel. More time for the gas to spread. I smelled the gas. Good, I thought, almost there. Only need another . . .

The front door blew open! Pieces of the door and frame flew everywhere. Glass breaking, smashing sounds came from the back! To my front, light beams in all directions! Cops went to the left. And right. I fired again.

Slamming into my chest was a huge, burning pressure, like a red-hot sledgehammer. Then nothing. I blacked out.

My end-of-life plan did not end my life. Surprise was my first conscious reaction when I woke up in an intensive care unit days later, thinking I should be dead.

Maybe two weeks later, a town cop came to the hospital and filled me in on what happened. By then, they'd removed the breathing tube, and I could talk, though only in a whisper and slowly.

His last name began with an H, I think. A big guy. He read me my Miranda rights and told me a court ordered attorney had already been assigned to my case. When I was well enough, I'd be arraigned and formally charged with kidnapping and attempted murder. I didn't care about anything else he said. The only thing I wanted to know was why I was still alive.

H explained, "Sorry, our mistake you're alive." Apparently,

when the cops broke open the doors, the inrushing air diluted the gas and spoiled my plans for self-immolation. Seeing my gun, the cops opened fire, hitting me three times, center mass, nearly fatally, but not quite. I do clearly remember another thing H said.

"The EMTs, the docs and nurses here. They're the reason you're alive. Maybe our officers need better marksmanship training. You should've fucking died right there."

I asked him where I was shot. H said, "Two in the belly. You're down to one kidney and short four feet of small intestine. Another through your left lungs. They had to take out half of that one."

"Eye?" I tried pointing to my right eye but couldn't. I forgotten about the restraints holding down my arms.

"Oh, that. It's gone. That wasn't us. Holt did that. Smashed your eyeball all to hell with his thumb. Big hole there. They had to take it out. Holt fractured your skull, too." The cop really enjoyed what he said next.

"Hey, you know what, Ford. You and Holt got something in common now. Down to one eye."

PART III

RESOLUTION . . . FOR NOW

CHAPTER FORTY-FIVE

CRIME SCENE

Harrison

Almost a month after I saw Ford in the hospital, the station called me at home. I had to get to a murder scene right away. Patrol officers were already there. A neighbor had called 911 to report gunshots.

In less than ten minutes, I was there, still in my slacks, dress shirt, and tie from work. Lights from three patrol vehicles spun madly about, along with those of two ambulances, adding to the scene's nightmarish feeling. One officer stood by the front door. Through the windows, I could see other cops moving through the house. EMTs with their gurneys stood by in the driveway but held their place.

There were two civilian vehicles. One I recognized. Oddly, it was parked at an angle with lights still on, the engine running, and the driver's door wide open. The other vehicle, a black SUV, I didn't recognize.

I'd like to say I approached the crime scene calmly and emotionally detached, but that would not be true. Like a nervous rookie, I bolted from my vehicle, intent on barging my way into Vic's home. The patrol officer at the door gently put out his hand in front of me, granting me the few seconds I needed to settle down before I made a fool of myself.

"Detective Harrison. Could you hold on before you go inside, please? I want to make sure it's okay." The officer was an old hand with the department. Sergeant Ed Sousa. "Yeah, all right. Of course, Ed."

Ed spoke into his shoulder mike. I didn't hear what he said, but I saw Ed nod. "Okay, Pete. We can go in but listen. There's no point in rushing in. What's done is done. Nothing you can do about all that. Let me brief you first on what we found."

"Is he . . ."

"Yes. It's bad, Pete."

Before I went inside, I slipped on a pair of latex gloves. I always kept a couple of pairs in my pants pocket, just in case. As an officer took pictures of the broken front door and foyer, I stepped around the glass shards to reach the alarm control panel. The panic button indicator was still flashing. Checking the video component of the new house security system could wait. I inspected the entire ground floor. No other broken doors or windows. Nothing else seemed out of order.

An officer called me from the top of the curved stairway to the second floor. "They're up here. You want to come up here."

A man's black sneakers came into view as I went up the curved stairs. The left foot hung over the step edge, the sole up. Reflection from my flashlight revealed flicks of glass in the sole tread. The toes of the right foot were still stuck on the step, as if he was about to leap up. Knees bent, the body had crumpled down a step or two. The shoulders rested just below the second-floor landing. The left arm had fallen close to his upper body, elbow bent upward. The body had curled up into an almost fetal position.

Facing to the right, the head lay on the second-floor landing. Along the body's right side, a trail of blood dribbled down the top three steps. Blood had streaked and sprayed on the short wall along the right side of the stairwell. Though the body seemed stable, I knew we needed to process the scene quickly before the body fell back and slid down the stairs. Determining his position at the time of death was important.

Maneuvering around to the body's left and up the stairs, I followed the same path as the other officers until I could see the face, careful not to step in the blood pools. Ed had told me about the fatal gunshot wound. It was unmistakable. A large caliber weapon, with entry just below his left eye, smashing the zygomatic bone. The round or rounds continued through his skull until it exited the center left of the rear of the skull, somewhere likely at the suture between the occipital and parietal bones. From there, they apparently smashed into the far wall near a front hallway window. The blast took with it a three-inch wide slab of hair-covered skull that smeared against the baseboard molding. Flecks of brain matter dotted the floor and walls.

The body's right arm extended forward, its elbow just below the end of the stairwell wall. The hand reached the hallway floor. Its fingertips barely touched the grip of a semiautomatic pistol, entirely black in color except for a new, randomly applied finish of red. The officer working on the scene had already marked four empty pistol shell casings, as well as two bullet holes in the drywall above the stairs.

Before I moved on, I summed up the body in my mind. White male, young, perhaps in his mid or late twenties. Short, brown hair. Dressed in blue jeans and a black windbreaker. No gloves. No hat or mask.

"ID on this one?"

The officer said he'd already patted down the exposed side of the body for a wallet, but his pockets were empty. "Rear pockets, that is. I didn't want to disturb it too much by checking the jacket or front pockets. Maybe we'll find something when we get it out of here. Or maybe from the SUV."

I nodded, agreeing with his restraint in dealing with a corpse perched so precariously.

For the second body, I didn't need an ID. It was Victor Holt. Barely eight feet away from the stairs, Vic lay on the floor just inside the door frame of his bedroom. He lay on his stomach with a visible gunshot wound on the left side of his neck. The blood pool reached three or four feet into the hallway. His 12-gauge was out of his hands and on the floor, the stock surrounded by blood.

"Looks like they shot each other. You think that's possible, Detective?"

I didn't answer. This was my first homicide investigation. On top of the burden of inexperience, I knew the victim. Trying to banish that emotional distraction from my mind, I focused on an inspection for further evidence. As I stepped over the body, I couldn't see anything obviously wrong. When I looked under the bed, though, I saw things.

I often find it useful to talk through my initial impressions of a crime scene, even if no one else is around. Luckily for me, I had an audience. Officer Denton was right there.

"Vic drives back home. He's in danger. Someone, that dead guy on the stairs, is after him. So, Vic runs inside, locks the front door, hits the alarm panic button, and then comes up here. He went for his shotgun. He told me he keeps it in his bedroom. Under the bed, there's a closed pistol case. We'll find a forty-five auto in it. But he went for the twelve-gauge first. And a box of shells he kept on the nightstand. He loaded it. When we break the shotgun breech, I'll bet we'll find only one spent shell. It looks like he dropped one shell. It rolled away under the bed. It's there now.

"Meanwhile, the guy smashed the front door glass, probably with his pistol, reached in and unlocked the door, and went upstairs. Maybe he heard Vic up here. The security video will help with that.

"So, Vic hit the floor, using the bedroom door frame for cover and aimed the shotgun at the top of the stairs. I'll bet the guy took cover behind that short wall before deciding to move on Vic. He starts shooting. Four rounds expended. Going around that wall, maybe he fired a couple of rounds in the blind. We've got two bullet hits in the hallway. I can account for a third one. The one that killed Vic. Entry wound at the neck. Vic either bled out because of a major artery wound, or the round made it all the way to his heart. That's possible. Yeah, anyway, we'll find out from the autopsy.

"And what killed that guy? Vic fired his one shell. That's the big entry wound on the guy's face. Look at the box of shells over there on the nightstand. Home defense double aught. Limited pellet number, but large shot size. One, maybe two, pellets hit him in the face. On the opposite wall, there's a shot pattern. So, yeah, they both got off a shot at the same time and at very close range. And maybe they killed each other."

Following the line of fire, I went into the bedroom, checking the bed mattress, walls, and window for any obvious sign of a bullet strike. I found it. The fourth round went high and into the far wall.

"You got any other thoughts on what you see here, Dent?"

"No. Not really. They shot at each other. Mr. Holt took the fucker with him." That struck me as an appropriate and succinct summation. Too bad I couldn't quote him in the official report.

I did one last thing before heading back down the steps. Vic's desk was just off the second-floor hallway, close enough to the action to catch a light spray of blood drops. The mist of blood caught his laptop, too, still on and charging. I flipped up the screen. There was a minimized document. Moving the cursor over the document icon, I saw it was labelled *Living Through Troubled Times*.

"Dent, no one touches the laptop. No one. I'll be coming back for it. Understood?"

"No one touches it. Got it, Detective." Having seen all I could, I went down the steps to meet Ed, who was still at the front door.

"Pete, a state police forensics tech and the medical examiner will be here soon. Maybe half an hour. Tell me, do you, ah, did you know Mr. Holt well? I mean, I'm sorry if you . . ."

"Thanks, but no. I didn't know him all that well. He was an active case, but we weren't friends, if that's what you're getting at."

"The grace of small favors, eh? Before you go, Pete, a couple of the neighbors are over there. They called 911. Steve and Lil, I know them. Good people. They want to know about Holt. I haven't told them."

"That's all right. I'll tell them." As I started to walk toward them, I turned to ask Ed another question.

"Media?"

"Don't know about that, but yeah. They're probably headed this way. I'll put an officer up at the intersection there to keep them away for now. Let forensics and the M.E. do their job. Get the bodies out before I let them get close."

I nodded and turned to walk over to tell the neighbors their friend had been murdered.

There was one more task before I saw them. I took out my phone. Bron wasn't going to hear about this on the news.

CHAPTER FORTY-SIX

LIFE'S END

Harrison

"You know, Bron, what terrifies me most . . . about what happened here?"

Chilled by a wind coming off the water, the two of us stood alone on the deck of Vic's house, looking at a spectacular September sunset. Earlier, Steve and Lil, as well as Vic's agent and his attorney, joined us for the release of Vic's ashes into the surf. No one else. Aided by glasses of wine, memories were shared, though Bron didn't say much. I said even less.

It had been two months since Vic was murdered. A disaster cleanup firm spent a month bringing the house back from being the scene of a killing. Blood and tissue wiped up. The ceiling, drywall, molding, and wood flooring torn out, replaced, sanded, stained, and repainted. A new front door, this time with better locks and less framed glass. In the end, it looked as good as new. Shame there's no way to scrub away the memory.

Vic's former attorney, Anthony, helped settle Vic's estate. Vic had updated his will out of prescient concern for what could happen to him. The house and all its contents would be sold and the proceeds divided equally between Bron and Vic's sister-in-law in

Maine, save for a small grant to the town's public library. Bron got all the rights to his books.

A For-Sale sign was still by the driveway. Though waterfront property usually sells in a matter of hours once it hits the market, no one was snapping up Vic's place. Murder scenes lack curb appeal. Though the will granted Bron the right to buy the place, she understandably couldn't bring herself to do that. How could she live in the home where her future husband was murdered? Until it was sold, Bron was the custodian of the house, leaving behind her former roles as attorney and lover.

Technically, the murder case is still open. Someday, I'll officially close it. After all, we know who did it. However, there remain frightening questions about the shooter's motivation.

Micheal James Donohue. White. Age twenty-six. Life-long resident here. High school graduate. Enlisted Navy veteran. Quartermaster rating. Six years of service aboard two destroyers. Good conduct medal, unit awards, and high marks on his evaluations. Honorably discharged one year ago. Nothing in his military record indicated any political involvement or a propensity for violence.

On the civilian side, the FBI and the State Police had nothing on him other than one traffic ticket. No arrests, no warrants, no complaints, no nothing. From the standpoint of law enforcement, he was clean.

A search of his apartment turned up nothing. No literature or books that indicated left-wing or right-wing affiliations or sympathies. The few books he left behind were classic science fiction novels by H.G. Wells and Heinlein. Donohue hadn't even registered to vote. No social media whatsoever. No manifesto left behind.

One curious thing. He had deleted his entire internet search history the day of the shooting. Deeper forensic investigation of his laptop is ongoing—there's always a trace of something—but so far, nothing. For all I know, all he wanted to do was scrub away his search history of anything embarrassing, like porn or whatever.

Donohue had a respectable video game collection. He seemed especially fond of the first-person shooter genre. It's anyone's guess if that has any meaning. We managed to identify two of his online gaming friends, but they volunteered nothing that hinted at what his end would be.

No employment issues. He worked at one of the local boat yards. Canvassing his coworkers and friends painted Donohue as a reliable, skilled, quiet, reserved type. Friendly, but not outgoing. They couldn't recall anything Donohue said that hinted at any radical political philosophy. No current girlfriends. Or boyfriends.

No connection that anyone knew of to a church. No athletic leagues.

His one lifeline to reality was family. Mother and father were divorced, and a younger brother was still in the Navy. Nothing remarkable came of interviews with his bewildered and despondent family.

No evidence that he was under medical care, psychiatric or otherwise. The autopsy was unremarkable. Somehow it would've been comforting if doctors had diagnosed him as a closeted psychopath, but no.

Well before Vic's troubles started, Donohue legally purchased the pistol he used to kill Vic. The apartment search did not find any additional weapons. He did belong to a gun club near here. Interviewing club members turned up nothing. So, Donohue was a law-abiding gun owner. Until he wasn't.

When did he get the idea to kill Vic? Was it somehow personal, unconnected to all the politics surrounding Vic? Did Vic wrong him in some way? As far as I could determine, their lives had never intersected. Hell, he didn't even have a copy of Vic's book.

Why didn't he shoot Vic away from his home? Did he know

about the home security system? Did he know Vic had guns in the house? Did he even care?

In the absence of evidence to the contrary, we are left with the conclusion that Donohue was just a quiet guy who kept to himself. A decent, normal, functioning human being. The life of Donohue would not cause anyone to give him a second thought. No one, law enforcement, family, or friends, has been able to uncover a motive. That could change, of course, with new evidence. For now, all we know is that this ordinary young man killed Vic. A mystery lies in Donohue's grave.

"Jesus, Bron. I'm so sorry this happened. You two had a life planned together. I'm sorry."

I'd offered Bron my condolences many times before. I guess I had, still have, a residue of guilt. That if only I'd worked a little harder on his case. If only I'd . . . done more, even if I hadn't a clue what "more" meant. An illogical feeling. Normal perhaps, but such feelings are of no purpose.

"You said Pete, something about how all this really terrifies you."

"Yes, I did. I should explain myself." I turned away to look out over the shore. It was easier to talk about this when I wasn't looking at Bron.

"It's the fact that Donohue's life was so goddamn ordinary. That's what makes him so terrifying. If he'd been in NSAG, or a guy radicalized by Smyth and Wright, or any other extremist. If they'd found anything in his family history, like his daddy was a KKK member or whatever. Anything that explained why he turned into a monster, like a brain tumor or a history of mental illness, that'd make it easier to understand."

"We want all the monsters to look like monsters. But they often don't. Is that what you mean, Pete?"

"Yeah, pretty much." I sipped some more wine before trying to finish my thoughts.

"I can understand, I can accept, people who make threats may lead themselves to violence. It's almost . . . rational. A rational and logical progression. But this kid Donohue, he comes out of the blue. Random. No one could've predicted he would do this. No discernible motive. No one can say why."

"Anyway, Pete, there can't be too many like him. I mean, really."

That seemed to me a reasonable hypothesis. Based on all the available evidence, the probability of another Donohue being out there was so small that it seemed unworthy of consideration. He's a statistical one-off. Yet this assumption, however fortified by science and common sense, left me with little comfort.

"Bron, yes, perhaps. I'll try to keep that in mind. Yeah, the odds are against another Donohue. Yet he did exist. I've got to assume that others like him out there, however rare. Before there was a Donohue, there was a Ford.

"That's what's so terrifying. We can never prove that another one does not exist. Can't prove a negative. We'll never really know, and it seems so far, the record isn't good."

Bron looked away at the sunset and finished off her Chardonnay before saying, "I'm good enough of a lawyer to know when a witness is not done talking. Finish what's on your mind."

"Okay. I'll accept that, for now, Donohue represents an extreme. Meanwhile, people like me will have to deal with God knows how many of what we could call run-of-the-mill extremists. Most of them, I could write off as frustrated, frightened, or misinformed, or whatever. A whole host of reasons. They won't go further than being angry. Given time, I hope their anger dissipates.

"Then again, it's from them we find the handful who want to kill people like Vic. Who rejoiced when . . ." I had to stop. I didn't sip my wine but took a fair-sized gulp before I went for the punchline.

"Donohue's a hero to these people. So's Ford. Martyrs for a cause. Freedom fighters. What's the evidence of their devotion?

I've been looking at all sorts of social media. There're tributes to them all over."

"I know. Seen them myself."

"Have you seen the latest trending thing? A conspiracy theory that I, the FBI, or even Vic set up Ford and Donohue. They say that because Donohue has such a clean record, he couldn't have done it. They take the same mystery about his motivation and turn it into a weapon. Jesus Christ, Bron, they're even saying I murdered him! Lot of them want my arrest and execution."

Bron interrupted with a professional assessment of that issue. "Ironically, it didn't help that the media played up that the police couldn't uncover a motive. That left the door open to those wild conspiracies."

As I continued, a tone of real anger came to my voice. "How in the hell did we get here? Christ, I don't know, but I can say what's obvious. Cynical and corrupt politicians have brought us to this. They've led people to a place where political violence, even murder, is understandable, excusable, justifiable, even necessary. Facts be damned. The rule of law be damned. Hard to believe we've come to this."

Bron stayed quiet during my little rant against things I could not change. I, however, refilled my glass of wine before continuing. I was on a roll.

"No. That's not . . . accurate. It's not hard to believe. A guy writes a book defending democracy, and people turn on him. I guess if we're to salvage anything, we start by believing we've come to this."

More wine was required to organize my thoughts before continuing. The big question was coming up.

"So, here we are. On social media, I've documented hundreds of new, unique individuals threatening me, a police officer, since Ford and Donohue. They say everything was faked. They're out there, and they're not done with Vic, and they're not done with me. I can't make them go away. They will not change. They will not stop."

"I know. Vic had the same thoughts."

"And Bron. Think hard about this. If they come after me, they'll come after you."

"I know. They already have."

At that point, as a police officer, I should have asked her for details with an eye toward opening an investigation. Instead, my fatigue with the whole situation took over.

"I see. Well, maybe you could fill me in sometime."

We let minutes pass silently, watching the sun start to dip below the horizon and the flat calm of the sea. Then Bron spoke.

"There's a Welsh saying. *Yma o Hyd.*" Bron repeated it again, slowly. Like a struggling language student, I tried to pronounce it, unsuccessfully, before asking, "And it means in English?"

"*Still here.* It's become a slogan for the Welsh to remind the world, especially the English, that the Welsh people and our culture still exist. Still resists. Still thrives. For the two of us, even after all this, we can say we're still here."

"That we are. Anyway, there's some business I wanted to go over with you, now that Steve and Lil are back home. It's about something Vic left behind." I reached into my jacket pocket, pulled out a letter in a sealed envelope, handed it to Bron, and told her to open it.

"On one of Vic's meetings with me at the station, he handed me this letter. It's for you. He wrote it and gave it to me just in case something happened to him."

"Jesus, why didn't he give it to me. I'm his attorney after all. And we were . . ." Bron's voice started to crack. "Why?"

"He didn't explain, but perhaps it was because you were . . . close. Maybe he didn't want to upset you or worry you. I haven't read it. I'm sure it's personal."

Bron opened the envelope, started to read it, then wiped a tear away before putting it back in the envelope. She said, "I'll do this later."

"One last thing, Bron. I recovered Vic's laptop from the scene. Did you know on his laptop he kept a diary of all that's happened?"

"Diary? No. Had no idea."

"Vic left me another letter. I didn't read it until after he . . . It told me about his diary. Or journal or whatever you want to call it." I showed Bron the letter.

"He intended to turn his diary into a book. From what I saw on his laptop, he'd already started working on it. A true-crime sort of thing. But here's the thing. The letter says that if something happened to him, he wanted me to find someone to finish it. And he wants me to add my part of the story. And get this. He even wants Ford to put in his story. Crazy."

"Crazy?"

"Really friggin' crazy. I've never written anything like, what, a book. I wouldn't even know how to start. So . . ."

"So, you're not going to do it."

"I didn't say that. Listen, I need help if I am to do this. Your help."

CHAPTER FORTY-SEVEN

SIX FEET BY EIGHT FEET, HALF BATH, DOUBLE OCCUPANCY, NO VIEW

Ford

A few more thoughts on paper before another hellish night comes. Another night in years more to follow.

Anyone driving on the interstate can get a quick look at my new home. Our state's oldest gated community: the Department of Corrections Maximum Security Prison. Locally, the average citizen knows this building as the CI, or Correctional Institute, but that's technically inaccurate. CI applies to the whole state prison system. Three prisons for men, plus another for the girls. I guess this building has been here so long, way over a century, that when the public hears "CI," they automatically think of my place. And it's quite a place. Built out of enormous granite blocks, it's surrounded by guard towers outside the old walls, linked together by high double walls of chain-link fence topped with razor ribbon. From a distance, it looks like something out of the past. A medieval castle without the drawbridge.

As to accommodations, I share rooms with 465 other gentlemen. The worst of the worst. Someday, one or more of them, just out of sheer boredom, will beat the shit out of me, or rape me, or kill me.

As of tonight, I've clocked three days over three months here at the CI Max. That's after two months in the hospital. I spent my first two weeks here awaiting arraignment before pleading guilty. Then another month here, held until sentencing.

The first time I met my court-appointed attorney, I was still in the hospital. She gave me this notebook and two felt-tip pens to write a statement about what happened. What they say about public defense lawyers is true. There's only a handful of them, and they have too many cases to handle. She spared me only ten minutes as she got right to the point.

In this state, she explained, kidnapping has a maximum sentence of twenty years. Attempted murder also maxes out at twenty years. The judge can make the sentences concurrent, meaning I serve both at the same time, and I'd get out in twenty. Sooner, if I keep out of trouble. Good behavior, they call it, just like in the TV shows.

"Stay out of trouble? You do know this place is filled with guys who could not stay out of trouble. That's why they're here." I almost said that to her, but I didn't. I kept my mouth shut and let her continue.

She then reviewed the judge's other option. Make the sentences consecutive. First, do the twenty for kidnapping. Then the twenty for attempted murder. Forty years in total. I'd be in my sixties before I got out.

Her best legal advice was simple. Plead guilty. Show contrition. If I agreed, she'd work with the prosecutor to arrange a deal for less than the max, though given the crime, they may not be in a deal-making mood. I understood why. This was not an impulsive crime. I thoroughly planned the kidnapping and murder. My lawyer said the prosecutor will seek the max because of my "forethought, malice, and cruelty." I think that's lawyer jargon, but I got the gist of it. Pleading guilty, while looking as pathetic as I can, might be the best way to avoid pissing off the judge. Consecutive sentencing comes from a pissed-off judge.

"You've got a hearing scheduled next week. Thursday. What's it gonna be?"

I didn't answer. "I'd like time to think about it. It's my life we're talking about."

My lawyer did not like that. "Look, Mr. Ford. Let me disabuse you of any chance of winning a court trial, if that's what's on your mind. That'd take a miracle that not even the Almighty himself has the juice for.

"Here are the facts. Your victim freed himself from the torture chamber you set up in your basement. Your victim fought you and managed to get upstairs and outside. I won't bother to review all the forensic evidence in your home. So, let me ask you again, what about the plea?"

Looking frustrated with me, she started to leave. Before she was gone, I said after her, "Fuck it. I'll plead guilty."

All she said was, "Okay. I'll talk to the prosecutor. See you at the hearing."

Though the prosecutors were willing to bend a little, the judge said I deserved the maximum sentence because of the depravity of my crime. He said something about how I tortured Holt and planned for him to die in agony. Whatever. I didn't listen to everything he said. Mom and Dad never even came up here to say goodbye.

Forty years. I'll have nothing but time on my hands. Funny thing, I do have a little project to help pass the time. That cop, Detective Harrison, the one who saw me in the ICU, visited me last week. He told me that Holt was dead. I admit that stunned me at first. Not because I was sorry he was dead, but that someone got to him before me. Then Harrison told me of Holt's last request of me. He and Holt's attorney are writing a book about what happened, and Holt wanted me to write my side of the story!

Since then, I've used the notebook to write down my story, beginning to end. Right up to taking Holt and being shown to my new home here in this granite castle. My days here start and end with writing.

Lights Out is the worst time. That's when I'm most afraid. Not because I think the guy in the bunk below me will strangle me in the dark. Not because somehow other inmates will get into my cell to knife me or rape me. So far, I've managed to escape the worst from the men in here, though that day will come soon enough.

The real monsters come out in the semi-darkness of Lights Out. My monsters. From inside my own mind, they come, torturing me with memories and doubt. They make me relive what I did. What I'm going through. What might happen to me in prison. I have become my own nightmare.

"Lights Out!" So much for memories. Except for the security lights, the darkness always comes quietly. Time to pull the blanket up and over my face and wish I could magically hide from my new life. The magic never happens.

And now, the night has finally come when I can write my last words and send them to Harrison.

Forty years. It doesn't matter. I won't last that long. Not ten. Not even one. I'm sure of it. I'll make sure of it.

I wrote down my story because I needed something to do. I guess it's done now. I suppose they'll edit it to fit into the book. There's an irony wrapped up in all this, aside from that other guy finishing the job I started with Holt. My words here will make me a co-author with the man I almost murdered. One more thing. I'm an author and a one-eyed Army vet writer, just like Holt was.

I will die in this prison. Soon, I am sure. Death is another thing I will have in common with him.

CHAPTER FORTY-EIGHT

THE LAST CHAPTER

Harrison

Vic's murder brought intense media attention my way. I hated every moment of it. The reporters relished the mystery that Donohue presented, feeding the conspiracy theories about him and me. For a time, Smyth and Wright joined in that feeding frenzy. That is, until Bron went after them again.

All I could do was keep my head down, gather all my notes, and find time to work with Bron on the book. I'd write something, and Bron would make it readable. Fortunately, Vic's neighbors cooperated. With their help, we were able to reconstruct much of what passed between them and Vic, with license taken with the dialogue for the story's sake.

We secured Ford's cooperation just in time. A couple of weeks after he mailed us his draft, he killed himself in prison. Ironically, he suffocated himself just like he planned to do to Vic.

It took almost exactly one year to write this book.

Now all that media attention is back. The book was published thanks to Ed, Vic's agent. Bron and I did interviews on the network morning shows, as well as a string of high-profile book signings. We were to do more, but we both found it so distasteful that we had the publisher cancel the rest. Nevertheless, the book sold well. Vic would be pleased by that.

I never want to write another book as long as I live. At home, my hardcover version of the book is stuck under a pile of other random books in the living room. Out of sight and out of mind.

Holt's house eventually sold. Even a grisly waterfront murder scene is still waterfront.

And what about Victor Holt? You, the reader of this book, might want to know how I really felt about Vic. The answer is simple. You will never know.

AUTHOR'S NOTE

Let me say first, nothing that happens in this novel has happened to me. While it's true that I've had two or three rough social media comments sent my way about my first novel, nothing ever crossed the line into a threat. Nor has anyone even remotely threatened me face-to-face. At least, not yet. Still, the possibility became inspiration.

I'm retired after fifteen years as a high school science teacher. Long before that, I served as a junior officer in the United States Coast Guard. In between, I bounced around from job to job with each military move—my wife is a retired U.S. Air Force officer. With retirement, I had imagined myself playing a good deal of golf. That didn't happen.

While the pandemic temporarily forced me to put aside my clubs, my enthusiasm for the game has waned to the point of extinction. I wasn't all that good anyway. So, what to do? I could still play golf, spend too much money, knowing that every time I walked off the 18th green, all I'd be left with was the memory of a poorly played game.

Writing, however, offers something of lasting value. Holding in your hand something of your own creation, something unique in the world, is a feeling that is unmatched.

Captive is my second novel. In a way, it continues with the political thriller genre of my first, *Refuge: A Novel of Lost Democracy.* This time, however, I narrowed the focus more, telling a fictional story of an author under threat because he wrote a novel that defended democracy.

Refuge: A Novel of Lost Democracy

What happens if democracy falls?

In *Refuge: A Novel of Lost Democracy*, democracy in America wasn't lost to invasion or foreign terrorist attacks. Nor to a global cataclysm, a military coup, or an economic collapse. Democracy fell because it was our choice.

An election was all that was needed. Gerrymandered districts. Laws suppress the vote. Disinformation and lies. Promises of former glory. Apathy and ignorance. Political violence and, above all, fear.

The story begins in Saint Andrews, New Brunswick, Canada, where American dissidents hope to start a new life. Mike and Debbie Whynot, both retired U.S. Air Force officers and leaders of their fellow expatriates, face threats from the new autocratic U.S. government. They will pay dearly for their continued fight for democracy.

Across the Saint Croix River in Eastport, Maine, others remain in service to the new U.S. government. A few will find the moral burden unendurable.

Refuge: A Novel of Lost Democracy explores what is possible. Even probable.

www.refugedavidschoorens.com

www.ingramcontent.com/pod-product-compliance
Lightning Source LLC
LaVergne TN
LVHW020659110826
845149LV00012B/2053

* 9 7 8 1 9 6 8 5 4 8 3 0 8 *